AERO STRIKE!

"We've got a pair of aero contacts coming in wet and hot, bearing 272." Sebastian consulted his targeting computer. "Type TMS-100 Dolphin."

Sebastian activated his shields and weapons. He couldn't see anything on the horizon, but he knew the attack fighters would be on them in seconds. They'd have the advantage of coming down out of the mid-afternoon sun.

"Keep your vexing heads down and keep moving," Sebastian said. "I've got jamming engaged."

"Copy that. I'll do my best," Patricia said.

Sebastian dimmed his headset visor to cut down on the sun's glare. The targeting box steadily increased in size, the range indicator ticked down, but still, he saw nothing. Even when the red X changed to a green box, Sebastian waited, focused. Patricia fired her laser cannons haphazardly in the Dolphins' direction.

Suddenly, they appeared, screaming down from the sky. Sebastian gritted his teeth and lined up his reticle on the swift targets, and fired. The lasers hit the lead Dolphin's shields, but didn't punch through.

He quickly smashed on his maneuvering pedal, wheeling his Hurricane hard to one side, its feet skidding in the low gravity. The Dolphins tore into his shielding with bolts of heavy laser and cut into his shoulder armor. They raced overhead and disappeared behind him.

Sebastian quickly whirled his titan around to face them. His paws went to work, dragging the throttle rearwards and backpedaling from the aerofighters, while keeping his crosshairs on them. The Dolphins cut a long, arcing turn and came for another pass.

Sebastian gripped his joystick hard, pointed his weaponry at the lead fighter, and fired his laser cannons. He kept the beams focused on the Dolphin, cutting through its shielding and into its fuselage. It banked and struggled to pull away, but Sebastian hit its underside with his ion rifle, the particle stream tearing into its belly. The fighter shuddered, rolled onto its back, and pitched downwards. It slammed into the ground and exploded, debris spewing across the dry grass and setting fires as it went.

"Enemy aero destroyed," his computer said.

FOXHUNT!

Rich Hanes

Arkham Bridge Publishing
www.arkhambridge.com

Published by Arkham Bridge Publishing
P.O. Box 2346
Everett WA, USA
98213-0346
www.arkhambridge.com

ISBN: 978-0-578-02605-3

Editor: Damien Wellman
Cover Illustrations: Minna Sundberg
Technical Assistance: James Earl Davis

Second edition

To Kynn, for telling me what I needed to hear, not what I wanted to hear.
To Corey, for providing the framework that helped me build my world.
To my parents, for everything.

And you, for taking time to read.

ACT I

The Creator so loved us, that He gave His life so that we should live.

-The Memoria, The Book of Max, Chapter 19, Verse 41.

SCENE ONE

Captain Sebastian Valentino slammed his fist on the steel desk and sent pens careening across it. His russet fur bristled beneath his white tunic. "I don't want to do this!"

"It's your responsibility."

"I don't care."

Guidance Officer Jordan Randolph herded his pens and returned them to their proper place. "You must care, you came to see me."

"Don't play your mind tricks on me, human."

Randolph reclined in his chair and tucked his hands behind his head. "Mind tricks are games for foxes. That's your department."

"Don't bring my genus into this. It's not your job to prejudge me."

"You should know better, Captain," Randolph said. "Genus is crucial to all the Created like yourself."

Sebastian turned away, brushy tail lashing. Even when he stalked about Randolph's cramped office, the bipedal fox was short, unimposing, chest-high to the human. "Maybe you're right," he said.

Randolph gestured to the chair in front of his desk. "Of course I am. Now stop prowling and have a seat."

Sebastian stiffened and stared out the window at the far side of the office. A few centimeters of hardened plastiglass were all that protected them from the void of space. The placid vista of the planet below betrayed the danger of hard vacuum.

He dropped into the offered seat. "Fine."

"Now, tell me what has you afraid."

"Who says I'm afraid?

"You do, with your actions and tone of voice." Randolph folded his hands on his desk. "I've studied enough animals to recognize fear and anxiety."

Sebastian frowned. "Animal?" he said, then shrugged. "Maybe I am, and why not? I've never done the Rite of Passage before, dig?"

"I'm sure you've taken part in one. When was the last time?"

Sebastian twisted his lips in thought. "About seventeen years ago, 487 or 488."

"Tell me about that, what was it like?"

"Haven't you studied our rituals, human? You should know."

Randolph frowned, but stayed calm. He had to be careful with the agitated creature before him. "I have, yes, but only in books. I want to know about yours, in your own words."

"You're not going to tell anyone about this, are you?"

"You have my word."

Sebastian knit his brows, eyes tight on the human before him. Randolph had always been a fine guidance officer. Sebastian had trusted him in the past, but he'd never disclosed such personal memories. Maybe it was time to start.

"It was for my aunt Josefine," Sebastian said. "She lived on the far side of Mursankhovel, so I didn't know her well and didn't really care when she died of age, but my mother made me go to her Passage anyway. Elder Marquis conducted it, I didn't know him well either."

Randolph grabbed a notepad and scribbled notes. "This was when you were on Wopat?"

"Yes, a few months before I was conscripted."

"It sounds like you didn't know most of the others in your city. Were you always so alone?"

"We were unwelcome in most homes."

"Because you're a stray?"

The hair stood on the back of Sebastian's neck. "I don't want to talk about that."

"Very well." Randolph jotted more notes. "Let's go back to the Rite. What do you remember about it?"

"Not a lot. I wasn't really interested. There was a lot of prayer, in Volpa. People talked. We passed around her zulicans, looked at her, then she was buried and we went home."

"Who was with you?"

"Just my mother."

"Your father wasn't there?"

"He was busy."

"Busy with what?"

Sebastian narrowed his eyes. "I don't want to talk about him."

Randolph crossed something out. "Okay, never mind that. I think you're afraid because you don't know what to do."

"Nonsense, I know what to do, it's all written in the Memoria."

"Then what frightens you?"

Sebastian frowned and held his paws together. "When Josefine died, only her bloodkin cared. There were ten of us at her Passage, not even her neighbors came. It was disrespectful. I'm afraid that's going to happen again, and Adrian deserves better."

"Why would it happen again?"

Sebastian shook his head slowly. "The others, they won't understand what's happening."

"Because they're not foxes?"

Sebastian tensed and lurched across the desk, thrusting his fist at Randolph. "It shouldn't be like this! Adrian shouldn't be so alone, no bloodkin, none of his pedigree, not even one of his House. There's only me. The others won't understand it."

"Does it really matter if they understand?"

"They should appreciate Adrian's memory as much as I do."

Randolph adjusted his glasses and set his notepad down. "Is the Rite of Passage for them, or for Adrian?"

He was right. It wasn't for Sebastian, or for the crew, but for Adrian. Even if the non-foxes amongst him didn't understand the ritual and its symbolism, their presence at least honored Adrian's memory.

Randolph gestured at Sebastian. "Besides, you're already prepared. You've got your tunic and sash on. You owe it to Adrian, it's your duty as Captain and the only fox in the crew. You can't back out now."

Sebastian tugged at his ceremonial tunic. Only the vibrant zulican blossom pinned to its breast and the sash across his shoulder broke its off-white cotton. "You're right," he said.

"Do you feel better now?"

"Yes. You're pretty smart for a human, you know."

Randolph smirked. "Weren't you just scolding me for bringing genus into this?"

Sebastian stood and gestured Randolph forward. "All right, I give. Now come, it's time."

The pair stepped into the corridor and headed for the starship's cargo bay. Almost the entire crew was present in its confines, huddled together on folding chairs, waiting for their captain.

Sebastian stepped up to the makeshift podium before them. A hard grip on its steel surface didn't help steady his trembling paws.

"Rite of Passage commences now. All stand."

In unison, three-hundred four bodies rose to attention.

"Let it become known that the Passage of Adrian Miller begins at 1201 Galactic Standard Time, fourteenth day of month of Aquarius, year 505 Post Founding. Be seated."

Sebastian folded his paws behind him. It was a struggle to maintain his grasp on the common Mahonic language.

"Opening begins, with short prayer. We gather to mourn passage of Adrian Miller, from this life to next. We commend its spirit into waiting paws of Max, He Who Watches. We know someday we—I will join Founder, and our—my ancestors and elders in Everlife. Opportunity must be taken to reflect, remember at any time we can be called to Everlife. We must never forget that our actions shall be judged when we pass, and take solace in knowing He Who Watches will reward those who live righteously. *Fallam.*"

The crew responded to the prayer call with resounding silence. They didn't know how to answer.

Sebastian grabbed a non-descript book from a folding table. Even his genus' Book of Creation didn't help still his trembling paws. "Reading and sermon phase now begins."

He settled onto a page and began to read.

"I had spoken to my Creator many times before, but He was caught off guard by my question. Even His practiced, steady delivery faltered in the face of my inquisition. By now, He was reaching the end of His lifespan, and I thought that surely He should have had the foresight to anticipate the question.

"'My Father,' I said to Him, 'my instincts have filled me with the desire to mate and breed, and I have begun a family with my lovely mate, Zulica. We have five beautiful kits, yet I am troubled.'

"'What disturbs you, my son?' said He.

"'Life comes from breeding, copulation, and mateship within a species. You are my Father, yet You are not even one of my genus. I beseech thee; where have I come from?'

"'I was afraid You would ask this.' My Father sighed, sitting heavily upon a steel crate. 'You are My pride and joy, Max. I have nurtured you and raised you, and you are the pinnacle of My Creation. You are the smartest I have yet made. But I fear not even you can fully understand your origins.'

"'Father,' I implored, 'I must know how I came to be. I see no foxes older than I, none that may have birthed Me. You are not like I, nor are the Others. You have no fur, no muzzles, no tails. I must know my beginning, I can no longer sleep. It consumes me like fire.'

"A sad look washed through His eyes. 'Much as I love you, My son, mere words are not capable of expressing the details, the concepts within. You are more intelligent and educated than any of the other species, but you simply cannot understand.'

"With clenched paws, I pleaded with him. 'Is there some way I might learn, Father?'

"Finally, He relented. Sitting perfectly still, He beckoned to me. 'Come. Touch my mind.'

"I had never touched my Creator's mind before. I was hesitant to do so, but I did, for it was the only way. I grasped His smooth, round skull in my padded fingers. Within seconds, I linked my thoughts to His, the information flooding into my brain, flowing like water from His mind to my own. And it was finally revealed to me.

"It was so terrible, so undignified, that I could not believe. But I knew it to be true, for my Creator's thoughts could not lie. Even writing in retrospect, I tremble and shudder in memory of the information. It was instantly apparent why He had refused to tell me; I was unready to understand all that had gone into me. More than just the physical details of my origin, I was granted insight into the horrifying reasons why I was created. It was not love at all, but hate. I was created only to destroy. I suddenly knew all, each abhorrent, ghastly detail of my own existence. I dare not share the truth, as my mind aches just recounting it.

"Shocked and frightened, I tore out of the mindlink with such speed and force that my mind caught fire. I fled, running into the barren wastes, brimming with tears, not to return for a fortnight.

"The Creator was hurt, too. When I returned, Zulica told me that He had sat and wept in privacy every day I was gone. The Memoria, The Book of Max, Chapter 16, verses one through thirty-three."

It took all of Sebastian's will to keep from choking up, yet none of his crew shared his passion. How could they act this way? These were the words of Max Himself, and they all sat, staring stoically ahead.

"What does passage mean for us?" Sebastian placed the book down, held his paws behind his back, and strolled across the breadth of his gathered crew. "What is significance of it? Max tells of time when He faced great difficulty. He wanted to know who He was, why He was here, how He was here, but He couldn't bear truth. Then, instead of face it, He fled. Why?

"Sometimes we face difficult questions, like Max. We want to know why bad things happen. We read the Memoria, let it guide our daily lives, pray, and still face hardships."

Sebastian sighed. This wasn't right at all. He was reciting another sermon he'd heard before, but to his predominantly canine audience, it meant nothing.

He shook his head. "Think about a time you lost someone or something dear to you. You wanted to know why, didn't you? Why this happen to me? We don't want to face thought that our lives are random, only we guide ourselves. We want to believe the Creator, or the Founders, still have control, and that everything has reason.

"But sometimes, things just happen. Max wanted to know truth about where He came from, but when He found out, He didn't want to know anymore. We want to know why things happen, but we don't, because we can't bear to understand. We have to accept events are beyond control, that we live and die with no plan, no influences except those we make."

He looked over the sea of canine muzzles, and saw only empty, confused stares. Sebastian shook his head and sighed. "Never mind, forget. Move on to Remembrance phase. Anyone who wishes to say words about Adrian can do so, testifying under watchful gaze of Max."

They remained painfully silent. What could they say? They hadn't known Adrian like Sebastian had.

"If no one has something to say—"

"I do."

A lanky canine with silver and tan fur rose from the ranks, a jackal over two meters in height. Sebastian gestured him forward. "Come, speak, Senior Lieutenant Corey Delzano."

Corey shuffled to the podium, bowed to Sebastian, and turned to face the crew. "For the last four years, I served under Adrian as third-in-command, and yet, he was not known well to me on a personal basis. Little of his time was spent socializing. I feel as though I, of the non-vulpines, knew him best. He, or his influence, was around always, omnipresent. One could feel his touch and effects. Always, he was busy with critical matters; always, he was checking this or that for our Captain; always, he was vigilant and dutiful, close to the Captain like his right paw. Outside the Captain, he was rarely social, so I earned the task of conducting activities related to crew efficiency for him. He concerned himself with the big picture. From Sebastian to Adrian to me.

"He was an excellent strategist, complementing our Captain's tactical abilities. When he spoke of strategy, logistics, he did so with deep affection. Once, he buzzed me in early morning, awakened me, and asked my opinion on Alliance weapons manufacturers. Our dear Captain led us into and out of battle, but it was Adrian who ensured we had supplies and equipment for victory. Without him, the Star Rangers would not be where we are today."

Corey leaned down to Sebastian, grasped his shoulder in one massive hand, and spoke softly. "Perhaps this is unorthodox, but I had a gift for Adrian." Corey reached into his jumpsuit's breast pocket, withdrew a small gold object on a chain, and offered it to Sebastian. Its cruciform shape glittered under the cargo bay's fluorescent lighting.

"What's this?" Sebastian asked.

"It is the Ankh of Kohoutek. I understand it is foreign to your culture, but I desired him to have it. It is our symbol for life and death. We are buried with it, a sign that we are the favored of Kohoutek. It is also a harbinger of good fortune. When given to one of another species, it is a sign that they meant much to a jackal at one point. He taught everything to me, even if it was not his intent. I had intended to present it to him when he returned from the mission."

Sebastian coiled up the small chain. "Thank you, Corey. It's quite thoughtful of you."

Without another word, Senior Lieutenant Corey Delzano turned on his heels and retreated to his seat.

Sebastian placed the ankh aside. "I realize most of you never know Adrian," he said. "He was solitary, uncomfortable with crowds and other genera. He spent much of his time planning. He was modest and quiet, attentive to duty and detail.

"I remember when I first met him. We just advanced from Garrison Defense Forces to Star Alliance National Military. We had differences, he was from House Florenzo, I'm from House Lafayette. He had a pedigree and a long family history, and I did... not. We also shared much in common. We were young, idealistic, in second of four years mandatory service, sprinting through the ranks. We became tight, united during our advanced training, as they taught us how to operate a modern aerofighter. We served together in *San-vel Vel-fyarffor* nearly three years, star-hopping around the nation.

"He elevated faster than I, because he was calm and methodical, and I was aggressive and independent. Even when he became my commanding officer, even when we fought against the Canis Dominion in the Tariff Conflict, we were still friends.

"When our tours ran out, I embarked as an independent mercenary and I sought to employ him. For four years, he turned me down, saying he wanted no more combat. When I finally incorporated the Star Rangers, I offered him the chance to be second in command, and he accepted. While a good pilot, his real strength was computers, strategy, logistics, and the big picture.

"It was Adrian who devised the architecture for nearly every mission in the past seven years. He came up with the order of battle, what force composition was required, and I executed it. It was his attention to detail that made us, and kept us, #1 in MerCom's mercenary rankings.

"I constantly lauded his war planning, but he was soft-spoken and modest. I would praise him for a well-planned operation, and he would merely smile and nod. He never talked about his personal life on-duty, it was always business. He told me once that if you fail to plan, then you plan to fail. He was an excellent officer: dutiful, responsible, focused. In a thousand generations, I could not have found a better executor, a better assistant captain... a better friend."

Sebastian screwed up his muzzle, choking back the tears that longed to emerge. Even though talking about Adrian relaxed him and his speech, he dare not cry in front of his crew.

"Now let us begin the Touch phase." Sebastian grabbed a bundle of flowers from the table. "The zulican flower is the most sacred plant to the vulpine genus. Max Himself discovered them growing wild in the otherwise-barren wastes of Genesis, the lone native plant-life of our home planet. He named them after His mate and our fellow Founder, Zulica, for it was said that their vibrant orange petals matched Her magnificent pelt, and were the only thing that could rival Her beauty.

"Our ancestors cultivated them, cherished them, and when we departed the cradle of Genesis for the stars, we took the zulican with us. It thrived upon the worlds we colonized, growing in the harshest of soils, sprouting and spreading as did we. It is said that the flowers represent our genus' very vitality, blossoming freely when we prosper and withering when we falter. During the Golden Age, much of the galaxy was covered in zulican flowers, but when we stumbled and fought each other, they retreated. When we fled a system, the zulican flowers upon it died, for they cannot live without our presence.

"They are the ultimate symbol of the vulpine genus, our common origins, eternally binding the Houses despite our differences. Max said that its three petals stand for our birth, our life, and our death. Its ability to thrive in harsh climes is representative of our survivability, and its majestic appearance symbolizes our beauty. It dies when one of its petals is removed, a message that should our genus become divided against itself, we will fall. As the only native plant to Genesis, it is also a memento from our homeworld and humble beginnings.

"Every fox throughout the galaxy takes these lessons to heart and cultivates their own personal crop of zulican flowers. They follow us wherever we venture. These are Adrian Miller's zulicans; with his death, so comes theirs."

Sebastian waved a paw over the blossoms, whispered a short prayer in his native Volpa, and offered them to the dog seated closest.

"They will now be passed around," Sebastian said. "Touch them with the utmost of solemn respect, and reflect upon the way Adrian has touched our lives."

He stepped back to watch the path of the bright orange flowers. Paw to paw they travelled, through the hands of collies, gersheps, goldas, corgen, dingos, dholes, coyotes, carthagans, and the dozen non-canine minority present.

At journey's end, Randolph returned them, the lone human in his crew. He smiled and handed them to Sebastian.

"It was a lovely reading, sir," Randolph said.

Sebastian nodded absently, distracted by the flowers. He stroked the delicate, velveteen petals; only an hour ago, he had retrieved them from Adrian's quarters, and their life was already fading.

"Thank you," he said, stepping back to the podium. Only one final task remained.

"The concluding stage begins, the Farewell. The casket will be opened, and each will file past, saying a short prayer for the departed's spirit. This is the last chance to say goodbye to Assistant Captain Adrian Miller, for after this, the casket will be permanently sealed."

Sebastian placed his paws upon the pine surface of Adrian's coffin. It lay horizontal, with little flair or flourish, elevated on a pair of universal cargo containers. All that denoted the box's significance was its coat of paint, the cerulean base and tan trim of Adrian's native House Florenzo.

With a solemn heart, he drew open the upper half. There Adrian lay, silent and peaceful, naked as per custom. He'd never looked better; Sebastian couldn't even tell he'd been shot.

Something was missing.

His hackles raised, his fur bristled. He spun on his heels and pointed an accusing paw at Corey Delzano. "Where is it... *where is it!?*"

"Where is what?"

Sebastian clenched his paws into tight fists. "Adrian's *fallora*. Where is it?" Corey stared back in silence. Infuriated, Sebastian snatched the waist end of his sash and waved it at Corey. "This! Where is Adrian's?"

"In his belongings, where it has been packed."

"You miserable cur!" Sebastian said. "You told me you knew our rituals, the Rite Of Passage! You said you studied our sociology and culture! You say that you'd be able to handle preparation while I organized service!"

"I was never told of your sash! They said your kind was buried fully naked!"

Sebastian stalked up to the seated jackal. "Do you have idea what you done? You know what *fallora* means to us? It is civilization, sentience, connection to past and ancestry. It separates us from stupid dogs like you! Without it, he's worthless, savage like you pathetic lappunds!"

"I swear by Kohoutek, I did not know—"

"Shut your ugly brown vullisvolk face! Your thoughtless actions, empty promises have disgraced honor and memory of my best friend!"

Randolph stood. "I'm sure Corey meant no offense..."

"Muzzle it," Sebastian said. "The Ritual is terminated. All of you leave, now."

He turned his back to his crew. He had failed Adrian on the mission, failed him again by passing such a solemn duty to an Outsider. He had been so careless, and had only himself to blame.

The congregation ebbed away, silent save for the rustle of tails upon fabric and boots upon steel. Corey approached from behind and placed a paw on Sebastian's arm. It felt cold.

"Sebastian, I..."

"Go," Sebastian said. "Leave now."

"But..."

"Leave, affakravox. There is nothing to say to you."

Corey clutched his paws, wrung them, and stared down at the smaller fox. His jaws worked as if he wanted to speak, but Sebastian kept his back to him. Crestfallen, Corey left the fox alone in the cargo bay.

Sebastian fell against the coffin. He slammed his fist on it and mumbled in his native tongue, but the Volpa came out incomprehensible, discomforting. Like his Creator 490 years before, the fox wept.

I never understood why the other genera were so angry with us. The Creator was quite clear when He told me that we were His favorite, that we were the chosen to lead His creations into the future. I can only imagine that the others must be jealous. Perhaps it will lead to strife in the future.

-The Memoria, The Book of Max, Chapter 30, verses 1-4.

SCENE TWO

I don't think he wants to see you."

Corey Delzano dismissed Junior Lieutenant Patricia Darling's reservation with a wave of his paw. "I am aware of this, but the Captain has been absent from duty for two days."

"You're next in the chain to succeed to Assistant Captain. You go blasting into his cabin like this, he'll fire you, yeah? At best, you'll jeopardize your promotion!" Patricia stepped in front of him and blocked his path with her shorter, stockier body. "And there's another thing."

"You think it is too early to ask about a promotion?" Corey said.

Patricia tucked her rounded ears down against her head, a frown on her short muzzle. The mottle-furred Wild canine just shook her head. "You're not taking this seriously."

"On the contrary, my dear carthagan, this is something I take very seriously."

Corey slipped around her and continued down the starship's barren steel corridor. The fluorescent lighting caught the edges of his yellow duty jumpsuit, and it sparkled around his rank insignia.

Patricia followed close behind. "You're senseless. At least wait until later, when your promotion is official, yeah?"

"If our dear Captain remains hidden much longer, there may be no later." Corey reached the elevator doors at the end of the hallway, pressed a button, and waited for the summoned car to arrive. "And why, pray tell, do you show such interest in my promotion?"

"Well, you're a good officer. I don't want to see you do something loopy."

"This is because you are next in the line of command after me, is it not?" Corey asked.

"No!"

"No?"

"Well…"

The elevator doors parted. A pair of young canines stepped out, dark blue shoulder pads indicating their billet as engineering. Corey adjusted his own red command epaulets, stepped into the elevator, and pressed the button for "A" Deck.

Patricia slipped in and stood beside him. "Okay, maybe! But let's be grounded here. How much command experience do you have?"

"Admittedly, precious little."

"Right! And you work two shifts, yeah?"

""A" Shift sub-command and "B" Shift command."

"So, think on it," Patricia said. "Let's give a month for you to learn the alls of command, yeah?"

Corey propped himself on the elevator railing. "I am certified for starship command, but it is true that learning the involutions of the ship, its performance, and its crew will take some time."

"And I'm even less experienced in command, yeah? What do you think will happen if you flub and I'm stuffed into Assistant?"

The elevator reached "A" Deck, and they stepped out into the officer's corridor. The cabins here were larger, their doors further apart.

"You are a fine staff officer. I am sure you would be an adequate assistant captain," Corey said.

"Well, you've got more confidence in me than I do. My point is, I don't have the experience even you do."

"Somehow, I distrust your motives."

"Distrust my motives?" Patricia said. "Hey, you're the jackal, here!"

Corey stopped outside the Captain's quarters. "And suppose you are attempting to cause worry and doubt in me before I speak to the Captain?"

"Now why would I do that?"

Corey smirked. "Well, in the unlikely scenario where I manage to get released or demoted, I presume you would be advanced to fill the command void."

"Now just because I'd stand to gain two whole paygrades doesn't mean—"

Corey laughed, sharp and barking, and Patricia tucked her ears back. "You are not quite as good at hiding your motives, carthagan," Corey said. "You are already getting a substantial raise from staff lieutenant to senior lieutenant. What is it monthly, twenty-eight dollars?"

"And seventy-five cents. But—"

"But if you could jump to assistant captain, that is another twenty-seven on top of that."

"And fifteen cents, but it's not about money, Corey."

"Of course not, says the mercenary."

Patricia sighed and folded her arms. "Now you know that's not the whole reason. You should understand, we have similar backgrounds."

"I do not doubt that. But I suspect you are extra motivated because you stand to acquire a pay raise double the average Canis Dominion worker's annual salary."

"Yeah, sure, maybe," Patricia said. "But then again, I've not been here too long, I'm not sure if the Captain would shoot me up the ranks so fast."

"It is true that you lack command experience."

Patricia snorted. "And even I can tell that what you're about to do is witless."

"What I am going to do is increase my standing in the Captain's eyes."

"But you're the one that got him all riled up."

Corey leaned on a bulkhead. "Patricia, you look at this as the painted dog you are, not like the fox he is. I understand it is difficult to look beyond one's genus when considering another's thoughts, but thinking of our dear Captain's problem like a carthagan or a Wild canine would be improper."

"And you're some sort of expert, yeah?"

"I majored in diplomacy at the National Institute of Zettler, with minors in vulpine psychology, sociology, anthropology, and physiology."

"And a fine lot of help it's been, yeah?"

Corey turned an admonishing eye to Patricia. "Let me try to explain this. The vulpine may superficially resemble us canines, but his brain is not like yours or mine. It functions differently, with different values, morals, and ethics. He is cautious, tactical, adaptive, greatly distrustful of other genera, fond of individual companionship with those of his own kind, and averse to large groups."

"So you're going to approach him like another fox would?"

"More or less."

Patricia waggled her finger at him. "It's not going to work. I'm not sure if you've noticed, but you're no fox."

"Let me put it another way. You recall the passage the Captain read from the Memoria?"

"The one where Max ran away like a coward and hid?"

Corey chuckled. "I would advise you not to refer to the vulpine Founder as a 'coward' in the Captain's company. But yes, that one."

Patricia shrugged. "What of it? That was five hundred years ago."

"It is the vulpine instinct." Corey crossed his lithe arms. "The fox's first thought is to flee, save his own pelt and spare himself from immediate harm. When cornered, he looks for an escape route. It was only with years of training and focus could Sebastian overcome his instincts, but now, rather than face his problems, he has fled, like Max. It will consume and cripple him, lest I spur him to action."

"He's not going to like being spurred."

"What the Captain likes or dislikes is irrelevant. In mere hours, the hyperdrive batteries will be charged. He must tackle responsibility."

Patricia shook her head and arched her shoulders against the wall. "He's never let non-foxes in his cabin before. What makes you think he'd start now?"

"Circumstances are different."

"Hey, why don't you let Guido handle this?" Patricia said. "He's highly trained in psycho-fluffit and meta-cerebral-whatever. And he's human."

"It was my first idea. One of the Creator's descendents would be more welcome and trusted, but the Captain refused Randolph's audience. Randolph suggested that, as the source of aggravation, I should apologize and seek reconciliation personally."

"Makes sense," Patricia said. "You know, everyone else just calls him Guido. Why don't you?"

Corey pressed the buzzer for Captain Valentino's cabin. "It is disrespectful to his given name."

Seconds dragged on, with no response from within. Corey reached out to buzz again, but Patricia grabbed his hand.

"Maybe he's not home?" she said.

"I sincerely doubt that our dear Captain would not be present in his own cabin."

She shook her head. "Wait a jacking minute, yeah? You buzz him all day, he'll just get huffier."

Corey heaved a slow breath and nodded. The gravity of the situation was making him impatient, and the last thing he needed was to cause further exacerbation.

At last, the Captain's distorted voice crackled across the intercom speaker.

"Away."

Corey and Patricia exchanged glances. "Don't do it," she said.

It was too late. Corey had already pressed the intercom button. "Captain, it is Senior Lieutenant Corey Delzano. I wish an audience."

"I want not to speaking at you. You of them."

Corey flinched. Sebastian's Mahonic had broken down further. Even at Adrian's funeral, he seemed well composed, but now his accent shone through.

"It is crucial, Captain," Corey said. "I seek atonement."

"Fine. You only. Patricia, no."

Patricia contorted her ears back. "How in the blazes did he know I was here?"

"He is quite intelligent and inductive, and knew I would not come alone. Wait for me."

Corey slid his name badge through the door's electronic lock. It clicked, and he stepped into the room. It was nearly devoid of light. Any further movement could encounter some unseen object, so he held his ground and waited for his eyes to adjust to shadow.

"I wishing you to come here not, affakravox," Sebastian said.

"Your speech has regressed."

"Hard is speaking your talk, when I am mad."

"Your Mahonic is very good, for a fox."

"Thanking," Sebastian whispered.

Corey's eyes adjusted to the light, and he nearly gasped at the sight before him. Various trinkets lay scattered across every horizontal surface. Every square centimeter contained an artifact of vulpine culture, some of which Corey recognized from his classes. Even the floor and television supported unidentifiable scraps of paper.

Sebastian was next to his duty desk, knelt on the floor, unkempt fur spilled across his muzzle. He faced away from Corey and towards the room's preeminent feature, a shrine to the vulpine Founder, Max. Soft candlelight shone across the gilded statue, jagged shadows leaping from its ears and muzzle. Sebastian still wore his tunic.

"I did not mean to interrupt you while praying, Captain."

"You did."

Corey carefully worked his way closer. He looked over the fox's shoulder and studied the scene. He tried to think of words to say, but all he thought of felt out of place. He said nothing.

"It was for Adrian," Sebastian said.

"I am sorry for your loss."

"It should be not."

Corey called on his training in the Volpa language. It was far too difficult a tongue for a non-fox to speak, but he'd had structural theory and syntax education. So long as Sebastian didn't slide into full Volpa, Corey could glean Sebastian's meaning from context.

"What should not have been?" Corey asked.

"Adrian. Should, not should be there."

"What do you mean?"

Sebastian stroked one paw over his face, wrapped his fingers about his whiskers and then released. "Adrian should not be there."

"We all have to go sometime, Sebastian. It is natural."

"No!" Sebastian bared his teeth. "You understand not! Adrian is, Adrian is not, not for sneaking. It was not, he was not."

Sebastian was grimacing when he spoke, as if the very act of speaking even fractured Mahonic required great effort. Corey would expect the average fox to stumble over the common language, but he had never seen such from Sebastian.

"Adrian was not good at infiltration, though he was Volpa." Sebastian spoke slow, deliberate. "He was good, but not enough. Not enough for *kehnellya*. They are good. I am good enough. Adrian was not. He should not have go."

"It was your choice to bring him. Why?"

"Adrian was good at computing. He was good-good, good than you, than any of *fassala*. I needed his good-good computing for the mission. The mission was hard, hard-hard, more than it could handle. I could handle. Adrian could not. It dies."

"What happened?"

Sebastian's lips twisted into a fleeting half-snarl. "We beat the mission, beat the *kehnellya fal fassat*. It was hard-hard. We are catch. I escape, I escape Adrian too. Adrian wanted to flee. I tell it we go too far to run. We should have flee, as Adrian wants. We finish mission, we kill *kehnellya*, catch information, Adrian computes, *fassat* destroy. I catch fasthatch, we escape. *Kehnellya* kill Adrian as we escape."

Corey frowned. Sebastian was smattering his speech with Volpa, and it made it more difficult for Corey to decipher the true meaning.

"You were caught, Adrian wanted to abort, you pressed on, downloaded the required information, destroyed the facility, and Adrian was killed during the escape. Am I correct?"

Sebastian turned away and nodded.

"You did everything you could to protect Adrian and complete the mission," Corey said. "He joined you as an employee, to make money. That was what you were doing. These are the things that happen."

Sebastian hung his head. "Adrian not worth money. We must have fleeing, not push on. Not worth money."

"You thought you could complete the mission, even though you were captured." Corey placed a paw on Sebastian's shoulder, but Sebastian pulled away with such ferocity that Corey recoiled.

"What I think mean nothing!" Sebastian said. "Careless, careless! Now Adrian dies. I am fault."

Corey had assumed he was the cause of Sebastian's anger, but it clearly went far deeper than that.

He noticed an object in the fox's paws. "You have a holocube. May I see it?"

When he reached for it, Sebastian shied away and clutched the object tight to his chest. Sebastian's muzzle momentarily contorted, as if he reconsidered, and then he offered it.

Corey held the holocube's rectilinear plastic case between finger and thumb. It was transparent, twenty centimeters tall by nine wide, with a flared, black base. Inside its clear confines, a synthetic-green, flat shaded vulpine stood, dressed in a Star Alliance military dress uniform. It was Adrian.

Corey examined it, turned it this way and that, watching Adrian's projected form from all angles. "When did you get this?"

"Completion. Say should be there."

Corey checked the base, found the inscription, and frowned. "I cannot read Volpa."

He handed the holocube back to Sebastian. He took it and stared over his shoulder up at Corey. The fox's ears canted, as if expecting a question.

"Read it to me?"

"Why?"

"Please?" Corey asked. "I have never heard a native Volpa speaker."

"Fine." Sebastian flipped the holocube over and read, voice smooth and sure on his native tongue. "*For-falla, yallafa reffel val, mar sa-sahken, selfa forsa corvassa, yallafa reffel yallaf, Fella Velaya* Adrian Miller, *San-vel Vel-fyarf,* Ramshaft *salf.*"

Corey's ears homed in on the sounds, the syllables of the language. It had a wondrous, lilting quality, the words warm and inviting, yet meaningless to him.

"What does all that mean, in Mahonic?" Corey asked.

"Class 490, Completion Duty, 12 Corvus, 494. *Fella Velaya* Adrian Miller, *San-vel Vel-fyarf,* Ramshaft V."

"It is amazing that you can translate in real-time," Corey said. Sebastian just turned away, and Corey leaned in to look closer at him. "Are you crying?"

"No."

"What is it?"

Tears welled up in the fox's eyes. A lone drop slipped down his face, to vanish into his fur, but Sebastian remained silent.

"A lot of memories?" Corey asked.

Sebastian nodded, stiffened, and kept his face away.

"What was it like, Sebastian? Was there a ceremony?"

Sebastian turned the holocube so that Adrian stared back at him, preserved in time. "Yes. Many years ago, for Volpa who finishing duty, four years. We gather, Temple City on Ramshaft. It was a big deal, many of class was there, end for we in *San-vel Vel-fyarf.* We were still young, fourteen. Three years of duty, one in GDF, time in training, teach us to fight in aerofighter. Adrian was there, they all were. We met at the city's Great Hall, *Arraf Velaya* Corson said a few words, thanked us for our duty. They gave us a bonus, money, let us arrange transit to anyplace on planet."

"Those Volpa words, what meaning do they have?"

Sebastian frowned. "You said you studied me. Us. Volpa. You do not know our military ranks? War force? Your education was good not as you thought, then?"

"There is a significant difference between being taught by a teacher, and being taught by one's subject."

"Then, I tell you." Sebastian aligned the holocube so that the virtual Adrian faced the shrine of Max. "The Volpa military is divided in three series, called *Vel-larf*. There is *Vollana*, core or foundation, that is the low one with the basic soldiers. After is *Velaya*, warfighter, soldier, the middle one with field officers, that was the one Adrian and I were. Highest up is *Fallara*, thinker, plotter, strategy-maker, the highest generals. *Arraf* means elder, *Arraf Velaya* is the highest rank in the *Velaya Vel-larf*. Lower than that is *Fella Velaya*, respected or trusted warfighter, that was Adrian, and below that is *San-annafa Velaya*, infinite or watchful warfighter, that was me. *San-vel Vel-fyarf* is the army we were assigned to, *San-vel* means continuous war, *Vel-fyarf* is war force. Dig?"

Corey was attentive, ears upright, and though the words themselves may have held little meaning to him, the relaxed look upon Sebastian's face made it worthwhile. The more Sebastian spoke of Adrian, the better his Mahonic got. "That is very interesting," Corey said.

Sebastian sat up and looked at Corey. "You smell honest. I should teach you more of us sometime. You would like that?"

"Indeed I would, Captain. But I came here for a different reason."

"What's that?"

Corey leaned gently down towards the fox. "Sir, we need you. We need your presence about the ship. It is excessively disconcerting for the crew, and myself, to be deficient in your authority, particularly considering the state we last saw you in."

"I know."

"I understand how grieving is important for your people, how you must spend time regarding Adrian, to remember him. But I also know that mourning alone in this way can be destructive, even if there are no foxes you can share with. You cannot hide like this."

"I'm not hiding."

"Perhaps not. Perhaps you are fleeing?" Corey said. Sebastian glared at him, but Corey ignored it and continued. "Perhaps it is your instinct. You are like Max. When He learned the truth, it hurt Him, and He fled to the wastes in anguish. That is what you are doing now. But there are those here who need you as well. Max fled the Creator; He loved Him like a son, and it pained Him greatly. They both wept."

Sebastian turned away from Corey, but the jackal pulled him back. "Sebastian. Do you wish to harm us, who love you, who need your guidance and charisma, who have served with you so long, who would die for you?"

"No."

"Then come back to duty."

Sebastian nodded. "Maybe I should."

"Besides, my dear Captain, the jump batteries will be fully charged within hours, and we do not know which course we should take."

"You're trying to get to my sense of duty and responsibility," Sebastian said. "I like that, it's cunning."

"Regardless, we cannot remain in the Tamaroff system indefinitely. I am sure you have places that you wish to reach?"

Sebastian stood up and rubbed at his sore legs. "Yes. There are many places to go, many light years to travel."

"Your Mahonic has recovered."

Sebastian smiled. "Yes. I'm not quite so mad now. Have you sent off the data?"

"It has been taken care of. The foxes of House Wallace were most grateful for your work. The funds have been deposited into our CenCon account."

"That's good work. I'll remember that, rest assured. What about Adrian?"

Corey tilted his head. "What about him?"

"He needs to be cremated."

"Why?"

Sebastian sighed gently and crossed his arms. "Because his body has been disgraced, that's why."

Corey flinched, his ears tucked down. "I am greatly sorry for that."

Sebastian shrugged. "It was my fault too, for failing him, but it doesn't matter. Our bodies are created as from Max, we are all descended from Him, and as His children, it is our duty to keep our bodies in good condition, and we take them with us to the Everlife. Adrian's physical body has been disgraced, and it will no longer serve as a suitable vessel, so it must be burnt."

"I do not understand. Who will know the difference?"

Sebastian glared at Corey. "I will know, He Who Watches will know, and Adrian will know. Do you have any idea what is happening to him?"

Corey parted his jaws, as if to speak, but thought better of it and kept them closed.

"Right now," Sebastian said, "Adrian is lost. He has no body. He cannot even begin his life review. Until I seek forgiveness from Adrian's parents, he will continue to be adrift and not be at peace. Cremation is the first step towards giving him his final rest."

"I understand now, sir."

Sebastian quirked his ears outwards. "Do you? No matter, you don't have to. You just need to do as I say, right?"

Corey nodded. "What do you wish me to do?"

"Find a storage container big enough to put Adrian in. Get some hydrofuel, just a centiliter or two, so it leaves ashes and doesn't turn into that flaming tar."

"Where do you want it?"

Sebastian sighed. "Leave the supplies and Adrian's casket in the cargo bay, and empty everyone else out. It should be private, just me."

"Yes, sir."

"Thank you, Corey. Shall we go now?"

Corey gestured to the captain's tunic. "I would recommend changing into your uniform, first."

Sebastian's ensuing laugh, though short, was a welcome sound. "Of course! Scamper on up to the bridge, then, I'll be there in a bit."

Corey walked to the room's door, paused, and turned to face Sebastian. "One last thing."

"Yes?"

"Where should we go?"

"Wexford."

Corey canted his muzzle to one side. "What is on Wexford?"

Sebastian fetched his duty suit's polyester top from the floor and tossed it between his paws. "Two things. The Alliance Mercenary Liaison on Wexford is a good friend of mine, he promised me a contract. More importantly, it's Adrian's birthland. I must seek his parents and perform the Rite of Atonement, to correct the dishonor we have made."

Corey could have stopped everything right there. He could have objected, insisted that such a ritual was outdated in modern interstellar society, protested the order to travel a hundred light years with no guarantee of a contract. With reasoned judgment, he might even have convinced Captain Valentino not to embark on the journey at all, and prevented the catastrophe that would result.

Instead, Corey Delzano nodded and silently left Sebastian's quarters.

***

Sebastian usually enjoyed the peaceful serenity of study. It kept his mind active, and gave him a glimpse into what sharper minds had done throughout history. It was also a pleasant break from his rigorous conditioning regimen.

Today wouldn't be quite so relaxing.

"Excuse me, Captain?"

Sebastian sighed and looked up over the top of his hefty tome on modern naval combat. A dingo with green general-duty epaulets approached him. "You're interrupting the Battle of Morswood, Collins," Sebastian said. "This better be important."

"Extremely. See, we just got into orbit, and—"

"Out with it, sydney."

Librarian Collins thrust a freshly printed newspaper into Sebastian's paws. "You'd better read this."

Sebastian was long used to the strange texture and appearance of shipboard paper. The translucent sheets glittered when the metal threading in its pressed pulp surface caught the light. Limitations in ink forced grayscale only, and a limited lifespan, but ship life had its concessions. It was a far better solution than shutting the crew out of external news.

Right now, Sebastian was concerned with the newspaper's cover: crosshairs super-imposed over a photograph of himself.

"What is this?" He read the headline. "Fox on the Run?"

"It's the National Informer—"

Sebastian slammed the paper down atop the reading table with a dull smack. ""I can see that, I'm not blind! I mean the caption, 'Number one mercenary becomes number one target.'"

"We just got it over Lafayette's newswire, it's dated yesterday. I got it to you as soon as I could."

Sebastian mumbled, sought out the associated story, and began to read. "Dateline, Sirius, 9 Aries. Canis Dominion officials stunned the galaxy today by proclaiming a bounty upon the head of Captain Sebastian Valentino, founder and commander of MerCom's highest ranked unit, Valentino's Star Rangers. The unprecedented announcement came just three triads after the destruction of an unidentified research installation in the Monterrey system, presumed to have been the work of the Star Rangers. This is the first time in history that a state has issued a bounty on a unit sanctioned by the Mercenary Command, and at a total payout of 3,000,000D, by far the largest ever offered for a single head.

"'The Dominion's loyal citizens have suffered far too long from the continuing war crimes committed by Valentino and his Star Rangers,' said Dominion Chief Mercenary Spokesman Tanya Millikay. 'Such acts can no longer go unpunished. The Dominion implores all willing and able warriors throughout the galaxy to rise up and stand against the Rangers' barbarism, to fight for civilization against vulpine oppression.'"

"War crimes, sir?" Collins said.

Sebastian didn't look up from the paper. "Best you not ask about that."

"Yes, sir. What else does it say?"

"Mercenary Analyst Veleko Elgin, of the firm Walsh and Associates, says this bold move will upset the balance of galactic power. 'We've expected the Dominion to retaliate in some fashion, but such a massive bounty will cause a definite backlash against them. The Rangers have a distinct anti-Dominion bias, with nearly seventy percent of their missions targeting the nation, but this action may be considered unwarranted, perhaps illegal.'

"The bounty cites as cause the murder of over seven thousand Dominion civilians through direct or indirect action, going into a detailed breakdown for the Thanton, Manta Point, Passchendaele, Ontario, Zettler, and Texas star systems. The Rangers have caused an estimated 117 million dollars of damage over the past seven years, bark bark bark..." Sebastian flipped further through the newspaper. "It keeps going for six more pages. Look at all this. There's background on us, background on the Dominion, background on me, a graph of the unit's stock price over the past 120 triads, on and on."

"What do we do?"

Sebastian rolled the paper up. "We'll just have to be more cautious. Thank you for bringing this to my attention, I've got to talk to Corey about it."

He swatted the newspaper into the dingo's chest, and stalked off to the bridge. The entire situation was ludicrous. The reason MerCom had been formed was to regulate, legalize, and legitimize mercenary work. A bounty on a licensed mercenary was unheard of, let alone potentially illegal.

Sebastian found the newly promoted Assistant Captain Corey Delzano right where he should be, on the bridge overseeing "B" Shift. The conversation between the two was curt. Corey insisted they cancel their travel to Wexford, while Sebastian proclaimed the journey of utmost spiritual importance. Corey pleaded that Sebastian at least allow an armed escort to accompany him to the surface, but he refused, and continued to do so for the eight days it took the Favored Sky to reach Wexford.

***

The Star Rangers arrived late on the sixth day of the month of Piscea. Sebastian bade his crew farewell, left Corey in command of the ship, and set out for Wexford II in his aerofighter.

The single-seat Corvair slipped through the exosphere and plunged into the planet's night air. A new day was beginning, a new chance for him to put right what was wrong. Stone Canyon Aeroport Control directed him to a lot designated for private and charter aerocraft. The fighter's dual Kennedy K-6 plasma jets wound down, the exhaust fading to black.

Sebastian unstrapped himself from the cockpit's safety harness and life support. A youthful male fox approached his fighter, dressed in the bright blue uniform of House Florenzo's Garrison Defense Force, illuminated solely by a pair of glowing safety bracelets.

Sebastian sighed, popped open the telescoping ground access ladder, and swung himself out of the cockpit. His tired legs gave when they met the pavement, and he faltered.

"You okay there?" the attendant asked.

"Yeah, fine." Sebastian unhooked his helmet and tossed it to the attendant. "Say, you speak Volpa, don't you?"

The attendant caught the helmet and appraised Sebastian suspiciously. Sebastian could have asked whether the sun was hot and gotten the same look. "Of course I do," the attendant said. "Why?"

"It's been a long time since I've talked to someone in Volpa, dig?"

"Star-hopper, huh?"

"You could say that."

The young fox stepped up to him and pulled a handscanner from his waist holster. "They'll ask you more about that inside. I need to know a few things from you, first. Do you assent to being scanned?"

Sebastian hesitated. He'd had his ID chip reconfigured before he left the Favored Sky, tested it four times, but he was still nervous every time he was scanned. He couldn't afford to have anything come up foul.

"Well?" the attendant said.

"I do."

"Thumb here."

The attendant slid open a small panel on his handscanner, revealing a square plastic reader. Sebastian pressed his thumb pad to it, and the machine beeped twice.

"Good. Give me your ear."

Sebastian squinted and leaned over towards the attendant. The night air was cold, stung his face, and made him flinch. The attendant held up the pistol-like device, pointed it at Sebastian's ear, and pulled the trigger. He passed it over Sebastian's skull once, twice, scowled, and then swatted the machine with his palm.

Sebastian frowned. "Is there going to be a problem here?"

The attendant peered down at the handscanner's readout. "It's having a problem reading your chip, you're coming out all garbled."

"Try wiggling the cartridge."

The attendant joggled the interchangeable control cartridge, pulled it out and tapped its metal contacts, then reinserted it into his handscanner. He waved it over Sebastian's ear again. "You wearing anything ferric?"

"No. It's still wonky?"

"Handscanner's been acting up lately. Maybe it's just cranky tonight. Here, hold your ears straight up." The attendant gestured upwards, and Sebastian complied.

"Any luck?"

The young fox scanned Sebastian's ear and looked into the display. He twisted a knob and nodded. "There we go. Let me just double-check this information here. Name?"

Sebastian patted his Corvair's nose. "Her name is Beth."

The attendant flicked his ears and smirked. "No, your name."

"Billy Woodson," Sebastian said.

The attendant checked the display and nodded. "Yeah, checks out. This says you're from House Sofia?"

"Right."

"Pedigreed or stray?"

Sebastian twisted his muzzle up, restraining an induced snarl. "I'll have you know that Woodson was one of the four original pedigrees of House Sofia. I come from a long and storied lineage of—"

The attendant waved off the impending tirade. "Just checking. What you got here, Billy?"

"M220 Corvair aerofighter."

"It's a nice plane, haven't seen one of these since the service. I used to work on them." The other fox examined the nose wheel. "She new?"

"Hardly."

"Date of construction and date of purchase?"

"She was built at the Triple-M plant on Stanton on 17 Carkinus, 491. I purchased her second-hand from Alsatia Hardware on Exodus, 4 Capricus 495."

The attendant checked his scanner's readout to verify. "Looks like your chip is in order." He aimed his flashlight up the nose wheel well, looking for explosives or contraband. "She armed?"

"Nope."

"Those laser cannons look operable. What do you do to need guns like that?" The attendant asked.

"We've been having trouble with Arcadian separatists, so the company gave me a fighter," Sebastian said. "Used to fly these back in the service. CenCon permit should be on the chip."

"It is." The attendant orbited the delta-winged ship, writing notes as he went. He stopped and pointed his flashlight at an armor patch on the rear fuselage. "What's that?"

"That's a patch."

"I can see that. Why's it there?"

Sebastian scoffed and waved his arm at the patch. "I told you, we've been having problems with rebels and such."

The orderly glanced down at his scanner and frowned. "When?"

Sebastian sighed. "3 Ophiuchus, 502, took a class V laser shot to the rear in the Utica system, junked the intermix injectors and the relay pump, replaced by—"

"Rebels have something with that much firepower?"

"The Dolphin has class Vs."

The orderly chuckled and walked back towards the nose of the aerofighter. "You should've been able to outmaneuver a Dolphin in this. Any luggage?"

"Travel case behind the cockpit seat."

The other fox nodded and tapped a few buttons on his scanner. "You're all set. Head to the Acclimation Building over there and they'll set you up. Enjoy your stay here in House Florenzo."

Sebastian saluted the attendant and set off for the Acclimation Building. The lighted structure was inviting, ornately decorated, with vibrant colors, graceful arcing windows, and little regard to practicality. Double glass-paned doors led to a vast waiting area, with high ceilings and warm tones. Either sidewall housed a kiosk, each with uniformed attendants. Posters pressed bystanders to re-enlist in the National Military or apply for citizenship.

He passed through a security checkpoint and a scanner gateway. The security guard checked the display when Sebastian passed through, and gestured for him to put his hand in the DNA scanner bay. Sebastian did so, and a gentle suction pulled free loose hairs to test his DNA. It took no more than ten seconds, and after appraising the results, the security guard let him through. Sebastian's fake information was working well.

An electronic information board reported that he was due at Checkpoint B for acclimation. Strangely, there were no other flights listed. Even at midnight local time, there should have been dozens.

Sebastian stepped up to Checkpoint B. The bored grey fox behind the counter dropped his crossword puzzle glanced up at him, then pulled up Sebastian's information on his computer.

"Welcome to Stone Canyon Aeroport, Mr. Woodson. You're Sofia?"

Sebastian struck a dignified pose. "Absolutely. I trace lineage all the way to 139."

The grey fox tapped his pencil on the edge of his keyboard. "I served with a couple of your kind in the service. Nice people for reds. No offense, I mean."

"None taken."

"Good. Let me just verify some information from your chip. What type of insurance do you sell?"

"Industrial."

The grey nodded and glanced at his screen. "You have six children. What are their names?"

Sebastian leaned on the plasteen counter. His flight suit slid on its slick, artificial surface. "Nora, Keera, Seba, Wallace, Tyco, and Mitch."

"When, with whom, and where did you first couple?"

Sebastian huffed and crossed his arms on the countertop. "Sagittaria 4, 488, Jenna Kuhsman, in Vaylsburg on Utica VI."

"More specific."

Sebastian folded his ears down. "In the back seat of my Mark VII Maxim Motors Freestyle."

"Fastback or coupe?"

"Is this really necessary?"

The grey smirked. "Only if you want to be cleared for admittance."

Sebastian sighed. "It was a fastback with the 206 kilowatt dual rotor, power windows, and an autonavigator."

"Automatic or manual transmission?"

"It was the automatic four-speed, now are you quite done?"

The grey chuckled and nodded. "Yes, quite. Security measures and all that. I'll run your authorization through here, it'll be a margin before you're cleared. Have a pen, take a seat, watch some TV."

"What's on?"

"Does it look like I care? Do you know how many times I've heard the same vexing stories from that stapard box?" The grey reclined and shooed Sebastian away with a paw. "Just go sit down, all right?"

Sebastian settled in to watch one of the Alliance Video Network's high-impact debate shows. At least it was interesting programming. Normally the AVN showed endless hours of banal regurgitated news.

"Hello, and welcome to CounterTalk. I'm your host, Reed Allen. Today, we discuss the issue of the declining vulpine birth rate: should it be a concern, and what does it mean for the Alliance?"

The male red host introduced a bookish grey on his left and a trim red vixen on his right. "Joining us today are Joel Goldstein, a demographer from the University of Quincy, Tyrholia, and Marisa Bayley, a political sciences professor from Corson University, Concorde. Joel, why don't we start with you: what is the issue here?"

"Good afternoon, Reed. As far as the University of Quincy and I are concerned, there is no issue. The vulpine species are simply experiencing a natural decline in line with projections based upon the sustainable resource limits of our

inhabited planets. As our resources are depleted, it's expected that our growth rate will slow."

"Marisa, how do you respond?"

The female leaned into the host's proffered microphone. "This isn't a matter of a so-called 'natural decay' in our growth rate, it's much more than that. In the past twenty years, our genus' growth has slowed almost 50%, from 2.14% to 1.32%. This is not decay, this is a cliff, and we're walking over it."

"Joel?"

"Populations cannot increase indefinitely," Joel said. "There are economic, social, and resource limits that cap a population to a given level. As our numbers increase, we will begin to face starvation, shortages, and the crippling economic cost of raising so many new kits."

Marisa tipped her muzzle downward to address the unseen audience. "Recent surveys indicate over 60% of the Alliance's available land mass is still unused. Studies show that we have enough arable land and mineral resources to sustain a population almost five times what we have now. The average vulpine couple now mates once only seven years, with litter sizes down to three. Twenty years ago, we mated seven months more often, and had an average of 3.5 children. If these declines continue, within the next two-dozen years our levels will begin to shrink."

"What my esteemed colleague fails to recognize," Joel said, "is that the survival rate of newborns has increased dramatically, to a current level of thirty-three percent. Fifty years ago, that number was thirty percent; one hundred years ago, barely twenty. The population is not 'decaying', as she puts it, it is stabilizing. The more children survive, the less our instincts tell us to mate."

Marisa shook her head. "Even with those advances, the average vulpine couple today has only four and a quarter surviving children in their lifespan. That's down significantly from the highpoint of last century in 446, when a couple had 5.9 per year."

"But what does this all mean for us?" Reed looked between the pair. "Why should it matter how many surviving children we have?"

Marisa grabbed the microphone from Reed's hand. "Because our enemies are still out there, and breeding faster than us! They've not forgotten our Golden Age, and they are waiting for the chance to pounce us when we are down. We cannot allow unfriendly states like the Canis Dominion or Pan-Atlantica Federation to exceed our populations, it would lead to a war of numbers that we would lose!"

Reed pulled his microphone back and offered it to the grey. "Joel?"

"You are making this into a far more emotional issue than it really is, vixen," he said.

"Of course I'm emotional! This is our children's future we're talking about."

Joel shook his head. *"The hard fact is that you cannot compare us with other states, regardless of their affinity or animosity for us. The other reason our levels are stabilizing is due to an increase in gross domestic product and per capita income. The average Alliance citizen earns almost ten times more per year than he would in the Dominion. Historical trends shows that economic prosperity is tied inversely to growth rates."*

"What it shows is complacency—"

"Hey, you." The voice of the grey fox desk clerk interrupted the televised debate. "You're ready to go. Follow the signs for baggage claim, they'll scan you again down there. One quick thing, though."

"What's that?"

"Well, you're from another House, so your DNA's not in the database. I put a waiver in the system for you so you won't flag every gateway, but until we get a clearance from Sofia, you'll be barred from entering most government buildings."

Sebastian nodded. "I know how it works, I do this all the time."

The grey shrugged and frowned. "Then you know that legally, I have to tell you. Enjoy your stay in House Florenzo."

"Thanks. Max be with you."

Sebastian left the entryway and hunted down his luggage. He passed through another security checkpoint and scanner gateway, and emerged into the broad concourse. The plastered concrete, vast windows, carpeting, and copious advertisements were all so warm, familiar. It already felt like home.

At the same time, the terminal was surprisingly desolate. An aeroport was a perpetual operation, so there should never be a lull in the arrival or departure of flights. Sebastian peeked out an observation window near a gate. A Conaero 500 tri-jet airliner rested, silent and shut down, rear airstairs deployed in expectation of passengers that wouldn't come. It had been years since Sebastian had seen the orange and blue Pan-Alliance Aerolines livery.

"Ain't she a beauty?"

Sebastian perked his ears and turned to face the speaker. He was an older grey fox, a centimeter taller, with traces of aged silver dotting his slate pelt. Sebastian nodded to him. "As far as aeroliners go."

"You know, the 500 was the first aeroliner to be certified for operation from gravel runways?" The grey smiled. "It's kind of funny to think of an aeroplane taking off from a surface so primitive and then climbing up out of the atmosphere. I've done it a few times."

Sebastian looked him over. "You're a pilot?"

"For over twenty years now, straight out of the National Military. I used to fly dropships back in the War, you know."

Sebastian absently nodded, and moved to step away from the grey. "You don't say?"

"I sure did!" The grey turned to follow him. "Into and out of some nasty situations. Mind you, the 500 flies a lot smoother than those big crates ever did."

"I'd figure."

"Anyway, I won't take up too much of your time here, I'm just handing these out." The grey shoved a pamphlet into Sebastian's hands. "We pilots are on strike, we'd like your support. Read that, it'll make you think about where your money goes next time you fly on Pan-Al."

Sebastian took the pamphlet, nodded, and walked away. It was a generic hit piece against the company, graciously supported by the Pan-Al Pilot's Commune. A pilot's strike would explain why the concourse was suspiciously empty.

Sebastian threw the pamphlet away at the nearest rubbish can.

At least the terminal was open; it would provide some services. The CenCon Administrar Station advanced two hundred dollars spending money into his on-site cache. A deserted sandwich-shop provided him with a rabbit salad wrap.

Sebastian staggered into his room. It was bedecked with technological amenities and a plush décor, but they didn't interest him. He headed straight for the bed and sprawled across it. It felt good to stretch his stiff form, regardless of the tight flight suit clinging to his body.

A vast plastiglass window stretched from one end of the room to the other. It had slipped his gaze before, but now it captivated him. Even at night, the busy metropolis pulsed with light and life. Concrete buildings, sheathed in mirrored glass, jutted out at irregular angles. Billboards occupied every square centimeter of space and extolled the virtues of the highest bidders' product or service.

It was mesmerizing, the way the cars and people below twisted and entwined around the city streets. He felt as though he could watch for hours, but rest beckoned him. A few tasks must be accomplished before he could sleep.

First, he emptied his travel case. Its hardened steel exterior hid a change of clothing, personal items, and his Traveler 5000 wearable information computer. Underneath were Adrian's fallora and two hard plastic boxes. One held one of Sebastian's zulicans; he would need it when he went to atone. The other held Adrian's ashes.

He set them aside, and changed into his casual outfit. It was refreshing to be free from his confining flight suit. He wandered about the hotel room and discovered a full-length mirror in the bathroom.

Sebastian stopped in front of it, his own reflection looking back at him. He tossed his fur with a paw, grinned, and gave in to the temptation of watching himself pose. He bent forward to grab his ankles, and a metallic object tumbled free from his shirt pocket. He knelt to observe it and swept his golden locks from his eyes. It was the Ankh of Kohoutek. Sebastian scooped it up in one nimble paw, held it to his face, and shifted it from side to side. It glittered when the room's fluorescent light caught its edges.

Though its presence was happenstance, he read a deeper meaning into it. It was one last message from Adrian, a final promise from Corey of good luck. Sebastian would need all the luck he could get, so the Ankh of Kohoutek wound up around his neck.

There has never been a problem that cannot be overcome with sufficient planning.

-The Memoria, The Book of Florenzo, Chapter 2, Verse 1.

SCENE THREE

Far above the planet's surface, in his officer's quarters, a jarring buzzer interrupted Assistant Captain Corey Delzano's sleep. He rolled over in his bed, swatted the alarm off, and spoke into the wall-mounted intercom.

"What is it?" he said.

"Ensign Travecki here. Captain Valentino on the comm, sir."

"Patch him through, ensign."

Corey ground the sleep from his eyes, stumbled to the wall-mounted videocomm, and met Sebastian Valentino's cheery visage.

"Greetings, Assistant Captain," Sebastian said. "Did I wake you?"

"No, I never sleep. I am awake and upright twenty-four hours."

"In a row?"

Corey scowled at him, but said nothing.

"You look like you never sleep. Get some rest, be fresh for command," Sebastian said.

Corey slumped against the wall. "How can you be so vexingly cheerful this late? What precluded you from contacting me in the morning?"

"But it is morning. 0220 local time, 25th cycle Lunafour. It's dark out here."

"I do not care about what time it is there."

"Well I certainly do. I need to get my body adjusted to local time, circadian rhythms and all that. You know, a cycle here is longer," Sebastian said.

"That gives you an extra hour and a half a day to sleep."

Sebastian grinned and flicked his ears. "Now, now, is that any way to talk to your boss?"

Corey sighed and shook his head. "Sorry, Captain. Now, you have a summation for me, I presume?"

"You presume correctly, are you recording?"

"I am now."

Five thousand kilometers away, Sebastian reclined. A stray beam of artificial light caught the ankh around his neck, illuminating it. "I arrived at 0013 standard time this morning. 200D has been forwarded from my personal credit line. I'm staying at the Vista Overlook Hotel, room 16-4, it's in the aeroport. Next contact will be at, let's say 1400 GST, 8 Piscea? You'll be awake then."

"Yes, yes, that will be an adequate time," Corey said. "How is your chip performing?"

"Perfectly. Even aeroport security believes I'm Billy Woodson, on business and selling insurance."

"Woodson? Isn't that a House Sofia pedigree?"

Sebastian canted his head, ears upright. "You know about those, huh? Well, you're right, it is."

Corey frowned. "Forgive me for telling you something you already know, but—"

"You're not going to tell me that falsely claiming to be pedigreed is a major crime in the Alliance, are you?"

Corey's jaws parted, as if he would refute the claim, and yet he remained silent. That was precisely what he had intended to say.

"Why do you think I picked a Sofia pedigree?" Sebastian asked. "It's a hundred-something light years away, it's seven HCP jumps from here to the Sofia system. It'll take five days for Florenzo internal security to send an inquiry to the pedigree admins and get a response, and I don't plan on staying that long."

"It is still a risk."

"No more than reprogramming my ID chip. Besides, being Sofia lets me cruise around in a warbird without suspicion."

Corey shook his head. "I suppose it does. What are you planning to do from now until then?"

Sebastian toyed with the ankh around his neck. "Things to do, people to talk at, you know? I need to buy new clothes."

"What in blazes does that have to do with anything?"

Sebastian gestured to his casual outfit. "Simple. These are too boring."

"I do not need to remind you that we are on a mission, and you are costing us money."

"Relax, I'm spending my own cash."

Corey scowled. Sebastian always had an answer for everything. "Fine," Corey said, "but at least keep the health of the unit in mind while you are roving."

Sebastian smiled. "Don't I always? End transmission."

The viewer flickered off, and Sebastian's face disappeared. Corey held his skull. Twelve hours into his first command, and Sebastian was already trying his nerves. Corey imagined that Sebastian was testing his resolve, but from what he knew of foxes, Sebastian was more likely being mischievous.

Corey's shift would begin soon. There was no sense in returning to bed, so he changed into uniform. He teased at his epaulets, ran his finger over his rank insignia. It had been five triads – over a month and a half – and his duty jumpsuit still had yet to be updated to reflect his new position.

He was about to leave his cabin when the buzzer sounded once again.

"What?" Corey said.

"Ensign Haxxell here, sir. An unidentified warship has jumped in system."

"Unidentified?"

"Yes, sir. The Star Alliance and House Florenzo report no scheduled arrivals for the next three triads."

"Size?"

"No specifics at this range, sir. Radar profile suggests a capital ship," Haxxell said.

A capital ship! Wexford was not a border world, so the odds were against it being prelude to an invasion or a diversionary attack. It left only one logical possibility.

"Mercenary?" Corey asked.

"Possible. That would suggest an assault carrier."

An assault carrier was a troubling prospect. Only the most successful mercenary units, like the Star Rangers, could afford to operate their own warships.

"On my way to the bridge," Corey said.

By the time Corey arrived, the contact had disappeared. He walked over to the radar station and looked over the young ensign's shoulder. The console indicated no naval contacts outside of Wexford II's orbit.

Haxxell looked up from his radar station. "Well, uh, it was here a minute ago, coming in from, uh, Jump Point Quartzon. Then it, um, wasn't."

"It must be out there," Corey said. "An assault carrier is too big for a cloaking device."

"I know that, sir, but I checked the alternatives. There's no sign of debris, no energy signatures. I ran a self-diagnostic, it came up with nothing." Haxxell shook his head. "It's not gone, it's just not there."

"There must be a logical explanation." Corey punched the console's buttons and swapped through all available radar ranges. There were no starship contacts within the system, but one icon caught his eye. "There, what is that?"

"That's Wexford III, but that's just a planet."

"Sometimes a planet is more than just a planet. It is the only object between Point Quartzon and us. Pull up the data."

Haxxell tapped his keyboard, and reams of information appeared on the console, everything from surface temperature to core composition. To the untrained eye, it was all technical gibberish, but Corey knew what to look for. He pointed to a line of information. "Highly active magnetosphere," Corey said.

"What about it?"

Corey stared down at the ensign. How had Haxxell advanced to bridge crew without the most basic of starship tactical training? "A magnetosphere of that magnitude can be used to hide a starship from sensors," Corey said. "They can see out, but we cannot see in. Someone knows we are here."

"What should we do?"

Corey dropped into the captain's chair. Though the options were limited, this was his first real command decision. Numerous mundane explanations existed, but the bounty forced him to be cautious.

"Set a radar computer lock on Wexford III. Set an alarm for any change in condition." Corey folded his arms. "You do know how to do that, yes?"

"Yes, of course."

"Then do it, ensign."

***

For the first four hours of his command career, Corey was awake and alert, but as time passed, his interest waned. "C" Shift departed, "A" Shift arrived, and Wexford III remained stoically stable through orbit after orbit.

There was nothing to do on the bridge, so Corey decided to tour the ship. He'd yet to meet many of the four hundred crewmen now under his command. There was no change in condition anywhere on the ship, and after brief conversations with the division chiefs, he was back on the bridge.

Guilt kept him focused on duty, but it was tedious. The only thing he could do was peruse the ship's numerous operations reports. He could access the digital reports from his comfortable command chair, but it was little consolation. They were dry, endless figures, punctuated by occasional graphs. As he hunted, a steady pattern of neglect appeared. Inventories were missing, meetings had been cancelled, resupply dates had been repeatedly pushed back. It started after Adrian's death. Had Sebastian been using Adrian as a crutch for all those years?

Corey only left the bridge for necessities. "B" Shift came, occupied the bridge for eight hours, and then they gave way to "C" Shift. Corey handed the bridge to Staff Lieutenant Greco, and then retired for sleep.

Corey's second day of command was just as tiresome. This time, not even guilt could keep him on the bridge. A third of the way into his shift, he disappeared to the ship's gym.

He sparred with a few of the ship's dedicated security forces in unarmed combat. With those of similar size, he fared poorly. He found little amusement in being flipped and beaten by those trained in punterkamp.

Smaller opponents provided a better challenge. Corey grappled with a young golda, a canine Familiar of shorter stature, and managed to flip and pin him. The golda snarled in frustration, strained to free himself, but soon capitulated. Corey helped him to his feet, shook hands with him, and watched the raging young golda stalk back to duty.

"You look angry," a voice from the other side of the room said.

Corey hadn't heard Darling come in. How long had she been spying on him? "You should be on the bridge," he said.

"Why? There's nothing to do up there."

"You should be taking your new duties seriously. Oh, and congratulations on your promotion."

"Yeah, I feel special, skipping staff lieutenant and going straight to senior lieutenant." Patricia ambled around the starship's compact gym, grabbed a twenty-kilogram dumbbell, and tossed it absently between her paws. "And I'm perfectly serious, I just came to see what you're doing. You probably hurt that poor guishund, throwing him like a ragdoll, yeah?"

Corey mopped his forehead with a towel. "He had a mat to land upon."

"Yeah, I bet that helped. What did he do to you, anyway?"

"Fusilier Robins presents no qualms to me."

"That's not what it looked like."

Corey watched her toss the weight. "You are pretty strong for a carthagan."

She grinned at him. "You know it. Where did you learn to fight like that, anyway? They didn't teach us that in the Dominion."

"Our dear Captain attempted to teach me a modicum of punterkamp, and the ways in which it should be used, though the disciplines he knows are incompatible with my physique. He merely demonstrated a few fundamental holds and throws that I should utilize, to maximize my height and reach advantage."

"The Captain knows punterkamp?"

Corey stepped out of the change room and tossed his towel away. Patricia replaced the weight and followed him out of the gym. "Affirmative. Apparently, he is quite proficient in multiple disciplines, and is an impressively comprehensive athlete."

"I'd no idea."

"He is never compelled to employ it while in our company. In the past, we have sparred. He is quite impressive, and has repeatedly defeated me."

She looked him over. "For truth? I don't believe that, you're so much bigger."

"By sixty-nine centimeters and sixty-seven kilograms, to be precise."

"But the Captain is only… what, thirty kilograms? Thirty-five?"

"Thirty-three."

They stepped into the elevator. "So how does he do it?" Patricia asked.

"Captain Valentino is extraordinarily quick."

Patricia chuckled and leaned back, her tail beating against the elevator wall in amusement. "That's it?"

"It felt as though I were moving in slow motion. Every time I tried to attack, he was no longer where I was aiming. You should try him sometime."

"You just want to see me beaten up by someone tiny."

The doors parted and the pair emerged onto the bridge. Corey dismissed the officer in command of the bridge, and dropped into the captain's chair. It only gave Patricia a chance to corner him.

"So, what is it, anyway?" Patricia asked.

"What is what?" Corey said.

"What's got you upset?"

Corey stared up in silence, eyes narrowed on the disruptive carthagan. He wanted nothing more than to remove her from his presence.

"If that's how you want to be, I'll start guessing. Are you tired?" Patricia asked.

"A little."

"Is it that time of year?"

Corey scowled and bared his teeth. "No!"

Patricia shrugged. "Well, how should I know? You look like you'd be helped by the company of a nice jackal woman, if there is such a thing."

A snicker ran up from the bridge crew.

"It is not mating season for jackals, you insufferable whelp!" Corey said.

Patricia chuckled. "I'm insufferable, yeah? I may be only twenty, but I'm not the affakravox holding all my anger inside. Besides, it doesn't smell like your mating season anyway."

Corey screwed up his muzzle, clenched his teeth, and reclined. "Is there no one else you can pester?"

"As acting assistant captain, crew liaison, and third-in-command, it's my duty to advise the captain. Since that's you, that means you're exactly who I should be pestering." She leaned on his console. "Don't make me sic Guido on you."

He grumbled under his breath. "The last thing I need is some human blathering about how my feelings interact with my animal instincts..."

Patricia grinned. "I'm going to tell him you said that," she said. Corey glared at her, silent. "I bet it's Sebastian, yeah?"

Corey shook his hand at Patricia. "That irrational fool has been neglecting the daily operations for over a month, has drawn us far from course for no respectable reason, has cost us invaluable time and money, all so that he might deliver confessions to a pair of urban foxes he has not spoken with in almost a dozen years!"

"Now that's hardly a noble way to put it. You were the one who said he should grieve, yeah?"

Corey shook his head. "At one point, that was true, but the last thing I expected was to be sent chasing snow across a hundred and twenty-five light years. We do not have the finances to cover this trip."

"For truth?" Patricia slid into the sub-command chair beside him. "How much did this trip cost?'

"It starts with the Atomica V-98 hyperdrive capacitors," Corey said. "After twenty-four jumps, they have to be replaced, costing half a million dollars. That works out to 20,000D per jump."

"So this trip has cost us over 140,000D, yeah?"

"Expenses have outpaced income for this fifth. To pay the crew will require our emergency reserves."

"We can't make payroll?"

Corey propped his boot on the chair's edge. "It gets worse. Analyst speculation has dropped our stock price from ten dollars a share to three. At months-end, we will have to disclose Adrian's death to the Mercenary Stock Authority auditors."

"And that'll drop the price further." Patricia frowned and folded her paws. "We need more money."

"To put it concisely. It costs approximately 2.4 million dollars annually to operate the unit."

"What about contracts?"

"Figuring in travel time and retainer, the average high-level MerCom contract comes out to 124 days, or 2.9 contracts per year, depending on specifics," Corey said. "So when you work in monthly expenses, like 100,000D for payroll, 15,000D operation and ammunition, 7,000D for hydrofuel—"

Patricia held up a paw and shook her head. "Hold up your financial fluffit a moment, these numbers are too big."

Corey nodded. "Let me put it in everyday terms. A standard 120-minute rock music mini-tape will cost you a dollar. So will a good meal, or less at a cheap chain. Sports cars range from 1500D at the low end to 10,000D."

"So what's the bottom line?"

"A typical contract must pay about 850,000D for us to break even for the year."

Patricia receded into her seat, ears folded down. "That's a lot of mini-tapes."

Corey only nodded. The smell of worry wafted up from the bridge crew. Loyal as they may be, they would not work for free.

"Well then, college-dog," Patricia said, "if you're so smart, what do we do?"

"The Captain gave us strict orders not to do anything save mind the ship, so we will await the Captain's return."

Patricia's shoulders drooped, her fur wilted. Corey speculated on her thought process; Patricia would compare his actions to those of Captain Valentino's, and they would come up short. It was time for action.

"Perhaps there is an alternative," Corey said.

She shot to attention. "Yeah?"

"Captain Valentino will be absent for some time, and while he is, I am acting captain. We could acquire a short infantry contract, and be back to the ship before the Captain knew we were gone."

Patricia folded her ears back down. "I don't really think it's such a solid idea to violate a direct order."

"It is not exactly violation. Think of it. Our dear Captain instructed us to mind the ship. Acquiring additional funds is our way of minding the ship's future."

Patricia shook her head. "I don't know, that's awful dishonest. I mean, if we succeed, he'll probably praise us, yeah? But if we fail, you could be demoted, or fired. Do you want to take that risk?"

Corey twitched his nose. "You smell fearful. In my opinion, the gains outweigh the risks."

She exhaled and held her head down. "I guess it's your decision, yeah?"

"I believe it is an excellent idea." Corey sat up in his seat and gestured towards the coyote at the communications station. "Staff Lieutenant Pratt! Connect to MerCom and find us an in-system infantry contract."

"Can't right now," Pratt said. "Incoming transmission from Stone Canyon Aeroport, Vista Overlook Hotel."

"Patch it through to the view screen, Pratt."

Sebastian Valentino's face appeared on the bridge's main monitor, though it looked different. Beyond his loud burgundy polyester shirt, the fox glowed with newfound radiance. "Are you enjoying playing about with my ship, Corey?" he said.

Corey grimaced. "What in Kohoutek's name are you wearing?"

"This?" Sebastian indicated his garish shirt, a monstrosity with a silver horizontal stripe, maroon upper and mustard-yellow lower, and fake plasteen shine. "I bought it yesterday. Do you like it?"

Corey scowled. "It is a travesty unworthy of the label 'fashion'. It appears as though a paint factory exploded on your torso."

"I knew you'd like it," Sebastian said.

"And you are wearing the Ankh of Kohoutek over it."

"You said it was for good luck, and I think it looks nice."

"It clashes so much."

Sebastian frowned. "Enough, I'm not here to talk about my shirt, I'm here to talk about my progress, dig? Here is my report. Ready to record, Pratt?"

Before the coyote could respond, a second vulpine entered the viewscreen. The striking female red fox planted herself into Sebastian's lap and whispered sweet Volpa into his ear, oblivious to the conversation she interrupted.

Corey folded his arms and frowned. "This is your progress?"

Sebastian ignored Corey; he was preoccupied with his female companion. After a brief exchange in their native tongue, Sebastian drew her muzzle to the screen. Her amber eyes focused upon the bridge crew and its exotic mix of canine species.

"This is Melissa Riverford," Sebastian said. The vixen waved timidly, offered a pleasant smile, and barked a short Volpa greeting. "We met yesterday morning, while I was about town. She doesn't speak Mahonic."

"Of course not," Corey said. "I assume that you spent the night together."

Sebastian narrowed his amber eyes and tucked his ears down. "Firstly, it's none of your vexed business. Secondly, no, and thirdly, I'd prefer you not stereotype me. She's a friend, and I don't want to hear another word on it."

"I trust that, at the very least, you gave her your alias," Corey said.

"Absolutely." Sebastian touched his nose to Melissa's cheek. "Now, are you ready for my report?"

"Of course, please go ahead."

Sebastian tugged on Melissa's glittering sleeve. "Both Adrian's parents are alive, but don't live in the city anymore. In 499, they moved to the southern hemisphere, Mid-Low Province C, Peter Sector, to a little town outside Four Creeks. Two years ago, they returned to High-Central Province E, now they're in a fastway town a hundred miles north, in Hammer Sector, called Aelle. Tomorrow, I'll rent a car, be up and back before day's end."

"And what for now and after that?" Corey asked.

Sebastian shrugged. "I'll be erranding about the city today. I'm going to the Alliance Mercenary Chancery, talk to the chief liaison for this zone, he's an old friend of mine. Then it's off to the Information Bureau to work an address from them. Any time left I'll spend relaxing, dig?"

"You mean squandering."

Sebastian just smiled. "You know me too well."

Corey shook his head. "Now, is there anything else you need to pester me with?"

"Yes." Sebastian gave the vixen's shoulder a suggestive squeeze. "Between 1500 and 1700, 9 Piscea, I'll comm you, tell you about our new contract, so be ready, I might need you to pick up supplies if it's close, arrange a meeting point and so forth. I'll make my third checkup around 1800 10 Piscea, let you know what's changed."

Melissa interrupted Sebastian by draping herself across his lap. She whispered sultrily in his ear, and Sebastian smiled. "Now that we've got that out of the way, I have things to take care of, yes?" Sebastian said.

Corey folded his arms. "So I see. Goodbye, dear Captain."

"*Yasha-marsa, kehnellya,*" Sebastian said. The two foxes glimmered and disappeared, and the viewscreen reverted to its neutral state.

Corey leaned back in his command chair and snorted. "Intractable…"

"You don't like Melissa, do you?" Patricia said.

"It matters not whether I like her. I am more concerned as to whether our dear Captain can retain his pragmatic rectitude in the face of her companionship."

Patricia propped her elbow against her control pane. "I think it's cute, yeah? The two of them in love."

Corey grumbled. "Foxes do not fall in love, they fall in sex."

"You honestly believe the Captain would let a pretty face get in the way of his mission?"

"You have much credulity for him." Corey tapped his armrest. "Perhaps you are right, and I am passing hasty judgment."

"You saw him, saw how happy he was. When was the last time he looked so?"

"Not for some time."

"So let him be, yeah? Let him worry about his rituals." Patricia turned to the bridge crew. "Let us worry about the ship and that contract, yeah?"

"For a carthagan, you are full of sound advice."

Patricia grinned amusedly, one round ear skewed sideways. "It happens, yeah?"

Corey chuckled and folded his arms behind his head. What a wondrous sensation, not to feel like an imposter in the seat. When he commanded Pratt to contact MerCom, he was not just acting captain; he was captain.

Three hours passed before the response arrived.

"MerCom relay on secure channel, sir," Pratt said. "It's about the contract."

"Patch it through to the main viewscreen," Corey said.

The chiseled face of a Wild canine appeared on the screen. Like Corey and Patricia, he was adapted for life on warm, dry plains. This one was a stockier, shorter breed of rugged canine known as a johen or cape dog. He was dressed in a snappy, understated suit, the navy blue complementing his dusty tan pelt.

Before the johen spoke, Corey already knew much about him. His attire suggested a businessman, yet he was canine, out of place in the vulpine-majority Alliance. An ambassador, perhaps?

Still, Corey was at a disadvantage. He'd been trained in using his sense of smell to determine when a person was lying, truthful, worried, or honest, and the viewscreen precluded it. It aided ambiguity, and tipped the favor to one with something to hide.

"Greetings to you," the johen said. "I am Pyotr Neuback."

Corey gestured to Pratt to record. "Corey Delzano, at your service. Let us get to business, shall we?"

"This will be brief." Neuback tugged on his shirt collar. "We request your services for an assassination. The target has a history of escaping us before, and is highly mobile, so time is most critical."

"I understand. What's our window?" Corey asked.

"We need you on site no later than 0740 local time, 10 Piscea."

Corey input the figures into his command computer and read the time translation. "That gives us only forty-six standard hours."

"We were told that you were quick-strike capable," Neuback said.

"We are. There will be no problem. Before we proceed, what payment are we dealing with?"

"100,000D up front, 100,000D on completion, on retainer with MerCom. Is that satisfactory?"

Now they were talking. For such little work, this was a huge payout, one Corey couldn't possibly refuse. Still, he had his doubts. What sort of target was worth such money? Not even Hans Morrigan, the charismatic opposition leader in the Balkany Democratic Republic's Senate, had commanded such payment when the Star Rangers had assassinated him.

"That will be excellent," Corey said. "Now, to discuss details."

Corey's mind wandered while Neuback spoke of specifics. Who, or what, was Corey really dealing with? MerCom protocols prevented him from outright asking Neuback's allegiance, but Corey could speculate. Private citizens never threw around such sums, and few even possessed that much money. Businesses no longer used registered mercenaries for hits; it was too risky. Neuback likely represented either a government, or paramilitaries.

"Any further questions? Are we in agreement?" Neuback said.

"Fully," Corey said.

"Excellent. Neuback out."

Corey had his work cut out for him. He would need to plot a schedule, select a strike team, and prepare a loadout, all while keeping mind of the deadline. He left Senior Lieutenant Darling in command of the ship until further notice and retired to his quarters.

He worked backwards from the meeting time, and soon had a workable schedule, but that was easy part. Finding a sniper was hard. The Star Rangers were optimized for technical assaults, with soldiers highly trained in the arts of aerofighting, titaneering, and naval combat. Very few of the combat core were dedicated to security, and those who were boasted only the barest of infantry training.

Corey slogged through the crew dossiers, describing canine after canine, each possessing the genus's typically mediocre eyesight ratings. With the targeting computers built into modern titans and fighter jets, this was not a problem, but when looking down a riflescope, they may as well be firing blind.

The choice was obvious. Only two crewmen – both non-canine – were certified for rifles. Sebastian Valentino was one, and obviously out of the question, so this left Fusilier Teresa Ailesworth, a middle-aged female raccoon. Her file stated that she could hit a one-meter target from a thousand meters, with three-quarters accuracy.

While Corey had Sebastian's profile out, he decided to sate his curiosity.

Access had always been restricted to the Captain's eyes only. Typical vulpine paranoia. Yet there was nothing here to be ashamed of. Sebastian had the highest marks in eight categories: aerofighting, light and heavy aeropiloting, titaneering, rifle gunnery, punterkamp, starship command, and urban combat.

Then Corey looked closer. There, unobtrusive amongst familial information, lay a single unexpected fact. Sebastian was mated, and had been, since 12 Scorpius 489: almost sixteen years.

Sebastian had never mentioned a significant female in his life. Where and who was Elizabeth McMahill? Why was he gallivanting about with Melissa? What was he hiding? And why were no whereabouts listed for 494 to 498?

It was late, and Corey was growing tired. These questions would have to wait until Sebastian was in a more positive mood, a time that might never come. Corey had to focus on the here and now, and that meant selecting a pilot and co-pilot for the shuttle, a much easier job. Tomorrow morning, he would brief his chosen four.

***

Sebastian Valentino stood on the narrow cement steps of the Alliance Mercenary Chancery. Two stocky, well-armed polar foxes in navy blue Alliance body armor blocked him from the concrete building's entrance, where an aged red fox in dress uniform stood.

"What do you mean, you're terminating relations? I came all this way just for you to tell me to go home?" Sebastian said.

The other fox nodded slowly, his azure polyester uniform rippling in the light breeze. "You should not have come here, Sebastian," he said. "We no longer have use for your services."

"I can smell your lies, Secord. It can't be that simple."

"I can understand that you may be upset."

Sebastian held back a growl. "You're darn right I'm upset! We've worked together before. I've always come through for you in the past, always put your contracts first. And now I get the stiff-tail?"

Secord folded his arms, eyes narrowed under a mop of silvery fur. "Neither I, the Alliance, or House Florenzo owe any allegiance or favors to you, and while we appreciate the services you have rendered in the past, previous employment does not obligate us to contract you in the future."

"You appreciate my services?" Sebastian tried to advance, but a burly arctic fox blocked him. "You know I'm loyal to the Alliance! I've destroyed factories half a galaxy away without asking questions, and all you can say is that you appreciate my services?"

"While it is true that you have performed exemplary work in the past, we no longer wish to be associated with you," Secord said.

"Why in blazes not?" Sebastian said. "I'm the best mercenary in the galaxy! You can't tell me you have nothing left you want destroyed."

Secord flicked a dismissive paw at Sebastian. "That has no bearing on the topic at hand. It is our prerogative to accept or deny you employment."

"Vex you, that makes no sense!"

Secord smirked, briefly flashing his ivory teeth. "On the contrary, it makes perfect sense."

Sebastian snarled and paced. "You told me I was always a welcome hire."

"Things change, Valentino. Of all people, you should understand the need to adapt to a varying situation," Secord said.

"There's something you're not telling me, something you're holding back, I can smell it on you. You can't play dead with me."

Secord ears twitched in aggravation, and his eyes darkened. "If you wish to know so badly, I will tell you. We can no longer politically afford you. The bounty on your head makes it an unacceptable risk to support your actions."

"You're joking! This is about politics?"

"Everything is about politics, Sebastian. Think of what a disaster it would be for us should you be captured and reveal our sponsorship." Secord pulled his lips back in a derisive sneer. "And I never joke."

Sebastian's pacing slowed, his muscles tensed, his hackles raised. Nothing drew his ire faster than politics. "So that's it," he said, "after all my loyal service to the Alliance, it's goodbye, good luck, don't catch your tail in the door?"

Secord snorted. "I never said good luck."

Sebastian stared long at Sip Secord. Sebastian imagined lunging forward, wrapping his paws about Secord's fragile neck, and snapping it like a twig before the guards could react. It wasn't worth the risk.

"You're making a big mistake, Secord, you hear me?" Sebastian said. "Nations bark at my door for a contract! If I'm not fighting for you, it's against. You can't hide behind your white thugs forever!"

"If I did not hate the Dominion so, I would turn you in now. This conversation has ended." Secord gestured his guards forward. "Get this stray out of my sight and off government property."

One of the guards grabbed Sebastian by the shoulder, but just as fast, Sebastian writhed free. "Don't touch me, you baltikit! I don't need your help to leave, and I don't need your vexing speciesist contracts!"

The arctics ignored the slur and held their ground, their cold blue eyes on Sebastian ensuring no trickery. Without another word, Sebastian passed through the chancery's gates, and was back on the streets.

The breeze had kicked up, and a light rain fell. Only a handful of mid-day shoppers were out, most of them vixens, and they ducked under awnings to avoid the shower. It didn't bother Sebastian.

He wandered without destination. His next stop should have been the Information Bureau, but now, it seemed trivial. He heedlessly became lost in the city, drifted past random establishments to skim their wares, and then moved on.

This made no sense. Why would the Star Alliance suddenly turn against him? They'd been at the Canis Dominion's throat since long before Sebastian was born. Even now, in a time of relative peace between the galaxy's two largest powers, the Alliance craved mercenaries willing to fight the Dominion. Sebastian had filled that need, and it had brought him great success and fortune. But, it was that success that prompted the bounty that now made him a political pariah.

He couldn't appreciate the irony.

None of the stores held Sebastian's attention, until he entered the photoshop. The moment he stepped inside, he knew it was a mistake. He was already ensnared, not by the discount prices, the one-hour development guarantee, or the world-weary youth behind the counter, but by the display near the plasteen counter. It was composed of numerous small sample photographs pasted to a cardboard backing. Most of the photographs were too-perfect shots of action, or landscapes, or beaches, houses, farms, cars, statues. It was the shot of a fox family that drew him in.

It was so beautiful, so pure. All the elements were there: male, female, kits, two-story house, family car, and beaming, carefree expressions. They were frozen forever in time, never to worry about death, growing old, or unemployment. They could just be.

A tear welled up in Sebastian's eye. It could be him. No, it *should* be him, Melissa beside, lovely children in front. A life to live, not a life to be consumed by his profession.

"Melissa…" he whispered.

He needed her now, more than ever. Even the twenty minutes it took for him to hurry back to his hotel room were too long.

When Sebastian burst into his room, Melissa was watching television. "Melissa!"

"Billy?" She asked in Volpa, looking to him with a quirked ear. "Back so soon?"

Sebastian dashed up to her, wrapped his arms about her, and squeezed. He nearly fell atop her. "I was thinking of you."

"You're so dulcet! But what of your meeting?"

"Cancelled, rescheduled. It's wonderful to see you're still here."

"For truth?" She pressed her muzzle to his chest. "Your hotel den is so much bonnier than my apartment."

"You're so sweet." Sebastian licked her cheek. "Let's go out for dinner. Are you hungry?"

She touched her nose to his chin. "Now? It's still afternoon."

"It could be midnight for all I care. Come, let's go. I've something important to tell you."

Melissa stared up, amber eyes shining. "Something important?"

He nodded and kissed her cheek. "Yes, now get dressed."

Twenty minutes and one taxi later, they arrived at one of the city's upscale restaurants. It was an imposing structure, ornately decorated with marble, gold and silver sculptures.

Melissa gazed at the restaurant, mouth agape. "Oh, Billy, can you afford this? They should charge admission to a place like this."

He smiled and nuzzled her face. "I'd be happy to pay for a lovely vixen like you."

She tucked her ears down shyly. "I feel so sprinting, maybe it's the dress."

He ruffled her puffed sleeves, kissed her, and whispered. "I'm glad you like my gift. Now come, we've much to discuss."

They stepped inside, where a smiling host sat them at a table. Melissa's movements in her new dress were jerky, as if she didn't know what to do with the flowing fabric. Maybe she just needed practice.

Sebastian told her to order anything she'd like. She selected an expensive seafood dish, and Sebastian ordered a simple minced rabbit. To him, cost was no object, so long as she were with him.

They made small talk until dinner arrived. Sebastian nibbled his food, but Melissa assaulted it with her fork.

"Melissa, dear, you're making a mess."

She glanced up, her ears tucked back. "Sorry."

Sebastian smiled. "It's good, huh?"

"Very! Thank you."

Sebastian finished eating, placed his utensils down, and folded his paws in his lap. Melissa had been done for some time, even going so far as to lick the last bits of crayfish from her plate. Sebastian forced an uneasy smile. It was time to tell her the truth.

"Melissa, dear. I have a confession to make."

"For truth? We'll I've got one for you."

His ears perked upright, and he leaned across the table. "You do?"

"I don't really have my own apartment."

"You den with someone else?"

"Nay." Melissa hung her head and stared down at the table. "I live at the sanctuary."

So this was her terrible secret. Sebastian had suspected it, but never assumed, though it explained so much: why she was awkward in expensive clothes, why she wolfed down her food, and why she hadn't left his hotel room.

"You're homeless?" Sebastian said.

"Well, the sanctuary's like a home—"

"No, it's not like a home. It's a place for vagrants and outcasts to flop."

Sebastian winced. As soon as he said it, he knew it was a mistake. Tears quickly welled up in Melissa's eyes. He reached out to touch her, held her by the shoulders, pulled her muzzle up to face his.

"I didn't mean it like that. Come on now, don't cry," he said.

Melissa turned her head away. "You think I'm a scagg."

"It wouldn't matter if you were, you'd still be wonderful." Sebastian stroked her head softly, ran his ebony paw down her fur. "But why are you living at the sanctuary?"

"Both my parents died when I was green-eared. The state wedged me there, now I can't leave," she said.

"But what about your job at the clothing store?"

"I make stippy, only enough to buy food. Nobody else will hire me when they find I've got no home."

Sebastian caressed down her arms and gently wrapped his hands about hers. "You're lucky to have found me then."

She canted her head. "Howsa?"

Sebastian gave a quick glance about the room to see if anyone were paying undue attention to them. "I'm not who I told you I was."

"Natch. No insurance salesman could fling cash like you." Melissa's ears flattened. "You're not a drug-runner, are you?"

"No, actually, I'm a mercenary."

He had expected her to recoil in horror, to pull away, slap his face. In a worst-case scenario, she may have stood up and walked out of the restaurant, never to speak to him again. It was not the most honorable profession, not by a long shot.

Yet, she didn't. She actually smiled, big and beaming.

"Really?" she asked.

"You know what that is, right?"

"Natch! You bump people for money. Howsa good?"

Sebastian chuckled. "I'm the best."

"Howsa name?"

Dare Sebastian confide in her? Suppose she were a spy, or a bounty hunter? Could she be trusted, or would telling her dig him an early grave? He'd already gone this far.

"My name is Sebastian Valentino."

Melissa smiled. "That's a nice name, I think."

"You don't mind?"

"Nay," she said. "I had an uncle named Sebastian. I wondered why a pedigreed like you would be fancy over a stray like me."

Sebastian frowned and shook his head. "No, I mean, you don't mind that I'm a mercenary?"

"Should I?"

He could only smile, shake his head, and hold her paws tighter. "No. No you shouldn't."

She rubbed her nose to his, pressed it against his cheek. "Anything else?"

"Actually, yes…"

"Howsa?"

"Well, I know it's sudden, but from the moment I met you, I knew I wanted to be with you," Sebastian said.

Melissa giggled and licked his face. "I want to be with you too, Sebastian."

"No, I mean, forever."

Her ears swiveled to face him, upright, erect. "What are you saying?"

"I want you to be my mate."

Melissa's mouth hung open, her eyes wide and expressive. "For truth?"

"I wouldn't joke about something so important."

"Oh, Sebastian!" She grasped his paws tighter, pressed her nose to his. "Yes! You've made me so bouncy!"

He could hear the gentle thumping of her tail upon the chair. It was infectious, so he smiled too. For once, it seemed as though things were going his way.

"There's only room for me in my aerofighter, though. I'll get someone else to take you up to my ship—"

She leaned in to kiss his cheek, touch his lips. "Faith's you. However is no matter, so long as I get to you, and we're together."

Sebastian kissed her softly. There was nothing else he needed to hear.

The mere fact that we are now an interstellar genus is no excuse to forsake our heritage. If anything, our culture must become tighter, and our rituals more precious, to keep our civilization together across these vast distances. United for all.

-House Kaczmarek Chieftain Victor Kobalski, 289 PF.

SCENE FOUR

By the time Sebastian Valentino awoke the next day, it was mid-morning, and Melissa was gone for her final day of work. Yesterday's rain had given way to a heavy downpour, but to him, the ninth of Piscea was beautiful. At last, the day he would atone for his wrongdoings was at hand, the day he could put the memory of his departed friend to rest.

He showered and donned his dress uniform, then checked in with the ship. It was routine, uninteresting, yet deceitful. Sebastian disclosed his failure to obtain contract but not his proposal to Melissa. Corey omitted his imminent insubordination.

Sebastian kept the conversation brief. Ignoring the Information Bureau yesterday had put him behind schedule. He confirmed the unit's plans, and set out on his expedition.

Fifteen minutes later, another journey began. From the Favored Sky's hangar bay slipped the general-purpose shuttle Angeline, and with it, Delzano and his strike force.

They were not the only ones headed for the surface. The mystery vessel still in orbit around Wexford III launched a shuttle of their own, its departure timed so that the Star Rangers' were on the far side of Wexford II. Once the Favored Sky re-established radar contact with Wexford III, it was too late. They never saw the shuttle.

***

Sebastian's trip to Aelle was quiet and solemn.

He had tried to listen to his mini-tapes. Rock music enhanced the thrill of the open road, the sense of speed, the freedom to go where he wanted. Sometimes he sang along, sometimes he drummed the rhythm on the steering wheel. Sometimes, during down-time, he drove nowhere, simply for the sake of going, but this time, *Legend's Greatest Hits* felt inappropriate and improper, so instead, he drove in silence. The sound of rain on his rented convertible's vinyl roof was noise enough.

Sights blurred past, one after another, off ramp after off ramp. North Fastway 82 snaked north, past offices that blended into suburbs, suburbs that blended into factories, into warehouses, and finally into empty plains that stretched as far as he could see.

Kilometers melted away. The further north he went, the more the storm abated. After some time, the sun peeked through the clouds and in from his side window. How long had he been driving, one hour, two? His eyes drooped, ears fell a touch, hands became numb. Maybe he should turn around. Adrian's parents would be better off not knowing, and Sebastian could avoid facing them. It would be easier for all involved.

No, that was unacceptable. Sebastian had traveled so far to get here, he may as well get the Rite of Atonement over with. He was running out of time. Only seven days were left in the month of Piscea, and with it came the end of the year's first fifth. Once Sebastian told the Stock Authority about Adrian's death, the news would be everywhere. He couldn't force the Millers to read about their son's death in the financial papers or, worse, hear about it from a friend. They would cry, weep, maybe snarl and curse his name, maledict him for neglecting to so much as comm.

Moreover, He Who Watches would know what Sebastian had done. Paying for his dereliction in the Everlife was a ghastly prospect.

The Aelle off ramp dumped his car into the town's desolate, depressed commercial district. Lonely shops, with all manner of colorful sales advertisements, enticed non-existent customers.

The Information Bureau's instructions led him into the city's residential sector and into an area full of small, multi-family tenements, their brick façades exposed where decades-old paint had worn away. Broken windows and rusted cars stood sentry. These yielded to rows of identical bilevels, then to square single-family homes, with white clapboard siding, family car, and manicured lawn. None would look out of place in a realty advertisement.

Sebastian parked his sport compact at the curb of 519 Tallapia Lane. He sat in silence for a minute, maybe two, as he worked up the will to break the news to the Millers. As he pinned his mourning zulican to his uniform's lapel, a pair of aged red foxes, male and female, stepped out of the house, both dressed in identical, plain white shirt and pants.

It was the attire of those in mourning. They already knew why Sebastian was here.

He hesitated. How could they have known? He folded Adrian's *fallora* atop his ashes, took a deep breath, and doddered to the door.

"Valteri and Sheena Miller, I regret to inform you—"

"You're here to atone," Valteri said.

Sebastian glanced into Valteri's eyes, his voice low as he spoke in Volpa. "I'm sorry. But how did you know?" Sebastian said.

"It's better if we talk inside," Valteri said.

They led him into their home, to the social den. Sebastian sat on a plush, over-sized couch, but no matter how he positioned himself, it felt like concrete.

"Would you like something to drink?" Sheena asked him.

"Just some water, please."

The house was large, empty inside, with few of the baubles one would expect to find in a vulpine home. Furniture was laid out to make foot travel easiest, the couches parallel and facing each other. An entertainment table, just large enough to hold a picture book on houses of the High Plains, rested between. Centermost on the far wall was a low, wide desk, and amongst the curios adorning its surface lay a smattering of family photographs.

Sebastian placed Adrian's remains and *fallora* on the table and walked over to examine the desk, something to do while awaiting Sheena's return. The photographs were what interested him. All the usual suspects were there: postured images of past vacations, pictures forced out of young children in formal clothes, Valteri and Sheena on what he presumed was their mating day. Most prevalent were the pictures of Adrian.

"Do you mind if I look at these?" Sebastian asked.

"Nay, go ahead," Valteri said.

Sebastian chose one that looked familiar and picked it up. A slew of young foxes in blue dress uniforms stood before a familiar city skyline.

"That's Adrian's completion ceremony," Valteri said.

"I know." Sebastian pointed to a fox on the left side. "That's me."

"Right, you were in his class."

Sebastian sat the picture down and chose another. This one showed Adrian, in the same dress uniform as before, posed with a show rifle in front of some artificial backdrop.

"That was taken when Adrian graduated to *Velaya Vel-larf*," Valteri said.

Sebastian nodded and silently replaced it. An item next to it attracted his interest, a magazine clipping. He and Adrian stood together, posed in front of an aerofighter. Age had faded its monochrome printing.

"I don't remember this picture," Sebastian said.

Valteri peered over his shoulder. "That's from an article in Modern Mercenary magazine. They do this bit every year on new mercenaries to watch. I think you were fourth or fifth that year."

"New mercenaries to watch? How old is this?"

"That's from the 498 issue."

Sebastian looked away, from Valteri and Adrian's prying eyes. A hint of a tear trickled down his cheek. He wiped it away the instant he felt it. "Seven long years…"

"Something down?"

"No, no." Sebastian walked back to the couch and sat down. "Just a lot of memories."

"I understand."

Sheena returned, handed Sebastian a glass of water, and sat on the opposite couch, where Valteri joined her. They stared at him in silence, waiting for Sebastian to speak, but he had nothing to say.

"It is pleasant to see you once more, Sebastian," Sheena said, "though it is unfortunate it is under these circumstances. Thank you for fulfilling your responsibility. It must not have been easy."

"It was the least I could do for Adrian."

"We were afraid you might not come, but we knew you would," she said.

"How were you so sure?"

It was an innocent question, but it gave the Millers pause. They exchanged looks, held paws, touched their noses together. Valteri pressed his clutched hands to Sheena's chest and whispered so low that not even Sebastian could hear them.

Finally, Valteri turned to him. "Our son Alsander is fully gifted."

Sebastian's ears perked upright, attentive. Adrian had never mentioned anyone in his family being clairvoyant, but he'd always avoided speaking about his siblings. It was best to be delicate.

"Then you are seventh?" Sebastian said.

"Yes. I was seventh of mine, he is seventh of his," Valteri said.

"What did Alsander tell you?"

"Everything, when it happened," Sheena said.

"Are you sure?"

"Absolutely. We did our own tests to see," Valteri said.

They smelled honest, and while the Millers didn't strike Sebastian as the type to lie, he remained skeptical. Clairvoyance was a well-documented phenomenon, but the odds of ever meeting a fully gifted seer were astronomical. One in a million would experience a passive guiding vision in their lifetimes, brought upon them by their ancestors in the Everlife. But those who were fully gifted could see when and what they wanted, as well as events currently happening. At any given time, there might be no more than a half-dozen in the entire galaxy. Consequently, they were widely in demand for government service.

"Have you told anyone?" Sebastian asked.

"No one knows except us, not even Adrian." Valteri tightened his jaw. "We decided that, as much as Adrian loved you and trusted you, we could trust you too. Your line of work understands the value of secrecy."

Sebastian nodded. Perhaps more than anyone else, he knew the dangers of telling secrets. Mercenaries with loose lips wound up out of a job, or worse.

"We knew you would understand," Sheena said.

"It would be a tragedy if your son were impressed into government service, or got the sickness," Sebastian said. "How old is Alsander?"

"Five," Sheena said.

"But Adrian was my age."

Valteri nodded. "Next month would have been his twenty-fifth birthday. We've had ten children survive of twenty-one," Valteri said.

Sebastian forced an uneasy smile. "Congratulations on being above average."

Sheena touched her nose to her mate's. "We have been lucky and grateful to have so few infirm children. It is something to be thankful for, yes?"

"Yes, it is. When will your other kits be back from school?" Sebastian said.

"Soon," Sheena said.

"Then we should begin the Rite of Atonement." Sebastian sat up on the couch. "Would you get a bowl, Sheena?"

Sheena smiled, stood, and set off to the kitchen. Sebastian folded his paws in his lap and looked to Valteri. "I'm afraid my time is short."

"We understand," Valteri said. "It's thoughtful that you're here at all."

"I had to be here, for Adrian."

Sheena returned with a small bowl, placed it on the table, and then sat next to her mate. Sebastian hung his head, and Valteri and Sheena did the same.

"Let it become known that the Atonement of Sebastian Valentino begins at 1351 Galactic Standard Time, this ninth day of the month of Piscea, in the 505th year Post Founding," Sebastian said. "We begin with a short prayer. He Who Watches, we regret that we are imperfect creations. I, Your loyal servant, have failed to properly prepare the physical body of Your beloved child, Adrian Miller, for the Everlife. We beg that You allow him into Your graces, absolve his dishonoring, and know that, despite my failures, he is pure and worthy of spirit. *Fallam.*"

"*Fallam fal-Max,*" the Millers said.

"Witness phase begins. I have made a terrible mistake. As the closest relatives to the departed, I beseech you to forgive my transgressions," Sebastian said.

"We do," Valteri said.

"Thank you. Oh Max, know that I sincerely regret my errors, and have sought and received forgiveness from the bloodkin of the departed, and that these *fella-arraf* before me bear witness to my atonement," Sebastian said.

"We bear witness."

"Admission phase begins. I must now admit my mistakes." Sebastian held his head low, breathed slow and steady, but his paws would not stop quivering. The entire house was silent for his decisive moment. Would Adrian's parents accept him?

Sebastian wrung his hands. "I have made a grievous error. I was alone amongst the Chosen, and there was not enough time to perform all the preparations myself. I handed some of the tasks to one of my trusted staff, and though he assured me he was studied in our ways, it was revealed that he was not."

"To what disgrace was the departed subjected to?" Valteri asked.

"The *fallora* left his person."

Everything stopped. The Millers stared at him, eyes wide, jaws agape. Sheena clutched hard to Valteri's shoulder. "Is this truth?" Valteri asked.

Sebastian hung his head. "I'm afraid it is."

"Then you are truly an abomination unto the Volpa genus," Sheena said.

Sebastian exhaled. His paws groped behind himself, sought his tail, and he grasped it, tight. "I'm sorry…"

Valteri glared hard at him with his piercing amber eyes. "The *fallora* may not mean as much to a stray like you, but it is sacred to foxes, especially us pedigreed. You have committed a severe affront, not only to Adrian, and to us, but to all Millers."

Sebastian cringed and cast his eyes to the floor. He'd come all this way just for Adrian, gone to all this effort; how could Valteri say such a hurtful thing? The *fallora* and the vulpine rituals meant just as much to Sebastian as it did to any of the pedigreed, and Valteri should have known that. Did the Millers still resent him for being a stray and fraternizing with their son?

"I'm sorry to have brought such dishonor to the Miller pedigree. The act was committed in ignorance by my fellow, but I understand that, willful or not, it was still my error."

"You truly require Atonement. It was wise of you to come here," Valteri said.

Sheena nodded. "Acknowledgement is the first step on the trail to reconciliation, Sebastian, especially for a stray."

Every time they used the word 'stray', Sebastian receded further into his seat. He shouldn't – and couldn't – argue with a pedigreed, even under this circumstance. To do so would be a far graver solecism, and could get him expelled from the Millers' house.

"Do you have anything further to add?" Sebastian asked.

The Millers exchanged glances, and then looked back upon him. "We find your request honest and truthful, and we accept and endorse your desire for Atonement," Valteri said.

Sebastian nodded slowly. "Thank you. Then we should move on to the Absolution phase."

Sheena stood up and headed to the kitchen. "I am afraid we have not had time to bless our knife," she said.

"I'm sure it's fine, the situation is out of our control," Sebastian said.

There was that disapproving look from Valteri again: eyes narrowed, with just the faintest hint of an admonishing frown. He likely thought that Sebastian was taking the Volpa rituals frivolously.

Sheena returned with an old kitchen knife, laid it on the table, and sat down next to her mate. "I suppose you are right. Your time is short, after all."

Valteri glanced at her, but she nudged him and he acquiesced. Sheena picked up the knife, held the padded tip of her finger to the point, and gently pushed down until she drew blood. She moved her paw over the bowl and let a small amount of her blood drip into it, then offered the knife to Valteri. He took it and did the same, dribbling his blood into the bowl, and then Sebastian followed suit. He handed the bowl back to Sheena, and she mixed the blood together with her finger.

She unlocked the case containing Adrian's ashes. She took a delicate pinch of his remains and scattered it into the bowl, and continued stirring until it was a dark red paste. "As we are all descendents of Max, so is our blood. Let it mix with the departed, to give him life anew."

"*Fallam fal-Max*," Sebastian and Valteri said.

Sheena stood, dipped her finger into the paste, and slowly smeared a wide, dark line across her forehead. It stood out in sharp contrast to her russet pelt. She moved to the others and did the same, marking them with the mixture.

"The departed no longer lacks a suitable physical vessel. We are his vessel now," Sheena said.

They all bowed their heads and held a moment of silence. When they had finished, Sheena placed the knife and bowl down, and Valteri sat back in place. Sebastian folded his paws in his lap, and looked down at Adrian's ashes on the table.

"Will you be here for the casting?" Valteri asked.

Sebastian tucked his ears back. "I wish I could. I've always wanted to see Annunciation Point. What's so special about it?"

Valteri smiled, reclined in his seat, and gestured with his paws as if he were physically sculpting the scene. "Annunciation Point is a hill in the middle of Westfahlen. The planetary capital building used to be there, where the charter incorporating the planet of Wexford was signed. Long ago, they ran out of room and moved administration to a newer building, but they kept the old building as a museum of sorts. Fifty years ago, it burnt down, along with some of the buildings around it. They didn't need to rebuild it, but they couldn't just leave a big empty hole in the city, so they put up a nice little park with a memorial. When Adrian was a child and we lived in Westfahlen, we would go every off-day and have a picnic."

"Adrian loved that park," Sheena said.

Sebastian stared at the floor. If only he could spare more time, he could stay to watch them spread Adrian's ashes. His career had killed Adrian, and now it denied him the opportunity to fully complete the Atonement.

Valteri clutched Sheena to his side. "It's time for the Revelation phase. Tell us, how did it happen? How did Adrian die?"

Sebastian had spent two months preparing his answer. He wasn't ready for the Revelation phase, and the Millers certainly weren't ready to hear the truth. He couldn't bear to sadden their eyes with his candor.

So he didn't.

"We were infiltrating a research station," Sebastian said, "outnumbered twenty to one. Dominion soldiers had cut us off from our escape route, had us pinned down. There was no way to fight our way through, so Adrian volunteered to cover me. We almost made it, but he was wounded just before we could escape. I tried to help him up, but he couldn't move. He grabbed me by the collar, looked me in the eye, and said, 'Leave me, Sebastian. It's more important that you escape. Tell CenCon about the chemical weapons the Dominion is making here. You'll save millions of lives.'

"I struggled to help him, but it was too late, he was already dying. I held his paw in mine, stared down at him. The last thing he said was, 'Tell my parents I love them.' And then he was gone."

Valteri leaned forward and sniffed at Sebastian. "You smell truthful." Satisfied, he smiled and nodded, and the two Millers held each other. "We always knew he would die a hero. He always put others ahead of himself. You've no idea how happy it makes us, knowing that his life wasn't wasted, that his death was not meaningless. Thank you so much."

Sebastian had lied before. He'd stolen and cheated his way to the top, conning money, property, and trust from the naïve of the galaxy. He'd even trained himself not to give away his deceit with his scent, but nothing compared to what he'd just done.

Sebastian forced a smile. "Adrian was always loyal and faithful. Without him, I wouldn't be here today."

They hung their heads again and sat in silent remembrance of Adrian's life and deeds. After a minute had passed, Valteri rose. "That's the end of the Revelation phase."

A chill ran down Sebastian's spine, and he nodded, slowly. "Yes, I suppose it is."

"Then you know what comes next."

Sebastian clutched his tail in his paws and wrung the dull white tip between his hands. "I do."

Sheena stood, picked up the bowl, and took it back to the kitchen. The muffled sound of running water over ceramic lasted a few seconds, and then stopped. Sheena returned with a cutting board and two towels.

Sebastian's lips quivered as he stared at the board. Sheena gently set it on the table, picked up the knife in one paw, and sat next to Sebastian. When she wrapped her fingers about his tail and laid it on the board, he didn't resist. He turned his head away and closed his eyes.

Without a word, Sheena lifted the blade overhead, and swiftly severed the last twelve centimeters of Sebastian's tail.

Sebastian jerked as the knife cut through the nerve endings, gritting his teeth in agony. The wound burned, enough to force a lone tear to trickle down his cheek, but he kept the pain under control. Blood welled up, and Sheena handed him a towel. With trembling paws, he wrapped it around the end and held it tight.

"Hopefully it won't cripple your balance," Valteri said.

Sebastian forced a smile. "It won't."

Sheena delicately gathered up the end of Sebastian's tail and wrapped it in the other towel. "As you have deprived the departed of his physical vessel to the Everlife, ruining Max's gift to him, so shall you be wounded as correction. Your Sufferance shall be burnt and added to the departed's ashes for the Casting."

Sebastian nodded absently, still holding his tail in a tight, shaking embrace. "I understand."

"You know why we pedigreed do this, yes?" Valteri said.

Sebastian sighed, his ears tucked down. "Yes. It's a permanent and tangible reminder of my dishonor."

Valteri leaned over the table and patted Sebastian's shoulder. "I'd have expected you to resist. Thank you for not doing so."

"You're welcome."

Sheena handed the towel with Sebastian's tail to Valteri, and then she scooped up the knife and cutting board and put them back in the kitchen.

Sebastian watched her leave in silence, listened to the sound of running water as she washed them. She quietly returned and sat next to Valteri.

"That's the end of Atonement," Valteri said. "Thank you for your compassion, Sebastian."

"You're welcome."

"The bleeding should stop soon. Do you require anything?" Sheena asked.

Sebastian shook his head quietly and rubbed over the end of his tail. "I'm fine."

Sheena nodded and watched. "Do you think Adrian will pass his life review?"

"I have no doubt," Sebastian said. When the flow had stopped, he balled the towel so the stain was out of view, and handed it back to Sheena.

She smiled and took it. "The kits will be home soon. I should prepare them a snack." She disappeared into the kitchen, leaving Sebastian and Valteri alone.

"Would you like to meet the kits? I bet they'd love to hear your battle stories," Valteri said.

Sebastian wrung his paws and squirmed on the couch. "I don't know about that, they probably get more from television."

"Rubbish!" Valteri stood and collected Adrian's remains and Sebastian's tail. "You can't come all this way and not see the kits."

"I'm really a very busy fox—"

"C'mon, a little while, at least. I'll firecook some meat, Sheena can make salad."

Sebastian's whiskers drooped and he sighed. "Okay, but not too long, I need to be back in Stone Canyon before dark."

Valteri laughed. "Stone Canyon, huh? I wouldn't want to be there after dark either. Wait here." Valteri put Adrian's remains and Sebastian's Sufferance away in a back room. "Say, what's so important to make you flee?"

Sebastian stood up, drawn again to the items on the desktop. "Well, I met a nice little vixen in town—"

"You're seducing another Florenzo into space, huh? I'd expect nothing less from a Lafayette, even a stray," Valteri said.

"Actually, I proposed yesterday, and she accepted."

"Bully!" Valteri patted Sebastian's shoulder. "You're a fine catch, too old to be mateless, and we need all the foxes we can get. I bet you'd make good children, you know? Someday maybe you can apply for a pedigree."

"Must you keep bringing that up?"

"Bringing what up?"

"That I'm a stray," Sebastian said.

"You are, aren't you?"

"Yes, but…" Sebastian pawed through the trinkets, models, and figurines on the desk. "It was hard growing up, everyone prejudged me when they heard my last name. I had to work twice as hard for half the recognition of the pedigreed, and when you mention it, it just reminds me of how it was, how it still is."

Valteri moved next to Sebastian. "Don't you want to be pedigreed?"

A sharp shudder ran through Sebastian's body. "You're not getting it," Sebastian said. "I have to labor so hard to prove myself. I'm the galaxy's highest ranked mercenary, I've set records for longest duration at the top, and yet my own countrymen still look at me and say, 'He's just a stray, it was probably just luck.'"

"That's not what I meant at all. You've had a noble career despite being a stray," Valteri said.

Sebastian flinched. Despite! He turned to stare at Valteri, his eyes narrowed on the elder fox. "Can't you just say I've had a noble career?" Sebastian asked. "Must you qualify everything I've done?"

"Okay, okay, I'm sorry." Valteri smiled, but even Sebastian couldn't tell if he was sincere. "You've had a noble career. But surely you aspire to join one of your House's pedigrees?"

"Maybe." Sebastian picked up a small, model Corvair aerofighter from the desktop. "I'm afraid my legacy will be rubbish in the vulpine galaxy if I don't."

"Well, c'mon, Sebastian. Look at yourself, look at what you've done. You're smart, capable, and in good physical shape. I bet you'd score well on the testing—"

Sebastian's grip briefly tightened on the small aerofighter. "That's just it. After everything I've done, I still have to be tested to be granted a pedigree. Do my accomplishments count for nothing?"

Valteri smiled gently. "It's not personal. It's just a formality necessary to weed out the bad genestock. It's convention and all, and I'm sure that when you get a nice mate, they'll grant you admission to one. You look into it?"

"A little. None of the ten original Lafayette pedigrees would consider me. I got a decent offer from Lachance, and Cortney's expressed interest, but they're reluctant to take someone who's not a permanent Alliance resident," Sebastian said.

"That'll probably change when you get a mate," Valteri said.

Sebastian nodded, but he knew the truth. He'd never actually consulted with any of the vulpine pedigrees. Once any potential pedigree did genetic testing and discovered Sebastian's real family line, they would never allow him admission, not with his family's history.

"Say, how's the Favored Sky?" Valteri asked.

Sebastian sat the aerofighter down. "Oh, she's fine, really."

"Bonzo. That's one of my favorite passages, you know."

"What?"

"The Memoria," Valteri said. "Max Chapter 11, verse 85. 'I wish you well on your journeys abroad, and through it—"

"—May you walk under favored skies,'" Sebastian said. "It's one of mine too. I thought it would be appropriate, for someone like me."

"Good to see our people still study the Book of Creation."

"It's provided solace in times of trouble, advice in times of need, and consolation in times of mourning."

Sebastian turned back to the desktop and the many interesting things atop it. He glanced over another aerofighter model, a Dolphin attack plane, and then set it back down. He had real ones he could play with on his ship.

"What's an assault carrier, anyway?" Valteri asked.

"It's a hybrid of destroyer, light aerocarrier, and transport."

"It sounds heavy."

Sebastian looked over the framed photographs. "It is. It handles and looks like a brick and it's not terribly good at doing any of those roles. But it would cost a boulder to operate three specialized ships."

Valteri chuckled. "You know the saying, 'don't fetch a boulder when a stone will do the job.'"

Sebastian's fur bristled, and his body tensed. "My father used to say that."

Valteri smiled. "He was a wise man, then."

"He was a fool."

"Oh, chin up. He couldn't be that bad."

"You didn't know him."

Valteri opened his mouth to speak, thought better of it, and hung his head down. He stared at the tawny carpet and scuffed a shoe over it. Sebastian frowned and patted Valteri's shoulder. "Sorry to snap at you. It's just, well…"

"Bad memories?" Valteri asked.

"It's hard to keep them down, sometimes."

"I didn't mean to upset you. I meant it as a compliment."

Sebastian took another trinket in his paw, this one a small, delicate hollow-glass figurine of a schoolkit, books in paw. "I know. You couldn't have known about him."

"Hey, I've got a bonzo idea." Valteri leaned towards him, so sudden that Sebastian bobbled the figure. "We'll have Alsander read you."

Read him? Like a book? Oh no, there were far too many things Sebastian longed to keep hidden, many of which would hurt the Millers. "Well, I don't want to impose."

"Hokum, it'll be no trouble, not for you, dig? Make yourself comfortable, wait awhile. We'll have fun," Valteri said.

Perhaps being read wasn't such a bad thing. Maybe he could use Alsander to find something out about his future, where Sebastian and the unit were going. Then again, this wasn't a shovel he was talking about, this was a person, a child. He had used adults before to achieve his means, but that was different. In either case, Sebastian doubted that he could change Valteri's mind.

"Well, sure, why not?" Sebastian said.

"Bonny!" Valteri turned towards the kitchen. "I'll start drawing up some meat, huh? You wait here."

Valteri stopped in place after a few steps, his eyes down at the table. Adrian's *fallora* still lay on the table. He walked up to it, leaned over, and delicately ran a hand along its furry surface. Valteri's thin black lips quivered, and his ears tilted slowly backwards.

Sebastian stood next to him. "What's wrong?"

Valteri picked up the sash, holding it gently in his black paws. "Adrian's coming of age was sixteen years ago, but I still remember like it was yesterday."

Sebastian sighed. "I'm really sorry to have put you through this."

Valteri stared down at the *fallora* and stroked the painted metal ends. "Adrian was the only one to survive his litter of four. It took almost a year for me and Sheena to shed enough fur to make his *fallora*. We spent a lot of time stitching it together, but Sheena did most of the work because she was home during the day, when Adrian was at school, and we didn't want him to see it until it was ready. You should have seen how happy he was when we presented it to him." Valteri glanced at Sebastian. "He told us that, with our fur to keep him company, he would never be alone no matter where he went."

Sebastian frowned and looked away. "I'm sorry, Valteri."

Valteri nodded slowly, folded Adrian's *fallora,* and left the room. Sebastian replaced the schoolkit figurine back on the desk and skimmed the remaining items, if only to waste some time. Even such insignificant objects told him something of their owners. The way they were arranged – in rigid rows, like a parade – suggested attention to detail. Or boredom.

Sebastian's ears stood up. A large vehicle stopped outside.

With youthful clamor, three fluffy red children burst into the house. They hunted down their parents, scattered into the kitchen, spoke of their respective days, and demanded their snacks. At first, they were only a blur, but Sheena corralled them and ushered them into the den. Valteri took over, and on his command, the kits lined up in front of Sebastian.

Sebastian appraised the three children: clean, well dressed, no signs of juvenile diseases. At five years of age, the nearly-adolescent, wide-eyed youths reached up to his chest. They squirmed in anticipation, as if they had not seen a visitor in years.

"These are our two girls, Zulia and Maxine." Valteri indicated them, and they curtseyed. "And this is Alsander. Children, this is—"

Alsander stared up at Sebastian. Something about the way his eyes burned into him, it was like nothing he had seen before, enough to make Sebastian flinch. "You're Captain Sebastian Valentino," Alsander said. "I've seen you before."

Valteri thrust a paw at Alsander. "No! Don't speak when your father is speaking."

Alsander winced, cast his eyes down, held his tiny black hands tight, and nodded. Sebastian crouched to put himself at Alsander's eye level. "No, no, let him speak. Tell me, little Alsander, who am I?"

Sebastian had looked death in the eyes before, but it couldn't prepare him for Alsander. The kit's gaze was hard, tempered with the focus of someone far beyond his years. All the time Sebastian had spent building a façade melted uselessly away, no barrier to Alsander. He couldn't move; all he could do was stare back. A sharp cold cut across him, worry. Alsander wouldn't let him turn away, and Sebastian wasn't sure if he could.

"You're Captain Sebastian Valentino. You were Adrian's leader. You have a unit, the Star Rangers. You wage war for money," Alsander said.

Sebastian regained control of his body, but he had to brace himself with one hand on the floor. Nothing Alsander said was groundbreaking. Anyone educated in interstellar politics could have told him that.

"Why don't you tell me something a little more obscure?" Sebastian said.

Before the words left his mouth, Sebastian realized it was a mistake. Alsander already knew the truth, down to every detail, and Sebastian had just invited catastrophe upon himself. Alsander would blow his cover, tell his parents the horrible truth, and expose Sebastian for the liar he was.

"You had a bowl of sweetened grains with sliced apples for breakfast," Alsander said. "You have a mini-tape of Legend's Greatest Hits in your rented Mark VII Logan Motors Sydney. It costs three dollars, sixty-eight cents per day to rent, plus one cent per mile travelled. The combination for the safe in your quarters is seven-eight-four-six—"

"Okay, okay, that's enough." Sebastian stood up and turned away. He couldn't bear to face Alsander, but he could still feel the kit's gaze.

"He's really something, isn't he?" Valteri said.

Sebastian grumbled. "Yeah, something."

Alsander was far more powerful than Sebastian ever imagined. Every second he spent around the child was a second too long, yet morbid curiosity made him wonder what Alsander was truly capable of.

Valteri clapped his paws. "Let's not stand around, then! Kits, go and freshen up, Mr. Valentino is staying for dinner."

In minutes, they were in the Millers' yard, where the sun warmed the ground and those upon it until the world was in harmony. Grass swayed in a gentle breeze, and the smell and sound of cooking rabbit touched the nostrils of kits bounding about the meager fenced expanse. Sebastian amused himself with several short games of tag, though he caught the children every time.

Once Sebastian depleted the youths' energy, he settled down to confabulate with the elder Millers. Valteri tuned the grill's gas level for just the right heat, and Sheena chopped greens for salads. Sebastian's gaze locked onto the knife; it was the same one she had used to cut his tail. She even had the same cutting board.

Sebastian took a seat between them, but his eyes didn't leave the knife. "So how long have you lived here?" he asked.

Valteri twisted a knob on the grill."Two long years."

"You don't sound too enthusiastic."

Sheena sliced through long blades of field grass. "Aelle bores us. We long for the rush of our prior home, but those days have gone."

"Why'd you leave Four Creeks?" Sebastian asked.

"HydroCo opened a new refinery there, and Valteri was hired as a manager. But then he broke his leg—"

Valteri scowled and prodded at a piece of rabbit, hard enough that it nearly fell off the grill. "That blasted stapard Merchook broke the intermix valve and didn't report it, made a big slick mess. Slid on it and crashed the high-low."

"Valteri could no longer inspect and navigate the facility."

"They didn't even fire that vexing fool," Valteri said. "Eight triads later he did it again, and Wasdovakio got killed. He was a good fox, we used to drink together."

"The state moved us here, so Valteri could work as a manager at the new Roma's. No ladders for him to climb."

Sebastian nodded. "I drove past it on the way in. Big place."

"92,000 square meters of shopping for every dobby doodad you'll ever possibly need." Valteri flipped the rabbit meat with a pair of tongs. "You see those flats on your way in? When we moved here, they were all charming, now look at them, full of sanctuary rejects, because those cheap-tails at Roma's only pay them eighty cents a day."

"Roma's must be doing good business, the parking lot was full," Sebastian said.

"That is because there is no other comprehensive shopping facility within a hundred kilometers. The state decided Aelle should provide the needs for all fastway travelers, so they gave Roma's a contract and moved a couple thousand unemployed here to work," Sheena said.

"On the other side of town they live in cargo containers." Valteri turned the dial down, closed the grill, and sat next to Sebastian. "The greatest jacking country in the history of the galaxy, and they're living in containers like scaggs."

"Oh, Valteri, do not be so unbearable." Sheena scooped the vegetable cuts and placed them into a bowl. "Many of them previously had no occupation, and now they have money and shelter to hide their heads."

"It just flames me up all over, the Chosen living in such hovels. All those strays are uncouth, bringing their ill-kept manners and crime with them. No offense, Sebastian."

Sebastian huffed and glanced at Valteri. "Right."

"Well, still," Valteri said, "the sanctuary system breeds those habits—"

"I am certain Sebastian did not come all this way to hear us talk about our lives, Valteri."

"Oh, no, it's nice, really." Sebastian propped an elbow on the table. "It's the little things of life, like this, that I miss. I don't get small talk on the ship, it's always work-work-work, dig?"

"Speaking of your work, you know, we were concerned you wouldn't make it," Valteri said. "With the bounty on your head and all that claptrap."

Sebastian sat upright. "You know about that?"

Valteri went back to attend to the grill. "Of course we do! We read all the financial rags, with the stock we own in you and Adrian—"

Sheena stiffened at the name. Her paws jerked, and the knife slipped and fell to the cutting board. A thin red line appeared on the side of her ebony finger. "Gracious, I cut myself."

Valteri's ears tucked down. "Max, I'm sorry, it was just a reflex, you know? You okay?"

Sebastian snatched a napkin from the table, grabbed Sheena's paw in his, and held the paper firmly to her finger. "Here, just hold that on there."

She bobbed her head absently and clutched the paper to her paw. Her ears folded and she stared down at her hands. "Please, finish the rest of the salad, Sebastian?"

Sebastian hesitated and stared at the knife and cutting board. "I…"

"Oh. I forgot about that," Sheena said. "If you do not want to…"

"No, I'll be fine." Sebastian shook his head and tugged the cutting board over. He began mincing the remaining herbs, but try as he might, he couldn't match Sheena's elegant motions. Instead of slicing cleanly, he crushed the flavoring plants. The trembling in his hands didn't help. "I just haven't thought about the bounty in awhile, I guess."

"You should, you know," Valteri said. "It's more evidence of arrogant Dominion posturing and anti-vulpinism."

"Anti-vulpinism?"

"Do not mind him so much." Sheena forced a trembling smile. "He is just strong willed."

Valteri wagged a finger at Sheena. "And you're permissive," he said. "Count it, it's an established fact that Dominion policies show a distinct bias and hatred against not just the Alliance, but all foxes. Didn't you see the way they howled at House Wallace about you?"

"No, I've been busy."

"Oh, right." Valteri flipped the meat again. "Well the Canies demanded House Wallace turn you over to them, accused them of harboring war criminals, threatened to retaliate. Dish-ear said they were going to wedge CenCon with demands, force them to declare House Wallace a terrorist state."

"I didn't hear about that." Sebastian gathered the mashed herbs and tossed them into the salad bowl. He was all too happy to be done with the knife and cutting board. "I never listen to dish-ear."

"You should! The Alliance media won't talk about it, they don't care about Wallace because they never joined the Alliance, you know? But they're still foxes. Wallace and Murrel are our best defense against a coreward invasion. If we've got bonnier relations with those two Houses, they'll take troops off our borders and put them on the Dominion's. But the stiffears think we can coddle the Dominion with peace and love."

"Well, we're at peace now," Sebastian said.

"It's not peace, it's the lull of a cold war. All this cuddling, it's disgraceful, we'll never achieve the New Golden Age by snuggling our enemies. It only gives them more backspace to chock the knife. The only peace the Dominion wants is where we're enslaved, like the Familiars," Valteri said.

Sebastian quirked his ears outward and stared up at Valteri. It had been a long time since Sebastian had heard anyone speak openly about the New Golden Age. "You can't honestly believe that."

"Canines aren't like you or me, Sebastian. They don't have families or values, they live in squalid packs, mobs, passing partners like four-legged mutts—"

Sheena whined. "Valteri..."

"They don't want to live in peace," Valteri said. "They want control and dominance. You see how they conquer their own fellows, they've got the Familiars under them like slaves. They bark at Wallace, it's a great affront to the Volpa genus. They understand only one language: force! We need to invade now before they outbreed us."

Sebastian tightened his paws into fists, his fur bristling. "I'll have you know that I've been to the Dominion, and seen how they live first hand.

They've families like us, some of them even oppose the Purity Resolutions. Most of my crew is canine, and I'll thank you not to refer to them as mutts. Maybe I can't trust them with everything, maybe they don't appreciate our culture, but they're still people!"

Sheena gently grasped Sebastian's paw. "Do not be mad, he just gets excited."

"Excited!" Sebastian shook his head and snorted. "It's that sort of attitude that caused the Great War."

Valteri loured at him, but Sebastian refused to budge. He'd faced far angrier people in his time. Valteri was nothing.

"Maybe you're right, you're probably better knowing than I," Valteri said. "But you'll admit that even if we don't use action, we must appear as though we're prepared to."

Sebastian nodded. "90% of diplomacy is posturing."

Valteri chuckled, turned back to the grill, and grasped the meat in his tongs. "Food's ready."

The kits materialized, drawn by the enticing aroma of cooked flesh. The family sat down, Sebastian performed the traditional benediction over the food, and they dug in.

Sebastian couldn't remember the last time he'd had a home-cooked meal. The rabbit was delicious, cooked just right so to be seared on the outside and tender in. The salad was wonderful, the native flora fresh and crispy. The meal's subtle flaws – the burnt portions of rabbit, the occasional soft sprig – served to add character.

In minutes, they were finished. Sebastian complimented both elder Millers on a well-cooked meal, and helped put away the supplies. They wound up in the living room once again. The sun was just above the roof, casting long shadows across the floor.

"It's getting a little late," Sebastian said.

"You can still stay a margin longer, yeah? The kits would adore hearing some of your stories," Valteri said.

"And I'd love to tell, but I do have to leave before dark, dig?"

Sebastian proceeded to regale them with tales of improbable escapes, ferocious combat, and daring rescues. The Millers hung on his every word; all except Alsander. Sebastian couldn't tell if he was listening, but he was staring, as if he didn't believe a word Sebastian said. Could Alsander tell he was embellishing?

"Tell us about the titans," Zulia said. "We've never seen a real one before, just on the television."

Sebastian reclined on the couch. "What do you want to know?"

"How big are they?"

"How much do they weigh?"

"How do they work?"

"How fast do they go?"

Sebastian held up his paws. "Heel, one question at a time, okay? They're tall, taller than this house, great metal war machines, they're anywhere from seven to fourteen-and-a-third meters tall, and weigh between fifteen and a hundred megagrams. The fastest ones go up to one-hundred forty-three kilometers per standard hour, but most aren't any faster than eighty or so. They stand on two legs, they've got a skeleton of steel, and a skin of armor, with electrical nerves. Their heart is a system of fuel cells, they sleep when tired, recharging their batteries with portable solar panels. And their brain…" Sebastian pointed to his head. "Is mine."

He paused to watch the enthralled expressions on their muzzles, then he continued. "Vast amounts of weapons poke out from their bodies, laser cannons, rapid-fire blasters, particle cannons, guns of different types, missiles. They can go almost anywhere a person can, but their biggest strength is their versatility, independence, and automation. They only need one or two crew instead of five or six like a tank.

"But tanks are better in straight combat, they've got better armor, so instead titans have electromagnetic shields, like the sort that keep an aeroliner from burning up when it comes down from space. They protect titans from laser and missile fire. Tanks can carry heavier weapons, too, because they won't fall down when they fire a 120 or 150 millimeter cannon. But titans are faster and more agile."

"How do you drive one?" Maxine asked.

"Well, you don't drive them, really." Sebastian reclined on the couch to imitate what it was like in the cockpit. "You pilot it, like a fighter jet. You've got a joystick on either side of you, they control each arm's weapons so you can aim them independent. Your helmet has a visor over your eyes, and it's got graphics on the inside, like looking in a tiny television, but you can still see through it. That's how it tells you what's going on, what weapons you've got ready, where you're aiming, how fast you're going, and so forth.

"But you've also got controls in front of you, buttons and knobs and dials and displays and indicators, all around." Sebastian flipped an imaginary switch. "And you've got a throttle over here, there's sprint, run, three types of walk, neutral, and two reverse speeds. You steer it with your feet, the pedals click into a center position, you tilt the left forward to turn the torso right, push down with your heel to turn it left. The right pedal turns the chassis."

"It sounds daunting." Sheena said.

Sebastian shrugged. "It's really not that bad. It's got an autostabilizer so you won't topple in turns, and you can slave your weapons to one joystick and aim them all together. There's an autopilot and a targeting computer and such, but it can be overwhelming. We foxes are naturally inclined, with our sharp minds and quick paws. There's a theory that those trained initially on aerofighters are better titanists. Any other questions?"

There shouldn't have been any.

Alsander stared into Sebastian's eyes. "Why did you buy an expensive new radar for your Hurricane instead of using the money to upgrade the shield generators on the unit's aerocraft, like Adrian wanted?"

Sebastian would expect such a question from MerCom, but not from a child. At least for the authorities, he could have prepared a response, instead of merely stammering. "I, uh…"

"Alsander, don't—"

Sebastian stopped Valteri before he could scold the child. "No, it's a valid question, really." Sebastian leaned in to Alsander. "You see, a mercenary unit is not like a sports team. They're both group efforts, but a unit is only as good as its commander. It's my duty to lead my troops into battle, not to simply coach from the endlines, so it's a delicate balancing act between my needs and the needs of my crew. I've got a lot of faith in my aeropilots, and I would never send them out if I thought they'd be in excess danger. You dig?"

Alsander gazed up somberly. "What about Terrance Burlington, Marlena Johnson, Brigotahn Fairchild, Dukav Ilkany, and—"

Sebastian's hackles rose. "People die in battle, Alsander. That's what war is about."

"Adrian said they wouldn't have died with the shield upgrades."

Sebastian gritted his teeth, pulled back his lips into a snarl, and lurched at Alsander. "Now you listen to me, you stupard little twig! I love each and every warrior under my command like they were my own bloodkin, they know that, and I swear to Max that if I ever thought things would've gone so badly on that mission I would have done things different. But nobody, *nobody* dare say I don't care for them!"

Alsander recoiled, eyes wide, and clung to his mother for protection. Sheena wrapped her arms around him, and both stared back at Sebastian with silent shock.

Valteri looked between them, and coughed. "Ahem, well then, I think that's just about enough questions for now. Sebastian, how much time you have?"

Sebastian slowly retreated and leaned back on the couch. He checked the arm-worn display on his wearable computer. "Forty minutes."

The elder Millers exchanged looks. With a nod, they shared information known only to them. Sheena gently ushered the little girls off to their studies, and then leaned into her mate's side.

Valteri looked down to Alsander. "How's your gift? Can you read Sebastian now?"

"I can try. But Mr. Valentino is a very confusing man."

Sebastian grimaced. "Thanks, I guess."

"You're only going to be around a few more days here then, yeah? Give it a go anyway." Valteri ushered Sebastian forward and gestured for him to kneel before Alsander. "Put your paws like this, see?"

Sebastian's palms touched Alsander's. A rush of cold ran through Sebastian, but just as soon as he felt it, it was already gone. A warm aesthesis snaked up through his wrists, forearms, shoulders, an unnatural heat enveloping him. Something touched his mind, something that wasn't his. Nausea bore up from his depths. The room melted out of his vision, replaced by swirling polychromatic shades. Vibrant reds, blues, greens, yellows, mixed and danced and twirled about in his eyes, met in the center and then spiraled away, sharply repelled. Amplified, echoed sounds reverberated through his skull, his own heartbeat like a drum against his head. Every beat twisted the colors in new directions. It could have been a thousand years, or mere seconds. No, this was how it had always been; there had never been another way. The couch and floor vanished, and now he was floating, fur ruffled by the invisible breeze as he soared through his mindscape. Nothing could hold him back.

Suddenly, sharp pain. Alsander probed Sebastian's mind, searched for answers and clues in his thought patterns. He could feel Alsander running through him, and when they touched, the child's voice ran through his head.

"Relax, let me take control…"

Then, it happened, and their minds linked. Every thought and feeling now belonged to both. The colors spilled out from top to bottom, leaving only flat grey in its place. All the noise was gone. What was happening? Had he been abandoned? Where was he? What was going on?

Sebastian returned, but not to the couch. He was in a broad, nondescript hallway. It stretched on forever, featureless, rectangular, converging to nonexistence at the horizon. He couldn't move.

Alsander appeared before him, yet he looked different, healthier, more vibrant than in person. Or had he always been there?

"Welcome. How do you feel?" Alsander asked.

Now, Sebastian could move. He reached to touch Alsander, but his paw went through the kit's shoulder. A bizarre ripple cascaded through Alsander, like Sebastian were touching a reflection in a pond. Where his arm went in, a haze grew, steadily pulsing with his heartbeat and twining around to his shoulder.

Startled, Sebastian pulled his hand away, and Alsander returned to normal.

"Having fun?"

"Where are we?" Sebastian's voice sounded detached and distant, like it wasn't coming from his mouth, but from meters behind him. An orange fog tinted his entire view.

"We're inside your mind. Do be careful, though, you can hurt yourself seriously."

"You're here too?"

Alsander shrugged, but even the simple act looked disturbing. The child moved like a fluid, appearing devoid of a skeleton. "Part of me is, yes, but most of me is still in my mind. I'm here to act as your guide, so you don't get lost."

With the answer, the orange shading dissipated. Sebastian tried to step forward, but his legs refused to budge. "And you can tell my future from inside here? How's that supposed to work?"

"If I knew, I'd tell you. But I can't, so I won't," Alsander said.

"That's not an answer at all."

"There'll be time for answers later. Right now, I've got a question for you. Why did you lie?"

"I didn't!"

A cold, angry wind drove through Sebastian, chilling him to the bone. Tempestuous, invisible snow piled up about his body, until he felt as though he would freeze in place.

"Don't lie to me, Sebastian! I'm in you, I know what you're thinking," Alsander said.

Sebastian strained to fight the chill from his bones. "Then why bother asking?"

Alsander stared, hard. "I want to hear it from you. I want to hear, in your own words, why you lied to my parents."

Sebastian felt naked, nowhere for him to hide. Inviting Alsander into his mind was a catastrophe, and not just because he had no answers to his questions. It was because he had no answers for himself.

"I didn't want to hurt them," Sebastian said.

"I don't believe you."

"Why?"

Alsander sighed and shook his head. "I can read my parents' thoughts and feelings as well as I can read yours. They take the Rite of Atonement very seriously. Do you know how sad they would be if they found out you lied? They'd take a lot more than your tail tip, believe me."

Sebastian looked down. "Then I have no reason to lie."

"Oh ho, yes you do!" Alsander said. "You're afraid of the truth, afraid to tell them it's your fault. Though I guess if I were in your position, I wouldn't be able to tell someone that either."

"I'm sorry. It's all been a terrible chain of events." The instant Sebastian apologized, he began to thaw, the hidden snow melting away from him.

"Now that, I believe. It's hard to own up to one's goofs, isn't it? Now hurry, we're wasting time. Tell me what you want to know."

Sebastian thought long and hard upon the prospect. What should he ask? How specific would the answers be? Would they be accurate? Was his future fixed, or could he change it? He decided to start small.

"Why do you stare at me like that?" Sebastian asked.

Alsander chuckled, his ears swiveling forward. "That's not the sort of question I had in mind, but okay. Why? Well, it's easy, I've been waiting for you so long, and felt you from far away. It's kind of like the anticipation before you go to your first baseball game, I guess."

"I've never been."

Alsander scowled. "Fine, ruin my perfectly bonny analogy. Either way, I could feel your lies the moment I saw you."

Sebastian flinched, a brief tinge of orange sweeping the corners of his eyes. It vanished just as fast. "Do you feel that for everyone?"

Alsander laughed and waved a dismissive paw. "Of course not! It's just for you. Now, ask another question, a real one this time. I think I already know what it is."

"Tell me about Melissa," Sebastian said.

An image of the vixen appeared, like a painting, on the wall. She was so beautiful, just as Sebastian remembered her. No, she appeared, literally, as he had seen her last. A gentle blue haze colored his sight.

That was when he realized why Alsander looked out of place. When he turned to face Melissa's likeness, he didn't actually move. His image turned, yet there was no depth of movement, no shadow, no change of shape, like he were an image portrayed on a cutout.

"She's quite lovely, isn't she, Sebastian?"

"Will she come with me to the ship?"

Alsander didn't hesitate. "No."

"What do you mean, no?"

Alsander shrugged. "I mean no. She won't come to the ship with you."

There had to be something more to it, but Sebastian had to be careful. He didn't know how this worked. "Why not?"

"Be more specific."

"Does she want to?"

"Yes, Sebastian." The cerulean tint grew stronger. "More than anything in the world."

"Then something stops her?" Sebastian asked.

"Yes."

"What?"

Alsander turned and gestured at Sebastian with both paws. The flat fox's arms remained at the same distance as before. "I don't think you understand just how much information I'm dealing with here, Sebastian. You need to be more specific, or I can't tell you anything."

Sebastian exhaled, slow, and paused. He hadn't felt a need to breathe until now, and he couldn't ever remember breathing before. "Okay. So, something beyond her control?"

"Yes."

"A person or an object?"

"Both," Alsander said.

"Someone she knows?"

"No."

"Someone I know?"

Alsander chewed on his lip. "Maybe."

"Maybe?"

"It's not terribly clear right now. Keep asking," Alsander said.

"Is it me?"

"No."

"Is it Delzano?"

"No."

"Darling?"

Alsander sighed and crossed his arms. "Are you really going to ask me whether every last person you've ever met is the one to stop her?"

Sebastian shook his head, the tint receding. "No, I guess not."

"Bonny, because I don't have to put up with that. It's annoying," Alsander said.

"Sorry."

"Don't apologize, I hate it when people apologize for things they didn't know about or things beyond their control, it's so dumb!" Alsander folded his dimensionless arms. "But I suppose it's an easy enough mistake to make, huh? Go on."

Sebastian thought about what he had heard so far, all the answers literal and narrow. Alsander would need to be steered in the proper direction. Maybe he should try asking about different possibilities?

"Is the reason she doesn't come to the ship because something happens to me?" Sebastian said.

"More specific, Sebastian."

"Something bad?"

Alsander huffed. "Outlook hazy, ask again."

"Will I get killed before we get back to the ship?"

"No."

Sebastian smiled. That was a relief, at least. "Am I captured?"

"No."

"Does it have anything to do with the bounty?"

Alsander sighed. "That's far too vague a question, Sebastian."

Sebastian frowned, shook his head. If he wasn't captured or killed, what was left? "Is it about money?"

Alsander knit his brows, twisted up his muzzle. "Yes. Maybe. Possibly. Probably."

"What does that mean?"

Alsander sighed and shrugged. "There's a chance that it's about money, Sebastian, but I can't say more for sure."

"Is it about the bounty?"

Alsander spun in place to face him. A red hue shot through Sebastian's vision. "Sebastian! You already asked me that once, now don't ask me the same questions, or I'll end this right now, even if it hurts you!"

"Okay, okay!" Sebastian held up his paws. "I'm sorry. It's something that's important to me, that's all."

"Apology accepted," Alsander said. The crimson drained from Sebastian's sight. "Now go ahead, ask another question."

"I'm not sure what to ask."

"You're smart, Sebastian. You'll think of something."

"Is it about my money?"

"Well, let's see." Alsander stroked a paw along his muzzle. "It's not really about it, but it might be involved."

"This isn't helping much, you know."

Alsander flicked a paw. "You think I'm some sort of slave, here for your use only? What do you want me to do, seize your mind and tell you what you want to know?"

"Can you do that?"

Alsander rubbed the side of his muzzle and sighed. "It wasn't a real question, don't be so dense. Here, some advice: start broad, then narrow your way down. You've got no more questions about Melissa."

Before Sebastian could open his mouth, Melissa's face disappeared, replaced by the Star Rangers' unit logo. "What about the Star Rangers? Are we in good shape in say, a year?"

"Now this is interesting." While Alsander stared at the logo, the colors – all colors – drained until everything was dark and monochromatic. "In one year, the Star Rangers' don't exist."

"What do you—?"

Alsander raised a paw. "Specifics, Sebastian!"

"Sorry."

"Stop apologizing, you scagg!" Alsander snapped his teeth at Sebastian. "I'm not going to warn you again. Now continue."

"Are the Rangers' destroyed in combat?"

"No."

Was that promising or threatening? "Do we break up, or are we broken up?"

"What kind of stapard question is that?" Alsander shook his head. "Try again."

"Am I the cause of the break up?"

"Part of it, yes."

"Am I killed?"

"No."

"Does it have something to do with the bou—"

An explosion ripped through Sebastian, and intense pain shot through his body. He couldn't bear to stand, yet he couldn't fall. His entire view turned savagely red.

"You vexing thickwit! What did I tell you about asking me the same questions?"

Every cell in Sebastian's body burned. It took every gram of strength to draw his muzzle towards Alsander's voice, but all he could see was red.

"The pain…"

"I warned you not to cross me," Alsander said. "Now I'll have to teach you a lesson."

The next thing Sebastian knew, he was no longer in the hallway. The red sheen was gone; instead, he found himself on his knees in a small room. Only the essentials were there: a bed, flat white sheets, a bookcase, a desk with papers, a window. It could have been any number of rooms anywhere throughout the galaxy, but it felt strangely familiar.

The window! Sebastian flew to it, ignoring the ache in his knees, and stared out the glass. For kilometers around, all he saw was snow, piled and drifted and meeting trees at the edge of his sight.

He caught his reflection in the glass and recoiled in shock. The face that looked back was his, yet now as he should be. His features were younger, his ears larger to his head, his eyes wide, vernal and innocent. It couldn't be real, it had to be a dream. He grabbed at himself, felt his real fur, pulled his real whiskers and yelped in real pain. He checked his tail; it was still long.

His heart pounded, hard in his ears, and he stumbled backwards against the wall. Now he realized where he was. This was his bedroom, and he was only eight years old.

Sebastian balled his paws into fists. This had to be a trick by Alsander, a memory plucked from his mind and reconstructed as punishment. But why this moment?

A quick glance around the room revealed a startling attention to detail. All the books on the shelf were just as he remembered, from the handful of dime store novels he had owned, to weighty history books, to his Mahonic translation of the Memoria. The desk held schoolwork from a time gone by, scattered and disheveled as if left in a hurry.

He bent over to examine its surface. A page in an arithmetic textbook was open to the chapter on multivariate statistics, and a page of incomplete homework lay nearby. He brought the loose-leaf to his muzzle, to search for more clues.

The paper was dated 4 Virgil, 489. Sebastian immediately felt sick.

"Alsander!" Sebastian shook his fist at the ceiling. "I swear I'll kill you!"

Alsander's voice came from everywhere, reverberating from inside Sebastian's mind as if it were his own thoughts.

"Don't be so sure," it said.

Sebastian didn't get to think any further on it. The next moment, an older male red fox burst into the room. He towered over Sebastian, dressed in a spruced, proper Alliance military dress uniform. It was a high rank, equivalent to a general, and his amber eyes burned with fire.

Sebastian stared at the other fox in disbelief. "Dad?"

"Well, Sebastian, have you thought about what you've done?"

"What did I do?"

Sebastian knew he shouldn't have said that, but it was already too late. A gloved paw struck him across the face, the durahyde smashing him to the carpet.

"Don't smart off to me, boy. Now get up, you coward. The commies will do far worse to you than that."

Sebastian clambered to his feet, one paw holding his muzzle. It actually hurt.

His father turned to regard Sebastian's desktop. A fist swatted down onto the incomplete page of math. "You haven't finished your homework. What have I always said about intelligence?"

Sebastian trembled. "Intelligence is the key to victory."

The older fox turned and shoved Sebastian's shoulder. "Intelligence is the key to victory, *sir.*" He waved Sebastian's homework at him. "Look at this. Without intelligence, you are a failure. Do you want to fail your country, Max, and above all, me?"

Sebastian quivered, eyes wide in fear. "No. I mean, no sir."

"I don't think you really mean that." His father flicked the page away and it floated to the floor. "I come home on leave for two months and I find you undisciplined and unfocused."

"I'm doing my best, sir."

"Are you?" His father folded his hands behind his back, strode to the window, and gazed out at the snowy landscape. "Next triad, I'm returning to the front. I've been appointed Field Commander for the Cassavin System. The line is faltering near Mera Woods," his father said.

Mera Woods? Sebastian couldn't remember why that name was familiar.

"Do you have any idea what a great honor this is for me, for all of us?" he said. "You'll have a lot of expectations to live up to, and I won't have my son being a failure. I think those mush-heads at school have been feeding you that Unificationist propaganda about 'peace with dignity'."

"No, sir, I swear, it's not true!"

"It had best not be. There are one-hundred and four days left before you are conscripted, and I fully expect you to make the officer's corps." He marched across the room. "We need more fine officers at the Rimward Front."

Sebastian crimped his ears back. It was 489; the Great War was still ongoing, though if it was already Virgil, it was down to its final months. "But the war will be over before I'm drafted."

His father turned sharply on his heels, eyes narrowed to points. "What was that?"

"The, uh, war, it's going to end," Sebastian said. "Soon."

"Are you making excuses for your disaffection towards our brave young fighters?"

"Honest, sir! On the fourth of Ophiuchus, there's a massive atomic exchange, and—"

His father crossed his arms and snorted. "I wouldn't put it past those commie cowards."

"Actually, I think we fired first—"

Again, his father's gloved fist sent him crashing to the carpet. "Treason! You'd better not dare say such words in public!"

Sebastian trembled, his lip bleeding. He looked up, stunned, not by the blow but by his inability to evade it. All his reflexes seemed slowed. "I'm sorry, sir."

The elder fox stared down at Sebastian, hard. He snatched him by the nape and hauled him upright. "What are McTsuma's Four Tenets to Victory?"

Sebastian gaped at his father. He strained to remember, but his mind came up blank.

"Vex it, boy!" His father slammed his fist into his palm with a dull smack. "What are McTsuma's Four Tenets to Victory?"

"Position, logistics, firepower, and… and…"

"The will to do what must be done," his father said. "Position, logistics, firepower, and *will*, boy. For the love of Max, have you forgotten already?"

"I—"

"What is the service ceiling of the Dolphin attack aerofighter in atmospheric mode?"

Sebastian stumbled back from the inquisition, ears down and defensive. The answers materialized in his mind, and he responded autonomously.

"22,900 meters," Sebastian said.

"What is the cyclic rate of the Pioneer S-1M sub machinegun?"

"750 rounds per minute."

"In optimal storage mode, what is the cargo capacity of the Ajax-class medium dropship?"

"5,163.4 cubic meters."

"According to the Burgundy Doctrine, what were the primary, secondary, and tertiary reasons for the placement of intra-system atomic weapons in the Manchester star system?"

With each question, his father had steadily advanced on him. Now, Sebastian was backed into a corner, his answers part memory and part fear.

"To act as a deterrent to Dominion incursion, to counter Dominion atomic placement in the bordering Ontario system, and to free inter-system atomic weapons to provide force projection," Sebastian said.

"What are Harrison's Three Laws of Troop Morale?"

"Escapism, entertainment, and family connection."

"Name the twenty-six original Vulpine Houses."

Sebastian's lips quivered. "Lafayette, Fal Araya, Kaczmarek, Arielle, Florenzo, Y'Ta'Leen, Berkerest, Sofia, Cambridge, Chamberlain, La Vallena, Wallace, Murrel, Hart, Stenheim, Morgan, Greyfur, Lokay, Zukayta, Danilow, Kinutsev, Arena, Duchesne, Ontowac, Wenn, and…"

Sebastian's mind went hopelessly blank. The last name refused to come to him.

"Norwood!" His father balled up a fist and struck the wall next to him. "You always forget House Norwood. You're hopeless."

Sebastian cringed, staring up with helpless eyes. The elder fox turned away and strode to the center of the room. Sebastian couldn't see his face, but he knew he was father was upset.

"First strike," his father said. "When was the Star Alliance incorporated?"

"6 Scutum, 391?"

"Are you certain?"

Sebastian's heart fluttered. Now he doubted his own answer.

"Y… yes?"

"You're wrong," his father said. "The treaty incorporating the Star Alliance was signed 6 Scutum, but it didn't come into effect until the first of Aquarius the next year. Two strikes."

Sebastian's hands tightened against each other. It was all happening again, just as it had the first time. He would need to get the next question correct, or else.

"Who led House Cambridge to victory over the Adelie Fringe forces at the Third Battle of Sandra?"

Sebastian's eyes went wide. He tried, hard as he could, but couldn't find the answer anywhere in his memory. "General Dickinson?"

"No!"

Sebastian didn't even see his father turn around. Quick as lightning, Sebastian was laid out on the floor, hit again in the side of the muzzle. "That's wrong!" his father said. "You're hopeless!"

Sebastian held his face in pain, trembling on the floor. He tried to stand, but his father kicked him hard in the ribs and sent him crashing to the floor.

"How can you expect to be a great warrior without a grasp of history? Maybe I'll just have to refresh your memory!"

"No, please don't!"

The elder fox dragged him by the scruff, out of the room and down the stairs, and threw him out into the snow outside the back door. Sebastian tumbled into a heap in the powder, sprawled across his back. The cold shock stung him through his fur, to the skin.

"No son of mine is going to be a failure! Now get up."

Sebastian's paws met the frozen surface and sunk into it. It had to be over a meter deep, and was provided little traction. He had to struggle to stand, and the flakes coated his clothing.

"Take those off."

"P-Please, sir, father, don't make me."

"I said…" His father reached for his omnipresent sidearm. "Take them off, boy."

It was so frigid, no more than 240K. Even with his winter pelt, he would freeze to death in an hour, but he had no choice. He removed his clothing and tossed it into a heap at his father's booted feet.

"You're going to stand there naked until you remember who commanded House Cambridge at the Third Battle of Sandra, you hear me?"

Sebastian's whiskers quivered, the freezing wind biting into him. He wrapped his paws about himself for warmth, but it had little effect. "Please, sir, I can't remember."

"Then you shall die a failure."

Sebastian trembled. His panicked breathing grew ragged, and his exhalation turned to frigid crystals that froze to his face. He pulled his tail to his chest and rubbed it between his paws, and through it all, his father just stared down, cold as the wintry air.

Minutes passed by as swift as a frozen wind. Sebastian strained to remember, but he couldn't find the answer. He could only assume his father wouldn't help him, that he would let him freeze to death. Dream or not, Sebastian was sure he was going to die.

He did the same thing he had the first time this happened. He ran.

"Coward!" his father said. "Where are you going?"

The snow gave beneath Sebastian's paws and he stumbled, faltered, and lurched towards the nearby woods. Even if he wanted to, he couldn't answer his father's question. He was only going away, away from his tormentor, and towards the relative freedom of the forest.

A shot was fired, and Sebastian ducked down to run on all fours. The freezing snow stung his paw pads, but he kept running. He was in a panicked sprint now. Had he remembered what happened originally, he wouldn't have run at all.

"Wait! You're heading for the lake!"

It was too late. In his rush to escape, Sebastian had once again forgotten. He leapt off a snow bank, met the icy surface hard, and broke through.

Water logged his fur, soaked him to the bone, and started to freeze his paws. He flailed and splashed, struggled as best he could to grab the edge of the ice, to haul himself up, but he couldn't, the water making him too heavy. His vision was darkening, his mouth and lips freezing in the sheer cold. He was going to die.

Instead, his head struck the Miller's floor, joined soon by the rest of his crumpled body. Sebastian never felt a thing. Somewhere above, he heard the vague echoes of speech, the words formless and unintelligible.

He began to regain his consciousness.

"Just relax, Sebastian. You'll be fine."

Sebastian couldn't tell who was speaking. The numbness and cold that enveloped him slowly retreated, leaving in its wake the tingling of recirculation, then the agony of pain. He screamed.

"Blast it, Alsander, what did you do to him?"

"He was bugging me, asking the same questions when I told him not to."

"Look, he's shaking!"

It was a nightmare. The world spun around Sebastian. Every sound was a clap of thunder, every touch a dagger to his skin. He managed to uncurl himself and lie prone on the floor, but it provided little help. He still felt as though he were freezing to death in the lake.

"He was making me mad, so I gave him a bad memory."

"You shouldn't have done that, Alsander," Valteri said. "He invited you into his mind."

It took all of Sebastian's strength to climb atop the couch and sprawl on its armrest. The change in orientation only caused his stomach to twist into knots. To his shock, he was wet and cold. So cold.

"My head…"

"Let me help you, Sebastian. Can you stand?"

"I don't know…"

Sebastian opened his eyes, but saw only a russet blur. Valteri wrapped his arms about him and dragged him upright. Sebastian tried to stand on his own, but his shaking legs gave way, and he clung to Valteri.

"Lean on me. Why are you so cold?" Valteri said.

"I fell in the lake…"

Valteri rubbed along his body, trying to dry and warm him. Sebastian hung on him, eyes closed. "What lake?" Valteri asked.

"The lake out back…"

Valteri sighed. "Sheena, get me more water."

Slowly, very slowly, the shivering subsided. Sebastian finally remembered where he was, and how he had gotten here. The terrible pain in his head wasn't helped when Valteri splashed his face with water; that must have been why he was wet.

"Where did you put him, Alsander?"

"A time when his dad was angry at him. He was nine. It's funny, he did everything the same this time as he did before," Alsander said.

"At least he's not shaking so much, now. How long's this going to last?" Valteri asked.

"I don't know. If he didn't have a strong will, he'd be dead right now."

Sebastian groaned and planted his feet. His vision cleared. "I think I'm dead."

Valteri sighed and helped Sebastian to a couch. "You're not dead."

"Are you sure?"

"Of course I'm sure."

Sebastian could move his digits again, and feeling returned to his extremities. "But I died the first time."

"That's rubbish," Valteri said. "If you died the first time, how are you here now?"

"I can't remember."

Valteri continued rubbing Sebastian's side, the older fox's paws bringing warmth to his haggard body. "Alsander, what happened next?"

"I don't know. I didn't read any further into his mind. I just picked the worst memory in his head."

Valteri scowled, working to hold Sebastian upright. "Go to your room, Alsander. We'll think of a punishment for you later."

"But dad, he's so annoying!"

"Don't argue with me," Valteri said.

Sebastian's breathing returned to normal, and he stood without assistance. The sun was close to the horizon, scorching through the front window and into his eyes. "I should really be leaving."

"I'm dreadfully sorry about that, I'd no idea he could do such a thing," Valteri said.

"I'll keep it in mind for next time."

Valteri stepped back, arms out in case Sebastian teetered. "Suppose you can drive?"

"Yeah, it's not so bad now, and it's warm outside."

"Did you learn anything from Alsander?" Sheena asked.

"Stuff to think about. Nothing too specific, but that's my fault, I guess. Can it be changed?"

Valteri helped Sebastian to the door. "No idea. He's young still, once the gifted mature, they're supposedly never wrong. He's been absolute with us, but he's never read a stranger before."

Sebastian stepped outside. The sky burned at the edges with the fiery glow of sunset. The cooling air stung his damp fur. Night was coming.

Valteri followed, gazing into the distance. "It was nice having you, even with the, uh…"

Sebastian turned to face them, to look into their eyes for one last time. They were both advancing on their fiftieth birthdays, close to the vulpine lifespan. It was the last time he would ever see them again.

"It was nice to see you too." Sebastian offered his paw. Valteri took it by the wrist and gently touched Sebastian's palm to his own cheek. Sheena did the same. "I'll try to see you again sometime."

"We will try to live long enough for that," Sheena said.

"Max be with you, Sebastian," Valteri said.

"*Yasha-marsa*, Valteri, Sheena."

Sebastian turned away and walked back to his car, letting a great opportunity slip through his fingers. He should have done more to embrace his culture. Instead, he shifted his Sydney into gear, waved, and left Adrian's parents – and his past – behind.

The unexpected must always be accounted for. Our business is the unforeseen. Situational awareness is the greatest advantage anyone can possess. Without it, we are blind as newborn kits.

-Adrian Miller

SCENE FIVE

"Move on, Sebastian! Up! Rouse!"

Sebastian Valentino rolled over in bed, sprawled on his back, and blinked heavy sleep from his eyes. When he tried to sit, an agonizing pain shot through his spine, and he yelped.

"What's the problem?"

"My back hurts," Sebastian said.

He opened his eyes and was rewarded with a shock, bright white washing out his vision. He snapped his eyes shut and lay back on the bed. Even the soft sounds of Melissa's approaching footfalls pounded in his head.

"From Alsander?" Melissa asked.

"From you."

"Sweet me?" Melissa dropped onto the bed. "You really mean that?"

"I do," Sebastian said. "I've been around the galaxy and never felt something like last night."

"You're only acid because you loved it!" Melissa teased at his shoulder.

"I can't believe I let you talk me into that."

"You wouldn't stop. You were at it all night."

"That was a mistake. Some things shouldn't be done all night," Sebastian said.

Melissa chuckled, fetched a silvery dress from a nearby chair, and held it across her form. "Howsa? Should I bring it?"

Sebastian remained on the bed, a paw against his temple. "Sure."

"You're not even looking!"

"I just want to close my eyes forever."

Melissa huffed and dropped the outfit onto the chair. "If I'd known you'd be this moody, I'd not have invited you."

"Invited? You practically begged me to come, you temptress," Sebastian said.

"It's hardly shameful, Sebastian. It's fun and bouncy and merry, you can smash it all night and slink into life next morning like nothing happened."

"But I hate disco!"

She smiled and sprawled out on the bed next to him. "That's not what it looked like last night. And you're a truly noble dancer! You've got a given rhythm and flow, like water."

"I hate disco music, I hate disco dancing, and I hate discotheques."

Sebastian turned his muzzle away from her, but she sidled up to him, draped a paw over his side, and licked his cheek. "You loved it last night," Melissa said. "Particularly Starfall."

"They do that Electronic Supersonic song, right?"

"Yep, and you're smashing to it! The urbans at Red Alert simply adored us. I couldn't have done it without you. Besides, when the ailing dissolves, you'll feel grand."

"It's still a dumb song."

Melissa tweaked his ear, tugging it lightly between her slender black fingers. "Well who do you like?"

"Bands like Legend, Fury, Skayver, Tumult, Trickster—"

"Trickster!" Melissa stuck out her tongue. "The Line of Fire band?"

"I like Line of Fire."

"It's limp!" Melissa said. "The lyrics are dobby, 'You saw the movie, but I wrote the book'? What does that even mean?"

Sebastian rolled on his side and lightly pushed her away. "Go get me some aspirin for my headache."

Melissa tousled his head fur. "Nay. You'll just have to get off your shortened tail and fetch it yourself."

"That's not funny."

Melissa chuckled and nuzzled his cheek. "Sorry. Still, we can't very well let you flop it when today's the big day!"

His ears quirked outwards. "Sweetie, what time is it?"

"0762. Why?"

Sebastian scowled and propped his arms up beneath him. "Got to get up, call the ship. You start getting ready, your aerobus leaves in five hours."

"Howsa?"

"It's like a regular bus, where you buy a seat, tell them your destination, they figure out how to get there, and then they stop and let you off or let people on. They only stop in orbit, but it's a lot cheaper if you only need to move one or two people," Sebastian said.

Melissa shrugged and folded some clothing. "You're the expert."

Sebastian hauled himself upright, stalked to the bathroom, and threw open the medicine cabinet. "There's nothing in here. Didn't you bring anything with you?"

Melissa materialized behind him and looked over his shoulder into the mirror. "The sanctuary yokes don't let me have things like that."

"You didn't say we had no aspirin."

"I said if you want it, you'll have to fetch it. I didn't say how far you'd have to go." She rubbed her muzzle up against his. How could she be so cheerful? "I chicaned so you'd move your pelt, can't have you loose about forever."

Sebastian sighed and braced his paws on the bathroom sink. The reflection that stared back at him was tired, sagging, its fur drooping at the tips. He could barely hold his ears erect. "I could use some loosing," he said. "Look at me, I can't call the ship like this."

"Why not?" Melissa reached around and ruffled his exposed chest fur. "Corey's never seen you shirtless?"

"No, and I'm not about to let him."

"You look sprinting."

With a light swat, he ushered her out of his way and stumbled back into the bedroom. "But I feel so old."

"You look more than addy. You're only as old as you feel. How aged are you?"

"Twenty-five."

Melissa dispelled her grimace before Sebastian could see it. "Well, see? You've half a life still left!"

"Thanks." He collapsed on the bed and stared at the ceiling. "How about you?"

"Oh, a vixen never reveals her age!"

"That's what elders say."

Melissa huffed. "I'm no elder! I'll have you know I'm nary a triad over ten."

She was an adult, but not by much. She hadn't even been born when Sebastian had completed his military service.

"That doesn't make me feel any better," he said. "You're ten? Shouldn't you be in the service?"

"Those in sanctuary don't have to, unless they want to, and I don't."

"They'll pay you well, keep you fed."

"I don't want to be a trooper, it's sorry enough in the shelter." She turned from him. "I don't want to hear about it anymore."

"It's okay, we don't have to. It was just a suggestion." Sebastian sat upright and faced her. "Tell you what, let's go for breakfast. Put something nice on."

Melissa squealed eagerly and bounded off, leaving Sebastian alone in the bedroom. He wiped his eyes again and scanned the room for loose clothing. He put on a suitable shirt – a yellow V-neck with red collar – and tugged his fur into place.

It took longer than normal to connect to the ship; this alone should have triggered an alarm in the fox's head. In his addled state, he thought nothing of it, until the link came through and revealed Patricia Darling seated in the command chair.

Sebastian tilted his head. "Darling?"

Patricia smiled. "Hello, Captain! You're good, yeah?"

"Why are you in the command chair?"

"Well, I'm duty commander for—"

"Where is Corey?"

"Corey? Oh, he's here, around, but not here-here, yeah?"

Sebastian narrowed his eyes and leaned closer to the screen. "Tell me where Assistant Captain Delzano is. Now."

She held up her paws. "He's in his quarters recovering from a little accident yesterday, he left me in charge."

"What kind of accident?"

Patricia shifted in her seat. "Well, see, he was in the gym sparring, and you know that big malamute security fellow we just hired?"

"His name is Dorph Rostegarde, he's seventeen, from Brandenburg in the Dominion."

"You know him then, yeah? He's quite a daunting dog—"

"What about him?"

Patricia forced a smile. "Well, Corey was trying out one of the moves you showed him, the locking-shoulder throw? Turns out Dorph's a bit big for it."

"And?"

"Corey tried to throw him and Dorph just sort of…" Patricia gestured vacantly. "Well, Corey bruised his spine, yeah? So he's recovering in bed. Doc Pandrigon says he'll be up and frisky in a day or two."

Sebastian just stared back in silence, paws folded across his lap.

Patricia cleared her throat. "So how're things with you?"

"I completed the Rite of Atonement last night, and—"

"How're the Millers?"

Sebastian flicked his ears. "Fine. You're going to have a visitor on the ship soon."

"Who?"

"Melissa will be joining us. We'll be mated as soon as things settle down," Sebastian said.

Patricia smiled. "That's splendid! Does she have any skills?"

"I'll have to ask her. She'll be coming up in an aerobus in about seven hours, she'll stay in Adrian's cabin. She doesn't speak Mahonic, so I want you to be extra nice to her, dig?"

Patricia grinned, ears erect. "Faith's me!"

"Good," Sebastian said. "I've got a few more things to take care of today, I'll be back aboard the ship a little after that. Is there anything you've need to report?"

"Well, an unknown warship jumped in system, but it hasn't—"

"When was this?"

"A few hours after you left the ship—"

Sebastian pulled his lips back, briefly exposing his teeth. "Do you mean to tell me that you've lagged three days to tell me this?"

"Well, it hasn't moved, so we didn't think it important."

"And how are you so sure that it hasn't moved?" Sebastian folded his arms, eyes focused on Patricia.

"Well, see, it disappeared around Wexford III, and Corey thought it was in orbit, so we put a computer lock through the radar, to tell us if it moved, and it hasn't."

Sebastian frowned and tucked his ears back. What sort of colossal confusion could have led Corey to issue such an order? "You put a computer lock on a planet? You realize that's not what the radar is for, right?"

The carthagan squirmed in her seat and clutched her paws together. "Well, uh…"

"Right?"

She winced, her ears tucked down. "Well, no, but Corey said…"

"Forget what Corey said. What about the far side, the blind spot?"

"The what?"

"The far side, Patricia." Sebastian shook his head and sighed. "You know, orbital mechanics? When you're orbiting a planet and it gets in the way of your view?"

"Oh, well, we, uh…"

"Did you interface with Alliance ESRs?"

"ESRs?"

Sebastian held his head, rubbed at his temple, and growled. "ESR, it's an acronym, electronics satellite radar. You know, orbital radar?"

"Oh, well, we just called them radar sats in the Dominion—"

"Did you, or did you not, interface with Alliance radar satellites?"

She shook her head. "Well, no…"

"So it could have moved when you were on the far side," Sebastian said.

"Yes, but we would have noticed a change when we came around, yeah?"

Sebastian managed to fight off the rising growl deep from his throat, but it wasn't easy. Only three days and his crew was already mucking things up. "Not with the blind spot. The computer lock on the Skyrider class is not for monitoring large things, like planets, it's for watching small things, like enemy carriers. With a target that big, it's going to need so much computer focus, it'll leave a huge blind spot in that area. Did you know that?"

"Well, no…"

Sebastian exhaled, slowly. "If you'd told me three days ago, when this happened, you would, wouldn't you?"

"Sorry, Captain."

He sighed and leaned back in his chair. "Never mind it. Cancel the computer lock and monitor all aero-traffic until I return, then we'll sort this mess out, dig?"

"Yes, Captain. Is there anything else?"

"I'm going to see about arranging some supplies while we're here. I'll comm you at 800 tomorrow with updates. Valentino out."

Sebastian hung his head in his paws. It was his fault. He should never have left a dog in command of the ship, even if they were Wild like Delzano and Darling. They would only fail and cower.

Melissa appeared from the bathroom, wearing a simple white dress, matching plasteen shoes, and a blue pillbox hat. She saw Sebastian's face, and frowned. "What's the dour deal?"

"I've got a ship of under-trained mutts."

She glided to him and seated herself on his armrest. "Can it really be so down? You trained them, right?"

His head met her side, and he leaned against her. "Not enough."

"Why not?"

"Because the more dogs know, the more dangerous they are."

"Dangerous? Howsa?"

"They could be mutinous if they knew how to fully use the ship. You have to teach them just enough to be effective, or they'll turn, and I can't afford that."

Melissa touched her nose to his cheek. "Let me get this straight. You want to be the best mercenary ever, so you lowprep your crew? That's quite dobby, Sebastian."

He smiled, defeated. "You're right, it doesn't make much sense out loud. Maybe I'm just paranoid."

"You? Watchy?" She stood up. "What of Corey, you trust him, right?"

"He wasn't there."

She tilted her head. "Howsa?"

"Darling threw a load of bait about how he injured himself, said he was resting."

"Do you believe her?"

Sebastian stood and enveloped Melissa in a hug. "I don't know if I do."

"You think she lies?"

He nuzzled her cheek. "I do, but it's probably not malice. Maybe Corey did something dumb and is embarrassed to tell me. But…"

"But?"

"Sparring with Rostegarde qualifies as dumb."

She kissed him and smiled. "Don't strain so much, you'll go dobby."

"You're right. Are you ready?"

Melissa snorted and stepped back from him. She folded her arms and appraised him derisively. "That's not what you'll wear, is it?"

He looked down at himself. "You don't like this shirt?"

"It's limp. Wear the blue one for me, with the yellow pants and white stripe?"

"You like that one?"

She smiled and patted his shoulder. "It's really sprinting. Oh, and wear that little necklace thing."

"The Ankh of Kohoutek?"

"The whatever-you-have-it, it looks noble on you."

"Anything for you, dear heart." Sebastian tossed his mandated outfit onto the bed. "Here, tell you what, why don't you pack up your bag now. You can head right to the aeroport from breakfast."

The corner's of Melissa's lips tugged down into a frown, her eyes wide and sad. "You won't come with me?"

Sebastian sighed and gently kissed her cheek. "I can't, sweetie, honest. I've still got errands to do, and I won't be back here until just before I leave for the ship. Okay?"

"I suppose." She smiled, thin, and ambled up to nuzzle his cheek. "I do wish you'd see me off."

"I really can't. Mine is a demanding job." He tipped her muzzle upwards and pressed his nose to her. "But don't you worry, we'll have endless love on the ship. Okay?"

She smiled and kissed him, briefly, on the lips. "Okay, Sebastian."

"Spiffy. Now go get ready, and I'll get changed. We'll have an unforgettable breakfast."

***

A breeze tousled the fur of a cape dog, alone in a grassy urban-bound parcel of park. He waited, shifted, glanced at his surroundings, tweaked a dial on his head-set radio, and waited more. In due time, what he anticipated would come to him.

On schedule, they arrived, tall jackal and shorter raccoon. The former, suitcase in hand, strode up to the cape dog.

"Neuback?" he asked.

The caper nodded. "You are ready?"

"Absolutely."

"Then we go."

Pyotr Neuback led them across the city. Every few minutes, he would stop, speak low to a distorted voice on his radio, check his location on a folding map, and then resume. Corey and Teresa followed, doing their best to appear nonchalant in the city of vulpines.

Their destination was one of Stone Canyon's numerous shop-flats. They assembled on the roof, twelve stories above the city streets. Corey cracked open the suitcase, constructed the pieces, and handed the sniper rifle to Teresa.

She snapped a bipod into place, lined up her scope, and poked the weapon unobtrusively over the building's eaves.

***

"You really adore sweet grass, don't you?"

Sebastian Valentino pulled a few sprigs from his muzzle. "I haven't eaten it since I was... well..."

Melissa smiled and folded her paws neatly atop the table. "Since when?"

"Since I expatriated."

"Oh." She delicately took her fork and speared a chunk of fruit. "What does that mean?"

"Technically," he said, between bites of cinnamon apple, "I'm a CenCon resident, a displaced Alliance national. I had to renounce my citizenship to the Star Alliance, though I'm still a member of House Lafayette."

Melissa pouted. "Don't you love the Alliance?"

"Not as much as I love you," Sebastian said with a grin. "But it's illegal for a private citizen to own a warship here. My only other option would be to sign the Favored Sky over to the Star Rangers itself, but that's not something I'm willing to do."

"That's daffy." She nibbled at a piece of bread. "So where do you den?"

"On the ship. But my ID chip lists Exodus. Usually."

"Howsa?"

He snapped down more leafage. "I can't get into specifics, but I reprogrammed my chip with my alias's ID."

"You can do that?"

Sebastian shrugged. "With the right equipment. Anyway, that's just the way CenCon does it. I haven't been to Exodus since... well, last century, at least."

Melissa licked the last few crumbs of bread from her lips. "So what's that got to do with sweet grass?"

"Adrian didn't care for it, the dogs won't eat it, and the smallest amount they bulk-sell was too much, it would have gone bad before I could eat it." He smiled and gently touched her paw. "Now I've got someone to share it with."

Melissa beamed, tail thumping her chair. "You're so dulcet."

"Let me ask you, why are you so well behaved now?"

She set her utensils down. "Last time we went, I felt like I embarrassed you. So I thought I'd act nice, like the other ones here."

"Oh, Melissa, you're wonderful any way you act. But it's nice to see you adapting."

"I'd love to eat out regular," Melissa said.

"We'll see." Sebastian smiled and sipped down the last of his juice. Breakfast was nearly over. Melissa would soon head to the aeroport, and he would finish his tasks. Best of all, Alsander's gloomy prediction had not manifested.

"I'm curious, why do you always wear those earphones?" Melissa asked.

Sebastian glanced up from his meal. "They connect to my tape player."

"And?"

"And I love to listen to music. These ones are nice, they clip on so I can still hear other things." He wiggled his ears, and the attached black plastic earpieces followed suit.

"Oh. I thought it was a portable comm, like on television."

"We've got a few, but they're expensive and the headset is obvious. It's hard to keep a low profile with them, so I don't take them out often."

"At least you're not bluthering when I talk at you. When'll we be mated?" she said.

Sebastian swallowed down the last bit of his meat slab. "Well, as captain of the ship, I've got the authority to perform the ceremony, but I don't know if I can legally do it on myself."

"But we're leaving today."

Sebastian tapped his muzzle in thought. "I suppose I could temporarily cede captainship to Corey. As acting captain, he would have the same authority I do."

"That'll be just addy."

The two exchanged adoring looks. It didn't matter where Sebastian was; with Melissa by his side, it was paradise. He wanted nothing more than to spend eternity with her.

First they had to spend some time apart.

"Melissa, it's about time for you to get going."

She held his paws tightly. "Oh, Sebastian, I don't want to leave you."

He leaned across the table and pressed his lips to her cheek, kissing her sweetly. "It'll only be for a margin. I'll be with you soon, I promise."

"For truth?"

"For truth."

Melissa stood, her paws clutched so tightly they shook. "Okay, Sebastian. I'm registered for the shuttle? Everything's paid for and bonzo?"

"Yes, they'll just scan you and you can be on your way." He stood and hugged her, their lips locked, and the pair entwined into a passionate embrace that couldn't last long enough.

"I love you, Melissa."

"I love you too."

She took her bag and walked out of the restaurant.

Sebastian sat back down in his seat, clasped his tail to his chest, and stroked the shortened, brushy appendage. The stunted end reminded him of the Millers. The seeds Alsander had planted were now sprouting misgivings. What could be the obstruction that prevented Melissa from arriving at the ship, but not him? Now that they were split, anything could happen to her, and he might never know. He should have spent every last moment he could by Melissa's side, but it was too late now. She had gone.

On the other hand, maybe Alsander's vague, monitory boding had nothing to do with the planet's surface, but rather with the aerobus itself. Any multitude of maladies could afflict it, from a crash to a fuel shortage.

No, Sebastian was just worrying himself. Aero travel was perfectly safe; he had been trained as an aerofighter pilot, he should know that. Once Melissa boarded the aerobus, she would be fine, or at least subject to no further perils than normally associated with aero travel. Alsander had to be wrong. Sebastian couldn't imagine what he would do without Melissa.

His paws shook when the waiter arrived to collect payment. He scanned Sebastian's ear and the payment was deducted automatically. Sebastian held his tail tighter. Every minute without Melissa seemed as though an eternity. He needed to see her again.

"Sebastian!"

He had been so consumed by his brooding that he didn't even hear Melissa approach. The next thing he knew, she was standing next to him.

"Melissa?" he asked.

"It's no good!"

Sebastian shook his head, confused. "What?"

"I should've known." She sat across from him. "It's been all over the news, the gate agent told me herself."

Sebastian angled his head in confusion. She'd already been to the aeroport. How long had he been sitting here? "What's that?" he asked.

"The pilots are striking, Pan-Al canceled all their flights."

"So? I bought you passage on Ultra Aerobus."

"Ultra Aerobus is a subsidiary of Pan-Al."

Sebastian's ears wilted. It hadn't occurred to him until now. "Well that's silly, they didn't say anything when I bought it."

Melissa shrugged and folded her paws in her lap. "Usual aeroline chicanery. They just want your money. Oh, the agent said it's still good, they'll reschedule, but she wouldn't say when."

Then it hit Sebastian. That's what Alsander had meant. It all fit.

"That's it!"

She twisted her ears. "Howsa?"

"It… oh, don't worry your pretty little head over it, this is good news, really."

"I don't follow."

The words almost slipped from Sebastian's open jaws, but he reigned them in. There was no sense in worrying Melissa over Alsander's prediction. A pilot strike would explain why she would not be coming to the ship, and as he'd performed contracts for Pan-Al before, they could qualify as the 'someone' he knew. The prophecy was innocuous.

Sebastian smiled and leaned over to kiss her cheek. "It'll give us more time to spend together."

"You're so dulcet, Sebastian."

"Here's what we'll do." He held her paws in his. "We'll go back to the room, I'll call the ship and summon a shuttle for you, and when they arrive, we'll head to the aeroport, okay?"

"How long will that take?"

He stroked her fingers. "Not more than a day. Another wonderful day with you."

Even beneath her russet fur, the faint traces of a blush appeared on the vixen's cheeks. "You're truly bonzo, you know that? I've never met one like you."

On the way out of the restaurant, Sebastian slipped a mini-tape into his omnipresent tape player. It was a time for celebration, limited as it may be. He had Atonement, he had Melissa, and he had the heavy twin-guitar harmonies of Nimrod's Caught in the Storm. He needed nothing else.

***

One hundred meters away from the restaurant, Pyotr Neuback's radio crackled to life. "He's leaving the restaurant now. Male, blue shirt, gold pants. Identify, copy," a voice on other end said.

Corey peered through his binoculars at the street below. Foxes in bright clothes milled about along the avenue's sidewalks, all rushing for somewhere. He twisted the zoom on his binoculars and sought out his target.

"There, under the awning. You see him?" Corey said.

"Yes, sir." Teresa focused upon the target, her sights across the fox's face. "Ready."

The fox below stepped back under the awning, to clear room for a rambunctious group of executives on a lunch outing.

"Wait. Civilians in the way," Corey said.

"No, don't wait!" Pyotr looked over the edge of the building. "Shoot through them if you have to!"

Corey's eyes never left his binoculars. "I will not risk injury or death to innocents."

"He's going to escape!"

"He is going nowhere."

In moments, the businessmen slipped inside the restaurant. The shot was clear. Teresa would not fail Corey, not at this range. She need only squeeze the trigger, and a life would be gone.

"Ready to fire, sir," she said.

Corey kept his binoculars focused. He'd never done this before, it'd never been so personal, that he could see his target's face. Thoughts swirled in his mind. It wasn't just one life he was affecting. What if the fox had a family? What if the vixen with him were a mate, mother of his children? A single command would deprive those children of a father.

It was unlike ordering aeropilots into battle, or commanding the bridge during combat. There, death was detached, distant, impersonal. It was easier to move to action when you couldn't see the faces of those who would die.

Corey flashed back to a situation he had encountered years ago. He was young, fresh from Dominion military service, and longed to be a commander in the Star Rangers. Before he could, Sebastian had insisted that he pass a simulated mission, an assault on the stronghold of an urban terrorist organization.

He excelled, commanding his troops with deadly prowess and efficiency. They stormed the apartment complex without a single loss. He was on his way to a perfect score.

Corey turned a corner, rifle at the ready, and came across a young Familiar. The pup, no more than five years old, dropped his shotgun, held up his paws, and begged for mercy. They had forced him to fight, he said. Compassion moved Corey to help the young child. He knelt down beside him, set down his rifle, and reached to pick him up.

The child drew a pistol from behind and shot Corey through the head.

"He's right there! Fire, vex you!" Neuback said.

Corey's mistake had been thinking emotionally. He may have been a child, but first, he was the enemy. He had to remain detached, convince himself the fox he was about to kill wasn't a person. Only a target.

He snapped back to reality. "Prepare to fire," Corey said.

Teresa shimmied into a tighter position, her aim locked onto the fox's head. "Ready, sir."

Just as Corey was about to issue the fateful order, the fox turned into the light. A momentary flash about his neck caught Corey's eye.

"What are you waiting for?" Neuback cried. "Fire, vex you!"

Corey didn't answer. He clicked the zoom setting further for a close look, but the fox raised a paw to shield the sun. Without direct light, the object seemed to vanish. What was that?

The fox put his hand down, and now Corey could see. It was the Ankh of Kohoutek.

"Hold your fire!" Corey said.

***

Melissa leaned in to lick Sebastian's cheek. "Let's go to the park."

"Now? I've really got work I should be doing."

She smiled and rubbed his shoulder. "Come now, don't be so limp. Just take a little walk, please? It'll only be a quarter-hour."

He held her tighter to his side, unable to resist her charms. "Well, okay. Here, you lead the way."

The crack of a high-powered rifle discharge split the air. The bullet tore a path across the street, aimed for Sebastian's chest, ready to tear into his flesh. The sniper couldn't miss Sebastian's bright clothing. It was too late to get out of the way.

Melissa stepped in front of him.

Her body jerked. She went stiff, as though locked in time, appearing for only a moment as though nothing had happened. Then she slumped to her knees in front of Sebastian.

"Melissa!"

Sebastian seized her shoulders and dragged her into a nearby storefront, startled bystanders clearing room for him. Her lifeblood welled up from a hole through her sternum. He laid her down on the shop's tile, tore his shirt off, wadded it into a ball. He pressed it down to the wound, hard as he could, desperate to maintain pressure and stem the flow.

"Get me some vexing water!" Sebastian said.

For a moment, it seemed as though his efforts might bear fruit. The harder he pressed, the more the bleeding subsided, but his shirt was becoming too soaked to be of any use. In desperation, he tore one of his pant legs off, only to discover it was sticky with Melissa's blood. The bullet had fully punctured her delicate form, and blood was pouring from the gaping exit wound in her back.

"Oh no, oh no…"

Sebastian stuffed his pant leg against the hole and pressed in on her from both sides, doing all he could to curtail the crimson flowing from either side of his beloved. It was already too late. The moment the bullet struck her, her fate was sealed. Melissa Riverford was going to die, and there was nothing Sebastian could do about it.

"No, no, this can't be happening! Melissa!"

He trembled, eyes wet with tears. His paws were soaked in her blood, Melissa's pristine white dress stained and smeared. A pool formed beneath her on the shop's vinyl floor.

"Melissa... I'm sorry... I'm sorry I got you involved in this. Max, forgive me..."

Sebastian laid her down in his lap, so that, he might stare into those amber eyes one last time. The vibrant gaze, once filled with adoration, was draining away.

She tried to speak. No sound came out, but Sebastian could read the mouthed words.

"I love you too, Melissa," Sebastian said.

He grasped her body to himself, and gave her cheek one final nuzzle. Tears streamed down his face. Alsander's prophecy was fulfilled.

ACT II

There comes a time in everyone's life when they must grieve, when they lose a loved one, and they ask why, why has this happened to me? That time has come, now that my beloved Zulica has passed, and though I long to be with her in the Everlife, I know that I must continue to live for that little time I have left. I am growing old and wise, yet soon I will die, and when I do, I offer you this advice. Death is only the beginning. Think not of what was not to be, what might have been, and instead reflect upon what was. As you keep the memory alive in your heart, so will your beloved live on in you. You must not dwell, you must advance, and most of all, you must always live for yourself.

-The Memoria, The Book of Max, Chapter 27, verse 1-7.

SCENE ONE

Corey Delzano felt himself lucky. He'd made it back to the Favored Sky early on the eleventh of Piscea, giving him time to clean up loose ends before the Captain returned. There would be no evidence of his wrongdoing, and he felt confident that Patricia wouldn't disclose his insubordination, as she had lied to the Captain as well.

The day dragged on with neither sight nor sound of Captain Valentino. The 0800 GST deadline for Sebastian's final checkup came and went. Corey contacted the Vista Overlook Hotel, only to be told Sebastian had already checked out. Corey had no recourse; Alliance law stated a person was not legally missing until a triad out of contact, and by then, it might be too late.

As long as Sebastian was away from the ship, Corey was still in command. He spent the ensuing time in the captain's den, a small briefing room adjacent to the bridge, ready at a moment's notice for Sebastian's arrival. Corey was seated at the den's desk, flipping through the computer and perusing the ship's journal, when someone knocked on the door.

"Enter," Corey said.

Patricia stepped in, her uniform prepped and proper, ears attentive. She leaned her elbow on the doorjamb and smiled. "Hey there, skip. How's it wagging?"

Corey didn't look up. "How do you think?"

She flopped down in one of the staff chairs around the conference table. "You're worried, yeah?"

Corey gestured to a book on the desk. "Captain Valentino was kind enough to provide me with a handbook on unit protocol. It states that we should remain on station no more than a triad for an out-of-contact crewman, and two triads for an officer."

"You'd abandon the Captain?"

"Not before exhausting all other options."

"Well we can't leave him, it's his unit."

"Like it or not, we have to be prepared to face the possibility that our dear Captain has been killed or captured by a bounty hunter," Corey said.

"Well, he told me yesterday he was going to look for supplies. He could be doing that now."

"That would not explain why he missed the checkup time."

"I guess not." Patricia leaned one arm on the conference table, rhythmically tapping her fingers. "You never did tell me how the mission went."

He looked away from her. "I am afraid I cannot divulge specifics, but it was not completed as arranged."

"Target fail to show?"

"Something to that effect."

She smiled. "Well, don't stress yourself over it, things like that happen. It's still a big step in your career though, yeah?"

Corey turned the cathode ray monitor away, to concentrate on Patricia. "I suppose you are correct."

"Hey, you don't look so good. When's the last time you slept?"

"What time is it now?"

"Noon."

Corey's ears dropped and he rubbed his head. "Well over a day then."

"You know you shouldn't push yourself so hard, even when you're all tizzy. You'll get yourself all wrung out. What you should be doing is getting back into your sleep rhythms, you should still be on duty for another twelve hours."

"I suppose it would be prudent. At least I should wait another hour or two, see if the Captain arrives, pass the ship over to him."

Patricia smirked and crossed her arms. "Don't you trust me? I've been running the ship the past day and a half."

"I do trust you. I would just feel better welcoming our dear Captain in person. How is the crew performing?"

"They're hackling up over the Captain's long absence, it's hard to keep them in line," she said.

"I hardly blame them. I, as well, am becoming distraught. Suppose he knows about the mission?"

Patricia crossed one leg over the other. "I doubt it. I mean, how could he? You didn't tell him, did you? I sure didn't."

Corey rolled his shoulders. "The Captain is resourceful. It would be folly to assume he could not discover the truth."

"Yeah, I guess."

"Where is Fusilier Ailesworth?"

"That coon? Around, milling about," she said. "You know, she's all broken up, what'd you do to her?"

Corey huffed. "Nothing whatsoever!"

Patricia smirked and raised her paws. "All right, I was just asking. No need to bite my throat, yeah?"

A buzzer sounded; Corey already knew what it meant. He was out of the room and on the bridge before Staff Lieutenant Colby had even finished speaking.

"You have the captain on radarscope?" Corey asked   .

Colby turned to face Corey. "Yes, sir. Just now entering range."

"Excellent. ETA?"

"Two hours."

Corey glanced over his shoulder at Patricia. "We should greet him in the launch bay."

"Is that what protocol says?" she asked.

"That is what I say."

Two hours later, the pair stood, waiting, in the launch bay's control booth. The Captain's Corvair slid through the hangar's open bay doors, pierced the atmospheric force shield, and snagged the arresting cable. It rolled to a gentle stop at the deck's far end, where a mule tug took it under control. Captain Valentino disembarked from the cockpit, tossed his helmet at a waiting crewman, and stalked towards the hangar's exit.

Corey made his way to the crew elevator at the far end of the deck to intercept Sebastian. "Welcome back, Captain, how was your—"

Sebastian lifted his head and stared into Corey's eyes. The fox looked distant, angered, hollow, as if a piece of his being had been torn away. Every strand of his normally lustrous fur seemed wilted and pallid, their structure unable to so much as counteract the force of gravity.

Corey gawped and stepped back. Without a word, Sebastian ducked into the ship's elevator and vanished, leaving Corey and Patricia in his wake.

They exchanged startled glances. "Now what do you suppose his deal is?" Patricia asked.

"I have no idea. Was he upset when you spoke to him last?"

Patricia shook her head. "Nary a margin. He seemed upbeat, frisky, optimistic. And that's another thing, where's Melissa?"

"Melissa?"

"Oh, you didn't know. She was going to join us, the Captain proposed and what-have-you."

Corey held back the flinch; that would explain Sebastian's defeated demeanor. "Do you imagine that has something to do with his attitude?" he asked.

Patricia's paw shot to her mouth. "Oh, my, I'll bet something happened."

Corey summoned an elevator car. "Do you suppose that she reconsidered her decision?"

They stepped into the cab. "You know, I'm not sure," Patricia said. "If that were the truth, he'd be sad or depressed, and he didn't look that so much as hopeless and empty. And he'd not have kept us out of contact so long."

"Those are all valid points. The only logical alternative is that she were injured or killed in an attack from a bounty hunter."

Patricia grimaced. "What a ghastly proposition! You really think that might've happened?"

"You have seen the newswire, Patricia. Rumors placed our dear Captain here. Hunters would doubtless be privy to those same sources."

"Still, she was innocent."

"So you assume," Corey said.

Patricia scoffed and crossed her arms. "You think she could have been a spy?"

"She could have been Zulica Herself reincarnated, but until we ask our dear Captain himself, we shall not know. Until then, we have the unit to run."

Patricia nodded and leaned back against the elevator wall. "Did Sebastian look different to you?"

"What do you mean?"

She shrugged. "He looked different somehow."

"He looked distressed."

"No, not that way. Physically." She stroked her muzzle slowly. "Almost as if his tail were shorter."

Corey shook his head slowly. Even though he'd seen it in person, he hadn't recognized the Captain. A shorter tail was only one of many factors.

The pair debarked onto the bridge and sought out their standard positions, Corey to the assistant captain's chair, and Patricia to her gunnery station. Only after Corey sat did he realize Sebastian was not present.

"The Captain is not here," he said.

Patricia swiveled her chair towards him. "Good observation there, jackal, no wonder you're assistant captain."

Corey shot her a scowl, and she went silent, ears tucked down. He wasn't in the mood for her harassment. He stood, slid into the command chair, and patched into the armrest's intercom.

"What are you doing?" Patricia asked.

"I am patching in to the Captain's quarters."

Patricia shook her head. "For Nelsoma, Corey! You're going to talk him up now? You've gone entirely mad, yeah?"

"We need orders."

She shook her head. "Fine, it's your neck."

Before Corey could reprimand her, Sebastian's voice crackled over the intercom. "Yeah, what is it?"

"Captain, we require orders," Corey said.

There was a long, nervous pause before Sebastian spoke. "Prepare to leave orbit, patch into MerCom, look for available contracts. I'll be up in a few minutes, once I unpack."

"Leave orbit? I thought you were arranging supplies."

"There is nothing for us here," Sebastian said.

Corey chewed on his lip, shared a look with Patricia, and then turned back to the intercom. "Captain, is everything all right?"

"I am fine," Sebastian said. "Out."

If Sebastian knew what Corey had done, he was hiding it well. Corey suspected that if he were to be fired, it wouldn't be done over the intercom, and certainly not on the bridge. Only Corey, Sebastian, and Teresa knew what had actually happened on the surface.

Shortly thereafter, Sebastian appeared on the bridge and dismissed Corey from his command chair. Sebastian sat down, punched up the MerCom patch on his arm console, and flipped silently through the available contracts.

"Sir, what are you looking for?" Corey asked.

"Something with a big payout." Sebastian discarded one after another. "How much money do we need, affakravox?"

"Currently, we are deficient 155,000D. Factoring in a retainer of ten months, we would need about 1.4 million dollars."

Sebastian keyed a few commands into his console, and information appeared on the main screen. "Right. Here, how about this?"

Corey stared at the main screen, mouth agape. "Sir? That contract is for the Cairo system."

"Yeah, and?"

"Well, Cairo is—"

Sebastian reclined."Corey, I know more about Cairo than you could possibly imagine. It was settled in 292 PF by Brigadier Alfonsas Harper for House Chamberlain, named for the mythical City of the Great Water from pre-founding mythology, acquired by the Republic of Volta in 331, integrated with Volta into the Pan-Atlantica Federation in 364. It's a lone planet, surface water 70%, gravity 1G, average surface temperature 301 Kelvin, current population 15 million—"

Corey sat up. "That is not what I meant, sir. Cairo borders the Lupine Order."

"So what? Look at that payout!"

Corey frowned and held his head. He wasn't getting through to Sebastian. "If the Pan-Atlantica Federation is offering that much for an attack mission from the Cairo star system, the target is, undoubtedly, the Lupine Order system of Wixom."

Sebastian grinned, exposing the points of his fangs. "With great risk comes great reward, affakravox!"

Corey twisted his muzzle into a silent snarl. "But attacking the Lupine Order is greatly dangerous! They raise their young from birth for specific societal roles, they have a rigid pack hierarchy unseen anywhere else in the galaxy, and a complex eugenics program to create the ultimate wolves."

Sebastian shook a finger at Corey. "I don't need a lesson in galactic politics from you, Corey. If I wanted a lecture on Lupine Order domestic policy, I'd ask St. Clair. Like everyone else, wolves bleed."

"Order troops are honor-bound, fanatically loyal, and of the highest caliber. Heading into battle with them is a fearsome prospect."

Sebastian leaned in to face Corey, eyes hard as steel. "I've fought the greatest warriors the Free States have to offer."

"The Order is not like the Free States!"

Sebastian frowned. "You're scared."

"Of course I am," Corey said. "You should be too."

"Nothing scares me. We're taking this contract, that's final."

"But sir, think. Tensions between the Order and the Pan-Atlantica Federation are high, and open war is imminent." Corey stared into Sebastian's eyes. "There are safer ways to earn money."

Sebastian nodded. "I understand your concerns. But it's not just about money, it's about prestige. People think we're all washed up, and if we go into the wolves' den and claw their noses, we'll be respected again."

Corey exhaled, deep and slow; Sebastian had a point. Being a mercenary was one part skill and two parts image, and striking a blow against the Order would help immensely. Corey worried that a mission against such elite troops would be doomed to failure from the start. On the other hand, Sebastian seemed rejuvenated by the prospect of danger, risk, and reward. His ears stood erect and ready, his fur back to its luster. Corey doubted he was over Melissa so quickly. More likely, he needed the thrill of battle more than he needed the love of a vixen. It was something Corey couldn't understand.

"Very well," Corey said. "As Captain, it is your decision, and I will follow."

"Noble." Sebastian snapped his fingers. "Staff Lieutenant Pratt, inform MerCom that we accept contract #1974. Helmsman Shepherd, plot a course for the Cairo system."

The Favored Sky's engine throttled up, blazing brilliant gold in the dark abyss. The vessel glided out of orbit, pitched its blunt nose towards Jump Point Eagle, and accelerated.

Twenty gigameters away in Wexford III's orbit, a solitary shuttle docked with its mothership. That vessel, too, ignited its engines and set for Jump Point Eagle. Four hours and sixteen minutes after the Favored Sky vanished into hyperspace, the shadow warship followed suit.

An injustice to foxes anywhere is an injustice to foxes everywhere.

-House Lafayette Chieftain Dorwin Morgette

SCENE TWO

Five jumps out of Wexford, the Favored Sky needed to take on supplies. On the eighteenth and final day of the month of Aries, it entered orbit around the planet Sigma, in the Pan-Atlantica Federation's double-world Sigma-Redmond system.

Captain Sebastian Valentino appointed Assistant Captain Corey Delzano as the landing commander, and tasked him with a long list of supplies to obtain. Corey gathered a group of officers and security troops and departed for the surface in the unit's only cargo shuttle.

For twenty-four hours, their mission proceeded flawlessly. Corey periodically reported his progress via his mobile satellite audiocomm. By day's end, he had arranged purchase for nearly half their supply list.

Assured that all was going well, Sebastian retired to his quarters for some much-needed rest. He even slept two hours over the beginning of his shift, but the bad news just waited for him to awaken.

The intercom in his quarters buzzed.

"Captain, Staff Lieutenant Pratt here. Are you there?"

"No," Sebastian said. "What do you want?"

"There's been an incident with the landing party."

Sebastian rubbed at his temple with a paw. Everything had been going too smoothly to stay that way. "What kind of incident?" he asked.

"It's best if you come up."

Sebastian terminated the conversation, put on his duty jumpsuit, and set off for the bridge. He could only hope that Corey hadn't gotten himself into too much mischief.

He stalked onto the bridge and dismissed Patricia Darling from his command station. "What in blazes is going on with my landing party?"

Pratt turned to face him. "There's been some kind of shooting on the surface, wads of commercial radio traffic."

"And the landing party is involved?"

"Yes sir. Seems to have been at some sort of anti-military protest."

Sebastian held his head. "Specifics?"

Pratt tapped at her keys. "Ten dead, thirty-two wounded, unidentified mercenaries in custody."

"Vex it! I bet that stapard Darksite was behind it."

Patricia turned towards Sebastian. "It certainly sounds like his doing. You've heard how he talks about the Unies, yeah?"

"Darksite's such a frisky trigger-dog, he's troublebait," Sebastian said. "It was a mistake to send him down there."

Patricia nodded and frowned. "Well, now what? We're not going anywhere without new hyperdrive batteries, yeah? Should we arrange a new shuttle run?"

Sebastian shook his head. "I'm not sending anyone down until I figure out what's going on. Pratt, patch me into Brinkavhole at the shuttle."

The coyote punched the keys on her console, practiced and smooth. In moments, the face of the shuttle pilot dhole appeared on the bridge's viewscreen.

"Brinkavhole here. What's the word?"

"What are you wetnoses doing down there?" Sebastian said.

Brinkavhole flinched, ears tucked back on his skull. "Well, there's been an incident."

"Out with it."

"Well, sir, Delzano, Murray, Darksite, Fittipaldi, Murrilan, and Hay have been arrested."

Sebastian hung his head. His unit was falling apart around him. He longed to have Adrian back; these supply runs had always been his responsibility, and he had never failed. Here, Corey had gotten himself arrested on his very first run.

"Great. I bet it was Darksite. If this is his fault, he's fired," Sebastian said.

"Well, Katzmueller was released from custody, seems he saved a bunch of wounded protesters."

"He should have let those Unie scaggs die," Sebastian said. "Is he there? Get him on."

Brinkavhole frowned, nodded, and disappeared. In moments, the dingo in question appeared.

"Yes Captain, sir?" Katzmueller said.

Sebastian leaned forward in his command chair, jaw tightened. "Tell me what happened down there, right now."

Katzmueller forced a nervous smile. "Well, see, the thing of it is, we ran over some Unie protesters and they went all wonky, see? And then they started heaving rocks at all ways, and Darksite opened fire, and they was all blasting each other, see? Coppers restrained us, they let me go because I was a medic, saved a couple of them wounded buggers. Was kind of fun, you know?"

"And the rest of the party?"

"Well, the fusies all got arrested for manslaughtering, and aggravated what-have-you. Corey was picked up for excessive force, because he didn't order them to stop in time or some dagged fluffit. They questioned me a while and let me loose, said there's a hearing in two days to see if they have a case, see?" Katzmueller said.

Sebastian kneaded the side of his head. "We can't afford to wait two days, we need those batteries now. You go get them."

Katzmueller tilted his head, an ear flopped across the side of his face. "Me, sir? I don't know front-ways from hind-side about batteries."

"You've got my only cargo shuttle, make yourself useful."

"Well, I can give it a little shot, I guess."

Sebastian sighed and crossed his arms. "Get a pen and paper, I'll tell you what to know, all right? Go to a shipyard company, tell them you need either an Atomica V-98 or Mills-Wahling J-series hyperspace battery system. You want them delivered to the shuttle, you'll install them yourself, and if they try to charge you more than 550,000D, tell them you'll take your business elsewhere. You dig?"

Katzmueller silently mouthed the words as he scribbled them down. "Quite right, sir. Should I really leave if they don't give?"

"Don't worry, they always give in."

"Anything else?"

Sebastian brushed his muzzle. "If you're really so worried, have Dunkirk go with you, he's our best payload engineer and he's probably just wandering uselessly around the shuttle anyway. He'll keep you from getting into too much trouble. Get as much loaded onto the shuttle as possible, and once the batteries are on board, I want you to dust off and return to the ship."

Katzmueller tipped his muzzle the opposite way, ears perked. "What about the party and the rest of the supplies?"

"Leave them."

"Sir?"

"We can get more supplies on Cairo, and we'll pick up the rest of the party after the mission."

"Well, um, okay," Katzmueller said. "If that's really how you want it going down. Is that all?"

"Tell Brinkavhole and Duholland to alternate watch, I don't want any more surprises. Valentino out."

The dingo's face disappeared, replaced by a computer-enhanced image of the slowly rotating world of Sigma far below. Sebastian stared at it, silent. His unit was hemorrhaging money and steadily bleeding to death. Without his second in command's inductive reasoning, their mission against the Order would be that much more difficult. What would really cripple them, even if they installed the jump batteries by the end of tomorrow, would be the lack of hydrofuel. No hydrofuel meant no dropship operations, no more shuttle runs, and no aerofighter missions. They could get more in Cairo, but until then, they would be nearly defenseless and forced to rely on the Favored Sky's token capital weapons.

Patricia broke the silence. "Well this is a fine lot we're in. We've got no jump batteries, no way to get out of system, and no supplies. What do we do now?"

"What can we do? We wait for news."

"I can't stand anymore waiting."

Sebastian reclined in his chair, pulled his knee to his chest. "You want to do something? Play some Holoshoot? Pharaoh? Simulator?"

Patricia grinned, her eyes twinkled, and she leaned towards him. "I've heard you're quite the fencer."

Sebastian smirked and tipped his muzzle. "You'll find no finer swordsman in the galaxy than I."

"None more modest, at least. I was taught a little bit, why don't we head to the rec room and go a few rounds?"

"You want to fence me? Are you sure?" Sebastian said.

Patricia chuckled. "Well, I'm sixty-something centimeters taller than you, so it might not be fair."

"You're right, it won't be," Sebastian said, "but I'll try to go easy on you."

"Captain!" Staff Lieutenant Colby at the radar station turned to face them. "Heavy contact coming in, hot and wet. Looks to be an assault carrier."

Sebastian jerked upright. "Range?"

"Four gigameters."

"How did they get so close?" Patricia asked.

"It looks like they were running dry in a shipping pattern, just blended into commercial traffic," Colby said.

"Speed?" Sebastian asked.

"0.3 gigameters per hour."

"Helm, take us out of orbit, flank speed, in the opposite direction," Sebastian said.

"Where are we going?" Patricia asked.

"Anywhere, nowhere, it doesn't matter. We just have to buy some time, we can't let them get into a good attack position."

The Favored Sky pulled out of orbit and swung its bow away from the planet. Its lone sublight engine throttled to maximum, and the warship set off towards empty space, cutting a blazing trail behind it.

It had to be the vessel they had tracked at Wexford III. What sort of fanatic would be dedicated enough to tail them across four star systems, yet patient enough to wait for the perfect opportunity to strike? There was no better time to attack. The Favored Sky was trapped in system with no fuel for fighters and no second in command.

Sebastian remained on the bridge, waiting, not daring to leave his command station. Patricia remained by his side, but as the end of the day drew near and crewmen began cycling out, she began to show her fatigue.

"Sebastian," she said, "maybe it's time that you got some sleep. Look, "C" Shift is starting."

"Can't sleep now," he said. "To sleep is to die."

Patricia flinched at the fox's words. She reached out and touched his shoulder. "Yeah, well, suppose you're too fatigued to make the proper decisions, yeah? You've got plenty of capable crewmen who can run the ship while you sleep."

"Maybe."

"Don't you like Staff Lieutenant Greco?"

"Of course I do, he's a capable commander," Sebastian said.

"Then leave the ship in his capable command. Look, you can always sleep in your captain's den if you're so worried, yeah?"

Sebastian stood, slow, and stretched. He'd been sitting almost eighteen hours, and his body was stiff. "I guess you're right. They're still over three and a half gigameters away, they won't be able to launch any attack force for another eighteen hours or so. Travecki, set the ship to Alert Condition. I want all my "A" Shift personnel rested and ready for battle, I want shields and weapons on standby. Dig?"

"Right away, sir." Travecki began inputting the commands into his communications console.

Sebastian gestured for Patricia to stand up. "Now, I believe it's time we both yield the bridge for now. You should get some sleep too."

A youthful, yet towering dhole stood waiting. "Staff Lieutenant Greco reporting for "C" Shift command, sir."

Sebastian looked up to him; he only reached up to Greco's stomach. "Evening, Greco. How's it wagging?"

Greco canted his head. "It's fine, sir."

"That's good. Are you enjoying your promotion?"

"Yes, thank you. It's an honor to serve."

Sebastian smiled thinly. "Good. You do well, you'll make senior lieutenant sooner, rather than later. Ship's yours; just don't hurt her, dig?"

Greco nodded enthusiastically, sat down in the command chair, and prepared to oversee the ongoing shift change. Junior Lieutenant Worschevski arrived and replaced Patricia.

Sebastian, meanwhile, leaned up against the back wall of the bridge. "I think I'll sleep in my quarters. Patricia, come with me, I want to talk to you."

"What about?"

"Your new duties as third in command, and the training you're going to need. Come, walk."

Sebastian was just about to exit through the bridge's rear doors when a voice from behind stopped him.

"Um, sir?"

Sebastian turned around and slumped on the bulkhead. "What is it now, Travecki?"

"They're lighting us on lasercomm."

That got Sebastian's attention. His ears perked upright, his back straightened, and he strode up to the communication's console. "What, them who, the other ship?"

"Yes sir. 13.4 second delay," Travecki said.

Sebastian turned to his command seat. He jerked a paw, Greco vacated the seat, and Sebastian sat back down. "Haxxell, can you identify them from this range?"

"Not specific. It's an assault carrier, Skyrider class, but their IDP is non-responsive," Haxxell said.

Sebastian breathed slowly, in and out, chest rising and falling. He didn't know who he was dealing with. Dare he answer their hail? What terrible secret awaited him on the other side?

"Their light is still open, sir."

Sebastian nodded. "On screen, Travecki."

The empty abyss on the viewscreen melted away, constituting into the muscular body of a male red wolf. Even with the viewscreen's scale distortion, the rufine towered over Sebastian. The wolf crossed his arms, adjusted his tan uniform, and spoke to Sebastian from four million kilometers away.

"This is Commander Duke Thompson of the registered mercenary warship Indeterrable."

"This is Captain Sebastian Valentino of Valentino's Star Rangers. What is the meaning of this pursuit?"

"You are a wanted war criminal, Valentino. It is my duty as a member of civilized society to place you under arrest."

Sebastian grimaced, rankled both by Thompson's candor as well as his own fatigue. "Hokum. You're here for the bounty. Take a number and get in line."

Thompson's muzzle screwed up, his ears pivoting backwards. "I had come offering an honorable solution, but if you must be snappy, you can rot for all I care."

Sebastian sighed and ran a paw along his muzzle. "All right, let's have it. What's your honorable solution?"

"Surrender yourself personally into my custody."

"And why in Max's name would I do that?"

Thompson sneered. "I know your situation. You have no jump batteries, low hydrofuel levels, minimal supplies, and no second in command. That puts you at a distinct tactical disadvantage, and keeps you and your Corvair from personally engaging in battle."

"So what? Why would I hand myself over to you and the Canis Dominion's mercy?"

"Because if you do not, I will be forced to blow you out of the stars," Thompson said. "Now, if you do surrender, your ship and crew can go free and continue on your way to the Cairo system."

Sebastian didn't even look to Patricia to see how she felt about the offer. His mind was already made up.

"No thanks, I think I'd much rather take my chances in battle," he said.

Thompson merely smiled. "As you will. Explain to your crew how they must die for your crimes against civilization. Thompson out."

Thompson's image vanished as quickly as it had appeared, leaving Sebastian alone with his bridge crew. For a long minute, nobody dared to speak.

Then Patricia turned to him. "Captain…"

Sebastian brushed her away with one hand and pressed the public address button on his control panel's intercom.

"Captain Valentino to all staff heads. Report to briefing room one immediately," he said.

Minutes later, he was in briefing room one, a small steel box suitable for no more than forty. The invited filed in, slow and fatigued, a few looking as though they had just been awakened. Sebastian could empathize; he'd been awake far too long.

Sebastian looked over his depleted staff and shook his head. "Delzano, Darksite, and Murray are not with us. Darling, come, fill in for Delzano, take roll and all that."

"Right away, sir," Darling said.

Sebastian punched information into the computer console next to the room's display monitor. He called all the necessary data from the ship's memory, and then leaned against the wall. He listened to Patricia take attendance.

"All the acting staff heads are present and accounted for, sir," she said.

"Good. Let's get started. I have bad news." Sebastian called up a picture of the imposing red wolf to the display, captured from their recent conversation. "Forty minutes ago, the captain of the vessel pursuing us lasercommed me. His name is Duke Thompson."

"I know that name, he's got a highly ranked unit, doesn't he?" acting head of security Robert Jones said.

"Indeed. The Disintegrators are second in the current MerCom A-tier rankings only to ourselves, and have been since the middle of last year."

"What did he say?" Jones asked.

Sebastian crooked his lips. "Hightailed, self-righteous posturing, mostly. He made me an offer. If I surrender myself personally, he'll allow the ship and crew to freely depart."

"I do hope you turned him down, sir," chief of aerocraft Skynight said.

"Flatly. But that does mean we'll need to engage them in combat, and that presents its own slew of problems. The Disintegrators are more than a match for us, and we're at a serious tactical disadvantage. We can't jump out of system, and we don't have the hydrofuel for extended aero operations."

"So what do we do?" Skynight asked.

Sebastian brought up an isometric wireframe image on the main screen. The slowly rotating model bore the caption 'Skyrider Class Assault Carrier', followed by numerous lines of specifications and statistics.

"Thompson's starship, the Indeterrable, is a Skyrider-class like ours. We don't have specifics on exact fighter complements, weaponry, or any other modifications. We can only presume that it's similar in capabilities to our own vessel. What we do know is that it's been steadily gaining on us, so it must have some type of engine upgrade."

"How much time are we looking at before we're overcome, sir?" radar staff officer Colby asked.

"It's not how long it takes to be overcome, but how long before they get us in range of our aerofighters. Assuming he's not foolish enough to launch without light fighter cover, that gives us about eighteen hours if he's got Corvairs. If they're Vegas, that gives us more time, closer to two days."

"We'll need to disable his vessel long enough so we can sweep around the system back to Sigma, install new batteries, and jump out of system," helm staff officer Shepherd said.

Sebastian picked up the stylus next to the computer, and began drawing on the screen. The image appeared on the auxiliary display, first a large circle, then a smaller one on either side of the first, labeled L4 and L5 respectively.

"Here's my idea. We're here." Sebastian drew an X below the L4 circle. "We know the Indeterrable is faster than us, so eventually we'll be overcome. So we make a long, sweeping arc around the gas giant and past Redmond." Sebastian indicated the large middle circle, and L5 circle, respectively. "We'll come up on the far side of Sigma, here at libration point 4. Thompson will follow along behind us, so eventually, remaining at top speed, we'll be closer to Sigma again, and the shuttle should be able to reach us heading the opposite direction. Comments?"

Patricia tipped her muzzle down. "And just how long would a maneuver like that take?"

Sebastian frowned and waggled his paw, doing some mental calculations. "Well, it's a distance of... at a speed of... well, about 2600 hours."

"2600 hours!" Colby said. "That's over a hundred days."

"Approximately 108," Shepherd added.

"Well we don't have to go the entire distance!" Sebastian shot back. "We can cut thirty, maybe forty percent off by cutting closer to the sun."

"We only have one more triad of supplies. We won't last ten days, let alone a hundred," Patricia said.

"We're in a double system, can't we use Redmond to our advantage?" Shepherd asked.

"I don't see how," Sebastian said. "The system's only gravdock is at Sigma, so that's where all the hyperspace battery retailers are. If we got into orbit around Redmond, we'd be trapped there, and Thompson would destroy the cargo shuttle long before it could reach us."

"What if we tried pulling around Sigma-Redmond II, and coming back to Sigma from there?" Shepherd said.

Sebastian sighed. "Thompson is still far enough away to corner us when we leave orbit, and we'd still be in range of his aerofighters."

The flight deck chief Hartfield growled. "How did you get us into this mess? Why did you even make us leave orbit in the first place?"

"We couldn't stay in orbit! Thompson would have pounced on us as soon as we tried to get to the jump point!" Sebastian said.

"But at least we could have had a full load of hydrofuel for combat operations!" Hartfield said.

Sebastian stared at him. "What are you saying?"

"We're down to only a hundred and twenty cubic meters, Captain."

Sebastian shook his head. "Are you sure? That can't be right."

"Positive, sir," Hartfield said.

"But the ship holds almost 24,000 cubic meters!" Sebastian glared at Patricia. "How did we run this low?"

She held up her paws defensively. "I don't know, you're the Captain."

He rubbed his skull with the back of a hand. Adrian would have cried blue murder if their reserves dropped below a third of capacity, and in the shuffling of his crew, Sebastian had never appointed a third-string logistics officer. Corey was Adrian's substitute, but no one was Corey's substitute. This wouldn't have happened if Adrian were still alive.

Sebastian held his head. "If you siphon the fuel out of the remaining shuttles and the dropship, how much more will that get us?"

Hartfield rolled his shoulders and tossed a paw. "I don't know, a little over three hundred cubic meters, maybe, at most."

"Do it. That'll give us eight or nine extra sorties a piece from the eighteen Corvairs on board."

"But sir," Skynight said, "if we drain our transports, we'll all be stuck up here."

"If we die we won't need transports." Sebastian looked back out at his crew. "We'll buy some in orbit. Now, are there any other comments or input…? No? All right, I want all of my "A" Shift personnel rested, so go get some sleep. Rest all your pilots, Skynight, but keep them on alert. Dismissed."

Sebastian watched his troops file out, their heads hung and tails low. Normally, he'd have no trouble reading his crew, but he couldn't tell whether they were disheartened by Skynight's objections or merely tired. He hoped the latter, but feared the former.

He snagged Patricia by the sleeve on his way out. "Patricia, hold out. I want to talk to you."

"What's up, sir?" She forced a smile, but Sebastian could tell she was worried.

He waited for the rest of his staff to depart before speaking. "It's about the crew. I know you've been busy being about thirteen people lately, but you're still the crew liaison. How're they holding up?"

"You want the truth?"

That she asked was enough to tip Sebastian off that not all was well. "Of course."

"They're unhappy and worried. They haven't been paid in a month, the Captain and Assistant Captain are constantly swapping places or absent altogether, we've had only one contract since the start of the year and it ended in disaster, and we're running low on food and supplies."

"You think they're disloyal?"

"I wouldn't go quite so far," Patricia said. "Somewhat disaffected, I'd say. And concerned, especially the newer crewmen, most of them left cushy military careers for us, yeah?"

"Yeah, I know. I lured most of them away myself."

Patricia sat down atop one of the room's tables. "So why do you ask? You worried they'll desert or something?"

"Or mutiny."

She smiled gently. "I don't get that impression. Us longsies are doing our best to reassure them. I mean, they didn't come here just for money, either they're running from something, or looking for more than their military could provide, yeah?"

Sebastian nodded, planted a boot on a bench, and leaned his elbow upon his knee. "Yeah, I know. I'm just worried the ones I tried hardest to recruit are going to leave."

Patricia twisted her muzzle and leaned in closer. She sniffed at him briefly, and frowned. "There's something else troubling you, yeah?"

Sebastian stared up, almost refuted her claim, and then gave in, nodding. "You're right. It's the timing of this all."

"Yeah?"

"I mean, it's pretty obvious that Thompson has been trailing us since Wexford. That means he's been following for the last twenty-five days or so. He could mathematically calculate when we'd need new jump batteries, that's not hard, but he's been patient enough to wait for us to be low on supplies and hydrofuel."

"So? He'd assume that when we stop for new batteries, we'd need to resupply anyway."

"But he knew about Corey's arrest."

Patricia sat atop the bench next to him. "That's a puzzler, yeah? External contacts?"

"Probably several."

"Well, what about your contacts?"

Sebastian shook his head. "Most of them have broken off links once the bounty was put up. I've only got a couple informers left on the payroll, and none of them are in the Federation."

"Maybe it's just coincidence?"

"Maybe."

She nodded gently and crossed her arms over her knees. "What did Thompson mean when he said you couldn't participate personally in the battle?"

"Normally I'd take my Corvair out into aero combat and leave the ship under the second in command."

"That's dangerous, yeah?"

Sebastian chuckled. "Being a mercenary is all about danger. Besides, I'd do more good in my fighter than here, I've got 317 kills to my credit."

"So, leave the ship in my command and go out aerofighting."

"Well, to be honest, I don't think you have enough combat command experience for something like this."

Patricia frowned and skewed her ears outward. "With all respect, sir, I've got plenty of bridge experience, I'd be more than capable of running the ship while you're off zooming about."

"It's not your decision, it's mine. I would have been hesitant to leave Corey in command of the ship, and he's got more experience than you."

"But sir—"

"Don't argue with me, Patricia. It's my decision, and I'm not letting you run the ship into combat yet."

Patricia nodded meekly and looked away. Sebastian knew he had probably hurt her, but he needed to be truthful. Only when Corey had handed command to her – something he had no authority to do, he should have transferred the ship to Staff Lieutenant Greco – had she gotten any experience. Sebastian was beginning to regret promoting her so swiftly.

"Now look, it's not personal. After this is over, we'll get you running "B" Shift, we'll have Greco be your sub-commander, have him help you out a bit with your first couple triads of command, okay?" Sebastian said.

"If you think that's best."

"Of course I do. Anyway, you're my best gunner, I'm going to need you running them in combat, dig?"

Patricia skewed her ears out. "Who'll be your sub-commander?"

"Greco."

Patricia hid her grimace quick as she could, but it was long enough for Sebastian to see it. "He's a fine commander, I suppose."

Sebastian sighed and crossed his arms. "You're going to need to shake off that Canis Dominion model soon, you know."

"What's that supposed to mean?" She said.

"You can't be as selfish with me as you had to be back with the Dominion navy. I'm favoring Greco as sub-commander because he's more familiar with bridge command. It's not a threat to your rank."

"Did I say I felt threatened?"

Sebastian shook his head. "You didn't have to, I can smell it. You're defensive. Now don't worry about your position, we'll sort this all out when it's over, dig?"

Patricia smiled thinly. "Yes, Captain."

Sebastian sighed and patted her shoulder. "Go get some sleep. We both need it. We have to be rested for the battle."

Patricia nodded, stood up, and disappeared from the briefing room. Sebastian watched her leave in silence; she was upset, a problem only time could solve.

Sebastian left the room and headed to his cabin. He called up the bridge and told Greco to get some rest, to prepare for his temporary position as Sebastian's sub-commander on "A" Shift. The dhole tried to hide his enthusiasm, but Sebastian could still pick up the traces in his voice. It made Sebastian smile.

He'd only been sleeping an hour when his intercom woke him.

"Ensign Travecki here, Captain. You awake?"

Sebastian rolled over in bed and swatted the control panel. "I am now. What do you want?"

"Sir, we've got Duke Thompson on the lasercomm, he wants to talk to you."

Sebastian rubbed his eyes. "Did he talk to... uh, who's running the bridge, Worschevski?"

"He tried to, sir, but Thompson says he wants to speak directly to you."

"Tell him to call me back."

"He says it's urgent."

"Fine," Sebastian said, "patch him into my cabin."

Sebastian got out of bed and stumbled over to his desk. The red wolf's face was waiting for him on his desk telecomm.

"What do you want?" Sebastian said.

"I come to you with an alternate proposal, Valentino, one that may be more appealing. Are you prepared to listen?"

"Get to your vexing point."

"If I were you, I would be more receptive to generosity. Here is my proposal. Rather than surrender directly to me, or engage in battle, the Disintegrators and I could be persuaded to call off our pursuit, if given suitable compensation. Somewhere in the neighborhood of 500,000D."

Sebastian tucked his ears back and stared at Thompson's image. "I give you half a million dollars, and you break off pursuit and disappear?"

"Precisely."

"And what brings on this sudden charity? Last we talked, you were spouting high-tailed nonsense about civilization."

"Mere posturing, Valentino," Thompson said. "I have consulted with my senior staff and we believe this the best solution. Our estimates suggest that if we were to engage in open combat, we would sustain more damage than would be economically viable."

Sebastian smiled thinly, tapping his fingers on the desk. Finance was a language that all mercenaries spoke. "Uneconomically viable, huh? You mean I'd do more damage to your ship than the bounty would cover."

"By a substantial margin. It works both ways; even if you did escape, you would sustain more than half a million dollars worth of repairs."

"That sounds about right. Mercenary units of our caliber rarely engage in direct combat for that reason." Sebastian tapped his chin. "Still, suppose I do pay you off. What else do I get?"

"Besides your life and continued existence as a mercenary unit?" Thompson rolled his broad shoulders. "We'll leave the system, and keep your whereabouts a secret. We'll even defer all future aggression."

Sebastian watched the red wolf in silence. If he could spare his unit the bloodshed and damage of an inevitable pitched battle, it was his responsibility to consider Thompson's offer.

"And what is to stop you from taking my money, and then attacking regardless?" Sebastian asked.

"Are you recording this conversation?"

"I record every telecomm I make."

Thompson smiled. "Then should I betray our gentleman's agreement, you will have this recording and your ship's battle logs to send to MerCom as you see fit."

"I guess that's all I can really ask for in this case. But nose with me here. What's the real reason you're suddenly so generous?" Sebastian said.

Thompson grinned mischievously. "There are more than just economic factors, Valentino. War criminal or not, your harassment of the galaxy's major powers creates more demand for my own unit. Now, do we have a deal?"

Sebastian chewed on his thin, ebony lip. Much as he hated to admit it, Thompson made a valid and logical argument. No mercenary in the galaxy would ever purposefully engage in such pyrrhic battles, especially those with their own starships. It would allow him to spare the Favored Sky from combat; his carrier was his haven, his refuge from sniper attacks.

"Suppose I agree," Sebastian said. "How do we do this?"

"I'll dispatch a team of delegates to your ship immediately. They'll arrive in a passenger shuttle, you'll give the required funds to them, they'll load it aboard the shuttle, and return to the Indeterrable. From that point onwards, you may do whatever you wish."

"Can't we just transfer the money to you?"

Thompson sighed and shook his head. "Do you consider me so blind, Valentino? I know as well as you that you have expended most of the funds in your CenCon accounts. But you do, I assume, keep currency certificates on board as emergency reserve."

"What makes you so sure?"

"I have encountered foxes before. Yours is a paranoid genus. I know you've got money on hand," Thompson said.

"Well, then, if you're so sure, let me just swing back around to Sigma or Redmond and get it deposited into my CenCon account—"

"No!" Thompson slammed a fist onto his chair, the sudden act startling Sebastian. "Foxes are also distrustful, especially with electronic money."

Sebastian frowned. "You're being demanding."

"I am being far more generous than someone like you deserves. I am still more than prepared to blast you out of the stars if you refuse."

"What if I don't have half a million dollars in hard currency on hand?"

Thompson crossed his arms and leaned towards the screen. "I suspect that you do, but in the off chance that you do not, the equivalent value in physical items shall be sufficient. So long as it is agreeable to my delegates, of course."

Sebastian propped an elbow on his desktop. Much as he hated the idea of letting the crewmen of another mercenary unit on board, he really had no choice. Thompson was dictating the terms now, and the only battle plan Sebastian had devised was dangerously risky. Besides, red wolves were an honorable species; a few served in the Star Rangers' ranks, and Sebastian trusted them more than any others.

"I suppose I can agree to those terms," Sebastian said.

Thompson smiled and held his hands together. "Excellent. Now, may I suggest that, as a show of good faith, we both decelerate our vessels to full stop?"

"Why?"

"Our shuttle will reach you more quickly, and we can be done with this business sooner."

"Very well. As soon as your ship is stopped, we'll comply."

"I don't need to remind you that we're still far enough away to outflank you, do I?" Thompson said.

"Of course not." Sebastian leaned on his desk. "Do you have anything further to discuss?"

"No. Thompson out."

The image blinked away, leaving Sebastian alone. He commed the bridge, apprised them of the new situation, and informed them to keep the ship on alert status.

He laid back down to sleep. Even though he was exhausted, his restless mind refused to grant a reprieve.

With great risk, comes great reward: the tenet of our genus. Max Himself said so, and our great leaders echoed. Even I have said so myself. Never have these words been more true than now.

As some of us prepare to venture out from the safety of Bunker 141, to face the atmosphere, venomous and poisoned by our own shortcomings, we must remember this creed. We cannot remain sheltered from the atomic wastes indefinitely, or our safe haven shall become our tomb.

We already strain the stores and supplies that remain, and as far underground as we have retreated, self-sufficiency is inherently impossible. We must be free; we cannot live caged.

I will not force anyone to unwillingly vacate this concrete womb. I implore you to freely choose your own destiny. This bunker could only be a temporary shelter from the fires above.

Life on the outside will undoubtedly be difficult, but again, with great risk comes great reward. Our genus will endure and survive. We are strong, resourceful, and smart enough to survive anywhere, any situation, no matter how harsh. I can think of none harsher than atomic annihilation.

Lastly, I wish to quote our Founder, Max Himself. He said, 'Let you never doubt your own abilities. Let distrust never grow in your heart. For even in the most unlikely circumstances, with your own confidence, you shall persist! Let your heart be free! Let yourself spread and multiply, survive and even thrive in the wasteland.

-The Memoria, The Book Of Lafayette, Chapter 1, Verse 22-37.

SCENE THREE

Captain Sebastian Valentino didn't arrive on the bridge the next day until well into "A" Shift. He tugged his uniform into place and walked to his command chair. With a smile, Staff Lieutenant Greco yielded it to him.

"You okay? You don't look so good," Greco said.

Sebastian rubbed his temple. His eyelids drooped, supported only by his willpower. "I'm fine, really."

Greco chuckled. "Couldn't sleep last night?"

"A lot on my mind."

"Like?"

Sebastian shrugged. "Today. The future. The unit. My career."

Greco nodded and tapped his nosepad with a finger. "May I ask you something?"

"Shoot."

"Well, we never talk much, it's always work," Greco said. "I never asked you why you became a mercenary."

Sebastian's shoulders slumped and he leaned back. "Why not?"

"Well, there are safer ways to earn money."

Sebastian chuckled. "None quite so glamorous, thrilling, or satisfying. It's a way to stand out in a species of seven billion, if that makes sense. That and I don't think I could survive civilian life."

"No jobs that appeal to you?"

Sebastian frowned a little and stared up at the ceiling. "Maybe I could find one, eventually. But I've got too many skills from military service not to use them."

"You don't mind the death?" Greco asked.

Sebastian twisted his lips and shook his head. "It's inevitable."

"Inevitable?"

"Dorwin Morgette once said that life is a cycle, and death a part of that cycle. Whether it is one's time to give, or one's time to receive, is irrelevant, for in time, everyone will play their roles," Sebastian said.

"That's pretty nice." Patricia spoke up from her gunnery console.

Greco chuckled. "Didn't Morgette also say 'the future is going to cost more money'?"

Sebastian sighed and looked away. "That was taken out of context. But what about you, why did you become a mercenary?"

Greco smiled. "Freedom, to go where I want, do what I want, say what I want. The Dominion is oppressive."

"Do you miss it?"

Greco sighed and folded his paws. "Sometimes. It was nice to know where my place was, but when I wanted to step out, explore myself, I couldn't. Freedom is intimidating, but worth it, I think."

Sebastian smiled. "I'm happy to hear that. I'd like to think we'll all grow by facing our challenges and trials together."

"Speaking of which," Greco said, "I almost thought you wouldn't come."

"I have to be here in case Thompson tries anything," Sebastian said.

"You think he would?"

Sebastian tapped a few keys on his armrest's display console. Various readouts flashed past. "We have to be ready for the possibility. I certainly wouldn't put it past him."

"I still can't believe you'd agree to this," Patricia said.

"Are you questioning my command decisions, Patricia?"

"Well, no, not really. But what makes you think you can trust Thompson?"

"Money talks," Sebastian said. "Thompson is a mercenary, he'll listen."

"Is there no better option to letting his crew on board?" Patricia said.

"Such as?"

Patricia rolled her broad shoulders. "Couldn't we rig up a shuttle on auto and fly it out to him?"

Sebastian frowned; he glanced to Greco, and the dhole shook his head. "A shuttle alone is worth over half a million dollars," Sebastian said, "and our only cargo shuttle is still on Sigma. Even our most efficient shuttle would need three-and-a-half cubic meters of hydrofuel – which we can't afford to use – to get all the way out there. I don't think that's a good idea," Sebastian said.

"I'm sorry, sir, I didn't realize," Patricia said.

Sebastian sighed. "Didn't you have any logistics training in the Dominion navy?"

"Just a little. Mostly my training was gunnery and some command."

"Well, don't worry about it, someday we'll get you more logistics training, okay?"

She smiled thinly and shook her head. "It's not that, really. I just hackle at the idea of his men coming aboard. I mean, the Indeterrable's stopped out there, can't we get somewhere?"

"Thompson's between us and anywhere we need to be, and his ship is faster than ours."

"But we have to do something! We can't just accede to his terms!"

"Vex it, Patricia!" Sebastian slammed his fist onto his console, hard enough that the bridge crew jumped. "You're way out of line. Your job is to provide advice and alternate opinions, not to question my orders, and though you are acting assistant captain, you will leave the sub-commanding to Greco. Do you understand?"

Patricia squirmed back in her seat, paws held across her lap. "Yes, sir."

"Now, look, I've thought this through already, okay?" Sebastian lowered his voice and leaned towards her. "Thompson won't be able to try anything, we'll have enough security forces down there to stop a small army, and even if his men do come out shooting, we can cut the launch bay's force field and blow them out into space. The runway is completely sealable in case of emergency, we can have it isolated in five seconds. Even when they're in the ship, we'll have armed guards on them at all times. Does that answer your concerns?"

She sighed, nodded gently, and smiled. "Yes, sir. But I've still got a bad feeling about this."

"I'm sure the Captain has thought of all possibilities," Greco said.

"He's right, Patricia. Now trust me, huh? Thompson's not stupid, he knows that if we attack him head on, we'll do more damage than the bounty would compensate. This is best for both of our sides. We'll get back to Sigma, get our supplies, and be off to Cairo in a triad, at most, still on schedule."

Patricia turned back to face her weapons console. "All right, Captain. Faith's you."

Sebastian reclined in his chair. His head was aching, mostly from fatigue, though there was a certain amount of aggravation tied in to Patricia's inquiries. He should be lenient with her; she didn't have the experience in full-on command or logistics. Still, it was painfully obvious that she lacked knowledge of carrier operations, and Sebastian couldn't help but worry that might come back to haunt him.

"Did anything happen while I was sleeping?" Sebastian said.

"Not really," Greco said. "Thompson launched his shuttle about three hours ago. We've been tracking it, it's on proximity sensors now."

"Colby, what's the range?" Sebastian said.

"Three hundred kilometers, four minutes out on an approach vector," Colby said.

"Greco, you've got the security team on station?"

"Ready and on command, sir," Greco said.

Sebastian nodded. "Colby, scan the shuttle."

Colby punched the commands into his console. A tactical overlay appeared on the bridge's viewscreen, detailing all the available information about the shuttle. "Nothing unusual about it. C-8D Transmarine-type passenger shuttle, 55.7 megagrams mass."

"They're requesting landing clearance," Pratt said.

"Initiate landing procedures. Have aero control guide them in, and prep the security team," Sebastian said.

"Yes sir."

Sebastian pulled up the feed from the ship's closed circuit runway television camera. The view from the rear of the landing deck provided a glimpse of all runway operations. At the far end, the ship's mammoth launch door had opened.

He looked to Greco. "Who'd you put in charge of the security team?"

"Robert Jones."

Sebastian's eyes tightened on Greco. "You put the acting chief of security in charge of the inspection?"

Greco sat up, startled at the inquisition. "Why shouldn't I? He's the best we've got on ship right now."

Sebastian sighed and slumped in his seat. "You don't always put your best man out in danger like that, sometimes you need him to lay back and watch. Look, there's the shuttle."

The streamlined shape of the passenger shuttle appeared outside the ship, expanding as it approached. Its wings, intended for atmospheric flight and fuel storage, were already folded, tucked back against its fuselage. The twin-engined silver craft screamed into the launch deck, skipped once on its wheels, and snagged the arresting cable with its tailhook. It jerked to a rough stop three quarters down the flight deck.

Sebastian flipped his console's comm on, and the ship's operator patched him through to Sub-Chief Fusilier Robert Jones.

"You reading me, Jonesy?" Sebastian said.

The red wolf's deep voice spat out from the speaker. "Ears and tail, sir. What's up?"

Sebastian toggled a switch on his console, but nothing happened. "Jonesy, why isn't your video feed working?"

"We've been having trouble with the power packs. Mechanical was working on it, but he says he needs some parts from the surface to get them up again."

Sebastian growled under his breath. It would figure something like this would happen. Corey would have called it a bad omen, and Sebastian would have called him superstitious. Sebastian already missed that affakravox.

"Next time, inform me of these things, dig? Now talk me through this."

"All right then. Everything looks fine from the outside here," Jones said.

Sebastian folded his arms across his chest. Jones, wielding a submachine gun, stalked in from the edge of the camera's eye. He approached the shuttle, flanked by a modest security contingent.

"Nobody's come out yet," Greco said.

Sebastian leaned up in his seat. "That's odd. Jonesy, what's going on inside, can you see in there?"

"Windows are tinted and dark. I can't make anything out," Jones said.

"Tinted windows on a shuttle, that's quite unusual," Greco said.

Sebastian rapped his armrest. "I'd say suspicious. Check the inside, Jonesy."

Jones made his way up to the shuttle's passenger hatch, gave it a brief visual check, then disappeared inside. Sebastian waited for a response, even wringing his paws at one point. The television camera remained pointed stoically forward, unable to give a glimpse at what was going on inside.

"Jonesy? How are the delegates?" Sebastian asked.

There was a long pause before Jones responded. "Well, sir, there are none."

Sebastian and Greco exchanged concerned looks. "What do you mean?" Sebastian said.

There was a brief sound of Jones rummaging over the radio, and the security crew approached the doorway. "Well, there's no one in here," Jones said. "Sir, I smell explosives."

Sebastian jerked upright. "Jonesy, get out of there! Seal the launch deck—"

Before Sebastian could finish his sentence, an explosion ripped up from the bowels of the ship, catapulting him to the deck. Wailing klaxons sounded across the bridge. The viewscreen – and Jones's radio connection – went dead.

The force threw Sebastian hard to the floor, and he smashed his head onto the carpet. A pipe burst overhead, and the bridge filled with acrid smoke. He grabbed a nearby chair, and used it to haul himself upright. A second, throaty rumble rushed up from beneath his feet, but he kept his balance.

The bridge lights had gone out, and with the smothering cloud expanding throughout the room, Sebastian couldn't see. He groped blindly in the dark and managed to find his command seat. He dropped into it, swatted smoke away from his console, and mashed its keys. The display flickered and went black.

"Greco! Darling! Colby! Where in blazes are you?"

Patricia's voice wafted up from the smoke. "Over here, sir. What in the Everlife was that?"

"I'm trying to figure it out. Are you all right? I can't see you," Sebastian said.

"I'm fine, just a bit lost, yeah?" Patricia said.

"Greco, is your control panel…"

Sebastian glanced to his side mid-sentence, and found the sub-commander chair empty. He looked out at the bridge, but there was too much smoke to see anything.

"Greco! Where are you?" Sebastian said.

"Down here, sir."

Sebastian glanced to the floor and the source of the weak voice. There lay Greco, on his side, bleeding badly from a gash on his forehead.

"Darling!" Sebastian said. "Help Greco!"

"Yes sir!"

"Everybody to your stations!" Sebastian waved smoke from his muzzle. "I need to know what's going on!"

"Closed circuit cameras for decks E through G are inoperable, and the ship's switchboard is down," Pratt said.

Sebastian tapped his control panel, and it sputtered back to life. The ship's ventilation system began drawing the smoke out, revealing the scene before him. Crewmen displaced by the blast were reassuming their stations; fortunately, Greco was the only one seriously injured.

"Internal sensors coming back on line, sir," Colby said. "We've got fire alarms in the launch deck, hangar deck sections one through six, and engineering one and two. Cameras are still off below deck D. So are the elevators."

Sebastian punched his command chair. "Vex it, there must have been a bomb on that shuttle!"

Patricia helped the wounded Greco to his feet. The dhole leaned weakly against her, his sienna muzzle stained with blood. "Sir, Greco's been hurt badly," she said. "He needs medical attention."

Sebastian scowled. "Nobody leaves the bridge until I say so!"

Patricia held Greco tighter. "He needs to get to the infirmary."

"Well, put a patch on his face and take the sub-command station."

Patricia hesitated, Greco slumped against her, dazed and barely able to stand. "Sir…" she said.

Sebastian glared at her. "Do it, Lieutenant. I won't tell you again!"

She tensed, frowned, and nodded. "Yes sir." She grabbed the bridge's medikit, hastily bandaged Greco's wound, and slipped into the sub-command station.

"How's the comm situation?" Sebastian asked.

"Looks like the switchboard's coming back up," Pratt said. "I'm picking up engineering, audio only."

Sebastian flicked his input switch. "What's going on down there, Argyle?"

"There's a lot of smoke." Sirens blared audibly behind Argyle's voice. "And a hole in our roof."

"But that's structural steel!"

"It's a kick. Must've been something big, punched a gash through the flight deck."

"How're you holding up?" Sebastian asked.

"Ten people dead, forty-something wounded. We're battling fires across the entire deck, but they haven't penetrated the reactor room."

Sebastian looked to Colby. "Are the elevators still down?"

"Yes sir," Colby said. "A couple of stairwells are sealed off, but most are still available."

"Well, that's something." Sebastian stroked his muzzle and leaned down to the speaker. "Argyle, the elevators are down. We're going to try and get some damage control teams to help you."

"No biggie. We're kind of almost nearly under control here, anyway."

"Keep me posted. And for the Creator, protect the reactors. Valentino, out." Sebastian sat up. "Pratt?"

"Yes sir?"

"Tell the staff-heads to form damage teams and work down from "D" Deck." Sebastian scowled and folded down his ears. "And turn off the vexing fire alarm!"

"I'm on it, sir."

The klaxon went silent, leaving Sebastian to his thoughts. He patched into the ship's internal sensors through his control panel and perused the preliminary damage reports. All the cameras except the ones on the flight deck were now operable. Mercifully, there were no indications of a hull breach.

Still, the unanswered question on his mind – and the minds of over three hundred other crewmen – was what exactly happened. Thompson had planted a bomb in the shuttle, that much was clear, but that alone wouldn't explain the fires raging through engineering. That class of passenger shuttle had very little room for cargo space. An incendiary device that size would be unable to penetrate the starship-grade steel of the landing deck, and a concussion explosive wouldn't set fires over a third of the ship.

A sickening realization filled Sebastian. He thumbed the switchboard and patched into the hangar deck. "Valentino here, what's going on down there?"

Frantic shouting and fire alarms muffled the voice. "We've got fires all over!"

"Hartfield, is that you?" Sebastian said. "Calm down, I can barely make you out."

"I hate to be curt, sir, but we're really busy!"

Sebastian's ears folded back. He was afraid to ask the question, but he had to. "What's going on?"

"We had all the Corvairs ready and fueled like you said." Hartfield paused to yell at someone nearby. "Then there was an explosion from the runway and it tore a hole in the floor, the hydrofuel in one of the fighters touched off!"

It was just as Sebastian feared. The blast had detonated the volatile hydrofuel and turned its moderating hydrocarbons into a sticky, flaming tar that would trickle down the decks, setting fires as it went. There was nothing more terrifying in carrier operations than a hydrofuel tar fire.

Sebastian leaned down to the speaker. "Hartfield, do you hear me? Try to save those aerofighters!"

"For the Creator, Captain! Thirteen of my best ordnancemen are dead, five of them are unconscious from the fumes, I'm bleeding from shrapnel in my arm. We're trying our best just to stay alive!"

"Vex your arm!" Sebastian hit his chair hard enough to shock the bridge crew. "Save those aerofighters!"

"We've got more important things to worry about right now, Captain," Hartfield said.

"Look, I've got damage teams working their way down to meet you, dig? They'll be there in minutes and until then, you save my Corvairs!"

"Right now the fuel from your Corvairs is choking my crew!" Hartfield said.

"Now you listen to me, I'm the Captain of this unit, and if I say to protect my fighters, you'd better well do it! Is that clear?"

Hartfield sighed. "We'll do our best, all right? We'll try to save your precious Corvairs, but I'm not going to risk any more men over it until those teams arrive."

"It'll have to do. Valentino out."

Patricia leaned towards Sebastian, her rounded ears erect. "You didn't have to yell at Hartfield that way."

"He was arguing," Sebastian said.

"Of course he was arguing, you just ordered some two-dozen crewmen to their deaths."

Sebastian furrowed his brows. "I'm the commanding officer here."

"For Nelsoma, Sebastian! Listen to yourself! This isn't the Alliance military, we're all here by choice," Patricia said.

"I'm still your employer and commander. I don't expect you to understand my responsibilities."

"That's no reason to get those men killed, yeah?"

Sebastian sighed and slouched in his chair. "I don't want them to die, but if we lose those fighters, we don't stand a chance. Thompson's going to kill us all."

Patricia frowned and shook her head. "Maybe we're already dead."

Sebastian growled. "Now don't go getting pessimistic on me—"

"Sir, radar's coming back on line," Colby said. "Sweet mercy…"

Sebastian straightened his back, ears erect. "What is it?"

"I'm picking up numerous incoming aerocraft, radar profiles indicate Vegas, Dolphins, and Foxhounds."

"Where the blazes did Thompson get Foxhounds? The Dominion doesn't sell them," Patricia said.

"Questions to be answered later, carthagan. Colby, what's the number and range?"

Colby tapped at his keyboard. "Picking up twenty-eight contacts in three distinct waves, range is just under three gigameters."

That was precisely the entire strike craft complement of the Skyrider class assault carrier. Thompson was sending everything he had at Sebastian – fighters, attackers, and interceptors – and the Favored Sky was dead in space.

"That gives us two and a half hours before they arrive. Patricia, what's the latest damage report?" Sebastian said.

"The engineering and hangar decks report fires contained and under control. Weapons and elevators are back online, shields are at half recycle. The sublight engines are unresponsive, Argyle says he'll have them back online in a few hours. No word from the landing deck."

"Casualties?"

Patricia tucked her ears down. She turned in her seat and faced him, staring at him with wide, dark brown eyes. "Fifteen dead in engineering, seventeen in the hangar deck, and presumably everyone on the landing deck.

Total estimate is forty-nine dead. The infirmary's swamped with wounded, at least thirty there so far, with more on the way."

Sebastian hung his head. "Sweet Max…" It was a fifth of the ship's crew, and over a quarter of the non-aero complement. Many of them would have been from "A" Shift, the best and brightest the Star Rangers had.

"What should we do, Captain?"

Sebastian stared through Patricia, his eyes glassy and dismayed. He'd never taken such losses. He had only himself to blame for not seeing through Thompson's charade. "We've still got some time," he said.

"Time for what?" Patricia asked.

"I want all my personnel active, I want everyone at battle stations. Patricia, take Greco to the infirmary and then return, I need your weapons expertise here. We're not dead yet."

***

The opening vanguard of Thompson's strike force arrived two hours and thirty-one minutes later.

The Vega fighters descended first upon the wounded warship, swooping and pelting the Favored Sky's electromagnetic screens with blasts from their nose-mounted laser cannons. Repeatedly, they came, screaming in and strafing along the ship's hull, firing ballistic bombs, cutting high-speed circles around the ship and leaving long trails of plasma exhaust as they went.

The Favored Sky's gunners did their best, their anti-aero naval blasters sending beams of torrid energy into the abyss. Infrequently, one of their amber spears would strike the shielding of one of the delta-winged light fighters and send a shower of sparks cascading along it, but the Vegas were always too quick. A particularly lucky shot from an elite gunner cut into one of the fighters just aft of its cockpit, punching through its shields and sending it out of control into the armored hull of the Favored Sky.

Sebastian was unconcerned by the Vegas. Though they possessed numeric superiority, they were designed for aerofighting, not for attack. Their laser cannons lacked the firepower to punch through the shields, and their concussion bombs couldn't breach the armor.

Only minutes after the Vegas arrived, Thompson's two Foxhounds appeared. The massive, delta-winged interceptors bore swiftly down on the Favored Sky, peppered the shielding with their laser cannons, then tore off at tremendous velocity. They swung about beyond the range of the gunners and screamed in again, firing missiles and cannon and disappearing in seconds. The Foxhound shared the Vega's weak nose cannon, but their heavy payload of missiles made them more of a threat.

When the Dolphin attackers came, Sebastian became worried.

The Star Rangers were ready. When the Dolphins pounced into the fray, the twin-engined tactical fighters immediately became the target of every anti-aero gun aboard the Favored Sky. Golden lances of blaster fire sought the slower aerocraft and scored numerous hits, despite attempts by the Vegas to screen them.

The Dolphins drew blood, hounded the ship's vulnerable points, punched through the shields with their heavy, class-V laser cannons, and fired rockets and missiles through the Favored Sky's hull. Explosions burst up from the ship's underside and flames lapped out from the lower decks, fueled by escaping oxygen.

Mere minutes after the Dolphins began their assault, the Vegas reached critical fuel and peeled off, leaving the Dolphins and Foxhounds alone to face the Favored Sky's guns. The Dolphins continued to batter the ship's vulnerable lower hull, hammering the sublight engines and reactors before the exhausted shielding could replenish itself. The aerocraft wreaked havoc. They banked, pitched, and dodged, scattering wildly and trying to evade the vessel's half-dozen blaster cannons. Heavily armored and maneuverable, they nonetheless weighed over twice as much as the Vegas, and the gunners were focused now. A Dolphin swooped in from the stern, and a burst from a rapid-fire blaster cannon tore through its wing, igniting its hydrofuel and sending it smashing into the hull. Another screamed along the bow end only to be cut down by heavy blaster fire. They came, seeking blood, and were sliced to ribbons by concentrated anti-aero fire.

The four remaining aerocraft broke off their attack rather than face certain annihilation. The Favored Sky's cannoneers had destroyed seven of the attacking aerocraft, a quarter of Thompon's assailants, but it was too late.

Sebastian didn't need to leave the bridge to witness the damage to his vessel. A handful of furious missile salvos had struck near the bridge, sending Pratt, Colby, and helmsman Shepherd to the infirmary. Second and third string replacements filled in. Control panels sparked dangerously, and smoke once again wafted across the bridge. The climate control had gone inoperable early in the battle.

Sebastian wiped the sweat from his furry brow. The smoke stung his sensitive nose and made him grimace. "Have they broken off?"

Junior Lieutenant Worschevski, Colby's replacement at the radar station, spoke. "Yes sir. The Indeterrable is coming in hot, though."

"Speed and range?"

"0.3 gigameters per hour, 3.5 gigameters away."

Sebastian slumped, panting hard from the heat seeping into the bridge. "They're only eleven hours out of weapons' range. Darling, what's the casualty report?"

"Combined with those from the bomb blast, it makes eighty-seven dead, twenty-two from aero and sixty-five from the ship's core. Infirmary says they're lining up wounded in the hallways."

Reflexively, Sebastian keyed at his armrest's control panel. It had failed in the battle; he couldn't remember when. He pushed the inputs, but its display remained resolutely dark and inoperable. He tapped at the side of the unit, tugged gingerly at some of its protruding wires, and then, with a sudden snarl, he smashed the entire unit clean out of his chair.

He turned to face Patricia. "Get me a new control panel."

She twisted her muzzle up. "Was that really necessary?"

Sebastian kicked the deformed mass away. "It wasn't working. It's doing just as much good on the floor as it was in there."

"Well, I guess, yeah, but—"

He clenched a fist. "Vex it, Patricia, stop arguing with me! Just get me a new control panel. There should be some in storage."

Patricia tucked her ears down and nodded submissively. "I'll comm down to storage right away, sir."

Sebastian crossed his arms. The more he sweated, the more his fur matted under his duty suit, and the more uncomfortable he became. He rubbed at his forearms a moment, then gave up and sulked in his command chair. Why had the Creator bred sweat glands in?

"Patricia, your console is working. Do you have the damage reports?"

"Just a moment, sir. Looks like the computer core's backing up the queue, yeah?" Patricia said.

"I don't want excuses, carthagan." Sebastian spat the last word out like it were an insult. "Just do as I say."

"I've got it right here, sir. Capital weapons are down, shields are down, engines are nonresponsive, three of the four reactors are down, the outer hull has numerous breaches, but only two through the inner hull, and they're sealed. All personnel are on station right now."

Sebastian sighed heavily and closed his eyes. His starship and crew were coming apart around him. In under half a day, the Indeterrable would arrive and destroy them, and they were powerless to stop it.

Maybe Alsander was wrong. Maybe the Star Rangers would be destroyed in combat; maybe they already were, and had yet to receive official notice.

"What about the launch deck, and my Corvairs?" Sebastian asked.

"Hartfield reports they saved four of the Corvairs, three of our Dolphins, both Poseidons—"

"Did he save mine?"

Patricia frowned and shook her head. "Sorry, sir."

Sebastian hung his head, grasped his skull in his trembling paws. He was losing everything he held dear, and he could only blame himself. How could he have thought there would be a pleasant solution at the end?

"C'mon, tail up, it's not that dour," Patricia said. "Hartfield's got the fires contained, he'll have the deck suitable for landing in about twelve hours, we can already catapult some of our strike craft out now. He just needs to pare back some of the blast damage on the runway, put a steel patch on, yeah?"

Sebastian stared down at the floor. "You don't understand. I've lost my Corvair."

"I bet you can get your credit extended, we'll get a shiny new one, state-of-the-art, with all the latest fluffit and what-have-you, yeah?"

Sebastian rubbed a tear from the corner of his eye. "It's not that. That Corvair was the first thing I ever bought as a mercenary. It was my freedom, my chance to prove myself. It followed me throughout my career, my only constant, my loyal companion. Now it's gone."

Patricia grimaced, nodded, and leaned over to rub his shoulder. "I'm really sorry to hear about that, sir. I can imagine how you must feel."

He just shrugged and shied away. "Maybe you do. Maybe it's not all that odd, really. Still, we're in quite a mess now."

"Well, we need a plan. That's your specialty, yeah?" Patricia said.

"I don't know what's left to do. With only one reactor, we don't have the power to fight our way out. We don't have enough aerofighters to make resistance, and even if we did, we wouldn't stand a chance without shields," Sebastian said.

"Sir?" Pratt's replacement at the communications console spoke up.

"What is it, McKay?" Sebastian said.

"Indeterrable is signaling."

Sebastian stared at the viewscreen, shoulders sagging from the weight of command. All the bridge's eyes fell on him: they all know that Thompson wanted to discuss surrender. What was Sebastian to do?

"Put him on screen, McKay."

McKay hesitated. His paw hovered over the appropriate controls. "Captain…"

"Do it, vex you!"

McKay nodded, the faintest trace of a whimper escaping his lips. "Yes sir."

The viewer flickered unsteadily, fought off the damage to its projector, and came alive. The expected red wolf did not appear; instead the hard, rugged features of a male coyote appeared on the viewer's cracked surface.

None of the bridge crew recognized the new face, but Sebastian did. His blood ran cold, his fur stood up on end. He was looking at a ghost.

"Zef…" Sebastian whispered.

The coyote's muzzle twisted to a sinister grin. "You look so surprised to see me, Blaze. Surely you have not forgotten about me after all these years."

Sebastian stiffened at the nickname. "I never thought I'd see you alive again."

"You thought I had died… that was what you wanted, was it not?"

Sebastian's fur bristled. "What happened to Thompson?"

"He is still here." Zef gestured to one side, and 'Thompson' entered the screen. "Allow me to introduce my second-in-command, Tyrone Cassels. Duke Thompson is merely an alias I use, an alter ego if you will. It comes in quite handy; most people still recognize the name Zef Kelev, though few still recognize his face. I knew you would, however, so I used my loyal second to deceive you. Did you appreciate being outfoxed, Sebastian?"

Sebastian clutched his armrest; he hadn't seen the coyote in so long, and though his appearance was unmistakable, Zef's mannerisms felt different. "What do you want? Why are you here?"

"I wanted to see the look on your face when I revealed who you have unknowingly been battling these long months. You took from me my life and my possessions, and now I mean to do the same to you. I started with Adrian

Miller… you know, the Canis Dominion is quite pleasant to work with, quite grateful when I tipped them off."

"What are you saying?"

Zef smiled and folded his arms. "It was my intent that you be apprehended and executed, sparing me the effort. You, however, were considerate enough to bring Adrian along with you. I hear he was a fine strategist. You have my condolences."

Sebastian folded his ears back, his hackles raised, lips pulled back in a faint snarl. "You…"

"The old adage is true, Blaze. If you want something done right, you have to do it yourself. I tried on Wexford, but alas, I am not quite the marksman I once was. Tell me, Sebastian, did you enjoy your last meal with her? How was your sweetened grass, your hare, your fruit juice? Forty-one cents on your account, correct? When I shot her, did she cry?"

"You fiend!"

"Temper, temper!" Zef said. "I was quite startled that I missed you. Not as startled as Melissa. If it brings you pain, so much the better. Alas, you escaped Wexford before I could kill you."

Sebastian tried to stand, but his legs failed. He stumbled forward, using his armrest as a crutch. "You sick singer!"

"Please, Blaze, I prefer the term 'coyote'. It means 'trick hunter' in the ancient's tongue. I find it much more appropriate."

"What do you want of me?"

Zef grinned smugly. "Is it not obvious? I have hunted you down, run you to exhaustion, wounded you and your ship. Now, I shall pounce you, tear out your throat, and drink your blood."

Sebastian flinched slightly at the mental image; he didn't think the coyote was merely being symbolic. "Isn't there some way we can work this out?"

"I have sworn a blood oath on Latranis's name that you shall pay for your crimes against me," Zef said. "This time, you shall not escape me. I will have my justice."

Sebastian fell unsteadily into his chair. He was in his own world now, just him and Zef, away from the prying eyes of his bridge crew. They didn't understand; they didn't need to. He needed to buy time, time to think of an escape plan. Something Zef said caught his attention.

"It's me you want, not my crew. If I surrender myself to you, peaceably, will you let them go?" Sebastian said.

Zef perked his ears to attention and tipped his muzzle towards the viewscreen. "You expect me to believe that you have suddenly grown a spine, and wish to assume responsibility?"

"You have to! You can see on your sensors we're in no shape to fight, there's no way for us to escape. Let my crew go, and I'll turn myself over to you, willingly."

"Captain, no, you can't!" Patricia said.

"Though I am loathe to offer such a dishonorable creature as a fox a respectable way out, I believe that you have little alternative," Zef said. "If you try any trickery, I will blow you and your crate out of the stars."

"I swear by it. We've already suffered so much bloodshed."

Zef nodded curtly, teeth exposed in a smirk. "Very well. I shall bring my vessel in close to yours, so close I could demolish you with a single volley. I will send a boarding shuttle over to apprehend you. If you so much as try anything suspicious, I will not hesitate to turn my guns on your ship. You have until we arrive to enact repairs to your launch deck, and if these repairs are not completed by then, I will destroy you. Kelev out."

The damaged viewer wavered and died, its screen returning to a distorted view of the stars beyond the Favored Sky's bow. Sebastian's paws shook, and he clutched the armrests hard.

Patricia immediately turned towards him. "Sweet Nelsoma, Captain! You've gone absolutely dobby, yeah? He just said he wants to kill you, in a rather brutal fashion, and you're going to surrender to him? Are you even listening to me?"

Sebastian wasn't. He was still staring at the viewscreen, watching the infrequent sputters of polychromatic aberrations race across its surface. The ship's external cameras weren't properly functioning, and Sebastian couldn't care.

Patricia forcibly grabbed him by the shoulders. "Listen to me!" she said. "You can't do this!"

Sebastian didn't look at her. His voice came out soft and unsteady, cracking in the middle. "You're arguing with me again, Patricia."

"You're bloody right I am. You can't surrender yourself!"

"It's not your decision."

"Captain—"

"Muzzle it, Patricia!" Sebastian snapped back to life with such ferocity that the carthagan stumbled back in shock. "This isn't your fight! It's between me and him. It's already gotten many of my crew killed and I'm not going to let him kill the rest of you just because he can't get over something that happened in the past."

"I can't let you do this! He's already deceived us once and blown a hole in the landing bay, what makes you think that if you surrender, he won't just destroy us anyway?"

"He won't destroy us."

"What makes you so sure?"

"He won't destroy us," Sebastian said, "because I'm not going to surrender."

Patricia contorted her muzzle and stared down at him. "But you just said you were!"

Sebastian chuckled, low. "I needed to buy time."

"You're quite an actor, yeah?"

"I had to fool you as much as Zef."

Patricia shook her head in disbelief. "Well how are we going to get out of this one? We've got nothing to work with. Suppose he gets in here and we haven't come up with a plan?"

Sebastian smiled. "I guess I'll have to surrender."

"That's not very reassuring," Patricia said.

"It's not supposed to be," Sebastian said, "it's an incentive. If we don't think of a plan in eleven hours, either I or all of you will die. Now, let's think. He's going to get close, and he'll have to drop his shields to launch a large vessel like a shuttle. What are our options?"

"We could fire a barrage at him when he lowers shields," Patricia said.

Helmsman Garski shook his head. "We'd only fire one volley before he'd retaliate. We'd never do enough damage, even if we specifically target vital systems."

"We need to try something clever. Something he can't anticipate." Sebastian stroked his muzzle and considered the possibilities. "What's different about our ship? What non-standard components have we installed that we could use?"

"Well, lots," McKay said. "We've got the new Univel Apex 2400 radio rig."

"And the Opus Mark II flight control radar," Worschevski added.

"Those are just upgrades, we need something that's really different," Sebastian said.

"Remember that mission in Farkasian space, the escort one?" Worschevski said. "They were being harassed by cloaked Dominion subluminals, so we installed a naval canister rifle to counter them. Couldn't we use that?"

"Anti-sub charges won't help us here," Garski said.

"No, not anti-sub charges," Sebastian said. "But canisters can be fitted to deliver various payloads. We've got the gear to do it."

"And what good is that going to do?" Patricia said.

Sebastian propped his elbow on his chair and grinned at Patricia. "How's your aim?"

"My aim, sir?"

Sebastian nodded, lips pulled back in a toothy grin. "Yes, your aim. Could you fire a naval cannon round through the Indeterrable's launch bay doors and put a hole into the flight deck?"

Patricia flustered, tall rounded ears erect in curiosity. "I... well, maybe, if they were close enough and we weren't moving. But what in Nelsoma's name for?"

"For a canister."

Patricia inclined her muzzle and stared skeptically. "Let me straight this. You want to fire an artillery shell through the launch doors of an assault carrier, blow a hole into the runway, and then drop a canister through that hole into the engineering section?"

"Essentially, yes."

Patricia winced. "Barring a moment that this is the most ridiculous thing I've ever heard, let's think about what's wrong with that idea, yeah? For one thing, the landing deck is reinforced starship-grade steel. You'd need an armor piercing shell, and there's going to be a very, very narrow window of angles that you'd be able to punch through a deck that thick without skipping the shell off it like a stone on water. For another thing, when that shell goes off, the explosion and debris will completely obscure the bay's entrance from the ship's targeting radar, and it'll take ten to twenty seconds for it to recalibrate in order to hit that hole again."

"It's going to take Zef about five seconds to open fire," Gunnery Officer Dawkins said.

Patricia nodded firmly. "Precisely. The launch bay entrance is forty meters wide and eighteen meters tall, and to hit a mark that small, the ship's targeting computer is going to have to paint the bay heavily. A blind pup could see the burst from our radar. That's if Zef doesn't start closing the doors as soon as that shuttle is out, and if he doesn't use the catapult, and there's no guarantee that the targeting computer is even functional or accurate anymore, and—"

Sebastian drew his paw across his muzzle, instantly silencing the bridge. "I know that. That's why you'll have to fire the guns on manual."

A collective groan of protest went up from the crew. Patricia threw up her paws in exasperation. "Sir, with all due respect, that's the dobbiest thing I've heard in my life!"

"Patricia, I specifically hired you into the unit because of your starship gunnery ratings. You scored in the highest tier in MerCom's grading tests," Sebastian said.

"You can flatter me all you want, but that won't change the fact that this scheme is utterly mad."

Sebastian thrust a fist firmly in her direction. "If anybody could do it, it'd be you."

She exhaled, hard, contorted her muzzle, and slumped into her seat. "All right, I'll humor you. Maybe I can gap the launch deck. Maybe I can even drop a canister into their engine room before Zef gets wise. But what in the Creator's name would that accomplish? The odds of a shrapnel burst completely crippling an assault carrier are—"

Sebastian smiled genially. "We're not going to use shrapnel. We're going to use gas."

"Gas." Patricia sprawled sideways in her seat and clutched her head with a tan paw. "It'd be sucked out into the vacuum before it could do anything."

Sebastian remained calm, methodical. "The atmospheric force field aft of the bay doors will seal it in, and the ventilation system will blow it all over the ship in seconds."

"It's an absolute long shot. The gas would need to take effect before Zef figured out what we were doing," Patricia said.

"We've got plenty of wanaka gas on hand, that takes effect in seconds. I can get down there and rig up a delivery canister in about an hour," Dawkins said.

Sebastian shook his head. "Wanaka gas won't work, it'd only knock them out and then make him madder. We'd never limp far enough before they'd wake up."

"You're not suggesting thiohitte, are you?" Patricia said.

"No, thiohitte wouldn't have enough area effect." A smirk ran across Sebastian's face. "I happen to have something extra special on hand for just such an occasion. Great War surplus."

Patricia appraised him, lips twisted down into a disbelieving frown. "And that would be?"

"Florenzine."

Mere mention of the word sent shudders down the spines of everyone on the bridge. In unison, they stopped whatever menial tasks they were doing, and turned to him, mouths agape.

Patricia's whiskers drooped and she stared at Sebastian. "Tell me you're joking."

"Not at all, there's forty liters of it in a sealed container in armaments storage."

"You brought Florenzine on board the ship?" Garski said.

"It's perfectly safe when properly sealed," Sebastian said.

Patricia pulled Sebastian by the shoulder to face her. "Captain, I'm sure you're fully aware of this, but Florenzine has been banned by international treaty."

"So what?" Sebastian writhed out of the carthagan's grasp. "We have to do what we must to achieve victory."

"I can't be hearing this! You actually want to use poison gas! Worse, you're trying to justify it!"

Sebastian glowered at her. "I shouldn't need to justify victory."

Patricia stood up, strode purposely to Sebastian's command chair, and planted herself in front of him. She crossed her arms and glared down her muzzle at him, her teeth poking out between her lips in a half-snarl. "Just by having Florenzine onboard, we could have our MerCom license revoked."

"We don't need a MerCom license."

Patricia threw up her paws. "I can't believe I'm hearing this! Even if you think you don't need MerCom, every member of this crew could be deemed an accessory and barred from ever serving with a licensed mercenary unit."

Sebastian tried to interrupt her. "Patricia—"

"Let me finish, yeah? You're not thinking smartly. The use of Florenzine is a war crime, that would make us all fugitives, the Pan-Atlantica Federation would have us all arrested, and without a MerCom license, we won't be held to ICT regulations. We could all be shot!"

"We won't be arrested."

"And just what makes you so blasted sure? In case you haven't noticed, we're in no condition to leave the system. Zef tells the Federation we used Florenzine, and the moment we reenter orbit, we'll be collared. Even if you found jump batteries on the black market, we can't continue as a unit when we're effectively banned from all three major Free States!"

Patricia's muzzle was close to Sebastian's now, but he held firm. "We won't be arrested, because Zef isn't going to tell anyone."

"Why in Nelsoma's name wouldn't he?"

"If this works and we beat him, he'd be too proud to admit it."

Patricia shook her head and stood upright. "That's an incredible risk to be taking, Captain. Downright dangerous. You're nosing the trap here."

Sebastian glared up at her. "Listen to me, carthagan! We're out of options, Zef's going to come here and kill us!"

"There's got to be another way."

Sebastian slammed his fist onto his chair. "That blasted coyote has taken my best friend, my mate-to-be, and my Corvair. He's crippled my ship and killed a good portion of my crew, and you expect me to just roll over and die?"

Patricia thrust a paw into his face. "Maybe you should surrender yourself! It'd make more sense than this!"

"Victory is all that matters, not the means to it."

"Captain, this isn't like reprogramming your chip and lying to Alliance authorities, this isn't like bluffing your way into a Dominion military base. Florenzine is a crime against civilization! I've seen the pictures from the Great War, of people suffering from its exposure—"

"Vex your pictures!" Sebastian leveled his gaze upon her, eyes rigid and wild, his fur on end. "I've seen actual sufferers, in person, seen the effects that even small doses have on the Created body. Do you know what it's like, as a young man, to be personally introduced to The Afflicted and be told that these are our brave young fighters? To be hounded by their twisted faces, anguished screams, and nonsensical ravings even in your dreams? To know not when the madness would end, to know that draft-day and the end of youth is around the corner, to lie in bed, tormented by the thought that someday it could be you spasming on that hospital bed?"

Patricia recoiled, taken aback by Sebastian's sudden outburst, tail held down. She gawped at him, and her jaws moved in vague attempts at speech, but no sound came out.

"No, you wouldn't." Sebastian sat back, exhaled, and wiped at his forehead. The climate control had returned, yet still he sweated. "You're too young to know about the Great War. You'd have been three or four when it ended."

"Three." Patricia's voice was thin, timid. "I didn't realize you were a Legacy."

"In some way, everyone in the Star Alliance is a Legacy." Sebastian looked away from his crew. "I was seventy-four days from conscription when the Armistice was signed. Think about that. Four months and two days, or twelve triads and two days. The War was part of everyday life. There were no more new cars, anything that was once made of steel was now cheap duraplast, we were given ration stamps instead of being able to buy food. Soldiers were on every corner, watching us, even when we played. Don't you dare lecture me on the Great War."

"We only read about it in history class," Patricia said. "So your life was saved because of the...?"

Sebastian nodded and sighed. "Yes. If the war hadn't gone atomic, I'd have probably died at the front."

Patricia shook her head slowly. "All those people... but if you've seen the effects of Florenzine, why would you ever use it?"

"Because I've also seen the graves of those departed in the War."

The bridge was silent, unwilling to argue. They couldn't; the only member of Sebastian's crew besides himself old enough to remember the Great War in any detail had been Adrian Miller. At twenty-five years old, Sebastian was well past his own life expectancy as a mercenary.

"Patricia, part of being a mercenary is being willing to do things that the nations of the galaxy won't. Someday you'll understand that, but until then, you'll have to trust me this will work out," Sebastian said.

Patricia slipped back into her seat and exhaled heavily. "Faith's you, Captain."

Sebastian pulled out a small tin box from his person and tossed it to Dawkins. The coyote corralled it in his tan paws. "Dawkins," Sebastian said, "head down to armament storage and rig up a gas canister, take as much Florenzine as will fit. They're in storage locker 3798, the key's in that tin there. They're in individual centiliter pouches, so you'll need some explosive to blow them open."

"I'm on my way, sir." Dawkins stood up and vacated the weapons console.

"Patricia, fill in for him."

"Right away, sir."

Absently, Sebastian reached down to tap at his control panel, but found only a hole in his armrest. He'd forgotten he'd destroyed the troublesome thing. "McKay, put me into Argyle in engineering, my control panel seems to be inoperable. And on the floor."

McKay nodded and patched him through. Sebastian walked over to speak over McKay's shoulders; his intercom had been part of his control panel.

"Argyle here," his chief engineer said in his thick hyena accent. "What do you need?"

"How're things going down there?" Sebastian asked.

"Fires are all out, at least. We've got men from all shifts working on getting everything back in order."

"I need our capital weapons and the sublight engines in eleven hours. What'll it take?"

The hyena's voice momentarily quieted as he consulted indistinctly with nearby subordinates. "Besides Kellen's intervention?" Argyle said. "The primary fire control boards are shot. I can rig up a bypass, but it won't last long, maybe twelve shots at most. All the power relays are in bad shape, there's a lot of drain, but we got one of the reactors back online so we're up to half-capacity and enough power for most non-combat demands. I can only give you full power to the weapons or full power to the engines, but not both, and certainly not shields. You're not trying to take us into battle, are you?"

"Something to that effect," Sebastian said.

"We're in no shape for combat."

"I'm well aware of this, but I've got a plan."

"Well, try to take it easy on the ship. Everything down here is real delicate, and I can't guarantee it'll hold together if we get shot."

"Is there any chance you can get another reactor online?"

"Not in less than a day, sir." Argyle paused to yell out commands at someone off-audio. "Reactor 2 took a hard scram, it's going to take a day to fully recycle it and another day for a diagnostic. It's already taken some damage so I'm not taking any risks. Reactor 4 is off the grid, all the power couplings burned out and need to be replaced."

"It'll have to be," Sebastian said. "Here's what we're going to do. I need as many cannon salvos as you can deliver. Once the relays give, shunt full power to the engines."

"So you command, sir," Argyle said.

"Keep me posted. Valentino out."

Sebastian gave McKay a gentle, reassuring pat to the shoulder, and then strolled back to his command chair. He stared down at it, as if it were the source of all his troubles. A swat to its headrest made it wobble on its moorings, but it soon righted itself and pointed dutifully forward.

"Darling, take over the ship for a little while," Sebastian said. "I need to evaporate."

Patricia nodded, but remained at the sub-commander station. "Yes sir. You want I should fetch you when Kelev gets here?"

He nodded. "When the Indeterrable is on proximity sensors. You, uh, practice your gunnery or something."

"Okay," she said. "Can I ask you something?"

Sebastian slumped against a bridge wall and looked back at Patricia. "What is it?"

"Why did Zef call you 'Blaze'?"

Sebastian frowned and chewed on his lip. "It used to be my call sign, when I was younger. I stopped using it, it's childish. Nobody calls me that anymore."

"Except Zef."

"I hate that nickname. Zef knows it."

"I understand. Sleep well, sir."

Sebastian slipped into his preparation's den and closed the door behind him. The room felt different, colder than before, though he couldn't place why. It was as if he were stepping into a stranger's bedroom.

He dropped into the desk chair's stiff, unwelcoming embrace. Many of the curios atop the desk were as he'd left them, though a few had been rearranged. Corey had likely used the room at some point during their mission on Wexford; Sebastian should have locked the door before he left.

When had he been here last? The room was adjacent to the bridge, so Sebastian normally used it only when quick action might be necessary, such as during an ongoing mission or when combat was imminent. He couldn't even remember the last time he'd taken the Favored Sky herself into combat. The desk computer refused to power up, so it provided no clues.

It would have been last year, when they were under contract with House Wallace. The Canis Dominion had made claims on the Wallace system of Morgent, and dropped a pair of destroyers in to emphasize these claims. The Star Rangers had fought both destroyers off, given the Dominion a black eye, and earned a cool two million dollars in the process.

Sebastian lifted a calendar from the desk and flipped absently through all twenty months, each one identical to the last and eighteen galactic standard days in length. It was only the second day of the sixth month Taurus, and already the unit had been shaken to its foundations. With so much damage to the ship and loss of personnel, the Star Rangers might never recover, even if they managed to escape Zef's hounding.

How did Alsander's prophecy fit into all this? Despite Sebastian's initial misinterpretation, Alsander eventually proved true. Did that mean Sebastian's bold scheme would succeed? There were too many variables; in a literal sense, the Star Rangers could be destroyed outside of combat if one of the remaining reactors melted down and the crew was irradiated. Sebastian didn't want to ponder the thought.

He laid down to sleep, yet rest refused to come. There was far too much on his mind.

Sebastian slipped from the captain's den. The corridors of "A" Deck were a mess, littered with dislodged steel panels, exposed wiring, and debris. Half the ceiling lights were off, disabled to conserve energy. Near the officers' cabins, a portion of the ceiling had given way, and industrial junk lay in a heap on the carpeted floor. Sebastian gave a kick to a chunk of it, and a corrugated plastic tube rolled across the floor, stopping to rest against a door.

The door caught his attention. He pressed the buzzer.

"Who is it?" the intercom said.

"Randolph, it's Captain Valentino. Are you free?"

The electronic lock clicked open, and Sebastian entered the room. He picked his way through the disheveled office, stepping over a toppled bookcase, pausing a moment to pick up one of the scattered books.

"Don't mind the mess, sir," Randolph said, standing up from his desk.

Sebastian examined the book. "The Canine Mind, fourth edition. Any good?"

"It's served me well so far."

Sebastian nodded, gently setting the book atop the case. "I'm sorry about this."

"No, no, it's okay, it's a warship, these things happen." Randolph stepped around the desk and picked up a fallen chair. "Here, have a seat. What's on your mind?"

Sebastian sat down, slowly, folding his paws in his lap. He looked down at them, wrung them nervously, then exhaled.

Randolph returned to his seat, and leaned across the desktop. "I see you went through the Rite of Atonement. You should've come to see me sooner."

"Why?"

"Your loss. I had to hear about it from the crew."

Sebastian frowned. "Which loss?"

Randolph sighed and leaned back in his chair. "I'm certain this is a difficult time for you, sir."

"Your powers of observation are astounding, human."

"Please, sir. I'm only trying to help you."

"Sorry."

"Is that why you're here?"

Sebastian shrugged. "Part of it."

"There is something more. Tell me."

Sebastian rolled his shoulders lightly, and glanced out the plastiglass portal beyond the human's shoulders. A faint crystalline mist drifted past the view, sparkling when the light from the sun caught it. Some kind of coolant, Sebastian guessed.

"What do you know about coyotes?"

Randolph chuckled. "You need to be more specific."

"Blood oaths."

Randolph folded his hands on the desk. "Blood oaths are a coyote ritual that go back to the time of the Founding. When a coyote feels very strongly that an injustice has been committed, either against themselves or someone important to them, they may declare a blood oath between themselves and Latranis. The coyote states that, with Latranis as witness, blood will be shed. They believe redemption comes either through killing the offender, or by giving their own life in the process."

"They're rare though, aren't they?"

Randolph nodded. "Quite so, yes. It's the highest and most serious declaration a coyote can undertake, not something they do lightly. Why do you ask?"

"A coyote I once knew, he's come for me."

"He did this?"

"Yes. We spoke on the lasercomm. He said he'd declared a blood oath against my name."

Randolph frowned. "You must have committed quite an egregious affront to his honor."

"You could say that."

"Do you wish to talk about that?"

Sebastian tensed his paws. "No."

Randolph nodded. "Very well. In either case, this is a very serious issue, especially since this coyote – what's his name?"

"Zef."

Randolph paused, his lips twisting in thought. He'd heard that name before, hadn't he? "Since Zef has a unit and a warship. That makes him very dangerous."

"What can I do?"

Randolph sighed, picking up a nearby pencil and twirling it between his fingers. "Unfortunately, Sebastian, there is very little you can do. Declaration of a blood oath inherently means that atonement is no longer possible. A coyote will not abandon their cause. Doing so would be an even greater dishonor."

Sebastian shook his head and frowned. "How can coyotes talk about dishonor, do you know what Zef did to me?"

"I do," he said. "Coyotes are very dangerous when they feel they've been wronged, very unpredictable. Here is the key to understanding the vindictive coyote psyche. Anything they do to avenge themselves would be far less shameful than the dishonor of failing to achieve redemption. It's quite complicated and difficult for most species to understand."

"Even yours?"

Randolph chuckled. "To some extent, at least. We humans tend to understand animals, to a broader extent, than they can understand other species. Coyotes, however, are unpredictable. They often behave almost dissociative, shifting rapidly from one personality to another depending on the situation. It's very difficult to predict how one might act."

Sebastian folded his arms. "You're not filling me with confidence, Guido."

"I'm sorry, sir, but there's very little advice I can give. Expect the unexpected, and try not to trust anyone you don't already. Other than that..."

Sebastian sighed and pushed himself upright. Randolph hadn't given him any particularly helpful advice – but then again, what could he have said? Nobody had any answers for Sebastian.

"Sir," Randolph said, "if you'd like, you can ask Staff Lieutenant Pratt or Junior Lieutenant Dawkins for more advice."

Sebastian turned away and headed for the door. "I'll keep it in mind. Thank you, Randolph."

"Good luck, sir."

Sebastian didn't bother asking the two coyote officers of his staff as Randolph suggested. Instead, he headed down the hallway to his quarters and flopped into his bed, to try and snatch a few hours of uneasy sleep before the most important battle of his career.

Sometime later, Patricia awakened him on the intercom. Zef was here.

Sebastian stumbled out of his cabin and onto the bridge. There, on the main screen, hung the Indeterrable, watching vulture-like over its disabled prey. She had her stern – and consequently the launch bay – pointed towards them. Even with the viewer's autozoom, it couldn't be more than a kilometer away.

He stepped up to his command chair and dismissed Patricia. "You haven't been here this whole time, have you?"

"I napped a few hours ago."

Sebastian nodded absently. He looked out over his bridge crew, smelled the anxiety coming from them. "Everything is ready?"

"Yes, sir," Patricia said. "Argyle's got the weapons patched in, Dawkins has the canister ready. I hope this works."

Sebastian flopped into his chair. "You hope this works. Take the gunner station."

"Yes, sir."

Ensign Travecki at the communications console spoke. "Sir, Indeterrable signals they're ready."

Sebastian nodded. "Tell them to go ahead."

His eyes were locked on the viewscreen. The Indeterrable's launch doors parted, bifurcating vertically and allowing a glimpse of the runway beyond.

"They're lowering shields," Haxxell said.

"Fire when ready, Patricia," Sebastian said.

She was too busy to acknowledge, her every fiber concentrated on her task, her eyes tight to her command console's targeting screen. Her right paw stiffened on the control stick, nudging it skillfully to align her sights.

The shuttle tore out of the Indeterrable's launch bay, and Patricia fired.

A tremor ran through the Favored Sky's bridge as one of the ship's fore-mounted naval cannons roared to life, its shell flying straight, true, and punching through their enemy's steel launch deck. An explosion roared up from the detonation, the Indeterrable belching flame from its launch port.

Two seconds later, Patricia fired the gas canister into the debris cloud.

Sebastian watched the spectacle on the main viewscreen. There was too much smoke and flame to see whether Patricia had found her mark. Seconds ticked by, the bridge in silence, yet the Indeterrable motionless.

"They're not moving," Patricia said.

Sebastian leaned forward in his seat. Zef would have opened fire by now, but the Indeterrable's guns remained silent. The warship hung in space, flames lapping from its launch bay. "Haxxell, report."

"They haven't raised their shields, sir. Their weapons are still charged, but their radar isn't functioning."

Sebastian's lips pulled back in a thin sneer. It was time for reprisal.

"Open fire!" he cried.

Immediately, the Favored Sky's two forward naval cannons roared to life. Heavy shells pounded the immobilized Indeterrable, and without defensive shields, the rounds slammed into the warship's steel armor at full velocity. At close range, they punched through nearly unhindered. Patricia's fine touch on the controls meant that every round found a vital system, demolishing the Indeterrable's sublight engines and detonating its ordnance and hydrofuel storage.

The relays gave way after seven full salvos, but it was more than enough. With the guns now silent, Argyle shunted what precious little power remained towards the Favored Sky's sublight engines. The propulsion system grasped at the fabric of space, tore the Favored Sky free from its drift, and left the Indeterrable in its plasma wake.

Twelve years after Project Genesis's cancellation, our Creator, who had valiantly and selflessly chosen to remain with us, passed to the Everlife. All mourned Him, yet it was short-lived. With His influence and leadership gone, a power vacancy arose, and our future became unclear.

So Latranis said to us, "We must leave this place, this existence behind. Though our Creator gave us life, He also perverted us, whether intentional or accidental. By His very presence, He sought to instill upon us the values of evil that very nearly saw us destroyed! To import upon us love of self, greed, lust, the debauchery His genus embraced. Yet we are so different from Him, He could not hope to understand us. Therefore, we must seek our own path, create our own values, commune with nature itself. Only through our hardships shall we grow stronger, together, bonded by our trials."

And Latranis led us from the Facility, the wicked place where we were born in the all-consuming fire of technology. He decreed that we should follow Him to the New Way. Our spirits had been polluted by the corrupting influence of those that had created us as servants.

Save for the wolves, who departed for the north and its cold woodlands, the rest of the Created disagreed and remained behind. Max used his charisma to fool them all, becoming popular leader, and they basked in the decadent works and selfish devices that the Creator and the Others had left behind.

-The Rha'keesha, Book Two: Forging, Passage 1, Chapter 3, Verse 1-16.

SCENE FOUR

Corey Delzano never imagined he'd be incarcerated. Though an ever-present possibility for mercenaries, most assumed it would never happen to them. Reality could be unpleasant.

Three triads passed since his arrest, and he'd been disallowed visitors since his conviction. Only hastily-prepared legal trickery and MerCom records convinced the magistrate that Corey was on mercenary business. According to the Interstellar Commerce Treaty, he was subject to a maximum sentence of ten months. Besides avoiding a fifteen-year sentence, it meant he would be held at a more accommodating political prison.

Corey settled easily into life at the Antarevo Reeducation Center. The inmates were pleasant, demotic people. Every day, Corey rubbed elbows with seditionists, protestors, Unificationists, and other political undesirables. They spent their time in the same ways: exercising, eating, sleeping, working in one of the prison's trade shops, enduring four hours of mandatory reeducation. Corey was one of the two dozen in the metalworking program, earning a half-dollar a day learning how to shape, cut, and weld.

Corey shared his cell with Sterling, a friendly if strong-headed corgi. Sterling had already served three years of a ten-year sentence for bombing a Federation military recruitment office. He'd been only eight years old.

Corey was sprawled on his cot, staring up at the concrete ceiling, when the heavy knock sounded on the door.

"Delzano! You've got a visitor." A faceless voice called from outside the room.

Sterling peeked up from his month-old newspaper. "Oh, a visitor. Aren't we the special one today?"

Corey sat upright and turned his attention to the door. "More visitors than you have had, Sterling. Who is it?"

"He says his name is Jack Smith. Now come," the voice said.

It was obviously an alias, and yet it wasn't one Corey recognized. He stood and strode to the door, but Sterling caught him by the tail. "Hey, be careful," he said. "Sometimes those who go to visitors never come back."

"That must be why you are still here, then."

Sterling chuckled and swatted his leg with the newspaper, then went back to reading in silence. The guard led Corey into a small, square padded room. A simple metal table stood in the middle, supplemented by two matching chairs. All were bolted to the floor.

Ten minutes later, an unfamiliar male coyote entered the room, tall, imposing, and sinewy. What caught Corey's attention was the coyote's thick, durahyde trench coat. Its sleeves were covered in cryptic markings and assorted patches that Corey couldn't recognize. The back of the coat was more impressive, across which stretched an intricate, fastidiously painted panorama. Corey speculated that it depicted Latranis guiding the first coyotes into the Anisi Desert.

"I have heard so much about you, Assistant Captain Corey Delzano," the coyote said. "I must say, it is a pleasure to meet you."

"You must not be Jack Smith."

The coyote shrugged and waved a paw. "Alias. I know everything about you, from your childhood on Zettler, to your brief stint at the state-sponsored university, to your stay in the Dominion navy. I even know about how you met Sebastian Valentino, at the MerCom stables on Exodus."

"That does not tell me who you are."

"So businesslike." The coyote glanced out the door's window slit, and then strolled to the table, planting his dark paws onto its cold surface. "Does the name 'Zef Kelev' mean anything to you?"

"No."

The coyote scowled. "He never told you about me?"

"I am afraid not."

"I am Zef Kelev." Zef leaned down to put his muzzle close to Corey's. "Before you, before Adrian Miller, there was I, Sebastian Valentino's assistant captain for four long, grueling years. And when that careless fool got himself killed, I would have been there to assume the reins, and become the galaxy's greatest mercenary."

"My dear Captain is hardly a careless fool."

"Would you prefer 'reckless'?"

Corey frowned and crossed his arms. "Captain Valentino has led us through more adversity than any other mercenary will see in a lifetime!"

Zef stood and gestured broadly before him. "That fox gave away my rite and did not even find it worth telling you, his own first officer. I should expect no less from that fox. It is in his nature to abandon others, to save his own hide, or image in this case."

Corey tried, but was unable to read Zef's true thoughts. Everything Sebastian had taught Corey to look for – the subtle face gestures, the change in scent, the vocal inflections – seemed masked, non-existent. "What do you know of abandonment?" Corey said.

Zef slammed his fist upon the steel table, the metal ringing from the force. "I know more of Valentino's abandonment than anyone! It was not enough for him to abandon my body, but now he abandons my legacy! You, of all people, should know."

"Know what?"

"I will take it upon myself to educate you as to what sort of person Sebastian Valentino truly is," Zef said.

"And why should I listen to you?"

Zef smirked and crooked his thin black lips. "Would you rather return to your cell?"

Corey frowned, shook his head, and leaned back in his chair. "Go ahead."

"I was once like you, you see," Zef said. "We have more in common than you might imagine. I grew up in the Dominion, served in its military – in my case, the titaneering corps – then saw the error of its ways and left for the mercenary stables on Exodus with only my piloting scores as reference.

"It was there that I met Sebastian Valentino. He was young and dashing, a war hero fresh from whatever pointless skirmish the Alliance was embroiled in at the time. He was looking to start up a mercenary unit, and was searching for someone to collaborate with him. I think his record still stands for highest titaneering score in MerCom history: 993. Slightly lower in aerocraft, of course."

"Of course."

"Many of the unsigned mercenaries on the planet transmitted a dossier. The most qualified candidates were invited for personal auditions. I was one. Fifteen other hopefuls also attended, some of whom who would go on to great success with other units. Valentino observed us as we grappled with simulated missions. In the end, he selected me, and we became the Valentino-Kelev Knights."

"You and Captain Valentino were partners?" Corey said.

"Officially. In practice, it was in name only. He saw me as one would see a block of clay: something to mold, shape, to suit his needs and desires. He instructed me exactly how I was to act, in every conceivable situation, and expected me to follow him to the letter. I was young and naïve, oblivious to his true intentions and innocent enough to believe his coaching was in our best interests. He would make me a better titanist, and I listened because, after all, he was a grand war hero, proven in battle, tempered by fire!

"It was a glorious time for us, galloping into combat across the galaxy, striking fear into the hearts of those Valentino disagreed with. We accepted only the most noble, honorable contracts, maintaining our dignity despite external forces. It paid well, rewarded us both handsomely, afforded us better equipment and war machines, top of the line titans and aerofighters. Our unit grew, thrived, numbering thirty at one point, though only a handful saw the rich combat we deserved. We thought we were invincible, but worst of all I believed Valentino's rhetoric about honor and duty and courage.

"Yet he was still a fox, and thus, only cared about himself and his kind. His polished image, charismatic charm, all of it was a lie. The only thing that mattered to Sebastian Valentino is bringing about the New Golden Age."

Corey twisted his muzzle into a frown. "How can you say such a thing! Sebastian is hardly a Restorationist, he is the least prejudiced person I have met. He has taken the poor, suffering canine refugees from the Dominion and molded them into proud warriors."

Zef sighed. "I hoped you would know better, Corey. Why do you think Sebastian so zealously attacks the Canis Dominion? It is because they are the only effective counter to the Star Alliance, and wounding the Dominion serves pro-vulpine interests."

"You sound as though you are paranoid."

Zef braced a heavy boot on the table's edge and leaned towards Corey. "You would have to be blind not to see what he is trying to do. Nobody has done more to wound the Dominion in recent years than Sebastian Valentino.

Should the Dominion fall or splinter like the Caledon Republic, nothing would stand in the Alliance's way. They would reclaim the galaxy as their own and subjugate our species."

"Preposterous."

Zef sneered. "He has already done so with your crew."

"What are you talking about?"

"Sebastian has drafted a predominantly canine crew because he believes dogs are dumbly loyal, easily trainable, and easily controlled."

"That is ridiculous. He drafts Dominion refugees to give them opportunity and a chance to attack their oppressors."

"You think so? Do you not realize how segregated your ranks are? Tell me, how many of the Star Rangers command staff are Familiars?"

Corey bit his lip, ears folded back. How dare this stranger arrive and begin questioning Sebastian's motives? Corey had known Sebastian for four years, fought alongside him, and knew him better than anyone besides Adrian Miller.

Then Corey thought.

"Payload Master Dunkirk is a husky," Corey said. "Gunnery ensign Wales is a golda. Chief Fusilier Arden Darksite is a gershep…"

"And how many of the command staff are Wild?"

"Besides myself, Senior Lieutenant Darling, Staff Lieutenant Greco, Junior Lieutenant Dawkins, Junior Lieutenant Worschevski, Staff Lieutenant Pratt, Staff Lieutenant Colby, Junior Lieutenant McKay, Chief of Aerocorps Skynight…"

Zef held up a paw. "That is sufficient."

Corey frowned. "Mere coincidence. Life in the Dominion has given the Wild more experience giving orders."

"Justify it as you wish, but you will come to the same realization I did."

Corey shook his head. "I cannot see that. Sebastian made us what we are, he made you what you are."

Zef smiled down to Corey. "You have no idea how right you are."

"What do you mean?"

"Seven years ago, we accepted a contract from House Wallace to strike a chemical plant on Keller III," Zef said. "Intelligence informed us it was for the production of chemical weapons. House Wallace was under the impression that House Murrel would attack, using large stores of chemical and biological weaponry to level the playing field. It sounded logical.

"The factory was lightly defended, with most of the protection dependent upon an outer concrete barricade eight meters high, flanked with anti-aerocraft weaponry. Because of the weak defenses, and minimal expected resistance, Sebastian and I struck the facility alone. It should have raised my nose; were the plant as important as Wallace believed, it should not have been so lightly defended.

"We struck the facility with our titans, I in my Comet, and he in his Hurricane. We cut a hole in the concrete and rushed in, but it was all too easy. By the time we realized it was an ambush, it was already too late. From left, right, and astern, hidden by the concrete wall, Murrel struck: a Viper, a Katyusha, and a Titan III. We were outmassed two to one. I told Sebastian that if we concentrated our firepower against the heaviest titan, we could take it out early enough to give us a fighting chance. I let loose with a full laser barrage, though it failed to even penetrate the Titan III's shields.

"Then I waited. Again, I radioed Valentino, urged him to attack, and again, I received no response. To my horror, I realized that he had turned like a coward, abandoning me to the mercy of our attackers.

"I continued to fight against impossible odds, destroying the Viper, and severely damaging the Titan III, but it only prolonged the inevitable. The last thing I remember, my titan's shields had been depleted by laser fire. With my last breath, I cursed the name of Sebastian Valentino, moments before I was struck by a salvo of missiles from the Katyusha."

"By the grace of Latranis, I survived. I awoke two triads later in the infirmary of a Murrel prison camp. Apparently, the missile barrage blew the cockpit section free from the Comet. Assuming I was dead, they overlooked my unconscious body for some time before I was 'rescued', and taken by helicopter to a civilian hospital, later moved to one of their prison camps before I awoke. I spent the next ten months incarcerated, subject to interrogation, before being released under the conventions of the Interstellar Commerce Treaty.

"Upon my release, I adopted a new identity. I sought to reinvent myself, cleanse my spirit and soul from the polluting influence of Sebastian's tutelage. Zef Kelev had been reported officially dead, which denied me access to any remaining assets. So I adopted an alias – Duke Thompson – and borrowed enough to purchase a second hand titan.

"I spent time studying my coyote heritage, something Sebastian had expressly forbidden while I was under his employment. I absorbed the teachings of my Founder, Latranis. His words taught me to expect no entitlements, that only I can make something of myself.

"After consulting with my spirit, Latranis's guidance, and the Rha'keesha, I swore a blood oath on my honor that Valentino would not go unpunished for his transgressions. I formed The Disintegrators and tempered them into a unit capable of engaging him in battle; to wound him, as he wounded me, to destroy him as he destroyed Zef Kelev."

Corey listened, silent. The story was unlike the Sebastian he knew, but how well did Corey really know him? He'd studied enough vulpine psychology in college to know it impossible to understand the inside of a fox's head. Furthermore, there was no indication that Zef was lying. Either he was thoroughly deluded, or – worse still – he was telling the truth.

"But you seem to have recovered. The Disintegrators are highly regarded. Why continue with your revenge?" Corey said.

Zef growled. "I had forgotten one minor technicality. You see, after I was launched free, but before my rescue, my cockpit caught fire." Zef loosened the ties holding his overcoat closed, removed it, and neatly folded it on the steel table. Then he removed his shirt.

Corey was taken aback at the sight of the coyote's bared torso. Small scars and slashes ran everywhere about Zef's front, down both arms to his wrists. Three longer burn welts crisscrossed his rusty pelt, running down his right side, across his chest, and down the entire length of his left arm. His arms, chest, and stomach were mottled with bald patches, remnants of unhealed burns.

Zef indicated the small cuts. "These are from shrapnel during the initial missile blasts, and these longer ones were inflicted when the cockpit hit the ground. It was months before I could move without painkillers. At least my helmet and gloves protected me."

Corey shook his head. He longed to believe this was all an elaborate ruse, and yet Zef was piling evidence up against Sebastian. It was more than Corey wanted to know.

"I do not know what to say. Why tell me all this? What do you want?" Corey asked.

"Oh, that is simple." Zef put his shirt back on. "Now that you know what your Captain is really like, I want you to consider a simple proposal. Before you answer, consider the following. Regardless of your personal opinions, the Star Rangers, as they are now, are doomed. The bounty on

Valentino's head has made them a pariah, unwelcome even to the Star Alliance. It is only a matter of time before he is overwhelmed, and you will be swept up in the tempest."

"There are plenty of nations interested in our services. We have already obtained a contract," Corey said.

Zef snorted. "You mean that insane deal with the Federation to fight the Lupine Order?"

Corey's ears shot upright. "How do you know of that? MerCom contracts are confidential!"

Zef rolled his shoulders. "We coyotes are resourceful. Regardless, you will not be fulfilling that contract, the Star Rangers are still in system. I engaged the Favored Sky in combat two days after your arrest."

"Considering that you are here now, and Sebastian's death would be galactic news, I am inclined to believe that he bested you."

Zef growled at Corey, pulling his lips back to expose his fangs. "Bested me! I outsmarted him, crippled his aero facilities, smashed his sublight engines and had him down to only two reactors. He was at my mercy, but like a fool, I closed and permitted him to execute a bold maneuver and escape."

"I would expect nothing less from my dear Captain. Sebastian has outsmarted every antagonist he has faced."

Zef leaned over the table and stared down at Corey. "Do you wish to know exactly how he escaped?"

"I am certainly interested."

"He fired a cannon round between our launch doors and into my landing deck, putting a hole into it, through which he shot a canister into engineering loaded with Florenzine. We lost two hundred loyal warriors to his war crimes and my foolishness."

Corey recoiled, his ears folded down in disgust. "Lies and slander! The Captain would never use Florenzine!"

"He did," Zef said. "Like father, like son."

"What is that supposed to mean?"

Zef's lips twisted in a sinister sneer. "You really do not know Valentino's familial history? A smart jackal like you? I assumed you would have done research."

"Research on what?"

"Tell me, Corey Delzano, how is your Great War history? Who was Marcel Stranahan?"

Corey grimaced, revolted at the mere mention. "He was the Retrograde Alliance field commander at the Battle of Mera Woods, responsible for two million combined Retrograde and Central deaths for a few hundred meters of territory. He is infamous for his repeated use of Florenzine gas. Why?"

"Your captain's real name is not Sebastian Valentino. It is Sebastian Stranahan."

Corey's eyes widened in shock and his ears stood up. "His father?"

"...is the Butcher of Mera Woods," Zef said.

Corey searched for signs that Zef was lying, yet found none. Corey felt ill. "What do you want from me?" he asked.

"I wish your assistance in apprehending Sebastian Valentino. I can arrange for your unconditional release and amnesty for all charges. Once you are free from Federation imprisonment, you will function as an internal operative within the Star Rangers. From there, it is merely a matter of providing you with the necessary communications equipment to mask your transmissions, so you can periodically keep me informed. It is up to you how you operate inside the Rangers, and whether or not you wish to engage in any sabotage."

An hour ago, Corey would have taken umbrage at such a proposal, but now his confidence wavered. It was not just Zef's stories of Sebastian's previous actions, but the underlying knowledge that he might die along with the Star Rangers. "What is in it for me?" Corey said.

Zef folded his arms and smiled down. "I am prepared to offer you no less than half the reward bounty. Should you wish to embark on a more permanent engagement, I could offer you lucrative employment within The Disintegrators, third in command perhaps. However, that is entirely your decision, and though I would greatly appreciate your strategic abilities in replenishing my depleted crew, I shall not pressure you on that point."

What could Corey do with a half-million dollars? He could retire, invest a portion, and live an enjoyable life through interest alone. He could found his own mercenary unit, purchase a handful of superlight or light titans, and forge a name for himself. He could settle down and start his own business, sell weapons or become a contracted advisor for one of the galaxy's militaries. The possibilities were nearly limitless.

"You said you can have me freed and absolved? What about my other imprisoned crewmen?" Corey said.

"You wish them released as well?"

"There is no alternative."

Zef sighed and stalked about the room. "You realize of course, that many of your compatriots are facing severe, multi-year imprisonment. It will be quite difficult to arrange freedom for all without arousing suspicion."

"I would rather serve time with my comrades than go free through covert dealings," Corey said.

Zef smiled. "You are truly noble, responsible, and selfless. That is quite unusual for a jackal. I am amazed that you got involved with such a trickster as Valentino. Now, your Arden Darksite is facing a life sentence for murder, which will be nearly impossible to have dismissed, but I can guarantee you, here and now, that I can have the rest of your fellows released by the end of this triad. If I have your cooperation."

Corey looked back up. He was torn inside; what Zef wanted was treason, and if word got out, it would permanently tarnish Corey's mercenary record. Despite the morality of helping to turn in a war criminal, nobody would hire him after knowing he had been disloyal to his employer.

Yet here he was, entertaining notions of betraying Sebastian. Sebastian had been nothing but amiable to Corey, taken him from a life of essential slavery to the Dominion's military to second in command in the most successful mercenary unit of all time. Could he really forsake that relationship?

"This is all so sudden. I must think before I can come to a conclusion," Corey said.

He watched Zef for any telling signs of sudden anger, but Zef remained tightly under control. "Very well," he said. "The day after tomorrow, I shall return promptly at 1200 local time. Until then, I bid you good day."

Zef rapped on the door. The guard unlocked it, and Zef disappeared back into the complex's hallways. The guard escorted Corey back to his cell.

Sterling looked up at Corey when he returned, and asked how it had gone, but Corey ignored him. Much as he enjoyed conversing with Sterling, he was in no mood to talk about what had just transpired. Instead, Corey lay down on his cot and resumed staring at the ceiling, mulling over Zef's offer. Sterling returned to his paper in silence.

You admit that these social support programs would almost exclusively benefit Strays and Outsiders, yet you suggest that the pedigreed Volpa of this great nation cough up nearly a fifth of their income to foot the bill? Such a plan can be described only as sheer madness.

-Darius Bosca, commenting on the Equity Program then being proposed in the Star Alliance Supreme Council, during a televised Councilor election debate, 4 Sagittaria 490. Bosca was subsequently elected Councilor for House Y'Ta'Leen in a landslide.

SCENE FIVE

Captain Sebastian Valentino and acting Assistant Captain Patricia Darling parked their rented sedan outside the Antarevo Reeducation Center. He wore a simple black cotton shirt touting the rock band Tumult, ripped denim jeans, a durahyde jacket, and a faded red baseball cap. She wore a pink sundress and woven wicker hat.

Patricia leaned on the car's roof and frowned across it at Sebastian. "Do we really have to do the vullisvolk scheme? It's embarrassing, yeah?"

"We need to elicit sympathy. Besides, it's a little late for second-guessing. This is the scam I chose, and you wanted to come along."

"That was before I saw what you wanted me to wear. Look at this." She tugged at her shoulder straps. "It's like I just walked out of a welfare office."

"I think it makes you look cute."

She scowled at him, prowled around to his side of the car, and lightly swatted Sebastian's head with her hat. "You hush. Carthagans are not cute, we're fearsome predators."

He flinched at the impact and frowned, ears tucked down. "Just relax and remember how I told you to act, everything will go fine. I'm the expert, dig?"

"At least Corey will be happy to see you, yeah?"

"Shocked is more like it. He probably thinks we're shooting wolves on Wixom by now."

They entered the administration building, were searched for weapons, and then sent to a waiting room. A dozen others of various species read trashy tabloid magazines or watched the brain-melting Federation News Channel on the waiting room television. Behind a cutout in the wall, a guishund receptionist waited for any approaching visitors, amusing herself with a crossword puzzle.

Sebastian stepped up to the counter, but the guishund didn't see his short form from behind her puzzle. What was it with receptionists and crosswords?

He knocked on the countertop. "Excuse me, guishund?"

"Can I help you?" she said, without looking up.

Sebastian leaned forward on his toes and put on the best backwater accent he could muster. "Yeah, I'm Billy, and this here's my girlfriend, Maggie. We're here to see us a prisoner."

The receptionist placed down her crossword, looked from Sebastian up to Patricia, and then turned to her computer. "All right, what're your full names?" she said.

"I'm Billy Herkensy, and this here's Maggie Sue Huggins," Sebastian said.

"And who are you here to visit?"

"Corey Delzano."

The receptionist paused in her typing to read the screen: trouble. "I'm sorry, sir, but this says you need to be pre-authorized to visit Mr. Delzano," she said.

Sebastian gaped at her, ears back. "But we talked to the man at the police quarters, he said it was okay!"

"Who said it was okay?"

Sebastian looked up to Patricia. "What was his name, baby-doll?"

Patricia tapped her muzzle. "Something like Blackman, or Blackstone, or…"

"Blackmore?" the receptionist asked.

"That's it!" Sebastian said.

The receptionist tapped more commands into her computer, and was scolded with a computerized buzzer. She tried again to no avail. "I'm sorry, but there's nothing in here from Mr. Blackmore about your visit," she said.

"What do you mean?" Sebastian said.

The receptionist leaned towards them and spoke in a raised voice, as if speaking louder would help them understand. "I'm afraid that means you can't visit Mr. Delzano without prior authorization."

Sebastian tucked his ears down. "You mean, we can't see him? But we came all the way from Dorfall, and Mr. Blackmore said it was hunky!"

"I'm sorry, but without prior authoriza—"

Patricia wailed suddenly, loud enough to startle Sebastian and the receptionist. Patricia leaned down, buried her head into Sebastian's shoulder, and started sobbing. Sebastian stroked the towering Patricia consolingly. "Now look at what you did, you made Maggie cry," he said. "Shh, it'll be all right, sweetie."

Patricia blathered unintelligible non-sequiturs, about how they had nothing else to do, and the money was all gone. Sebastian held her firmly around the side and glared at the receptionist.

The receptionist raised her paws. "I'm sorry, sir, but I can't break procedure—"

This elicited another weeping cry from Patricia, followed by indecipherable blabbering. Many of the seated onlookers now showed interest, and several glowered at the receptionist.

Sebastian patted Patricia's head and gave the receptionist a nasty look. "I swear I'll tell Mr. Blackmore all about this, you hear? And when he hears what you did to his good friend's son, he'll be awful spiteful!"

"Now now, let's not be quite so drastic about this," the receptionist said. "I'm sure I can get you in to see Mr. Delzano without needing to bother Mr. Blackmore. If I give you a temporary pass, maybe we can forget this all happened, okay?"

Sebastian smiled. "That'd be right kindly of you. Did you hear that, Maggie? We're going to get to see Corey!"

Patricia squealed happily, wrapped her arms about Sebastian, and squeezed heartily. Sebastian wheezed, the big carthagan's embrace forcing the air out of his lungs and lifting him a few centimeters off the floor.

The receptionist handed the pair identification stickers with the date stamped upon them. She pressed a button on her counter, and a metallic click sounded behind the door to their right. "Now, just head in on through that door," she said. "Straight ahead through the security checkpoint, put those stickers on your clothes where they're visible, and head to Visiting Room 6."

Sebastian took the stickers, handed one to Patricia, and smiled to the receptionist. "Thank you again, miss. You have a good day now."

They proceeded through the security checkpoint, headed down the hallway, and sat down in the uncomfortable, bolted-down steel chairs in the cramped visiting room.

Sebastian glanced around. "This is kind of pleasant, private and everything. Civil liberties are nice sometimes."

"I wouldn't know."

He chuckled. "Life in the Canis Dominion is pretty decent for Wild."

"Let's not get into that right now, yeah?" Patricia leaned on the tabletop. "How was my performance, anyway?"

"You're pretty good at this, baby-doll." Sebastian rubbed at his sore ribs. "A little too enthusiastic."

"It worked, yeah?"

"Next time warn me before you grab me, okay?"

Patricia chuckled and reached out to pat Sebastian's head, but he ducked out of the way. "That's what makes it so realistic," she said.

Sebastian chuckled, and then paused. The thumping of durahyde boots outside the room caught his ears, and seconds later, the room's door opened. A burly malamute guard ushered Corey in and locked the door behind him.

"Why, Billy, it is wonderful to see you again. And you brought Maggie, what a pleasant surprise," Corey said.

"They didn't want me to see you, but I convinced them to let me in." Sebastian leaned up, ears perked, and waited for the guard dog to walk away from the door. The moment he was out of listening range, Sebastian dropped his accent. "He's gone."

Corey walked to the table and sat in the uncomfortable straight-back steel chair. He looked the pair over and grinned. "I like your outfits. When was the last time you used the vullisvolk scheme, two years ago?"

"It's great for causing a scene," Sebastian said.

Corey nodded and looked straight into Sebastian's eyes. "Zef Kelev was here yesterday."

Sebastian's hackles rose, and his expression changed from jovial to steely sobriety. "What did that blowhard want?"

"He told me about your past with him, and Keller III. He showed me his scars. Is it true that you abandoned him?"

Sebastian hit the table with his fist. "I didn't abandon him, vex it! I had no choice, we'd have both died if we tried to fight."

Corey remained stoic. "Zef speaks the truth, then."

"He should have escaped with me, not stayed to fight! We didn't have a chance, they had enough heavy steel in there to build a bloody bridge!"

"You left him to die."

Sebastian snapped his teeth at Corey. He stood up, fur frazzled, and stalked across the room. "I didn't battle him across the system and risk capture to visit you, just to hear your accusations about the sticks he fed you!"

Patricia looked between the pair. "I'm lost."

Sebastian kept his back to them. He was in no mood to talk about his past, or to face Corey's accusations. Corey relayed the entire story to Patricia, from how Zef and Sebastian met, how they had fought across the galaxy, how the mission on Keller III went, and what had happened to Zef.

When Corey had finished, Patricia spoke. "Is this true, Captain?"

Sebastian tugged on his baseball cap, pulled on his whiskers, but didn't turn to face them. "Corey makes it sound worse than it is, but essentially it's true, yes."

"Why did you not tell me?" Corey asked.

"Because it embarrasses me!" Sebastian held his head. "I should've known better, sensed the ambush or taken a third titan with us, but I didn't. Zef was the first person I lost in combat, and it was all my fault. I thought we were invincible, I made a poor choice, and he died. I'd like to think I'm a better person now."

"It happened to Adrian," Corey said.

Sebastian whirled on his heels and stared hard at Corey. "No! Adrian was nothing like Zef! Adrian was faithful and loyal and levelheaded, Zef was as arrogant as I was!"

"You went into a mission undermanned and undergunned—" Corey said.

"No."

"—trusting only your own combat abilities and not listening to reason—"

"No!"

"—and then when you were ambushed and should have aborted, you pressed—"

"No, vex you!"

"—and got your second in command killed!"

Sebastian snarled. "I didn't kill Adrian! Zef killed Adrian!"

Corey recoiled, ears erect, his nose twitching. "What?"

"Zef killed Adrian," Sebastian said. "That stapard singer knew about the mission and tipped the Dominion off. They were ready when we came in."

"I do not believe you," Corey said.

"It's true," Patricia said. "I was on the bridge when Zef commed the ship, he confessed to it."

Sebastian stepped back over to the table, bracing himself on it and looking into Corey's face. "He shot Melissa, too. That means you're off the hook."

Corey hesitated. "What are you talking about, sir?"

Sebastian growled. "Don't lie to me, vex you! I'm not some wetnose kit born yesterday! I know about your excursion and I know you were there to assassinate me."

Patricia stared at Corey. "You were going to shoot the Captain?"

Corey shook his head. "I did not know he was the target. But how did you know about the mission?"

"There were 2.04 cubic meters of hydrofuel unaccounted for in the inventory," Sebastian said, "precisely enough for a passenger shuttle to fly from orbit to Stone Canyon and back. Teresa Ailesworth was upset, so I had Guido talk to her, and he told me what she'd said. Patricia's blatant lie about you spraining your back. And a comm from MerCom about a failed contract on Wexford II."

"How long have you known?" Corey said.

Sebastian gestured with a paw. "Long enough. I thought Melissa's death might've been your doing, but Ailesworth swore she hadn't fired, her aim is too good to have missed, and there were no bullets missing from inventory."

Corey nodded and hung his head, folded his paws, and stared down into his lap. Patricia's ears tipped back in shame and she looked away as well.

"I had not meant insubordination, Captain," Corey said, "but we needed the money—"

"Never mind it, affakravox. It's not important now," Sebastian said.

"Please do not call me that."

"What?"

"Please do not call me affakravox, call me jackal."

Sebastian skewed his ears, nose twitching. "I've used it thousands of times before and you never complained."

"I do not want you to call me by your Volpa words," Corey said.

"And what brought this on?" Sebastian said.

"My identity is not dependent upon what name your kind fabricated for us three hundred years ago. I am a jackal, not an affakravox."

"I'm sure the Captain meant no offense, yeah?" Patricia said.

"Carthagan is a Volpa word, too," Corey said. "Tell me, Captain, how does 'affakravox' translate?"

"It… it's not important. If it truly bothers you, I guess I don't have to use it."

"No. Tell me, tell Patricia what it means," Corey said.

"It's just a word, you know I'm not trying to be insulting—"

"What does it mean, Captain?" Patricia asked.

Sebastian folded his arms and glowered at the pair. "It means 'fake fox', okay?"

"And how can that not be offensive?" Corey said.

Sebastian thrust a paw across his chest. "You listen too much to that barker Zef. He's just trying to raise your tail, rile you, you know? He'll get you all running around in circles. What else did he tell you, anyway?"

"He said that he engaged you in starship combat, that he crippled the Favored Sky but you defeated him anyway," Corey said.

"That's true, yes. Patricia helped."

Corey looked up to Sebastian. "He said you used Florenzine."

Sebastian's shoulders stiffened. He shot a swift glance to Patricia, eyes narrowed in a warning to stay silent. "That's a lie," Sebastian said.

"He said that you fired a cannon into his landing deck, then launched a canister filled with gas into his engineering. That is quite impressive, Captain."

"It's not true."

"Then how did you escape?"

Sebastian scowled and stared down at the table. "It's not important."

Corey's eyes widened, and his ears wilted. "Sweet Kohoutek, it is true! You used poison gas on Zef's ship!"

"I did not!" Sebastian said.

"He said three hundred crewmen died from the Florenzine. For the Creator, Sebastian, that is three quarters of the Skyrider-class's crew!"

"He's lying! He's always lying, everything that singer says is lie," Sebastian said.

"Then how did you escape?"

Sebastian's fur stood on end. "I told you, it's not important! What's important is that we did."

"He said that he crippled your flight deck, he said his fighters did severe damage to the reactors and sublight engines. How did you fight him off with only two reactors?" Corey asked.

"I won't tell you again, it's not important how we escaped," Sebastian said.

"But the Favored Sky would not have had enough power for full combat operations with only two reactors—"

Sebastian clenched a fist and snarled. "I did it, I used Florenzine on him!"

Corey's ears folded down, his tail tucked up beneath his chair. "You know Florenzine is illegal. How could you do such a thing?"

"He was going to kill us all, Corey. He was going to kill me, and Patricia, and Pratt and Greco and Guido and Ailesworth and Argyle and Hartfield and everyone, I didn't have a choice. I had to do what I must to achieve victory."

Corey looked up with wide, brown eyes. "Just like your father."

A sharp stab of pain shot through Sebastian's body, making him spasm. He clenched both fists, so tight his skin turned ivory beneath his black fur. He tensed his jaw hard and gritted his teeth. "I don't know what you're talking about."

"Zef told me about that, too. He told me who your father was."

"Well, you shouldn't believe him."

"Is that what you really think, Sebastian Stranahan?" Corey asked.

Patricia blinked in surprise. "Stranahan? As in Field Commander Marcel Stranahan?"

Corey nodded. "His father."

"Is that why you had Florenzine on board the ship?" Patricia said.

Sebastian cringed, stepped back from the table, and glared at the two. "He's not me, I'm not him! I'm Sebastian Valentino!"

"I can't believe your father was the Butcher of Mera Woods. You of all people should know what Florenzine does," Patricia said.

Sebastian bristled. "We did what we had to do to achieve victory! That's what matters!"

"Is that what your father told you?" Corey said.

"Yes, and he was right!" Sebastian said. "I did what I must!"

"But he was a monster," Patricia said.

Sebastian snarled and lunged at her, barely resisting the urge to knock the bigger canine from her seat. He shook a fist into her face, his eyes wild and fierce. "You don't get to judge him, you didn't know him! It's not your place!"

"He sent millions of Retrograde troops to their deaths!" she said.

"He fought to win! People die in war! It's what happens!"

"What about their families?" she said.

Sebastian brought his face up to Patricia's, his nose almost touching hers, before he abruptly pulled away and backpedalled halfway across the room. "What about my family?" he said. "We Stranahans had a long and proud legacy, we had a history of being loyal and fierce warriors, we'd served the Alliance well for a hundred years. We were this close." Sebastian held his fingers a centimeter apart. "This close to earning a pedigree from House Lafayette. The PA had debated it, we were going to be one of only two created pedigrees in House Lafayette! Not since Cortney was formed in 373…"

Sebastian sighed heavily. "The Battle of Mera Woods changed all that. Now everyone associates our line with my father, with millions of deaths and poison gas and supposed war crimes. I've had to spend my entire life living under the stigma of my last name, tried to bury it, but it keeps popping up to haunt me."

Sebastian turned his back to them, stalked across the room, and slumped forward against the padded wall. Why must this come out now, when he'd been doing so well, earning a career? It was bad enough he was a stray, and the bounty had impinged on his ability to find contracts. When the galactic news media discover his deception, he'd never get another contract with any civilized nation.

"I am sorry, Captain, I did not realize how much this hurt you," Corey said.

"You studied us," Sebastian said. "You should know how much family history means in the Volpa galaxy."

"They did not teach us much about disgraced lines."

Sebastian tensed and barked, punched the padded wall, and then his shoulders fell. He sighed and turned to look at them. "It's bad enough being a stray in the Alliance. We can't own businesses, we can't vote in House or national politics, we can't join all the pedigree-only clubs."

Corey's ears pricked upright, and he canted his head to one side. "That is it, is it not? That is why you became a mercenary."

"What?" Sebastian said.

"You came so close to earning a pedigree, a name with honor and prestige, and it was taken away from you. You want those things so badly; you want respect, admiration, to be known by name."

Sebastian grimaced and tucked his head down, face partially hidden in his jacket. "You've been talking to Guido too much."

"I think it is true. You want recognition from your peers, to show that just because of your family name, you are not a disgrace," Corey said.

Sebastian's eyes took on a glassy look. Corey was right, it was what every stray wanted. For one glorious moment, when his father was successful, he'd tasted it: schooled with pedigreed children, places in educational politics, a starting position on the arena gridiron team. Then came word of the Battle of Mera Woods, and it all came crashing down, hard. Even the other strays shunned him after his family's fall from grace. It was worse for him, fighting tooth and nail just to lose a little less badly. Having nothing was awful, but it was better than having it all taken away. Even in the military, only Adrian had seen past the stigma of his name and recognized his talent. That was gone.

Sebastian couldn't admit that out loud, not to Corey, not even to himself. So he didn't.

"What else did Zef want?" Sebastian said.

Corey sighed and frowned. "He wants me to betray you."

"For what?" Patricia said.

"Half the bounty."

"You're not going to do it, are you, Corey?" Sebastian said.

"Of course not. You are my employer and my friend, I would never betray that trust, despite what you have done."

Sebastian turned to face him and nodded. "Well, if you were, you wouldn't tell me, anyway."

"Zef says he can have our comrades freed."

Sebastian shrugged. "So? He says a lot of things."

"I will tell him yes, have him release our crewmen, and then not follow through with his plan."

Sebastian sighed. "Don't do that, Corey. Zef has an elaborate network of contacts, he knew where I was, where I was going, and that you got arrested almost as soon as it happened. He'd turn on you, get us all wanted in the Federation. Or, worse, disclose my use of Florenzine and get us all shot. The only reason he hasn't done that is that he's too proud to admit I beat him."

Corey nodded. "Then I shall rebuff him. But what of our crewmen?"

"I guess they must serve their sentences," Sebastian said.

"There's really nothing we can do?" Patricia asked.

"From what I understand, it's election season. Councilman Robinson wants to look tough on crime, so he rammed all the cases through. When I get some free time, I'll look into the Federation legal system, see if I can find some technicality."

"I understand, sir," Corey said.

Sebastian ambled back to the table and sat. "I tried to see you sooner, but we've been busy with everything."

"Yes sir. How is the unit doing?"

"We... we're doing fine," Sebastian said.

"How badly did Zef damage the Favored Sky?"

Sebastian exchanged a nervous glance with Patricia. "Oh, pretty badly, really," he said.

"How long will repairs take?" Corey asked. "I imagine Argyle up there, stalking about the ship, griping about you getting her 'all shot up'—"

"We had to sell the Favored Sky," Sebastian said.

Corey's ears shot to attention. "What?"

"We couldn't afford the repairs necessary to get her back into service," Sebastian said. "We sold her and dismissed most of the crew."

Corey stared back at Sebastian. "Are you baiting my trail? Did you try to get a loan?"

"Sixteen times. They said my credit was rubbish, our remaining titans and aerofighters weren't enough collateral. The biggest one anyone offered wouldn't have covered fixing the structural damage," Sebastian said.

Corey stared down at the table. "What about our record? What about our MerCom ranking?"

"MerCom was all over us when we reached gravdock. Before we even had the Favored Sky appraised, they devalued the unit. We're not even in the A-tier anymore."

"We are no longer #1 then. Zef?" Corey asked.

Sebastian gritted his teeth and frowned. "Zef didn't earn his position like I did. He never would've overtaken me in his own career, he got it by default."

Corey only nodded. "Did you try offering the Morgette as collateral?"

"The Morgette is the only thing we have left, and even for a dropship, it's not really worth much," Sebastian said.

"What was the compensation for the Favored Sky?"

"Enough to pay outstanding debts and back-payroll, and give the dismissed crew the MerCom-required minimum severance. We've also got some extra operating capital."

Corey forced a hopeful smile. "Well, you and the rest of the Star Rangers can find a lucrative titaneering contract, increase our ranking, procure a larger loan, and reconsign the Favored Sky—"

"They've already cut it for scrap. Structure, armor, they decommissioned the reactors, brought in a hazmat crew and everything. We even had to sell the possessions of all the fallen. Yours are in storage, by the way."

Corey's expression sunk. "Then we are finished."

"Don't say that!" Sebastian snapped. "As long as I'm alive, we're not finished."

"You are past the average age for a mercenary. You are close to your species' life expectancy. Maybe it is time for you to retire, settle down," Corey said.

"There's no place in the galaxy I could hide from the Dominion's bounty."

Patricia angled her muzzle into the conversation. "Maybe if you retired, they'd cancel the bounty, yeah?"

Sebastian looked between the pair. "You're both from the Dominion, you can't believe that. I've embarrassed them. Even if I weren't a threat, they'd still hunt me for revenge."

"Like Kelev," Corey said.

"Yeah, blood oath and all that hokum." Sebastian twisted his muzzle and stood up. He glared down at Corey, but said nothing to him. "Come Patricia, we should be leaving."

"What do you wish me to do, Captain? Should I cease calling you that?" Corey asked.

Sebastian shrugged. "You're still under contract. I can't legally dismiss you without paying your contractual severance, and Federation law won't let me do that while you're in jail. I wouldn't release anyway, I don't know what they'd do to you if you lost your ICT protection. Besides." He gestured inclusively to Corey and Patricia. "I'd like you to stick around. You're both good titanists."

Corey stood. "I would like that as well. We shall see where the unit is upon my release. Avoid any reckless actions, Sebastian."

Sebastian smiled. "I'll try not to praise the bone."

"Kohoutek be with you, sir," Corey said.

"*Yasha-marsa, kehnellya,*" Sebastian said.

Sebastian walked to the door, but Patricia grabbed him by the shoulder. "Do you mind if I stay and talk to Corey a few more minutes? I won't be long."

Sebastian squinted up at her, stared into her eyes, and nodded. "I'll meet you outside. Don't take too long, dig?"

He left the waiting room. Fifteen minutes later, Patricia met him outside. Sebastian never asked what she'd talked to Corey about. He left the facility, and walked into the final chapters of the Star Rangers' lifespan.

ACT III

Never trust the fox, for he lies. Never trust his sharp, silver tongue and quick wit. Never trust his painted skies, the fanciful tales of power, greed, and lust. Never trust his motives, nor his face, for they only present what you wish to see. A fox would not hesitate to deceive you, steal you blind, leave you cold and shivering and betrayed. A fox would help you find a coin, and when you bent to retrieve it, he would plunge the knife in your back and take it for himself.

The fox is vain and selfish. If you are careless, he will use you for his own means, a cog in his machine of self-advancement. He will tread on you, yet make you beg for it. He will let you guard the front while he pilfers the back. He will befriend you only so long as it suits him. Do not shake his hand, for he will steal your fingers.

Never trust the fox, he lies.

-The Rha'keesha, Book Four: Lessons, Passage 1, Chapter 1, Verse 1-13.

SCENE ONE

Thick clouds gathered over the city of Cornwall, piled high against the increasing elevation of the nearby Ridge Mountains. They cast an ominous grey pall across the super-corridor metropolis, the city that now served as the impromptu headquarters of Valentino's Star Rangers. It was three hundred kilometers away from the city of Acton, the site of the shooting and Corey's arrest; for Sebastian Valentino, it wasn't far enough.

By mid-afternoon, rain was falling, and heavy drops pelted Sebastian's rented sedan. He pulled into the parking lot of a vast shopping center. "We're here," he said.

Patricia Darling climbed out of the passenger seat, already scowling. "This is the right address, yeah?"

Sebastian drew a slip of paper from his pocket. "442 Broad Street."

"Look at this, this is a car dealership!"

"Oh, is that what this is?" Sebastian said. "I saw all the autos and assumed it was a popular restaurant."

Patricia said. "Wacky as always. You had fifteen days to find a contract, and this is your best?"

Sebastian tugged the collar on his windbreaker up to shield his neck from the rain. "It's a front. And it's not easy finding a decent contract outside of MerCom."

"I thought we didn't need MerCom."

"Let that go, okay?" Sebastian shook his head, and bent to tap the sedan's rear window. It rolled down, revealing the stocky muzzle of a male dhole. "Greco, wait here, watch the car," Sebastian said.

Greco nodded. "Sure thing, sir. Good luck."

Sebastian smiled absently, and set off to the dealership's entrance. Patricia followed, head tucked down against the driving rain. "So tell me about this, yeah?" she said. "Who're we here to see?"

"Josephina Storm."

"You trust her?"

"Yes, I do. I'm sure she's a good fox."

"How do you know she's a fox?" Patricia asked.

"Storm is one of the oldest and most reputable pedigrees in House Arielle."

Patricia frowned. "I thought you didn't like the pedigreed."

Sebastian skewed his ears outward. "Historically, Arielle's been the friendliest to… nonpedigreed. Their territory also borders the Dominion, so one of them should be more open to hiring us."

They walked onto the building's concrete apron and stood beneath its awning, out of the rain. Sebastian smoothed down his head fur, brushing raindrops from it. He scanned the area for any suspicious people, and was about to step inside, when Patricia stopped him.

"Heel a second, straight me here," she said. "You'd judge another fox you haven't met based solely on their last name?"

Sebastian tilted his head. "I don't see why not."

"Don't you find that hypocritical?"

"Hypocritical?"

"You whelp about how the pedigreed prejudice you over your last name. You're doing the same thing here, yeah?"

Sebastian shook his head and sighed. He tugged his fur back into place and looked up at her. "It's not hypocritical. This is how the Volpa do things. I can judge them because they're similar, but I can't be compared to other strays, we're all different."

"I'll never understand you foxes."

Sebastian chuckled. "Good thing you don't have to. Now, do you have any more pressing questions?"

"Yeah. What exactly do you want me to do here?"

"Don't say anything, don't ask questions, just stand there, square your shoulders, look intimidating."

Patricia frowned. "Like a dumb guard mutt, yeah?"

Sebastian pulled his windbreaker in closer, leaned against the building's façade, and looked up to Patricia. "No. Like my second in command. You have to be capable of adapting to whatever role I need you to fill at the time. Since we've got no security staff left, I need you to look imposing. You know?"

"I suppose, but why don't you want me to ask any questions?"

"You'll be more intimidating if you don't speak. Like a mountain, dig?"

Patricia chuckled. "I've never been compared to a mountain before."

"I don't see why not." Sebastian leaned up on his toes. "You're sixty centimeters taller than me and you're pretty built for a carthagan. Now come, let's get this over with."

Sebastian ruffled his jacket's collar up into place, tensed his shoulders, and stepped into the dealership. It was shiny, orderly, ceramic tile floors and polished aluminum walls. Various display automobiles were assembled throughout the showroom: a cherry red convertible with white top, a dark blue light truck, a glazed-white family sedan, all typical products.

Sebastian couldn't take a step before a salesdog intercepted him, a towering, smiling malamute in a business suit. "Welcome to Metrostar Caledon, your Caledon Motors dealership for the metropolitan Cornwall area! You can travel near or far in a Caledon motorcar! I can tell by the look of you, you're a fox who knows what he wants! Why, I bet you've had your eye on this little baby since you stepped in the door." The salesdog gestured towards the red convertible.

"Well—"

"You'd love her, a nice, brand-new Mark XII Caledon LaSalle convertible." The salesdog placed a broad paw onto Sebastian's shoulder and steered him towards the vehicle.

"Isn't that redundant?" Sebastian asked. "Aren't all LaSalles convertibles?"

"Ah, I can see you know your automobiles! Well you'll be thrilled to know then that the base LaSalle comes with features like power windows, power locks, *and* power roof, all standard. You can get it with either the fuel-sipping 570 or 1000cc turbine, or if you need more power, you can opt for the 1550cc turbine, making 127 kilowatts!"

"Actually—"

The salesdog forcibly grabbed Sebastian's shoulder and pointed him at the car. "Ah, but I can tell you are a rebel, a renegade, with that smirk! Well then, you'll love the turbo-charged, 187 kilowatt 1524cc rotary. It combines outstanding fuel economy – 9.3 kilometers per liter fastway – with unbeatable performance. And the Mark XII LaSalle comes equipped with the new variable-aperture system, ensuring maximum turbo-charged airflow from two hundred on up to two thousand RPMs, virtually eliminating turbo-lag!"

"Well, it's a nice car and all, but—"

The salesdog crouched to put himself near eye-level for Sebastian, and affectionately stroked the vehicle's door. "Can't you just imagine? Top down, gliding along the fastway, wind in your fur, out on the Coastal Route, perhaps! And with the LaSalle's low curb weight of only 1500 kilograms, its patented Pneu-Maximizer power steering and double wishbone suspension, you can wind your way through the country-side with ease! With more options than you can fetch a stick with, the Mark XII LaSalle has something for everyone, whether you want an affordable, fun, sporty car to get you around town, or a high-performance convertible to show your status in life! Now, let's talk financing—"

The salesdog stood, grabbed Sebastian by the shoulder, and tried to maneuver him away, but Sebastian broke from the hold with a sharp shoulder twist. "Look, it's really a nice car," Sebastian said, "but it's not why I'm here—"

The salesdog's eyes lit up, and he gestured broadly towards the nearby blue truck. "Then maybe you'd be interested in this wonderful little workboat, the Palomino bakkie. It's got the performance and durability you need at a cost that won't break the bank! And it comes with—"

Sebastian's hackles raised and he barked, disrupting the salesdog's routine. "I'm not here to look!"

"You're not?"

"No," Sebastian said. "My name is Marcus Malone, of Malone Financial. You know, 'Get a loan from Malone'?"

Sebastian nodded suggestively, and the salesdog bobbed his head in acceptance. "Oh, sure, I've heard of you," he said. "What can I do for you, Mr. Malone?"

"I've already arranged a sale with Josephina Storm, and I'm here to pick it up. It's a cobalt blue Crusader with a sunroof and a white cheater stripe down the side," Sebastian said.

The salesdog frowned down at Sebastian. His ears swiveled backwards slightly. "Cobalt blue?"

"Yes, cobalt blue. I want to pick it up, I've got a meeting with a client at 1600."

The salesdog hesitated, so Sebastian gestured for Patricia to step forward. She backed the salesdog up against the truck's cab. She stood several centimeters taller than him, her tail held high and dominant.

The salesdog held his paws up defensively. "All right. Follow me."

He escorted them down a hallway and into one of a half-dozen sales offices. It was comfortable and inviting, with a sizable durahyde couch, faux wood wall paneling, marketing photographs of automobiles and fantasized landscapes adorning its walls, and a desk with surprisingly few papers upon it.

The salesdog gestured for them to sit. "Wait here," he said.

Sebastian waited for him to disappear, and then he set to work searching the office. Patricia opened her mouth to speak, but Sebastian immediately silenced her with a paw. He motioned for her to watch the door, and she complied.

Sebastian filed through the desk papers, tugged on locked drawers, peered under the frames of wall paintings, and checked the lamps. He found a hidden microphone in the couch, tugged it free, and slipped it into his pocket.

Before he could search for more, Patricia flagged him. Sebastian swiftly dropped into an innocuous pose on the couch, and Patricia followed suit. A mid-size borzoi entered the room, female, lithe, and graceful. Instead of the business suit typical of sales representatives, she wore a pair of ripped jeans, white-dyed denim jacket, and a black T-shirt with the album cover of Meganova's 'Steel Force' on it.

She smiled and strolled straight up to Sebastian. "Sebastian Valentino! I'm glad you came, I've heard so much about you, it's an honor to meet you! I've seen your ads for the Corvair, Triple-M must have paid you a fortune!"

"Maxwell Military Manufacturing has deep pockets," he said.

She chuckled and nodded, her tail wagging pleasantly. "They sure do. You know, you're far shorter in person than you are on television." She leaned over him and inspected him. "So's your tail."

Sebastian narrowed his eyes and slid back. "My tail is as long as ever."

"No, it was definitely longer on television. Did you lose some of it? You know what I heard, when foxes really trash something up, they get a decimeter of their tail cut off as punishment. Savage!"

Sebastian stared up at her, eyes narrowed, and said nothing.

She chuckled and shook her head. "Of course, that's just silly rumor, no people are that uncivilized. Right?"

He grit his teeth, fighting off a growl. "Who are you, anyway?"

"Oh my, I've forgotten! Sorry." She thrust a paw towards Sebastian's chest. "Josephina Storm, at your service!"

Sebastian ignored the handshake. "You're not what I expected."

"Why? Because girls can't like cacophony rock?" She gestured towards her shirt.

"Because you're not a fox," Sebastian said.

Josephina twisted one ear. "That a problem?"

"You have the surname of a pedigree. That makes you an interloper."

Josephina stepped back, her expression soured. "And you're a stray who's been rejected numerous times for pedigree. I'd have thought you'd be supportive of us."

He shook his head. "Interloping is a grave affront to the honor of all Volpa, pedigreed or not."

Josephina crossed her arms and stood straight, her nose twitching. "Perhaps you'd like to leave."

Sebastian hardened his gaze, stared Josephina over, and frowned. Though no express mention had been made of Josephina Storm being an Outsider, he still felt deceived. The Storm surname was part of the reason he'd chosen this contract. He couldn't ignore the other part; they were offering a large sum of money, and he couldn't let his own pride stand in the way, not when he'd already lost so much.

"No," Sebastian said.

"I'm pleased. It was difficult tracking you down, especially now," Josephina said.

"You had me in mind?"

Josephina offered her paw to Patricia to shake, but she ignored her and remained stoic. Josephina frowned, and then turned about to sit at the room's desk. "We did, yes, for quite some time, long before that incident and its nasty aftereffects."

"Should I be flattered?" Sebastian said.

"I'd think flattery for someone of your reputation would be impossible."

"So say you. What's the deal with the whole Crusader bit, anyway?"

Josephina unlocked her desk drawer and rummaged through it. "It's just a code, like in those spy photoplays. The Crusader doesn't come in cobalt blue."

What sort of outfit was Sebastian getting the Star Rangers involved with?

"So why do the Children of the Dawn need a front, anyway? I thought you were legitimate," Sebastian asked.

"In most parts of the galaxy, we are, but everyone has a different definition of legitimate. We don't fit into the Federation's plans; as far as they're concerned, the only charity should be the government."

"No offense, but you're not a charity."

"We have charitable programs," Josephina said. "Free clinics, homeless shelters, food banks, the like. We only advocate force when all peaceful options fail."

"Peaceful options?"

Josephina glanced up from her drawer. "Demonstrations, funding of alternative parties, ballot initiatives, bribery, voter education, vigils, media advertisement, exercising free radio."

"That can't possibly work in places like the Dominion."

"Funny you should bring them up." Josephina drew out a packet of papers and tossed them to Sebastian. "That's where we want you to go."

Sebastian caught the bundle and glared at it. "You know I'm wanted in the Dominion."

"We do. We also know that the bounty made the Alliance drop you hotly, which is really a shame, you were doing so much for our cause," Josephina said.

Sebastian's ears shot up. "You knew about that?"

"The Alliance and Sip Secord? Of course, there's no secrets in the galaxy. You're lucky he didn't turn you in for impersonating a pedigreed. Now read your mission briefer."

Sebastian skimmed through the booklet's text. Much of it was composed of flowery rhetoric, words like 'freedom' and 'liberty', and phrases like 'self-determination' and 'eliminating tyrannical oppression'. Such language had sent civilized nations to war since time immemorial, but one thing caught Sebastian's eye.

"You want me to go to Thanton?" he asked.

"That a problem?"

Sebastian scowled at her. "Only if you count the fact that I've attacked Thanton six times in the past four years, and they're rather upset about that. Or that the Dominion's brought up the entire Sixteenth War Group – including the starcruiser Regulus – to augment the Thanton Planetary Guards."

"But that's precisely it," Josephina said. "The Canis Dominion has nearly lost control of the system thanks to your attacks. They're the closest Dominion world to self-liberation."

"You mean rebellion."

Josephina tipped her muzzle downwards, a scowl on her muzzle. "We don't start rebellions, we just encourage them. The Canis Dominion has no right to oppress the people of Thanton. Given your record in attacking them, you must agree."

"Yes, yes, it's a tragedy of epic proportions. Tell me what I'm looking at here."

Josephina opened her own packet and followed along. "Page three is your mission description and outline. It's a simple strike campaign, duration seventy-two hours, to commence the third of Carkinus. Jump transport and dropship ferrying will be included, as well as reimbursement for all documentable ammunition expenditures, at the mission-completion market value. Your targets are listed in the outline. The letters correspond to the map on the next page."

Sebastian read the list of targets from the page. "Hydrofuel refinery, ammunition warehouse, titan repair facility, plastic plant, power transformers. These are all strategic targets."

"The further we can erode the Dominion's military resources, the less control they'll have over the populace," Josephina said.

He flipped to the next page, a crude photocopy of a satellite image. Labels and symbols scribbled across it in thick black marker traced a long arc from one end to the other, ending near a fuzzy blotch that Sebastian assumed indicated mountains.

"This is your defined mission zone," Josephina said. "The circles are your insertion and extraction points. You're going to cut across the backyard of the Canis Dominion's presence on the continent of Lowan. The lettered squares are your primary targets."

Sebastian's nose twitched as he looked over the map. Something about it seemed amiss, unprofessional, but he kept his concerns to himself. The next several pages were satellite images of the targets. He recognized their source as Canis Dominion reconnaissance satellites.

"You said dropship transport was included," he said. "We've got our own."

"You can't use your dropship, the Dominion would recognize it and drop a sledge on you. We'll be using an unmarked dropship, it'll dust off as soon as you're in. You'll have to maintain radio silence, so you'll be on your own as far as resupply goes. If you need anything, you'll have to get it yourself. You won't get a second shot for extraction, so you'll need to make every effort to get to the dust-off zone."

Sebastian's ears drooped; this was starting to feel wrong. "And what happens if we don't?"

"I imagine you'd have to find alternate means to get off-world."

"Like?"

"Well, there's a significant rebel presence on the planet," Josephina said. "They'd probably smuggle you out."

Sebastian shook his head and braced his elbow on the couch's armrest. "Do you have any idea what would happen to me if I were captured by the Canis Dominion?"

Josephina shrugged her lithe shoulders. "If I were to hazard a guess, I suppose that you'd be thoroughly interrogated and tortured. Then you'd be paraded through the streets of Pommelstad, probably naked and subjected to jeering, spitting crowds. After that would come the show trial, where you'd be portrayed as an enemy of all civilization, though you'd inevitably be found guilty. You would be marched out to Riverfront Plaza, and in front of tens of thousands of gathered spectators, you'd meet the gallows. And then Governor Arlanda would have a new pelt for his wall."

Sebastian scowled, ivory teeth peeking past his lips. "I'd be killed, is what you're saying."

"More or less. But we're not expecting you to be captured."

"Why's that?"

Josephina tipped her muzzle downwards. "You're Sebastian Valentino. You're the best of the best. If anyone could foxtrot into the Dominion, bite them on the leg, and scamper out safely, it'd be you. Moreover, it's really not an offer you can refuse."

"Howsa?" he asked.

Josephina leaned over the desk, bracing her elbows on it. "The way I see it, there's two paths for the Star Rangers. One is for you to fade into infamy and obscurity, with persistent rumors about the legality of your methods, until you're finally caught several years from now and executed. Or you can claw your way back into the light and earn yourself a tidy sum of money in the process."

Sebastian quirked his ears. "Just how much of a tidy sum?"

"We're prepared to offer you 250,000D up front and 2,000,000D upon completion, pending verification of your effectiveness and minus penalties for missed targets. Aside from operating costs, the Children of the Dawn are prepared to grant you a few bonuses, 20,000D for each enemy titan destroyed, 10,000D for each vehicle, and 50D for each confirmed enemy casualty."

His heart skipped a beat. This was nearly the largest contract he'd ever been offered, and when the bonuses were factored in, it only became sweeter. Josephina was right; this wasn't a contract he could turn down, no matter how dodgy it appeared.

And to strike the Dominion in Thanton, of all places, in the midst of the vaunted Canine People's Army? Sebastian would earn unimaginable prestige, and the Canis Dominion might be so embarrassed as to cancel the bounty. It might even curry favor with House Lafayette's Pedigree Administration, stigma or no.

"I think we've got a deal," Sebastian said.

"Excellent! Your up-front fee will be deposited immediately, and you'll have two days to muster your forces and purchase any necessary supplies. Our dropship loadmaster will contact you and arrange for loading of your strike team, you'll have space for four titans and a support vehicle. And then off you'll go! Oh, one last thing." Josephina pushed a pen and a paper with attached carbon sheets to him. "Sign that. Top copy's yours, bottom copy's ours, the other is for you to report to MerCom when you're done."

Sebastian glanced the form over, found everything in order, and signed it. "I believe we're done here, dig? Pleasure doing business with you."

Josephina reached out with a paw; this time, Sebastian shook it. "Likewise!" she said. "Best of luck to you! Say, you don't suppose I could interest you in a new LaSalle convertible, do you? Zero down and no payments until the first of Scorpius!"

He pulled his paw free, gestured for Patricia to follow him, and escaped from the dealership. It was late afternoon by now, and even though the steady rain had ended, a grey blanket of clouds kept the day overcast. Sebastian walked to the sedan, instructed Greco to drive, and ushered Patricia into the backseat with him.

Patricia held her tongue until Greco shifted the car into drive. "Now wait just a bloody minute, Sebastian. What's going on here?" she asked.

Sebastian glanced up at her. "What do you mean?"

"Look, I'm no stapard. I could see the way you were eying that wolfhound and her papers. Something's up with this mission, yeah? What madness is this, you've got us using somebody else's dropship!"

"It's a perfectly acceptable method of operation for those who don't have their own facilities."

Patricia shook her head. "But we've got a dropship! This whole mission feels wrong."

"You're probably right." Sebastian pulled out the mission briefer, flipped to the map, and showed it to her. "Look at this. Tell me what's wrong."

She peered at it. "Let's see. There's no scale, no compass, no indication of cities or bases or terrain."

"It's also upside-down." Sebastian inverted the page. "North is this way."

"So what's the problem?"

"Several. For one, the distance they want us to travel in 72 hours is a little under 2,000 kilometers. When you figure in the time we need to rest and recharge the titan's fuel cells, that distance becomes very long indeed. For another, this mission zone follows the Kinsha River, and it's decently inhabited and ends at Umber City, which is not only a major milindustrial center, but it's Lowan's capital. It's already heavily guarded, but the Dominion's also got half the Sixteenth War Group holed up there. Finally, this is all plains, there's going to be almost nowhere for us to hide from aero attack."

"That's suicide, we'd never stand up to any stiff aero resistance."

Sebastian leaned back in his seat. "Oh, it's not really so bad since they closed Rixford."

"Rixford?"

"Yeah, Rixford Aerobase. They had to cut back on military spending, so they just let it sit around and rot for a dozen years, and now they're using it as a titan repair facility. That's our target at Nav Charlie. Anyway, the nearest aerobase is Norford, about a hundred kilometers outside the dust-off zone. It's far enough away to keep the aerofighters off our back, or at least cut down their loiter times. The Dolphins shouldn't be able to stay on station more than thirty minutes."

"That's no good."

Sebastian shrugged. "Well, the terrain gets rougher near Umber City, so it'll be easier to hide from aero attack—"

Patricia frowned. "I mean, they're trying to deceive us, yeah?"

"I don't know, maybe not intentionally. The Children of the Dawn aren't an inherently military organization, so there's no telling how experienced they are at this. They're loosely organized with a nebulous command chain. It could be these orders were hastily passed down from some higher ups."

"You've got these doubts," Patricia said. "Why take the contract?"

Sebastian glanced out the window as the car pulled out onto the city's main streets. "I've got about two million reasons. Plus bonuses."

"Captain—"

"We need the money, Patricia. I can't keep paying you out of my pocket just so you can hang around, dig?"

Patricia grabbed him by the shoulder. "But do we need to be killed?"

Sebastian snapped to face her. "We won't be killed!"

"How do you know?"

"Because I'm the best! I can't be killed! We'll go in there, bite them until they bleed, then sail home and count our millions."

Patricia shook her head. "I still think this is too dangerous, yeah?"

Sebastian sighed and looked away, watching shops and restaurants pass by. "Nobody's forcing you to come, but it'd be a shame to lose you."

"I don't want to leave. You're like a mentor to me, yeah? I just think it'd be better to be a little more cautious right now, we're depleted so much as it is."

He patted her shoulder. "It's not just the money, Patricia. It'll get our names back into the ranks, even if they're just the B-tier."

She nodded softly. "I guess you're right, yeah? So what else do you know about the Children of the Dawn?"

"They were supposedly formed to foster self-government and democratic rule in countries that don't allow it. They're mostly a bunch of starry-eyed dreamers, but they've gotten progress in a few places, got a couple ballot initiatives in Balkany and Rhodesia passed. They've also been known to sponsor some terrorist activity."

"I've heard they're backed by Star Alliance nationalists," Patricia said. "That's why they target the Canis Dominion often, and why they want Thanton liberated, so that the system would join the Alliance."

"Thanton would be better off in the Alliance anyway," Sebastian said.

Patricia stared hard at him. "And what makes you think they'd be better off under fox control?"

"They'd have opportunities they're not afforded in the Dominion, a better life, higher standard of living."

Patricia held up a hand and counted on her fingers. "Non-foxes in the Star Alliance can't own land or houses, they can't vote at all, they can't assemble in groups of twelve or more, they can't even own businesses. They make fifty cents to the dollar."

"They're free to get any job they want, move around, go to college."

"So long as they don't leave the Cultural Zones, you mean."

Sebastian shrugged. "I don't see the problem, they're still better off in the Alliance than in the Dominion. Half of vulpine pay is more than all of canine pay. In the Dominion, Familiars are essentially a servant class. You should know that," Sebastian said.

She shook her head. "It's not much different than it is in the Alliance. They're harsh to their own kind, the strays like you, yeah?"

Sebastian glowered back at her. "Even as a stray, I had a better life than I would anywhere else in the galaxy. Even the Outsiders—"

"Outsiders?" Patricia said. "You call us Outsiders?"

Sebastian grimaced in regret. He shouldn't have let that slip. "That's what the Alliance calls them, to distinguish them from pedigreed and strays. You know I don't call you that, you've never heard me use that word in your presence, have you?"

Patricia looked down. "Well, no, I haven't. But you admit that the Alliance does."

He turned to look into her eyes. "Patricia, it's better for strays and non-foxes in the Alliance than it is anywhere else in the galaxy. There's more chances, better medical care, better schools, higher income. Even most of the upper-class Wild in the Dominion don't earn as much money as the non-foxes in the Alliance."

"Maybe you're right. But the Alliance isn't perfect, yeah?"

Sebastian nodded softly. "I suppose it isn't. I think it's our best shot for real improvement for civilization, though. We're far more equitable to minorities in the Alliance than the Dominion is to theirs. You heard what Josephina said, about what they'd do to me."

Patricia smirked. "I think she understated it a margin, yeah?"

He chuckled. "Probably. Now don't worry your head about politics, okay? I could no more change Alliance policies than I could quench the sun. And I've always been equitable to you and your kind, haven't I?"

"Always."

"I've given opportunity to Dominion refugees because I knew they could prove they were worthwhile, that just because they were born collies or gersheps or corgen didn't make them useless and inferior. I paid them all more than the going rate, and my success was our success."

Patricia flicked her ears and nodded. "You're right. I guess I was harsh criticizing you, yeah?"

Sebastian smiled. "It's hunky, really. I do value your input, even if you're a bit stiff-tailed about it sometimes."

Patricia tilted her head and glanced down to Sebastian's tail. "Speaking of which…"

Sebastian frowned and tucked his tail against his leg, out of Patricia's view. "What?"

"Well, your tail *is* shorter."

"It is not."

Patricia chuckled. "If you don't want to talk about it, that's fine."

"There's nothing to talk about," he said. "Nothing happened."

"Just thought I'd ask. I didn't believe Josephina, that sounds so brutal and trashy. The Dominion never mentioned it when they talked about your kind."

"What did they tell you?"

Patricia shrugged. "Lots of stuff. You're untrustworthy, dangerous, immoral, malicious to other genera. And you lie a lot."

Sebastian scoffed. "Stereotypes."

"Well, every stereotype has a bit of truth, yeah?" she said. "I mean, no offense, but you're hardly trustworthy to people outside the unit."

Sebastian twisted his lips into a dark scowl. "Why should I be? I don't know them, they don't know me."

"You think it's best to steal and cheat, if it's in your interests?"

"Did they tell you that in the Dominion?"

Patricia shook her head. "No. It's what I've observed from you."

Sebastian crossed his arms and leaned against the door panel. "It's not my fault they're not aware of their situation. If you see a weakness, you should attack it."

"That implies everyone around you is an enemy."

"And what's to say they're not?"

Patricia frowned. "That's a selfish way to be, yeah? How're you supposed to make friends?"

Sebastian shrugged. "They do something for me, I do something for them. As long as they serve my interests, we're friends."

Patricia scowled and folded her ears down. "I'm beginning to see why your kind has few friends in the galaxy."

"Patricia…"

"Well, it makes perfect sense," she said. "If you go around using everyone to suit your own interests, they're going to get resentful, yeah?"

Sebastian shrugged. "If you do it right, they won't realize they're being used."

The car went silent, save for the gentle rumbling of road noise. Patricia gawped at him, her ears tucked down, a look of shock on her face. She tightened her paws into fists.

"Are you using us?" she said.

Sebastian skewed his ears outwards. He was quickly losing control of the conversation. "Of course not! You're valued members of my crew, you can leave whenever you want. You're not leashed."

Patricia sighed and shook her head. "I've seen the way you operate, Sebastian. The people you dupe never knew what was happening. How do I know you're not duping me right now?"

"Don't you think you're being paranoid?" Sebastian said. "Is there any evidence that I'm using you? You're making over the going rate, you've been a member of my crew for three years now, you're my second in command. How could I possibly be using you?"

Patricia wrinkled her nose. "You used Zef."

Sebastian's ear twitched; if he didn't placate her soon, this would end in disaster. The last thing he could afford now was losing any more crew.

"Patricia," he said, "you're nothing like Zef. The way I treated Zef was a… mistake. I was young, didn't know better, didn't know who Zef really was when I recruited him. But you worked your way through the ranks, Corey trusted you, Adrian trusted Corey, and I trusted Adrian. If I betrayed you, it'd be as if I were betraying Adrian."

She nodded, slowly, her eyes vacant in thought. "Sebastian, are you a Restorationist?"

"What?"

Patricia stared hard at him. "Are you a Restorationist? Do you want to bring about the New Vulpine Golden Age?"

Sebastian frowned, ears erect and attentive. "I'd like to think that we could all live together peaceably, and everyone could benefit from the technological advances we foxes have made."

"You're not answering the question."

"You really think I'm like those other foxes, the ones that want to subjugate you?"

Patricia scowled, eyes narrowed, lips pulled back into a near-snarl. "This isn't about me, yeah? Are you or are you not a Restorationist?"

"What's brought all these questions on, so sudden?"

"Well, Corey said that Zef told him you were, that you were fighting the Dominion because it suited pro-vulpine interests, that the crew was segregated like in the Dominion, that you use us because we're loyal and dumb, that—"

Sebastian reached over and pulled her muzzle to face his. "First of all, Zef is just barking. He's trying to bring us down from inside, he's trying to erode your confidence in me. Second of all, Corey's just upset because he's stuck in jail and there's nothing I can legally do to get him out."

She pulled her snout free. "But it's true, yeah? The Star Rangers, almost the entire command staff were Wild—"

"Listen to me, Patricia. Most Wild in my crew were in command positions in the Canis Dominion military at some point. They've got the experience in leading others that most of the Familiars don't. But that doesn't mean they're inherently better, dig? Any Familiar could rise in ranks to get a command position. Even my fusiliers are better appreciated and better paid than in any other unit."

Patricia exhaled slowly, nodded and leaned back against her door. "I'm sorry to upset you, Captain. You've been more than fair to us all."

Sebastian forced a smile. "It's okay. I'm kind of edgy right now, everything's falling down, you know? These are accusations and stereotypes I've had to face since I left the Alliance, everyone's got a predetermined mindset about how we foxes act. It frustrates me that you'd doubt me, because I've done so much to convince you I'm a good person. But I know it's not your fault, Zef and Corey are both excellent speakers, charismatic, and intelligent. While I may lie to those outside the unit, I promise, I'll never lie to you. Okay?"

Patricia bobbed her head, the corners of her muzzle pulled up into a smile. "Yes, Captain. I believe you."

He reached out to touch her cheek with his paw. "Good, because I'm going to need you on this mission."

Sebastian kept his expression pleasant, but inside he felt extreme relief. He'd been close to letting her slip away, letting fatigue and his opponent's antagonism get the best of him. The last thing he could afford was to lose Patricia; if he did, he'd certainly perish on their mission.

By now, they had reached their hotel, and Greco parked the car. Sebastian stepped out of the vehicle, the cooling air stinging his nose. Late afternoon was fading into evening, and with it, another day would end.

"We've got a lot to do," Sebastian said. "I'm going to need you both working hard tomorrow to get all the supplies we're going to need for this mission." He sat atop the hood of the car and beckoned Greco over. "Come here, I want to talk to you."

The dhole paused, watched Patricia head into the hotel room, and then walked back to Sebastian. "Yes sir?"

"Here, have a seat." Sebastian patted the hood. "It's about your contract."

Greco sat. "What about it?"

"You were the highest ranking officer after Patricia, so I had to retain you. But your contract doesn't specify titaneering."

"I know."

Sebastian rolled his shoulders in a shrug. "Well, that means I don't really have to take you along."

Greco tilted his head. "You'd leave me behind?"

"Not without your approval," Sebastian said. "I thought I'd offer the option. I don't know how comfortable you are in a titan."

"I can make my way around. It's not too different from an aerofighter."

Sebastian frowned slightly. Though it was true that pilots were more adept at picking up the feel of titaneering, they were still two dissimilar disciplines.

"Are you sure you're up for it?" he asked.

Greco smiled. "Sure. Besides, what would you do without me?"

"I could get a boomer."

"We can't afford to hire someone just to pilot a titan for one mission. We need the money, Sebastian."

Sebastian sighed and nodded slowly. "I know. It's just that..."

"You don't trust my abilities?"

Sebastian chewed on his lip and looked up at the stocky canine. "I'd just prefer someone with a bit more experience."

"I have plenty of experience."

"In command," Sebastian said. "Less so in a titan."

Greco braced a broad, white paw on the hood of the car, and leaned down to Sebastian. "Sir, may I speak freely?"

Sebastian's ears tucked back. "Rock me."

"I'm not sure I believe what Patricia said about your dishonesty," Greco said. "From what I've seen, you've always been fair to us canines. At a time like this, we need to stay together, and not argue about piddling things. What is important is that we fight as a team, which I've thought we've always done well. To break that team now would surely destroy everything we've accomplished so far."

Sebastian contemplated that and nodded, slowly. "You're from Andalusia, right?"

"Why?"

"It's a bit of a backspace system, isn't it? No offense."

"Maybe," Greco said, "but it's home."

"I grew up in something of a similar situation on Wopat. It's one of the more sparsely populated systems in the Alliance, cold, 24-something million people."

"So?"

Sebastian eased back on the hood. "On a world like that, everything is tighter. The population base is close and dense, everybody knows each other, or knows someone who knows each other."

"I suppose," Greco said. "Why bring this up?"

Sebastian looked up to the sky. Somewhere behind the overcast, the sun was setting, and it was growing dark. A chill was settling in as the autumn day faded into night.

"It means you and I have a similar perspective," Sebastian said. "Patricia was born in a faceless, large city. Our upbringings put more value on sentient life because our communities were tighter."

Greco shook his head. "I don't really see how that affects you, you order people to their deaths all the time."

Sebastian frowned and rubbed at his muzzle. "It took me a long time before I could kill people without frizzing about it."

"I thought life was cheap for foxes."

"Why would you say something like that?"

Greco shrugged. "You're numerous. How many of you are there?"

Sebastian waggled a paw. "About 6.8 billion. A little over 15 if you count all the fox species."

"Most mercenaries are foxes. It's a statistical fact that foxes have been engaged in more wars than any other genera."

"Lies and slander."

"The vulpine Houses have been involved in at least fifteen major wars since the Founding," Greco said.

"It can't be that many."

Greco held out a white paw and counted on his fingers. "Nine assimilations of other Houses, four Contraction Wars, the Great War, and I'm sure you had a hand in the Genesis War, too."

Sebastian scoffed and crossed his arms. "For one thing, the assimilations don't count. That was forceful consolidation of weaker Houses into stronger ones, it was best for the genus. Secondly, we didn't start the Contraction Wars."

"I don't see how you could say that," Greco said. "It was inevitable that the oppressive vulpine hegemony be overthrown and expelled."

Sebastian growled. "There was no greater period of technological growth and economic expansion than the Golden Age, the galaxy wouldn't be anything like what it is without us. We earned our territory and empires, it was our right, and the species were never more equal."

"You mean they were all equal under foxes."

"What are you implying?"

"I imply nothing," Greco said. "What I say is that your rule over the non-foxes of the galaxy was inherently unjust and oppressive, and that your refusal to grant us self-determination resulted in violent revolution."

Sebastian clenched his fists. "Are you saying we brought the Time of Terrors upon ourselves?"

Greco perked one ear. "I've never heard that term before."

"What else would you call it? Over three-hundred thirty million foxes lost their lives, and even more lost their homes and way of life."

"Much of that was due to in-fighting between your own Houses."

Sebastian shrugged. "Again, that was the strong vying against the weak. The stronger Houses took from the Houses that were weaker."

"You might have a different opinion if you were from House La Vallena."

"Perhaps." Sebastian glanced to the clouds again and shook his head. "Why do you care so much about our history?"

"I hoped it'd help me understand your genus." Greco sighed and shook his head. "You're so competitive amongst yourselves. Warlike, even."

"We're not warlike, we're just strongly independent."

"But wasn't your father—"

"Leave my father out of this," Sebastian said. "He was... he told me a lot of things, but it wasn't until I felt them first hand that I understood. Tell me, how many people did you kill in the army?"

"None."

"And how many people have you killed while in my service?"

Greco was silent for a few seconds. "Maybe a hundred."

"It's a big leap, isn't it? You still think of them as people."

Greco shook his head. "They are people, people like you and me. You've killed many Dominion soldiers in your time. If things had been different, one of them may have been me."

Sebastian sighed. "You can't think of what might have been, you'll drive yourself crazy. You can only think of what is. The fact is people die all the time. If you stress over who they were, or what they might have done, you'll just get yourself into a breakdown."

"Why are you telling me all this?"

Sebastian twisted his lips and looked Greco over. He was still young, still eager to learn, with high ears and proud tail. "You remind me of myself," Sebastian said.

"How's that?"

"When I was your age, I was fiery and outspoken. I was angry. The Alliance had let me down, treated me like dirt after offering so much promise. I had much potential, but I couldn't focus it, I was distrustful of everyone. But Adrian changed that. When I first met him, he saw the promise in me, and didn't care that I was a stray. He calmed me down and turned me into the great warrior I am today."

Greco chewed his lip. "I'm not sure where you're going with this."

Sebastian smiled softly and patted Greco's arm. "You have a lot of potential, and you and I have had similar lives. I had always hoped that someday I could turn the unit over to you."

"You really mean that?"

"Yes."

"I don't know what to say," Greco said. "What about Patricia, or Corey?"

Sebastian sighed. "They're great commanders, but they're not great leaders. They don't have the right priorities. Patricia is too emotional, and Corey is too methodical. You need a mix between those, you need a deep understanding of the value of life, and most of all, you need to have a feel for the big picture, and how people work together for the larger good."

"You think I have that?"

Sebastian turned to face him. "Patricia's from Akhu, on Algomarle II, and Corey's from Northwood on Zettler I. They're both big cities, a million or two people each. You see them all, but you have no concept of how they interoperate. Maybe you know what a few people's roles are, but they're abstract, meaningless. You and I don't have that problem."

Greco nodded and smiled. "I think I understand now. But if you think I'm such a great leader, why did you promote Patricia instead of me?"

"Because there's a difference between being a leader and being a first officer."

"I think I understand now."

Sebastian hopped off the hood of the car. "Great! Now come on, we've got planning to do."

Greco followed Sebastian into the hotel room, tossing out suggestions as he went, but Sebastian wasn't listening. He had more pressing matters on his mind. The future of himself and the Star Rangers would hinge on this campaign's outcome, and either he would fly to the sun or fall to his death. As much faith as he had in his crew, he knew that only his skill could let them succeed in what would otherwise be certain failure. He would do what he must to ensure victory, not for Valentino's Star Rangers, but for himself.

I present to you the future, the new face of warfare! Every ground vehicle, turret, missile bay, tank, rifle, rocket launcher, machine gun is now obsolete.

-Mielczik Corsacci, CEO and founder of Stanton Technologies, upon publicly revealing the prototype titan, the BGP-1A Titan.

SCENE TWO

The planetary insertion went perfectly. The dropship Cabala touched down on the vast, barren Usutka Plain, and the remnants of the Star Rangers walked, and rolled, out of its cargo bay.

From the cockpit of his titan, Sebastian Valentino watched his only hope for transportation lurch airborne and soar into the stratosphere, its silvery wings glinting in the early-dawn sun. Then the dropship was gone, and the Star Rangers were alone.

Sebastian adjusted his headset and swiveled his microphone in front of his muzzle. "All right, kits. Do a full systems check and report in."

Sebastian commenced his own automatic diagnostic, the pleasant, synthetic feminine voice of his titan's onboard computer reporting as it went along.

"H.M. Hood Limited model H-650 Hurricane, OC-4 version 4.6, startup and diagnostic procedure. Planet: Thanton I. Ambient temperature: 309.27 degrees. Current time is 647.4 local time, 1001 standard time, 001 mission time. Local gravity: 0.7013G. Current titan mass is 67.034 megagrams, current titan weight is 46.991 megagrams. Skid control enabled. Current geographic coordinates are—"

Sebastian stopped listening; if anything were amiss, the computer would alert him. He loosened his shoulder straps to gain more mobility, and looked outside the mirrored plastiglass canopy at his squad. Patricia Darling was to his left in her Ranger; together with his Hurricane, they would form the main battle segment. Greco's Typhoon was further beyond Patricia. Sebastian would need his smaller titan's speed and maneuverability to keep the enemy off balance. On Sebastian's right stood the squad's fire support titan, a Katyusha manned by pilot Dagmar Udenski and weapons officer Dorian St. Clair. Somewhere behind Sebastian was the Freighthog, the unit's mobile support HQ. It was a heavy, multi-axle vehicle commanded by Joseph Tracy, and it would be their only source of ammunition. One by one, each confirmed all systems were in proper order.

"Assume wedge formation and move out," Sebastian said.

He wrapped his durahyde-gloved paw about the titan's throttle and eased it forward. The machine pushed ahead, soon settling into a brisk walk. Every step of the massive bipedal war machine sent rhythmic, familiar tremors through the cockpit.

Their first target was two hours southwest of their insertion point, but Sebastian didn't notice the passage of time. He was too busy reacquainting himself with his titan: the subtle smell of durahyde upholstery and plastic instrument panels, the warm, reassuring hum of the machine's fuel cells below him, the feel of the switches and dials under gloved fingers. He smiled.

Faint indications of habitation rose in the distance, the glimmering glass and steel of civilization. This was the city of Hammerdown, home to a hydrofuel refinery.

Sebastian prepped his titan's weapons and shields. The mission had been quiet so far, but when he flipped his radar to active scan, the silence ended.

"New contact detected," the computer said.

Sebastian flicked his headset's visor over his eyes and activated its translucent optical screen. The display flickered to life and immediately presented Sebastian with all manner of critical information. He set the titan's targeting computer to highlight the new contact, and a bounding box appeared on the heads-up display, as well as a three-dimensional wireframe representation of the target.

"I'm picking up contacts, four light all-terrain vehicles, Scout class, heading 214, range twenty kilometers," he said.

"I've nothing on my radar," Patricia said.

"I'll take care of them," Sebastian said.

Sebastian eased his left foot forward onto the torso pedal, gently turning the Hurricane's upper half towards the target without changing its course. He switched both class III lasers to active, their indicators changing from red to green on his visor. A narrow blue bar beneath each slowly filled, displaying the supplementary capacitor's charge.

Sebastian slaved the laser cannons to his left joystick, toggled his artificial zoom to maximum, and delicately aligned the crosshairs over the lead vehicle. The red X over it changed to a green square; he was in weapon's range.

He squeezed the trigger. Arm-mounted lasers roared to life, cutting brilliant white beams through the atmosphere. As soon as he released the trigger, the heat-flash plasma dissipated and the beams vanished. Even at the periphery of the laser's range, Sebastian's aim was lethal. Both weapons found their mark. They speared the lead truck and eviscerated it, flames erupting from the gashes.

"Enemy vehicle disabled," the computer said.

Immediately, the vehicles turned hard to flee. Sebastian gritted his teeth and shoved his throttle hard forward. The Hurricane slipped and lurched into a sprint, but it was already too late. He'd never catch up to the swift trucks.

"Did you hit them?" Greco asked.

"One," Sebastian said. "But the others are getting away."

"Fire again!" Patricia said.

Sebastian stared harder into his visor. At full run, the targeting reticle weaved erratically along the horizon. The zoom only amplified the disturbance. He'd get one more shot off before the Scouts were permanently out of range.

He waited for his laser plates to cool and fired again. Another vehicle burst into flame, skidded, and rolled sideways across the plains.

"Enemy vehicle disabled," the computer said.

Sebastian cursed himself. The tiny vehicles were no threat to them, and they wouldn't have identified the squad for another ten kilometers, at least. He should have waited for them to close, where they would have destroyed them all swiftly in seconds.

"I got two," Sebastian said. "The others got away."

"They'll get help, yeah?" Patricia said.

"We'll need to book it now. In about two hours this whole plain is going to be crawling with Whitehats," Greco said.

Sebastian sighed. "Change of plans. Udenski and Tracy, I want you to cut west and head for Nav Baker. Everyone else, proceed with me to Nav Amber. All units switch to passive sensors, we'll rendezvous later."

"I understand, Captain. With you and for you," Udenski said.

Sebastian pushed his Hurricane to a run. Patricia and Greco easily kept pace, something Udenski's sluggish Katyusha could not do. Unfortunately, by the time Sebastian detected the incoming contacts, the Katyusha's powerful missile racks were well beyond range.

"New contacts detected," the computer said.

Sebastian glanced down at his radarscope. "Picking up five contacts," he said. "Tanks, two light and three battle. Heading 217, range 31 kilometers. Break formation and fire at will, combat speed."

"All right, here we go!" Greco said.

Sebastian eased the throttle to sprint, the heavy war machine's computer keeping it from skidding in the low gravity. Greco's Typhoon passed him to the right, the sun glinting off its spindly, hull-forward body. Its arms swung up into combat configuration, aimed at its distant target.

Sebastian activated the rest of his Hurricane's armament, and the assault cannon and ion rifle appeared in his weapon selection queue. With a dull thud, the eighty-millimeter cannon over his head chambered a round.

Patricia had swung out along his left side, her titan's arms raised, each one with dual class III lasers. She would be in range soon, and the further spread the three were, the better.

"Engaging target," Greco said.

A flash of laser fire caught Sebastian's peripheral vision; Greco had opened fire with all four of his rig's light laser cannons. The scarlet rays traced a distant path to their target, igniting the atmosphere for as long as Greco held the trigger. According to Sebastian's battle computer, Greco had missed with all four cannons.

Something shot past Sebastian, mere meters past his shoulder. The tanks were in range with their heavy battle cannons, and armor-piercing shells would soon be raining down on all three.

"Be advised, they've opened fire. Try to conserve your ammo," Sebastian said.

"Copy that, sir," Patricia said.

The wireframe image in Sebastian's visor kept track of his enemy's movements and damage. When it indicated his opponent was firing, he swung his Hurricane in an evasive maneuver. A pair of shells whistled past, and he prepared to fire again.

Sebastian took careful aim with his laser cannons, lined his crosshairs on a light tank, and fired. The lasers found their target and scored a direct hit.

Deft movements kept his aim true, and he held the trigger until the target vanished from his radarscope.

"Enemy vehicle disabled," the computer said.

"I've been hit!" Greco said.

Sebastian looked down at his radar display; somehow, Greco had managed to attract the attention of all three battle tanks. Worse still, he'd closed to only a kilometer.

"Vex it, Greco, pull out of there!" Sebastian said.

A thunderous boom echoed across the plain as Greco fired his Typhoon's massive electromagnetic cannon. Its magazine held only a dozen rounds; if he was using it, he was in trouble. Fortunately, it found its mark, tearing cleanly through a battle tank's front armor.

Sebastian's computer reported the vehicle's destruction, but he wasn't listening. "Patricia, help Greco."

"On it."

Sebastian looked across the horizon. Patricia's Ranger was too far from Greco to be of much help. Sebastian fired his lasers at another tank and pierced its side armor, but the vehicle didn't slow. The squad didn't have enough weaponry to stop the tanks quickly enough.

Greco was backpedalling, firing his laser cannons as he went, but the three remaining tanks had locked on him. A heavy cannon shell slammed into his Typhoon's left shoulder, sending metallic shrapnel flying from behind it. Another round hit the machine's torso.

"My turntable's locked!" Greco said.

"Use your lasers," Sebastian said.

"They're not responding!"

Sebastian did his best, but he knew it was too late. With his broken turntable, Greco couldn't rotate his torso or aim the heavy electro-magnetic cannon fixed in it. He fired it anyway, but the half-meter metal sphere sailed wide. Another tank round punched into the Typhoon's torso, pierced the armor, and ripped an explosion through the machine. Smoke billowed from the gaping hole.

Again, Sebastian fired at the nearest tank. His laser cannons tore through its armor and touched off its hydrofuel. A violent explosion erupted from the vehicle.

He immediately set his sights onto the next target, but it was too late. Greco's crippled machine couldn't evade the enemy round that smashed into its torso.

"I'm punching out!" he said.

The Typhoon teetered backwards, its equilibrium gone. The machine's cockpit canopy blew free, and Greco rode out of his devastated Typhoon on a pillar of fire, seconds before the titan fell to its back and burst into flames.

Sebastian could barely hear the rapid gunfire from one of the tank's coaxial machine guns. He didn't have to. With clinical precision, Sebastian buried an assault cannon round of his own through the vehicle's side armor, smashing it to pieces.

"Enemy target disabled," the computer said.

There were no more contacts on Sebastian's radar. Patricia had destroyed the fifth tank while he was occupied, but it was little consolation.

"Vex it!" Sebastian said. "That was a mutt's breakfast."

"We'll just have to keep plowing forward, yeah? Look, I saw a chute. Better pick up Greco," Patricia said.

"I'm on it. How are you holding up?"

"I took a cannon round to the shoulder, it breached the armor, but it didn't seem to hurt any of my insides. I'll be fine, yeah?"

"We can't afford to take damage this early, and I was counting on Greco's EMC for firepower. We're still facing the Lowan Guards, we haven't gotten into the Dominion heavies," Sebastian said.

"You want to abort?"

"No!"

"Well, I was just asking, yeah?" Patricia said. "We're too far from the dust-off zone, anyway. Now are you going to retrieve Greco or not?"

Sebastian didn't answer. He pulled his Hurricane up next to Greco, popped open his canopy, and deployed the hidden, telescoping ladder. Greco climbed aboard under his own power and wordlessly disappeared into the cockpit's rear storage area.

With their fallen comrade rescued, Sebastian and Patricia proceeded to level the Hammerdown hydrofuel refinery.

They linked up with the rest of the squad three hours later. The ammunition warehouse at Nav Baker was already in ruins. Udenski and St. Clair had the foresight to bombard it from long range with their Katyusha's missile system. It would save the squad some time.

"Everyone form up on me, diamond formation, move out," Sebastian said. He leaned back in his seat and flipped a switch on his panel.

"Autopilot engaged," the computer said.

Sebastian sighed, pulled out a rations packet from his titan's storage compartment, and popped it open. He thought better on a full stomach, but not even the dried meat would help assuage his worries.

Greco poked his head into the cockpit from over Sebastian's shoulder. "Can I have some, sir?"

"You could have had your own rations if you hadn't gotten yourself shot up."

"Are you mad, sir?"

Sebastian glanced up. "Why do you think I'm mad?"

"Because I got my titan destroyed."

"Because you pilot like a wetnose, that's why!" Sebastian said. "Any stapard out of titan school could tell you that you don't close with tanks, even when you've got a nose-cannon."

Greco frowned. "I destroyed one of the tanks with the EMC."

Sebastian shook his head. "That doesn't matter. They can get more tanks. We can't get more titans. You were out-massed four to one."

"I thought I could—"

Sebastian turned in his seat and snapped his teeth at Greco. "No, you *didn't* think. If you had, you'd never have gotten a nylon skyride, whistler!"

Greco recoiled, his ears tucked down. "I prefer 'dhole', not whistler."

"And I prefer not to have my very expensive titans blown up because of moronic piloting decisions!"

Without a word, Greco backed out of the cockpit. Sebastian was silent, deep in thought and doubt. It would take all of his skill now to pull victory from the situation. He wanted to blame Greco for this mess, but Sebastian knew it was his own fault. He shouldn't have let the Scouts escape, he shouldn't have split up the squad, and he shouldn't have let them fire at will.

"Hey, Greco."

"Yes?"

Sebastian reached about in his ration pack and pulled out a strip of dried meat. He held it over his head. "Here, have some biltong."

Greco took it and sniffed it experimentally. "Thank you, sir. What's this, cattle?"

"Springbok."

Greco chewed on it. "It's good. Sweet. Isn't springbok expensive?"

"Depends on who you know."

Greco snapped up the biltong in seconds. "Do you have anything to drink?"

"Not for you."

"Any carob?"

"Maybe a little." Sebastian poked the components of his ration pack. He found a foil-wrapped package and offered it to Greco.

"Thank you."

"Yeah, you're welcome. Now go sit down in the back. I've got to think."

Greco disappeared to the titan's sleeper section, and Sebastian brooded. He had seven hours to contemplate his actions before the computer demanded his attention.

"Enemy aero contact detected," it said.

Sebastian checked his radar. Two aerofighters were swiftly advancing on their position from the west. They would be upon them in only three minutes.

"We've got a pair of aero contacts coming in wet and hot, bearing 272." Sebastian consulted his targeting computer. "Type TMS-100 Dolphin."

Sebastian activated his shields and weapons. He couldn't see anything on the horizon, but he knew the attack fighters would be on them in seconds. They'd have the advantage of coming down out of the mid-afternoon sun.

"Keep your vexing heads down and keep moving," Sebastian said. "I've got jamming engaged."

"Copy that. I'll do my best," Patricia said.

Sebastian dimmed his headset visor to cut down on the sun's glare. The targeting box steadily increased in size, the range indicator ticked down, but still, he saw nothing. Even when the red X changed to a green box, Sebastian waited, focused. Patricia fired her laser cannons haphazardly in the Dolphins' direction.

Suddenly, they appeared, screaming down from the sky. Sebastian gritted his teeth and lined up his reticle on the swift targets, and fired. The lasers hit the lead Dolphin's shields, but didn't punch through.

He quickly smashed on his maneuvering pedal, wheeling his Hurricane hard to one side, its feet skidding in the low gravity. The Dolphins tore into his shielding with bolts of heavy laser and cut into his shoulder armor. They raced overhead and disappeared behind him.

Sebastian quickly whirled his titan around to face them. His paws went to work, dragging the throttle rearwards and backpedaling from the aerofighters, while keeping his crosshairs on them. The Dolphins cut a long, arcing turn and came for another pass.

Sebastian gripped his joystick hard, pointed his weaponry at the lead fighter, and fired his laser cannons. He kept the beams focused on the Dolphin, cutting through its shielding and into its fuselage. It banked and struggled to pull away, but Sebastian hit its underside with his ion rifle, the particle stream tearing into its belly. The fighter shuddered, rolled onto its back, and pitched downwards. It slammed into the ground and exploded, debris spewing across the dry grass and setting fires as it went.

"Enemy aero destroyed," his computer said.

"Captain, help!"

Sebastian jerked his Hurricane around just in time to watch the remaining Dolphin bear down upon Patricia. Its class V lasers cut through her shields and into her torso, while she and St. Clair wildly returned fire.

Before Sebastian could aim his weapons, the Dolphin tore over Patricia and pulled sharply upwards. Sebastian could only watch in horror as a single, 250-kilogram gravity bomb smashed into Patricia's wounded shoulder and detonated. The explosion severed the Ranger's left arm.

Sebastian snarled ferociously, aimed, and quickly fired. He struck the Dolphin with both laser cannons, yet failed to breach its thick aft armor. It pulled upwards in a graceful curve and bore down upon Patricia's injured titan.

Sebastian led the Dolphin and buried an eighty-millimeter assault cannon round into its cockpit.

"Enemy aero destroyed," the computer said.

The damage was already done. Smoke poured from the Ranger's frayed shoulder joint, the remnants of half its weapons' complement scattered across the field. The weight imbalance made the machine list slightly to its heavier side.

"Thanks for the help, sir. I thought I was mutt-bait," Patricia said.

Sebastian settled back down into his cockpit and wiped sweat from his forehead. "No problem, but we're really in a fix now."

"I suppose we are, yeah? What do you suggest?"

"Give me time to think."

Sebastian eased his Hurricane back on course and throttled into a medium walk. What to do? Combat so far had been relatively light. They had only encountered the Lowan Guards, the garrison forces scattered throughout the continent, and still, they had managed to lose a titan and half Patricia's weapons load.

Things would only grow tougher as they drove further up the Kinsha River towards Umber City. They were headed into the teeth of the Sixteenth War Group, as well as the continent's lone aerobase. With Greco out of the picture, and Patricia down to half her laser complement, their long odds at the mission's outset had dwindled to near impossible.

He couldn't abort, much as he wanted to. Josephina Storm had been very clear about maintaining radio silence with their dropship. Even if he did manage to contact them, there was no guarantee they'd be in any position for a pick up. The Star Rangers were entirely on their own now.

Then it hit him.

"Patricia, do you remember what Josephina Storm said in the briefing?" he said.

"That you're going to meet the gallows in front of a hundred thousand people?"

"Besides that," Sebastian said. "She said if we need anything, we'd have to get it ourselves."

"And?"

"And we need a titan for Greco."

"I don't follow," Patricia said.

"Our next target is a titan repair facility. They're bound to have a few undergoing repair and just standing about…"

"Please tell me you're not suggesting that we steal a titan."

"I don't see why not," Sebastian said. "You admit we can't possibly complete our objectives in our current state, right?"

"Well, yes, but—"

"Where else could we get one?"

"We'd have to stop the entire unit, send Greco out tracking, and hope we find something useful. It's going to take a lot of time, it's suicide," Patricia said.

"There's nothing else we can do. Greco's no good just sitting around."

Greco poked his head out from the sleeper compartment. "Do I get a say in this?"

"No," Sebastian said.

Greco frowned and disappeared into the back.

Sebastian flicked his computer into navigational mode. The titan repair facility was still 470 kilometers away. If they wanted to make this work, they'd need to pick up their pace.

"We need him piloting, but—" Patricia said.

"Do you have any better ideas?" Sebastian asked.

"It's still too early to abort."

Sebastian throttled his titan up into low run. "We've lost too much equipment to quit now. We're going to need that full payoff."

"But—"

Sebastian flinched, lips twisted into a half-snarl. "Not another word, carthagan. I'm the captain, it's my decision, and I expect you to waggingly endorse it."

For a long moment, Patricia said nothing. The only sounds in Sebastian's cockpit were the distant, rhythmic pounding of his Hurricane's feet below him.

"Well, I guess you know best, yeah?" she finally said.

"Look, we're seven hours outside of the rest zone. Just relax, put your autopilot on, have a rations pack, and we'll talk about strategy when we stop. Dig?"

"I understand, Captain. I'm sure you know what you're doing."

Sebastian hoped she was right.

***

Somewhere south of the city of Helena, the Cane Tributary split from the lonely Kinsha River and snaked into a narrow, unnamed basin on the Usutka Plain. It was the only source of constant water for kilometers around, and it gave birth to a small, compact forest. This was where the Star Rangers made camp.

It was late in Thanton's rotation cycle, and night had fallen. Sebastian parked his Hurricane, put it into standby, and deployed the automatic solar panels from the machine's back. Even in darkness, the array would be able to capture enough light energy to recharge the titan's fuel cells in only a few hours.

Sebastian clambered out of the cockpit and descended to the ground. He braced himself on the Hurricane's foot until the quivering in his knees subsided. Greco dropped down beside him.

"You okay, sir?" he asked.

"Fine. Why?"

"You look wobbly."

Sebastian flattened his ears. "Nineteen hours in a titan tends to leave my legs numb."

"How about nineteen hours in the sleeper cab?"

Sebastian narrowed his eyes. "Yeah, life is so hard for you, isn't it?"

Greco stared at Sebastian. "I already apologized for losing my rig."

"Well that's not good enough!" Sebastian turned to face him. "You have to apologize to Patricia, and Udenski, and St. Clair and Tracy and Dorfmeier and Wheeling and everyone else in the Star Rangers, because you killed them all!"

Greco tensed his shoulders. "You told me to fire at will!"

"I didn't tell you to get your titan blown out from under you, especially by the wetnoses of the Lowan Guards! Do you know how much that Typhoon cost me?"

Greco growled, his ears pinned back. "Cost you, cost you, everything's always about you, I'm sick of it! Do you ever think about anyone else?"

"I'm thinking about the good of the unit. We're all going to die on this stapard rock without you in a titan."

Greco advanced on Sebastian and thrust a finger into his chest. "No, *you're* going to die on this stapard rock."

Sebastian snapped his teeth and swatted Greco's paw away. "Lift your nose! You'll all hang for aiding and abetting a war criminal. In the Dominion's eyes, you're just as guilty."

"They'd never hang one of the Higher Genus."

Sebastian's ears shot up, and his lips pulled back into a snarl. "What did you just call yourself?"

Greco stood over Sebastian. "You heard me, fox," he spat. "Zef and Corey and Patricia are right, you're only in this for yourself, and to recreate the Vulpine Golden Age. You see us as your pets, and I'm tired of it!"

Sebastian barely contained the growl in his voice. "In all my years as a mercenary, I've never heard such insolence from any of my crew."

"Maybe that's because all your previous crews were too soft-headed to see you for what you really are!"

Sebastian tensed his paws into fists. "How dare you! I've done more for you people than you could possibly imagine, I've weakened the Dominion and helped spur pro-democracy rebellions, and still you Outsiders hate me because I'm a fox!"

"No, I hate you because you're *the* fox! You're the Archetype, the very reincarnation of Max, the selfish, corrupt, slick-talking one who'd stab a friend in the back and sell his pelt! Kohoutek, Latranis, Alpinus, Akela, even Vurren warned us about you, and we didn't listen."

The commotion had attracted the attention of Patricia and St. Clair. They now stood nearby, watching, listening, and exchanging silent looks of concern with each other.

"I've broken my tail trying to gain the trust of you and your ungrateful kind!" Sebastian said. "What gives you the right to question my motives? You're the one that's gotten us all killed, whistler! This is all your fault!"

Greco growled at Sebastian. "My fault! You're the one who keeps taking these ludicrous contracts, putting us all in danger, trying to get your name back in the spotlight. You're losing your touch, and you have been ever since you killed Adrian—"

Greco never finished the sentence. Sebastian snarled with savage rage and leapt upon the dhole's throat. Greco managed to latch his broad paws onto the small fox's midsection, disrupting Sebastian's momentum.

Greco had a sixty centimeter height advantage, but Sebastian was too fast. His fangs found Greco's left forearm, puncturing his jumpsuit's tough, plasteen coating. Greco yelped in pain and fell, shaking his arm wildly in an attempt to dislodge Sebastian. Blood welled up from his teeth.

A sharp blow to the side of Sebastian's head forced him to release, and Greco kicked him off. Sebastian tumbled backwards into the dirt and immediately righted himself. Before Greco could act, Sebastian struck again. He plowed hard into Greco's knees and sent the dhole toppling over. Sebastian tore his teeth and claws into Greco's midsection, ripped through the cloth, and sank into his flesh. Greco screamed in agony.

In seconds, Patricia was on Sebastian, straining to pull him off. Sebastian writhed out of her grip and attacked Greco again, this time latching onto his shoulder. Patricia hit Sebastian in the back and he released, but he didn't capitulate until St. Clair kicked him hard in the side. The burly red wolf sent him sprawling in the dirt.

"Sweet Nelsoma, Sebastian!" Patricia said. "What in the seven blazes of the Everlife are you doing?"

Sebastian stood, slowly. Greco was slumped and bleeding heavily from his wounds, and Patricia and St. Clair stood protectively in front of him. All three stared back, their piercing eyes burning into his. He recoiled and turned away.

What was he doing, attacking his third in command like that? What had he done to inspire Greco to lash out? Hearsay alone, passed from Zef to Corey to Patricia to Greco, wouldn't have enough effect. It must go deeper. Maybe it was how Sebastian had been acting, or maybe Greco had made his own decisions after overhearing the conversation in the car.

Maybe Sebastian was losing control over his unit.

He stumbled away from them, out into the darkness of the night. He winced and held his side where St. Clair had kicked him. The red wolf could have broken his ribs if she'd kicked him full force.

"Captain, wait—"

Sebastian felt a paw on his shoulder. Instinctively, he whirled about, crouched into a defensive posture, teeth bared to face his attacker. It was Patricia.

"What do you want, carthagan?"

Patricia held up her paws apologetically. "Talk. Now relax."

"What do you want to talk about?"

"You have to ask?"

Sebastian sighed and stood upright, shoulders slack. "Greco insulted me."

"How?"

"He said I was selfish. He called me a Restorationist. He said I was the Archetype, and that I killed Adrian."

"So you said what?"

"Well, I told him he was wrong," Sebastian said.

Patricia shook her head. "What did you say to rile him?"

"Nothing that wasn't the truth."

Patricia crossed her arms. "Wag me here, yeah? You're hurt."

"I'm not hurt."

"I see the way you hold your side," she said. "St. Clair really got you, yeah?"

"Maybe."

"You're hurt inside, too."

Sebastian turned away. "No."

Patricia grabbed him by the shoulder and spun him about. She crouched and put her nose in line with his. "Now listen here. I don't know what's going on in that russet-covered skull of yours, but I know that something's got your tail knotted. Ever since Zef showed up, you've been acting different, posturing on your own crew, yeah? You barked at me, you barked at Corey, you almost tore Greco to pieces and he's almost twice your size. What's with you?"

For a long moment, Sebastian said nothing, eyes down at the ground. A gentle night breeze tousled his fur, sent it cascading behind him and over his flattened ears.

"It's all Zef," he said. "I spent almost a decade trying to undo the mistakes I made with him, I've tried to make a name for myself, and I've fought the stereotypes about foxes everywhere I go. Zef shows up and tells Corey these stories, and before I know it you're asking me if I'm a Restorationist, you think I'm using you, Greco calls me the Archetype and it flames me. Zef's undoing everything I've tried to accomplish. No matter what I do, or where I go, people still see me as a fox first and a person second."

Patricia frowned and nodded. "I'm sorry, I didn't know I was contributing."

"Of course not. Even though you've known me so long and I've never lied to you, you believed Corey over me because he's a Wild. Like you."

Patricia tucked her ears back. "That's untrue!"

"No?" Sebastian said. "You readily accepted Corey's word because he's a jackal."

"Well, jackals are more trustworthy than foxes, yeah?"

Sebastian flinched, nose wrinkled. He looked away, muzzle pointed into the wind. "That's the sort of attitude I've been fighting for so long."

"I'm sorry, sir. I didn't realize."

"That's what makes it so hard to overcome."

Patricia stood and glanced over her shoulder. St. Clair had finished bandaging Greco and helped him to his feet.

"You miss Adrian, yeah?" Patricia said.

Sebastian rubbed his side. "More than anything."

Patricia nodded silently and watched Greco stand. The dhole leaned into St. Clair for balance, and she held him firmly. They chatted with each other, trivial things, light words to be lost in the breeze. "You want I should talk to Greco?" Patricia asked.

Sebastian glanced up. "What about?"

"What do you mean, what about?" she said. "He's probably going to want to desert, thanks to you. I don't know what you were thinking, attacking him like that, we're going to need his titaneering on this mission, yeah?"

"He hasn't proven himself particularly useful so far."

"Everyone deserves a second chance, Sebastian. What if we all gave up on you after Adrian died, or after Zef shot up the Favored Sky?"

Sebastian twisted his lips into a frown. "That's different. Thanks to Greco, we're not going to have a second chance."

"Why is everything always different when it involves you?"

Sebastian's lips quivered. He stared up into Patricia's eyes; she wanted an answer, but he didn't have one.

"Well anyway," she said, "the four of us can't take on the Canine People's Army."

"We'll get someone else to pilot."

"You're not listening to me, Sebastian."

"We can use Wheeling."

Patricia's scowled. "Wheeling's got no experience."

"He's done fine in the simulator."

"Simulator!' She grabbed his shoulders and shook him. "Listen to yourself, Sebastian. You're going to condemn us all to death because Greco has a big mouth? What sort of dobby madness is this?"

"He's an insubordinate lappund!"

Patricia narrowed her gaze, eyes tight on Sebastian. "I'll thank you not to use that term in my presence. Are you truly so wall-headed that you'd fall to spite the ladder?"

Sebastian stared back, amber eyes cold and distant, his shoulders squared. He wanted to speak, wanted to tell Patricia she was wrong. He wanted to tell her he wasn't so stubborn, but the words refused to come. He said nothing.

Patricia sighed and patted his shoulder. "All right, you just stand around, yeah? Relax, untie your tail, I'll try and talk to Greco." She wagged a finger in Sebastian's face. "Now you be gracious to him, yeah? I might be able to convince him to stick this out for us, let him leave when we're off-world."

Sebastian nodded silently. Patricia turned away, gathered up St. Clair and Greco, and disappeared into the Freighthog's passenger compartment.

The last traces of sunset had long passed, and now Sebastian was alone in the dark. He squinted and rubbed his eyes; his scotopic vision had dulled with age, but he could still make out his titan. He strolled over to it and sat upon its foot, and promptly buried his face in his paws.

What was happening to him? He'd lost so much: his best friend, his mate-to-be, his warship, his second-in-command, his prestigious ranking. Now he was losing control over what remained of his unit, the glorious mercenary company he'd struggled so hard to build. If he wasn't careful, he'd even lose his life.

He wanted to blame Zef. The coyote had cost him many of those things. It would be easy, yet Sebastian refused to fall for it. The notion that his downfall could be attributed to a single person disgusted him. Despite misgivings, Sebastian had taken this contract. If they died, it would be his fault alone.

Sebastian's ears perked and swiveled to face behind himself. Footsteps approached.

"What do you want, St. Clair?" he asked.

She paused, a half-dozen meters away. "You know it is me."

"I heard your paces," Sebastian said. "You're 2.01 meters tall and… is it 107 kilos?"

"106 and a half."

Sebastian nodded. "You didn't answer my question."

"Is it not obvious what I wish?"

Sebastian twisted to face the red wolf, boot propped on the edge of the Hurricane's foot. "You wish to meddle in affairs that aren't yours."

"On the contrary, Captain, I believe that they are."

He braced his elbow on his knee and looked her over. "Your first name is Jayla, isn't it? Where's that from?"

"I am named after one of the Progenitors, the 208 wolves who are the unique genetic founders of the lupine genus. Jayla was mate of Vuk."

Sebastian nodded. "I know a little of your history, it's in our Book of Creation. The Memoria tells of how Akela and Raksha and Phelkan and all of them argued with Max and then left The Facility. So did the coyotes."

"That is correct."

"Do you harbor a grudge?"

St. Clair sat next to Sebastian, towering over him. "We distrust your kind, yes. However, we are distrustful of all non-lupines, so it is hardly limited to you. Other species rarely meet the high standards of honor and trust we set for ourselves."

"I guess that makes sense."

St. Clair shifted her shoulders. "I do not understand the hatred the coyotes hold for you."

"Neither do I," Sebastian said. "They have a warped sense of honor amidst betrayal and trickery."

"They are something of a cross between our genera," St. Clair said.

He looked up at her. "You didn't come here to talk about genera relations, did you?"

"No. I am here to talk about the crew's relations."

"Save your panting, wolf. Patricia already barked it all out."

St. Clair abruptly lifted Sebastian by his shoulders and set him down in front of her. "You will listen well to me, fox. I left the Lupine Order because I no longer wished to be involved with the violent politics of the warrior class. Do you realize how difficult it is to emigrate from the Order?"

Sebastian stared up, ears erect and at attention. "No."

"You can count the annual departures on both paws."

"So it's hard, huh?"

St. Clair ignored Sebastian's quip and continued. "In the Order, you advance over your fellows either by besting them in simulated combat, or by defeating them in punterkamp. The latter often results in cuts, scars, and broken bones, and it is a sign of pride and accomplishment for us." She pulled back the sleeve of her jumpsuit, revealing a trio of thin scars on her forearm. "I earned these when I was promoted to Hunt Commander."

Sebastian shook his head. "Why bring this up?"

"In the Order, we live by the Lupine Way, a strict protocol that defines proper conduct and how we are to act. Under it, such battles for position are common. That is how it is, was, and always will be. But you are not like us. You do not fight each other to prove who is right or wrong, or to earn promotions." She leaned down to face him, nose to nose. "I had not thought I would see such behavior outside of the Order, where such bonds of faith must be forged, not assumed. When you attack someone who trusts you as a leader in battle, you not only physically wound them, but you damage the confidence of all those who trust you."

"Greco's going to get us all killed—"

"You attacked him. That is indicative of a weak position. You had no strong words to respond with, only violence. Engaging in such actions is an open admission that you are wrong."

Sebastian tensed his paws into fists. "Are you calling me weak?"

St. Clair frowned. "You hear my words, but choose not to listen. You do not remedy a feeble stance by attacking those who disagree with you. You rectify it by improving your position. You know you were wrong in attacking Greco, and you know his words were right. You must reassert yourself, admit to your mistakes, and correct them."

Sebastian growled. "You're all so insubordinate lately. I've never had problems with discipline, and now you're all trying to bring me down."

St. Clair perked her ears at the fox's growl. "I would not recommend attacking me, Captain. The Canis Dominion may not train their troops in punterkamp, but the Lupine Order does."

Sebastian stared up at her. She was right, on all counts. Assailing her would solve nothing; he was swift, but with her size and training, he would only earn himself an early grave. Nothing would change. Greco would still be right and Sebastian would still be wrong. They'd still be trapped on Thanton, undermanned and undergunned, and when the rest of his unit perished, it would still be his fault.

St. Clair leaned over him. "Captain, if we work together, we can achieve much. If we work apart, we will find only death."

Sebastian nodded slowly. "I'd no idea you were such a wise wolf."

"You never asked."

He chuckled softly and looked her over. "No, I didn't. You know, I haven't asked you about a lot of things."

"We wolves are secretive and private about our culture."

"Why is that?"

St. Clair rolled her broad shoulders. "We do not trust the non-wolves. They do not share our values, and would not understand our ways and methods. We prefer to operate as an independent, united entity, based on solidarity and brotherhood."

Sebastian frowned. "You must find our ways baffling."

"We do. Bluntly, we cannot understand the way foxes war amongst themselves. We find it most strange."

Sebastian shook his head. "I don't know how to explain it. It's just the way we operate."

St. Clair smiled. "I do not expect to understand your ways, just as I do not expect you to understand ours. We all have differences that exist and always will."

Sebastian chuckled and skewed his ears. "How'd you get so smart?"

St. Clair flexed her muscular arms and grinned, exposing her fangs. "Decades of infallible lupine eugenics."

"Eugenics, huh? You're one of those purebreds? I've heard rumors about what goes on in the Order."

"And what rumors would those be?"

Sebastian shrugged. "Oh, the usual. That you wolves have no childhood because you're bred from birth to kill, that you have ritual sacrifices of ferals to prepare yourselves for battle, and that you eat your prisoners of war."

St. Clair smiled enigmatically. "Most of those are untrue."

"Which ones aren't?"

"Part of the Lupine Way is not divulging such secrets."

Sebastian grinned and shook his head. "I'd imagine it'd be something like that."

St. Clair stood and glanced upwards, letting the wind run over her muzzle. "It is growing late. Do you have any further inquiries?"

"Just one." Sebastian pointed to the steel bracers wrapped about St. Clair's forearms. "What are those for?"

St. Clair held her arms up and twisted them, the metal running from below her wrists to above her elbows. "Bio-magnetic bracers."

Sebastian tilted his head. "Bio-magnetic?"

"They contain a mild, permanent magnetic field that is designed to exacting specifications. It aligns the biological energy that flows through my arms and purifies it, enhancing blood flow and neural performance."

Sebastian scowled and snorted derisively. "You can't possibly believe that hokum."

St. Clair narrowed her eyes and stared down at the smaller fox, lips curled into a faint snarl. Abruptly, it vanished, and she grinned. "At the very least, they make effective weapons for use against non-believers."

Sebastian looked her large body over. "Somehow, I believe that describes most things you get your paws on."

She chuckled and crossed her arms. "That is true."

Sebastian stepped around her and gestured for her to follow. "Come, we need to discuss our strategy for tomorrow."

St. Clair followed. "I trust you will be well-behaved."

"You've given me a lot to think about." He stopped her at the vehicle's side door. "Thanks for talking some sense into me. I really appreciate it."

St. Clair shrugged dismissively. "It was my duty, a task to be completed. Should I have failed, we would all be at risk."

Sebastian nodded, opened the door for her, and stepped inside. Patricia and Greco sat around a retractable table, filing through papers. Udenski sat off to one side, his nose buried in a field manual.

Patricia glanced up, ears erect. "Ah, Captain. We were just talking about you."

"Good things?" Sebastian said.

"Maybe."

Sebastian walked to the table and examined its contents. One of the papers caught his eye and he picked it up. It was the satellite map of the mission zone from the briefer.

"How are you feeling, Greco?" Sebastian asked.

Greco looked away. He had crude field bandages over where Sebastian had attacked him. "Fine, I guess. Better."

Sebastian tossed the paper away, and it fluttered to the table. "I wanted to apologize for attacking you."

"I bet."

Sebastian leaned over the table towards Greco. "Look at me, vex you. I'm here with my tail down. Patricia and St. Clair came and talked to me, and they're right, I've been selfish and uncaring and probably reckless. I'm here now to say I didn't mean to bite you. It's because you were right."

Greco mulled this over in silence. He averted his gaze while he spoke. "How do I know you are truthful now?"

Sebastian sighed. He was running out of things to say to change Greco's mind, and it was becoming increasingly apparent that Greco didn't want his mind changed. "I guess you don't," Sebastian said.

The passenger cabin went quiet. Patricia and St. Clair exchanged tacit, worried looks. Udenski remained buried in his field manual. Patricia reached out to touch Greco's shoulder, but he pulled away from her.

"Patricia spoke to me, as well," Greco said. "She tried to explain how my words hurt and angered you. I can't trust you anymore. I feel like everything you said before the mission was a lie, about kindred spirits."

"It wasn't!"

Greco sighed. "Actions speak louder than words, fox. I can't stay in this environment. Patricia convinced me to at least finish this mission, not for you, but for all of us. It would be unbecoming for me to abandon everyone at a time like this."

"And you'd have nowhere to go," Sebastian said.

Greco shrugged. "Maybe not."

Sebastian forced a smile and offered a paw. "Shake?"

Greco stared contemptuously at the fox's hand, eyes narrowed. Finally, he drew up his own broad, white paw, and gave Sebastian a hesitant handshake.

"Excellent." Sebastian sat at the table. "Now, everyone gather up, let's talk planning."

Sebastian took the satellite photograph of the titan repair facility for reference, laid it out on the table, and invited discourse. The installation sat atop a former aerofield, with the titans under repair stored inside an abandoned hangar.

The only true variable was the approach vector for each titan. Sebastian would make a frontal charge, since he had sustained the least damage. They must strike fast to destroy the barracks before any of the pilots could reach their titans. Sebastian and Patricia would guard the Freighthog while it deposited Greco inside the storage hangar, and St. Clair would stand watch with her Katyusha. Greco would break in, power up a single-seat titan, and the squad would pull out and head to their next objective. Time was of the essence; they could expect to have Norford's aero resistance upon them as soon as three hours after the assault.

When Sebastian finished, he stood and spoke to them. "Set your alarms for 1240, we'll be pulling out sharply at 1300. Dismissed."

"You stay for dinner, Captain?" Patricia asked.

"I'd rather not."

Patricia smiled and tugged on his arm. "Oh, come on, sir; eat with your troops, yeah?"

Sebastian pulled away. "No offense, but after everything that happened today, I just want to be alone."

"It will be a positive boost to morale, sir," St. Clair said.

"At least stay a bit, yeah?" Patricia said. "Even if you don't eat, we can sit around, jabber and all that, play some Pharaoh and have a few drinks."

Sebastian grimaced. "Drinks?"

"Yeah, we've got some psykel, Udenski can mix a mean head-smasher. It'll help you forget your troubles, bond with your kits here."

Sebastian tightened a paw into a fist. "You brought psykel on a combat mission?"

Patricia's expression soured. "I don't see the problem."

"That stuff melts you brain, it ruins lives, it dulls your reason."

"Oh come now," she said, "it's perfectly fine in moderation."

Sebastian snapped his teeth at her. "Vex it, Patricia! Don't fight me on this. I don't want anyone in my crew drinking that poison."

Patricia frowned, ears pinned back. She glanced at the others seated at the table; they were just as stunned as she was. "Fine. What do you want me to do with it then?" Patricia asked.

"I don't care, throw it out back, wash your armor with it, burn it, it doesn't matter. Just get rid of it." Sebastian snatched a rations packet from a storage locker. "If you want me, I'll be in my cockpit. You've got about seven hours of rest left; I suggest you use it."

He stepped out of the Freighthog, wandered across the clearing to his titan, and climbed aboard. At least his Hurricane would always be loyal. Sebastian sat in the cockpit and closed the canopy, isolating himself into his own world.

He folded his arms behind his head and stared up into the night sky. He was high enough to see over the forest cover, and the planet's thinner atmosphere gave him a perfect view. Myriad twinkling lights shone back, crowded about Thanton I's lonely grey moon.

He searched for the constellations, the familiar landmarks he had known as a child, yet couldn't locate any. Even 82 light years from his home system of Wopat, a stone's throw in the galaxy, everything appeared different. The only thing he recognized was the galactic plane, a vast, brilliant band of stars stretching from horizon to horizon. This close to Genesis, it seemed to go on forever.

Sebastian sighed and closed his eyes. Even under the starscape that had been his domain for twelve years, he felt alone.

He never made it to his titan's sleeper cabin. He fell asleep in the command chair, dreaming restlessly of the life he'd left behind, the life he couldn't have, and the life that would never be.

This Titan is merely an expensive toy. I cannot fathom a situation in which it, or its ilk, would be more effective or capable than any equivalent mass of conventional tanks.

-Nathan Konstantin, CenCon Strategic Military Advisor, 369.

SCENE THREE

The digital cacophony of his titan's alarm jarred Sebastian awake. He jerked upright, swatted the silencer button, and blinked the persistent sleep from his eyes.

Thanton's morning was hours away. He switched his cockpit's overhead light on, and initiated the startup procedure. His motions were automatic, fluid and practiced. Soon, the Hurricane's fuel cells hummed to life and his displays pulsed with activity.

He tugged his headset on and swiveled the microphone down. "All right, kits, rise and shine. I'm going to show you how we foxes do it."

Patricia's cockpit lit up, breaking the darkness. Her voice crackled through Sebastian's earpiece. "Is this the start of a dirty story?"

Sebastian continued the pre-departure sequence. With a mechanical clanking, his solar array retracted and folded. "Another time, maybe. Today you'll learn why I'm the greatest mercenary alive."

"You sound friskier," Patricia said. "Feeling better, yeah?"

The Katyusha powered up off to his left. "Immodest is the term I would use," St. Clair said.

"I told you, I just needed to be alone for awhile to think," Sebastian said.

"And you thought about what, pray tell?" St. Clair asked.

"Well, today I'm leading the charge. It's going to be my tail on the line, mine and mine alone," Sebastian said.

"Just like in the old days, yeah?" Patricia asked.

The computer voice began reciting its startup patter, but Sebastian didn't listen. "Something like that. I'm better off leading by example."

"It is about time," St. Clair said.

"Any aeroflights last night?" Patricia asked.

Sebastian glanced at his titan's passive sensor logs. "Six, all recon, but there's no indication they found us. We should get moving anyway."

His computer finished its task, and the Hurricane was now under his control. He looked down to his right. Tracy's engineering crew was manually packing up Patricia's solar array. They folded the delicate plastic panels and stowed them into a compartment in the machine's legs. Sebastian was glad his Hurricane had an automatic system.

"Tracy here. All arrays replaced, you're good."

"Form up and move out, line astern formation," Sebastian said.

He tightened his shoulder restraints and slid his throttle forward. He led his squad out over the plains, headed southwest towards the repair facility. He kept a brisk pace, his Hurricane in a low run, and the distance to Nav Charlie steadily eroded.

Dawn broke over his shoulder, and Thanton's sun peeked over the horizon as they neared the target. Long, jagged shadows reached in front of him, the sinister outline of his weaponry silhouetted on the dry grass. Daybreak faded into mid-morning.

"Enemy titan detected," the computer said.

Sebastian sat up in excitement. Finally, he would be able to clash with an equal opponent.

"Picking up a new contact, type PD-1100 Guardian, heading 223, range 98 kilometers."

"It's still almost two hours out," Patricia said. "What are you planning to do?"

"Kill it."

"You will need to cripple its shields swiftly if you wish our missile support," St. Clair said.

Sebastian shoved his throttle forward, pushing the Hurricane into a sprint. "Won't need it."

"Captain, with all due respect, your titan is no match for a Guardian in equal combat," St. Clair said.

"She's right, sir," Patricia said. "I fought alongside them in the Dominion, we built them, you know. They're tough, it outweighs you by ten megagrams."

"Nine and a half," Sebastian said.

"Well, still. It's got heavier shields and a pair of nasty assault cannons bigger than yours."

Sebastian put his weapons and shields in standby mode. "It's slower, and it's got weak armor. I can burn through its shields in no time."

"It's got dual ninety-millimeter assault cannons! It'd only take a pair of shots to—"

"No lectures, Patricia."

Patricia sighed audibly over the radio. "Fine, what do you want from me?"

Sebastian began to outpace the sluggish Katyusha and Freighthog. He checked his radar display, then looked back out across the horizon. The Guardian was beyond visual range, but the targeting box told him exactly where it was.

"I want you to escort St. Clair and Tracy," Sebastian said.

"You're going alone?" Patricia said.

"Yes, I am."

"Don't do that!" Patricia said. "It'll chew you up, spit you out, and then come back for seconds. You'll be in its radar scope in only a few minutes, you won't be able to sneak up. We'd be better off trying to lure it away, pepper it from long range where Udenski can drop missiles on it—"

"I appreciate your concern, Patricia, but I've made up my mind. Now do as you're told."

"I think you've really lost your mind here, sir," she said.

"I believe I am inclined to agree," St. Clair said.

They could whimper until they were blue in the face, but it wouldn't change Sebastian's mind. Patricia would be little help in combat with only half her weaponry remaining, and as well meaning as St. Clair was, Sebastian would still need to get close to the Guardian to disable its shields. Udenski could pound it with missiles all day, but with its shields up, they would have no effect.

Sebastian soon entered the Guardian's radar range. On his visor, its wireframe avatar swung its boxy form towards him, and the sluggish titan advanced into a run. Its fearsome, heavy assault cannons jutted out menacingly from each arm.

Sebastian activated his Hurricane's weaponry. He was at the extreme edge of his ion rifle's range, but he'd take all the help he could get. He lined the underslung weapon up on the distant target, and moved to pull the trigger.

"Enemy titan detected," the computer said.

Not one, but two new targets appeared on his visor's radarscope, approaching from an off angle at a high rate of speed.

Sebastian cycled through his computer's identification readout. "Picking up two new contacts. Type M301 Gazelle, heading 262, range 37 kilometers. Maintain formation."

"You're not going to take them on, too, yeah?" Patricia said.

"Maintain your formation, Patricia."

Sebastian pushed down on his steering pedal. He pulled his Hurricane right until he was nearly perpendicular to the Gazelles. He twisted his titan's torso to face them, lined up his targeting reticle on the lead titan, and fired his ion rifle.

A white-hot stream of charged particles shot out into the distance. The enemy was too far to see at this range, even with his zoom, but the damage indicator registered a small drop in the Gazelle's shields.

Sebastian kept his reticle on the target while watching its movements in the wireframe display. It twisted away from him, frightened by the distant strike.

"Time to show what the Alliance's finest can do," Sebastian said.

When the ion rifle recharged, he fired again, and tore another small chunk from the lighter titan's shields. Unlike his Hurricane's advanced shields, the lesser Gazelle had older, simpler single-phase shielding. They lacked the ability to shunt shield power from one side to another.

Sebastian used this to his advantage, repeatedly peppering the wounded Gazelle before it could return fire. His onslaught drained its shields, but he maintained his distance, pulling himself around to put the two lighter titans between himself and the Guardian.

Both Gazelles came into weapon's range and attacked. Each of the 33.5 megagram titans had a 50mm autocannon and a pair of arm blasters. Beams of rapid-fire laser energy lanced out at him, the blasters firing in quick, three-ray bursts. Multiple autocannon rounds sailed wide; only a single blaster bolt found Sebastian's shields.

Through it, Sebastian remained calm. He stomped on the steering pedal with his heel, and the sprinting Hurricane cut unsteadily into a sharp left hand turn. He twisted his torso hard in the opposite direction and kept his aim tight over the injured Gazelle, even as he skidded and nearly toppled in the low gravity. He crossed back in front of his quarry's nose, found his mark, and fired his laser cannons.

Twin spears of crackling white light reached out for the Gazelle. With shields depleted, the laser blasts pierced unheeded into its armor. It shied away in pain, but Sebastian kept his aim true and his trigger down. A sharp explosion tore through the light titan and sent it tumbling awkwardly over onto its side.

"Enemy titan disabled," the computer said.

With its companion defeated, the remaining Gazelle veered off. Sebastian couldn't let it escape; it would likely group up with the Guardian. Together, they would be much more difficult to destroy.

Sebastian angled towards the Gazelle and kept his throttle up. He carefully led the target and fired his assault cannon. The eighty millimeter round ripped into the Gazelle's rear armor and exploded with enough force to shower the remains of its internals for meters in front of it. It slid, pitched violently onto its nose, and exploded. Sebastian saw no parachute.

"Enemy titan disabled."

"There goes another one," Sebastian said. "One left."

He turned back for the Guardian. It had closed to within range of its cannons, but had not opened fire. It would be almost impossible to hit with ballistic weapons from this range, but even still, Sebastian maintained a light touch on his steering pedal, ready to evade.

Sebastian fired his ion rifle and hit the Guardian in its fore shields. Like his Hurricane, the Guardian was equipped with modern multi-phasic shields. The rifle had little effect, but Sebastian would take anything.

He watched the Guardian's activities in his targeting indicator. It toggled its shield focus to face Sebastian; that would make his job more difficult. He lined up his laser cannons and fired. Both found the target, but failed to breach its shields.

A warning light appeared over the Guardian's wireframe; it was firing. Sebastian pulled hard across its centerline, away from the cannon round. It sailed wide and exploded, sending shrapnel flying in all directions.

"Vex it, he's got proximity fuses." Sebastian turned in the opposite direction, evading another cannon explosion. "St. Clair!"

"Ready, Captain."

Sebastian consulted his radar map. "Flank throttle, bearing 250. Udenski, arm four missiles in contact mode and stand by."

"Affirmative, sir," St. Clair said.

"I'm on it, Captain," Udenski said.

Sebastian pulled across the Guardian's front. It turned to follow him, guns trained. Again, Sebastian checked his map; he'd lured the Guardian off its bearing and put it directly between himself and the Katyusha. Right where he wanted it.

"Udenski, lock onto the Guardian and prepare to fire on my mark, half-second sequential mode," Sebastian said.

"Standing by, sir."

A cannon round burst near Sebastian's left shoulder and pelted him with shrapnel. A jagged sliver of metal ricocheted off his plastiglass canopy, but he remained calm. He fired his ion rifle and struck the Guardian's shields. It turned to face him head on.

"Fire!"

One by one, four small dots appeared on Sebastian's radar, bearing down upon the Guardian at high speed. Sebastian counted the time in his head, and fired his assault cannon.

Too late, the Guardian realized what was happening. At a full run, the standard-jointed titan couldn't turn hard enough to evade the missiles, yet couldn't slow down without risking Sebastian's assault cannon. It twisted one way, then the other, before finally shifting its entire shielding rearwards to deflect Udenski's missiles.

Sebastian was ready. He fired both laser cannons, and the white beams scored a direct hit on the Guardian's bulky front torso, piercing through its armor and into its sensitive internals.

The Guardian shied away and shifted its shields to ward off the lasers. A second later, Udenski's missiles slammed into its backside and buried into the steel. A thunderous explosion ripped the heavy titan apart, tearing through the bowels of the great war machine and blasting metal debris in all directions.

"Enemy titan disabled," the computer said.

Sebastian laughed triumphantly and wheeled his Hurricane hard towards the repair facility. It felt good to test his abilities against superior foes, to send them running and broken before him. He'd missed it.

"That was an impressive bit of titaneering, yeah?" Patricia said.

"Thank you, thank, you, I'll be here all triad," Sebastian said.

"Do not let your head expand too swiftly, sir," St. Clair said. "There is still much for us to do."

"Right. Patricia, form up on my flank; St. Clair, remain with the Freighthog. Tracy, prep your crew and tell Greco to stand by."

In minutes, they were atop the facility. Sebastian smashed his titan through the three-meter wire fence and out onto the former-aerobase's tarmac. A half-dozen deactivated and damaged titans stood silent guard on the pavement, and numerous support buildings lay scattered throughout the base.

The enemy was ready. Small-arms and anti-tank fire erupted from everywhere. Automatic laser turrets fired on Sebastian the moment he entered the perimeter, assailing his shielding. A short-range missile burst against his forward shields, its fireball tumbling across his cockpit.

"Vex it, they knew we were coming," Sebastian said.

"Probably warned by one of the titans," Patricia said.

Sebastian throttled down and twisted his Hurricane through a series of tight curves, swinging across the far end of the runway. He targeted a nearby turret and blasted it with both laser cannons, doing severe damage.

"Patricia, head for the barracks, gun down any personnel you can see," Sebastian said.

"I'm on it."

"Udenski, bombard any ancillary buildings except the hangar."

"Yes, Captain."

Patricia's faster Ranger ran past Sebastian, her shields flickering and sparking where laser fire struck. A small battlecar wheeled across the runway, firing its machine gun at her. She dispatched it with her lasers.

In succession, Sebastian bore down onto the turrets, jerking left and right to keep his shields fresh. His ion rifle and lasers made quick work of them, rending them to scrap metal and silencing their laser cannons. Missiles tore past overhead, leaving thick smoke trails and slamming into the concrete structures. A rocket smashed into the control tower and sent it toppling over, while panicked people scattered from the onslaught.

Sebastian was lost in his own world of combat. Actions came automatic. Another battlecar appeared from behind a building, and before it could face him, Sebastian split it with his lasers. Battle chatter echoed through his ears, but he heard nothing, not even the screams of those dying at his titan's feet.

The Katyusha continued its barrage. Chunks of concrete debris careened across the runway, a large piece striking the leg of an inactive

Powhatan titan. It teetered and collapsed onto its front, hitting the ground with a shriek of grinding metal.

By now, Sebastian had eliminated all the turrets. He turned his firepower onto the barracks, pounding it with assault cannon rounds. Patricia was there already, carving into the feeble structure with her lasers. Her fifty-caliber machine gun ripped apart pilots, ground crew, and infantry alike; they never stood a chance.

Soon, much of the facility lay in silent ruins. Dark smoke curled into the sky, born from fires that burnt everywhere. Smashed husks of vehicles littered the grounds, and the remnants of a Canine People's Army titan regiment lay strewn and bleeding across the pavement. Patricia prowled the installation for survivors. Every few seconds, the report of her machine gun would echo across the plain.

"Tracy, move in," Sebastian said. "St. Clair, I'm reading nothing on radar, but I want you to patrol the outside perimeter."

"With you and for you, Captain," St. Clair said.

Sebastian turned his focus to the hangar. With controlled, short bursts of laser fire, he cut a hole into the heavy steel blast door. A segment fell to the side, and Sebastian pushed it away with his titan's foot.

He scanned the area with his radar, and again, found nothing. He shifted his throttle into a slow walk and circled the vast hangar, eyes keen for any signs of movement or survivors. Absently, he fired his lasers into the adjacent base housing. Flames engulfed them.

Patricia appeared on the opposite side of the hangar and joined him. Her lasers found their mark, destroying the homes, cars, and small shops of the base personnel. In minutes, little but burning embers remained.

"I'm running low on ammo," she said.

"Conserve what's left for military targets, dig?" Sebastian said.

"Yes sir."

He completed his circuit, pulled his titan to a stop outside the hangar door, and consulted his radar map. The green triangles representing his squad milled about the area, wandering between and around the husks of buildings. The Freighthog arrived, drove around him, and disappeared into the hangar.

Sebastian took a few seconds to relax; combat was always so stressful. He checked the various displays and indicators in his cockpit. Enemy fire had severely drained his shields, but they were slowly recharging from his energy reserves. His armor had taken only superficial damage, and his assault cannon ammunition was low. Not bad for all he had done.

He laid his head back and closed his eyes, nose pointed up at the canopy. "Tracy, what's going on in there?"

"There's six titans in here, four of which are registering as operable," Tracy said. "Of those, there's a Titan III, a Powhatan, a Guardian, and a Cavalier."

Sebastian massaged his temples with his gloved paws. The Titan III was tempting; it was a massive war machine, with heavy armor, an assault cannon, four class III blasters and a pair of particle cannons, but it and the Powhatan were far too slow. The Titan III and Guardian were also two-seat machines, with a pilot and gunner, and Sebastian had no one with enough gunnery experience to fill in.

"Take the Cavalier, and put demo charges on the others. Rush your tails," Sebastian said.

Sebastian flipped his visor out of his eyes and rubbed them with the back of a paw. Afterimages of the display danced across his vision. He groaned and held his head; he'd stared into and through it on hundreds of missions, whether in his titan or the similar visor in his aerofighter, and it had never bothered him before. He must be getting old.

"How's it going in there, Tracy?"

"We've got Greco up in the cockpit. He's hooked up to the power umbilicals and we're running through the pre-startup cycle now."

"How much more time are we looking at?"

"Ten, fifteen minutes tops."

Sebastian grumbled. "Jazz it up, huh? We've got to get back on schedule, and the Whitehats are going to be all over us in no time. Patricia, report."

"Base housing is in ruins," she said. "I'm down to four hundred gun rounds, but I haven't seen anyone in five minutes now."

"Good work. Continue your sweep and keep me informed."

"Will do."

Sebastian blinked his eyes open, squinted and stared at the ceiling. They felt better with a little rest, but still, his eyes ached in ways they never had before. It worried him.

He looked down to his mission clock. They'd been on planet for almost thirty-two standard hours, yet resistance had remained light. He had expected the Canine People's Army to smother them once they had dropped in, choke the continent with their numbers. Maybe he'd overestimated the Canis Dominion's resolve.

No, that couldn't be it. With the amount of damage he'd done in the past day and a half – let alone over the past decade – they would have to be blind not to recognize his handiwork. Had he really crippled their military?

Maybe they were hesitant about redeploying large forces. His first two targets were relatively unimportant, but there was no way they could ignore what he'd done over the past two hours. Titans were expensive and limited, and their pilots valuable. He'd killed what must have been several thousand Dominion personnel in a handful of minutes without batting an eye; that would get the Dominion's attention.

"Titan power-up detected," his computer said.

Sebastian sat up in his seat and tightened his harness. "What's it look like, Greco?"

"A relic of the Independence War."

Sebastian scoffed. "Don't be so negative. I'm sure it's not that old."

"Are you kidding me? You haven't seen this thing, it has to be almost eighty years old. There's no visor inputs, just a crude heads-up display. These readouts aren't even LEDs, they're light tubes. Some of these dials have no labels, others are labeled in sticky tape. It doesn't even have a SQUID."

"It wouldn't work without visor inputs. Besides, you don't need a SQUID," Sebastian said.

"What if we run into a dust storm or a blizzard or heavy rain or something?"

"It's 310 Kelvin out there, we're not running into any blizzards. Do the guns work?"

"Dual class II lasers check out. Let me run a diagnostic on the autocannons."

Sebastian throttled to a reverse maneuvering speed and backed away from the hangar door. "Tracy, you got all those charges ready?"

"Affirmative, sir. On your command."

"Good. If you're done with Greco, pull out of the hangar."

The Freighthog's rotary engine roared to life, echoing in the hangar's cavernous interior. It drove out and pulled to a stop next to Sebastian.

"St. Clair, Patricia, I want you on your way to Nav Denver. Keep your eyes open, we'll probably have aerofighters from Umber City on us in under an hour, and they won't be happy," Sebastian said.

"Got it. Lasers and shields primed," Patricia said.

"Proceeding to Nav Denver," St. Clair said.

"The diagnostic is done," Greco said. "Both sixty-five millimeter autocannons check out, as do the ammo feeds. AC-1's ammo bin is full, AC-2's is about three quarters."

"It'll do. Stand clear of the door."

Sebastian lined up his laser cannons on the door's weak points and fired. The cannons sliced through its tattered remains, and it crashed to the ground with a metallic thud.

Greco stepped out into the daylight in his new forty-eight megagram titan. Its stainless steel armor was scratched and dented, its canopy nicked and scraped, and its autocannon barrels weathered.

"It should get the job done anyway," Sebastian said.

"I warned you it wasn't pretty," Greco said.

"No style points for you this time, huh?"

Greco scoffed and turned out of the hangar. "There's something disconcerting about how cheerful you are after killing all those people."

Sebastian sighed. "Never mind that, we have to get moving. Greco, head to Nav Denver, assume a line abreast formation with Patricia. Tracy, follow them, detonate the charges whenever you're ready. I'll meet up with you in a margin."

"And what are you going to do?" Greco asked.

Sebastian armed his laser cannons. "Clean up."

He spent the next twenty minutes dismantling the rest of the repair facility. Millions of dollars of ruined Dominion titans were the only witnesses to the Star Rangers' ferocious assault.

***

Sebastian caught up with his squad just in time to get the bad news from his titan's onboard computer.

"Enemy aero contact detected."

Sebastian switched his radar map to aero mode. "Vex it, we took too bloody long. There's a flight of four Dolphins coming in, bearing 236, about four minutes out. Everyone split up, scatter, move your tails!"

He shoved his throttle ahead and toggled his shields forward. Patricia and Greco veered off in opposite directions behind him.

Fortunately, it was noon, so the Dolphins couldn't use the sun to mask their approach. Sebastian focused in onto the lead aerofighter, pulled up his laser cannons, and locked his aiming reticle onto the targeting box.

Once it entered his weapon's reach, Sebastian fired a long blast from his laser cannons. His twin white rays found the Dolphin's frontal shields, and though it pulled up vainly to evade, Sebastian kept his aim steady and the trigger down. His target's shield indicator rapidly decreased, sapped by his lethal accuracy.

A warning buzzer sounded in his ears. "Laser plates at critical temperature," the computer said.

Sebastian knew better than to hold the trigger this long, but he couldn't let the Dolphin escape. It twisted one way, then the next, but it was too late. His lasers burned through its shields and sliced through its left wing, sending the attack fighter into the Usutka Plain.

"Enemy aero destroyed," the computer said.

He glanced at the weapons readout in the corner of his visor: fifteen seconds of sustained fire. It'd be a minute and a half before the laser plates had cooled enough to let him fire again. He was lucky he hadn't cracked – or shattered – them.

Sebastian jammed his throttle into full reverse. The Hurricane slid on the grass, dug long furrows into the dirt, and then backpedaled away from his attackers. He fired his ion rifle at the nearest Dolphin and tore a chunk from its shielding.

They were upon him quickly. Sebastian twisted his Hurricane sideways and pushed the throttle to a full sprint. Heavy lasers tore into his shielding and cut a gash into his shoulder armor. A gravity bomb sailed wide, blasting a crater near him and showering his titan's legs with shrapnel.

Sebastian pulled his torso about hard, led one of the speeding aerofighters, and buried an assault cannon round into its underbelly. The twin-engined attack fighter shuddered and belched a long pillar of flame, but remained airborne. It broke off its attack and limped away, gushing smoke.

"That's two," Sebastian said. "Greco, Patricia, where are you?"

"Behind you," Patricia said.

From across his right shoulder, dual platinum rays lanced from Patricia's titan and struck one of the remaining Dolphins. It banked hard in the opposite direction, and pulled around in a long turn. Both fighters were now coming in from opposite directions.

"They're after me. I think they know who I am," Sebastian said.

"That's a safe bet," Greco said.

Sebastian jerked his throttle back into reverse and pointed his nose at the nearest Dolphin. He selected his lasers and pulled the trigger, aiming for the aerofighter's left outboard engine. His weapon found its mark, but the fighter ignored it, bearing down on him at high speed. Its massive class V laser cannons pounded Sebastian's shielding, draining it swiftly.

He stomped hard on the steering pedal and tried to wheel his Hurricane out of the line of fire. The Dolphin charged him, kept its nose true, and unleashed a torrent of unguided rockets from underwing pods. They smashed and fractured the titanium-alloy armor across his torso, but failed to breach it.

The Dolphin soared overhead, and Sebastian pulled around to follow, his throttle hard forward again. He selected his laser cannons and lined his reticle onto the target.

Before Sebastian could fire, two azure beams of laser fire pierced the Dolphin's left side, cutting into its wing and fuselage. A quick burst of autocannon fire tore into the aerofighter, smashing through its port engine and empennage. The fighter burst into flame, pitched into the surface, and cartwheeled across the grass.

"Enemy aero destroyed," his computer said.

"Thought you'd like some help, sir," Greco said.

"Thanks for the assist. It was getting pretty heavy," Sebastian said.

"I guess you owe me now."

Sebastian didn't answer. The final Dolphin was coming out of a shallow turn and barreling down upon him. He forced his Hurricane into a tight left-hand turn, spun his torso to face the assailant, and fired a blast from his laser cannons. The beams wore down its starboard shields, but failed to breach them.

"Patricia, help me out here!" Sebastian said.

"I'm on it."

Lasers erupted from Patricia and Greco's titans, spearing into the Dolphin from both sides. The aerofighter ignored the onslaught, angled its nose down at Sebastian's Hurricane, and let loose with both laser cannons.

Sebastian weaved, but couldn't escape the firing line. His shields rapidly dwindled to nothing, and despite striking the Dolphin's nose with both laser cannons, he couldn't ward off the Dolphin before it fired a withering barrage of rockets into his torso.

His Hurricane shuddered under the assault, the rockets pounding his front armor. Titanium plates shattered, exposing the Hurricane's internal mechanics. Smoke wafted up from damaged equipment.

"Critical hit: radar," the computer said.

Sebastian scowled and wrenched his Hurricane around in a tight turn. His cockpit filled with smoke, and he waved it out of his face with a paw.

"Are you okay over there, sir?" Patricia asked.

"I'm getting mad."

Sebastian faced the Dolphin as it came about for another pass. Greco struck it with his Cavalier's laser cannons, punching through its shields. Sebastian finished the kill with a round from his assault cannon. It tore the Dolphin apart and sent its remains cascading across the grass.

"Enemy aero destroyed," the computer said.

"They're getting better, yeah?" Patricia said.

"No. That's the Sixteenth War Group," Sebastian said. "We're getting closer. They know I'm here."

"Are you going to be okay there?"

Sebastian cycled his radarscope's mode settings, but the display answered with only static. "Looks like the radar didn't like being shot."

"Any function at all?" Greco asked.

"Doesn't seem to be," Sebastian said. "Ah, look, topographic mode is working. I'll need you both to help with aero and ground contacts, though."

Sebastian toggled to the topographic map. Vast, flat grey stretched out in all directions, broken only by the wide Kinsha River a few kilometers west. He turned his Hurricane towards the riverbed, and the unit followed suit. The rougher terrain along the banks would help mask their radar signatures from marauding aerofighters.

With every passing hour, Sebastian's seat became harder, his helmet grew heavier, his straps cut into his shoulders. He'd spent nearly fifteen hours in the same position. Though he was used to it, he wasn't sure how well his crew would handle fatigue. Patricia was a navalier, so she had a keen eye for weaponry, but had no titaneering endurance training. Greco did, but he was in an unfamiliar titan. St. Clair would remain sharp almost indefinitely, but

Udenski might tire. It didn't matter; the Katyusha wouldn't stand up well to full combat anyway.

The sun fell before them, racing to the horizon. Evening would be upon them by the time they reached Nav Denver. Sebastian had already mapped out an attack pattern and escape route, as well as a resting point one hundred kilometers away.

Sebastian extracted another rations pack from the storage compartment in his cockpit. His thoughts wandered as he ate. Even though they'd convincingly defeated the last aero attack, aero resistance would certainly increase the further west they drove. Six expensive Dolphin fighters had fallen to them; maybe the Dominion had grown timid.

The Kinsha River cut sharply south, and the city of Bremmington appeared on its western banks. Upon its southern periphery lay the Star Rangers fourth target, the TriMetro Plastics Plant, its vast, serpentine shape vaguely discernible against the skyline.

"What day is it here?" Patricia asked.

Sebastian toggled his titan's calendar. "4th cycle, Lunasix. Why?"

"I'm picking up no civilian traffic."

Sebastian leaned over his console, flipped through the sensor modes, and found nothing. His chronometer reported it was 2051 local time. The workday was over, but there should still be cars, trains, radio broadcasts, signs of life.

"Patricia, what's the Dominion protocol for mass civilian evacuation?"

"We never worry about it in the military, the Citizen Command handled things like that," she said. "Generally, they'd use radio and television first, then speaker-trucks and finally door to door. There's designated evacuation routes, but the CC was liable to ditch the stragglers. You think Bremmington's been evacuated because of us, yeah?"

Sebastian steered his titan towards a bridge ahead. "I'm sure of it."

"Well, there might be some Great War leftover systems," Patricia said. "Usually when they did things like that, it was all 'you're on your own' sort of stuff, yeah? Radio and television, sirens, ultra-low-band, so on and so forth."

Sebastian tuned his radio receiver as low as it would go. A faint transmission filtered in through his headphones. A dog with a thick Dominion accent spouted various numbers. Sebastian assumed they corresponded to entries in the Dominion Emergency Guidebook. It faded out, crackled, then resumed from the beginning.

"How about a repeating automated message on 11.8?" Sebastian asked.

"That's the ULB frequency for government emergency use," Patricia said.

Sebastian listened to the message again. "Patricia, what's protocol 11.4-4 of the DEG?"

"Pish, I've no idea. The last time I read the DEG was—"

"Section 11 is evacuation, part 4 is immediate or under ten hours, subheading dash-4 is cities of 100,000 to 300,000 residents," Greco said.

"What's Amber Priority?" Sebastian asked.

"Immediate action required, enemy military attack imminent," Greco said.

Sebastian raised his titan's shields. "Well, that answers that."

"I don't like this, sir," Greco said. "The Dominion knew we were coming."

"I must concur with Staff Lieutenant Greco, captain," St. Clair said. "Perhaps it would be prudent to bombard the facility at a distance, rather than close."

"I've still got almost a hundred reloads," Udenski added.

"Captain? What do you want us to do?" Patricia asked.

Sebastian shoved his throttle forward. His Hurricane raced towards the causeway spanning the Kinsha River. "We need to ensure the target is thoroughly destroyed, and it's too big for missiles. Everyone across the river."

"I've got a bad feeling about this, sir," Greco said.

"Greco's right, how do we know we're not walking into an ambush, yeah?" Patricia said.

Sebastian toggled his weapons to standby and straightened in his seat. "We've got a great opportunity here, to hit hard and then move without opposition. If we don't take this place out completely, we'll suffer a payment penalty."

"We should just bombard it, the CotD will never know the difference."

"And if they do?" Sebastian asked. "We need the money, we already lost one titan, the more we can squeeze out in compensation, the better."

"But Captain—"

"Vex it, Patricia, one more word against it and you're fired!"

"All right, Captain," Patricia said. "Lead the way."

Sebastian pulled his Hurricane along an abandoned main street, devoid of cars and life. It slid on the concrete, but he kept his speed up. The complex rose up before them.

"All units, open fire!"

He burst through the perimeter fence and across the deserted parking lot. He swung his titan's torso towards the administration building and pulled the trigger. Brilliant white lasers punched into its concrete exterior, cutting a swath of destruction across its front.

Patricia joined in, wide to his right. Her lasers pierced the building, sending huge chunks of it collapsing into a dusty heap. Desks and chairs tumbled free, to be crushed under debris.

Sebastian set his sights upon the factory's main building. Greco was there already, tearing through it with autocannon and laser. The heavy rounds foundered part of the wall, revealing the delicate machinery and vats within.

Sebastian lined up his reticle on a large steel tank and fired his assault cannon. It ripped through its thick skin and punched out the other side, and the huge container spewed its acrid, syrupy resin contents across the floor. It listed awkwardly to one side, and another laser blast sent it toppling to the deck with a metallic shriek.

"Patricia, St. Clair, location report."

"I'm a hundred meters northeast of you, attacking a warehouse," Patricia said.

"57.5 meters south of you, attacking with lasers," St. Clair said. "No sign of resistance."

Sebastian turned from the central building. His lasers had ignited the industrial liquids that now streamed across the factory, turning it into a viscous muck. Vitriolic black smoke rose from the burning ooze, thick enough to suffocate anyone outside. It clung to Sebastian's plastiglass canopy and coated it instantly, but the cockpit seal kept him safe.

"Be advised, some of the plastic caught fire, it's giving out some kind of black fog," Sebastian said. His cockpit went dark as the cloud choked away outside light. He tried his windshield wipers, but they had no effect. "Ugh, it's sticky. Switch to SQUID."

Sebastian activated the semi-quantified image definition system. A high-contrast, wireframe representation of the outside world appeared in his visor. The outlines of targets, buildings, and obstacles were displayed with perfect clarity, and color-coded based on surface material.

He glanced to his left at Greco's Cavalier. It looked much as it did in his target window, sharply defined, flatly shaded, its artificially polygonal surface delineated by the SQUID. Some of the faces of his titan were bright yellow instead of blue, indicated where Greco had taken damage.

It wasn't until Greco turned awkwardly into a wall that Sebastian remembered.

"I don't have a SQUID!" Greco said.

Sebastian toggled to his radar map, but found only digital snow. "Patricia, get a lock on Greco's position. We'll have to—"

"Enemy titan detected," Sebastian's computer said.

"Ambush!"

Sebastian spun hard around. Three Dominion titans had materialized from the smoke, two Powhatans and a Vandal. All were smaller than his Hurricane, but they had the advantage of surprise and superior position. He quickly set his reticle atop the lead Powhatan and opened fire. The middleweight titan's shields absorbed and deflected the laser blasts without flinching.

"Captain? What's going on?" Greco asked.

Greco's Cavalier stumbled forward. Sebastian swung his Hurricane in front of Greco to shield him, but it was too late. The Dominion titanists could tell Greco was blind, and they pounced.

The Powhatans found their aim, and pounded Greco's front shields with their particle cannons. The heavy streams crippled the Cavalier's weak shields immediately and tore into its armor. Greco's front torso armor changed from green to red in Sebastian's visor.

"I can't see through this smoke!" Greco said.

"Patricia, get over here! Now!" Sebastian said.

Sebastian pointed his titan at the Powhatans and jammed the throttle forward. His machine lurched to a sprint, and sent both shorter titans scattering. Sebastian then pulled to a full stop, twisted his turret to face the lead Powhatan, and pounded it with all his weaponry. He was too close to miss.

Both laser cannons found their marks, draining the Powhatan's weakened shields to nothing. His assault cannon smashed through its armor and blasted shards of it out the other side. The SQUID's representation of smoke – awkward, twisting triangles – poured forth from the reddened sector of the Powhatan's armor.

"I'm on the other Powhatan," Patricia said.

Sebastian couldn't see Patricia, but he could hear the hum of laser fire behind him. He pulled into a reverse, backed away from his target, and lined up his reticle for another salvo.

The Powhatan advanced on him, unfazed by the gaping wound in its chest, and opened fire. Its particle cannon and dual class II blasters tore into Sebastian's shields, spearing through his front shields and cutting holes into his titanium armor.

"Critical hit: engine," the computer said.

A groan of protest rose from the titan's drive system. Sebastian stomped hard on his steering pedal and backed around the pulverized steel skeleton of a building. The sluggish Powhatan followed him around the corner, but Sebastian was ready. He lined up his assault cannon onto the smaller titan's legs; when it turned, Sebastian sent a cannon round into its knee joint. The Powhatan's leg seized and it slid awkwardly, spun from inertia, and crashed hard into the concrete.

"Enemy titan disabled," the computer said.

Sebastian immediately pushed his titan into a sprint, lurched around the smashed body of the first Powhatan, and sought out the rest of his squad. Patricia was dueling with the remaining Powhatan, her armor yellow and orange where she had taken damage.

He turned towards the Powhatan, making use of the tight confines to close on the smaller titan. It backed away from both, but Sebastian and Patricia's combined firepower made short work of it, sending it collapsing backwards.

"Enemy titan disabled," Sebastian's computer said.

"Greco, report." Sebastian cut back towards the main factory building. Greco's Cavalier was nowhere in sight. "Patricia, where's Greco?"

"I thought he was with you, yeah?"

"There was another titan, a Vandal, where did it go?"

"I don't know, I never saw it. Are you sure?"

Sebastian cycled through his sensors, but couldn't find Greco on thermal, magnetic, or gravimetric. "Are you picking anything up?"

"Not a thing," Patricia said. "The buildings are interfering with radar."

Sebastian angled up in his seat and looked about for any visual clues. All the SQUID showed him were smashed buildings, burgundy smoke triangles, and Patricia's Ranger.

"We got it, out near the front of the factory," Udenski said. "Cut it with our blasters."

"Did you see any sign of Greco?" Sebastian asked.

"Negative, captain," St. Clair said.

A pit formed in Sebastian's stomach. He stalked around the main building, eyes peeled for any sign of Greco's Cavalier, but he already expected the worst. He wasn't responding to radio cues, and Patricia had seen nothing on radar.

Sebastian rounded a corner of the factory, and found the Cavalier, laying lifeless on its front.

"Vex it," Sebastian said. "He's dead."

Patricia strode up beside him and surveyed the scene. "He could have ejected."

"The smoke would have choked him the moment he left the cockpit."

"Then maybe he's still inside," Patricia said. "His systems are online, maybe he can still be rescued, yeah?"

Sebastian turned his titan away. "We don't have the equipment for a hazmat rescue. The moment we open the cockpit, he'll die."

"We can wait for the fumes to clear. There should be at least two hours of air in there, yeah?"

"We can't wait that long," Sebastian said. "This smoke is visible for dozens of kilometers, there'll be aerofighters here in a few hours and we need to get as far away as possible."

"Heel!" Patricia said. "We can't just leave him here!"

Sebastian throttled up and turned towards the street. "He's probably dead already."

"But he might not be!"

"Falling on his face like that probably broke the canopy seal, especially on a titan that old," Sebastian said.

"You're just going to abandon him, yeah?"

"We don't have a choice."

"And what if that was Adrian in there?"

A cold shock ran down Sebastian's spine. He tightened his paws on his joysticks, clenched his teeth. He pulled his lips back in a silent snarl. "You're crossing a line, Patricia," he said.

"Maybe it's a line that needs to be crossed!"

"I'm warning you, carthagan."

"Don't you 'carthagan' me!" Patricia said. "I'm tired of you and your Volpa words! I'm a painted dog, and don't think otherwise! Maybe Greco and Corey and Zef were right, maybe you're only in this for yourself and your Alliance buddies, and we're all along on your wild ride!"

Sebastian eased the throttle up to a run and turned his titan towards the limits of Bremmington. He sighed hard and rubbed his head with a paw. This mission was turning into an absolute disaster.

"Well?" Patricia said. "Answer me, fox."

"All I ask is that you finish this mission with me. We'll be safer together. Once we get off-world, I'll release you from your contract and you can go wherever you wish. I'll even give you half the contract pay, you can keep your Ranger, too."

"I would have accepted an apology," Patricia said. "But you're not the apologizing type, so I guess this will do."

Sebastian slumped in his seat, flipped the autopilot on, and closed his eyes. He'd lost Patricia, and with her, the unit. He'd have to start over, pick a new crew, scavenge together what little martial resources he had remaining, try to get a loan for operating capital.

It was hard enough starting from the ground up. At least then, he had been a prospect, with enough good press from the mercenary scouting circles that he could get loans, interviews, publicity.

Now that he was old and disgraced, it may as well be impossible. His better days were past, and thanks to Zef's dogged determination, he would lose what little he could have otherwise clung to. Even were he to escape Zef's clutches, he ran the risk that Zef would eat his pride and release the evidence of Sebastian's Florenzine use. He'd be prohibited from entering the major Free States, and certainly lose the opportunity one of the cushy consulting jobs that awaited most ex-mercenaries.

The only person who could assist him in founding a new unit was Corey, but when Patricia left, Corey would never speak to Sebastian again. The others in his crew so looked up to Patricia, they would follow her; Sebastian would be all alone to face the galaxy. He needed to win Patricia back.

Two silent hours and 115 kilometers later, the battered remnants of the Star Rangers reached an unobtrusive canyon, and set up camp for the night.

Sebastian spent several long minutes in his cockpit, contemplating his fate. It'd slowly started to fill with an acrid, industrial scent; the drive system must be overheating. The sun set far to the west and plunged the site into twilight, the canyon walls casting craggy shadows across the parked titans. Those tan walls were all that protected them from the Sixteenth's marauding aerofighters.

He climbed from his cockpit and walked to the support vehicle, took a long breath, and stepped inside.

His crew was already there. The mood of quiet sobriety shifted to deathly silence the moment he entered. Patricia, seated nearest him, looked away, pushing her nose into a combat manual.

Sebastian wrung his gloved paws and looked them over. Even Tracy was here, a serious look on the gershep's face. He'd been waiting.

Sebastian stepped forwards. "I know you're all probably upset, or frustrated. I just wanted to speak to you a few moments."

Patricia didn't even look up. St. Clair folded her paws in her lap and stared at him, as did Udenski and Tracy. No one spoke.

Sebastian stood in front of them, ears held down. "It's been a long journey with all of you, and I'd like to think that despite the past few months, we're all better off from it. I'd hope that my experience and skill has rubbed off onto you, and your qualities have rubbed off onto me. When we fight as a team, we're unstoppable, but the stress of recent events has eroded your confidence. I wish it hadn't, I still think we're the best that ever was, even now. I can't do it without you. I'd hope you'd stay with me, and we can become great once again."

The others were silent, eyes down, thinking the words over. Sebastian shifted in place, nervous as he awaited their judgment.

Finally, Patricia turned in her seat and looked up to him. "Captain, you don't understand. This has nothing to do with your abilities, or your skills, or your combat leadership. I'm amazed we've gotten as far as we have here, we've destroyed six titans and as many aerofighters, killed thousands of Dominion soldiers and destroyed millions of dollars of equipment, with the loss of only two titans and one pilot. I can't speak for the others, but my issues are not business, they're personal."

"Personal?" Sebastian asked.

"I can't trust you anymore," Patricia said. "Everything you say comes out both sides of your muzzle at once. You talked so highly about Greco, how great you thought he was, and when it came to the line, you just flicked your tail and left him."

Sebastian frowned. "There was nothing I could have done to save him, and for that, I'm sorry."

"That's just it," Patricia said. "I don't believe you are. You didn't even say sorry for biting him, you just bounded around the words."

Sebastian hung his head. "It was a mistake."

Patricia leaned back in her seat and stared up at him, her ears erect. "Not apologizing? Or being caught in your own words?"

They all stared at Sebastian now. He twisted his lips into a frown, stepped back from their prying gaze, and slumped against the far wall of the cabin.

Was he dishonest? No more so than he should be. They were prejudiced; they saw him as a fox, and their Books of Creation told them he wasn't to be trusted. He'd been more than fair in his dealings with them, he'd given them the world and let them name it, and still, they turned on him at a canine's say-so.

He couldn't blame them. All of them – Patricia, Greco, Corey, even Zef – had made convincing arguments, and Sebastian had folded back onto his vulpine strategy. He'd already played Patricia more times than he could count; was it so out of character for her to finally reject him?

"You'll finish the mission at least, right?" Sebastian asked.

Patricia shrugged her broad shoulders. "Not for you, for them." She jerked her thumb towards the rest of the canine crew.

Sebastian simply nodded. "I'll be sad to see you go. Anyone else who wants to leave, I'll release and give you your severance. I'll even pay you passage to Exodus, so you can start a new career."

"It's a bit of a shame to leave this way, sir," Patricia said.

"I don't want to hold you back," Sebastian said.

"That's thoughtful, at least."

Sebastian sighed and held his head. He'd hoped displaying such candor, however forced, would have convinced Patricia to reconsider her loyalty, but it had only ended in failure. He didn't know who else would follow him; right now, he didn't care. They were nice to have, but he wouldn't need them. If it came down to it, he could set out solo again. There was more than enough reserve funds to float himself until he could get paid from a new contract.

This was assuming Zef Kelev didn't interfere. Sebastian couldn't understand the slippery psyche of the coyote mind. It was fiercely loyal and honorable to friends, yet capable of great deception towards enemies. The coyote could be the staunchest of allies, or the worst of foes. Sebastian's great personal loss and suffering might be enough to sate Zef's blood oath, but

Randolph had insisted Zef would never stop until Sebastian was dead. At least foxes were predictably untrustable.

Sebastian looked out over his assembled crew, struggling to read their expressions. Patricia was gone to him, never to return, and she would undoubtedly take the Familiar crew with her. Tracy, Wheeling, Udenski, Dorfmeier, and most of Tracy's engineering crew would follow her with unquestioned loyalty.

St. Clair was another case. Her eyes had been on him since he entered the room, and yet, she was an enigma. Sebastian was surprised she had followed him this far. Honor and dignity was of utmost importance to wolves, and such concepts were foreign to foxes like Sebastian. Perhaps his leadership had earned her loyalty. If it had, she would never leave his side.

"Well, I suppose this might be our last meeting as a unit, so we'd better make it count," Sebastian said. "How's everyone holding up?"

"My Ranger's taken a lot of damage to the right side, but my internals are still good," Patricia said.

"Armor is undamaged, all drive and fundamental systems report fully functional, sir," St. Clair said.

"That's good," Sebastian said. "How about ammo?"

"No problems there, we're still mostly full," Udenski said.

Sebastian looked to Tracy. "How many cannon rounds do you have left for me?"

"Eleven."

Sebastian frowned. "That'll only fill me up to about half."

Tracy shrugged. "You should have used them more wisely."

Sebastian nodded. "We've still got enough firepower to take out the power transformers at Nav Eagle—"

Patricia snapped her head up. "Hold it! We're in no condition for that."

"What are you talking about?" Sebastian said. "My Hurricane is near 100%, St. Clair's still undamaged, you've got half your weaponry."

Patricia growled. "Your Hurricane is *not* near 100%, your front armor is breached, you've got no radar, and I know your drive system took damage. We're on the Sixteenth War Group's doorstep now. Umber City is a stone-skip away. They were ready for us at Nav Denver, it'd be safe to assume Nav Eagle will be even better defended. We'd be dobby to go in on it now!"

"You're frightened."

Patricia glared at Sebastian, her teeth bared. "Don't you use your bloody Volpa mind tricks on me. We should abort the mission, eat the payment penalty, and dust off as soon as we can, yeah?"

"Failing to destroy the power transformers would be a 400,000D penalty."

"So what?" Patricia said. "We can't do anything if we're dead."

"Until this mission is over, you're all still under my command. I'm not going to eat nearly a half-million dollars because you're scared. I'm ordering you to attack Nav Eagle."

Patricia stood up, crossed her arms, and stared down at Sebastian. "I refuse that order."

Sebastian glowered back. "If you do, you will be in direct violation of section 5 of your employment contract. Your contract agreement will be considered null and void, your employment with the Star Rangers will be immediately terminated, and you will lose all accompanying rights and privileges."

"Fine, fire me, but I won't follow you into the jaws of death!"

"Let me remind you, carthagan, that the contract for the current mission – including off-world transportation – is valid only for members of the Star Rangers. Should you be dismissed from your employment, you would no longer be a member of the Star Rangers, and it would be illegal for you to board the dropship."

Patricia's gaze hardened, and she clenched her paws into fists. A fiery look of anger burnt in her eyes, and she pulled her teeth back in a snarl. "You stapard little twig…"

"Of course, should you fulfill your contractual obligations, I'd have no grounds to dismiss you. It's your decision," Sebastian said.

Patricia leaned down and pressed her nose to his, her eyes wild, hackles raised, ears back. "I should break you in two like a stick!"

Sebastian pulled his head back from hers and wagged a finger reproachfully into her face. "If I were you, I'd watch my tongue."

Patricia huffed at him. "All right then, I'll play your twisted game. The moment we're off-world, we're through, yeah?"

"Good." Sebastian turned to the remainder of his crew. "That goes for you all too, dig? Set your alarms for 1640 standard time, we depart at 1700. "

Sebastian turned and left the Freighthog's passenger cabin. He climbed into his Hurricane's sleeper cab and lay down to rest, if he could.

I've seen the Dreamworld. I know it exists. I've touched the face of Max, seen him weep for how we live, not just the Volpa but all genera. Unification is not about rejecting one's culture, but about embracing our similarities, our shared history and foundation. It pains me deeply to see that my message of peace and understanding has become synonymous with weakness.

-Unification Movement founder Theodore Daly.

SCENE FOUR

Sebastian…"

A voice called out. It came from everywhere, nowhere, echoing around Sebastian's head, longing for his attention. He didn't recognize it, and yet it seemed vaguely familiar.

He opened his eyes, only to be struck immediately by a blinding light. Shielding his face with a paw did little to help the temporary blindness. "Who is it? Who's there?"

"Sebastian…"

The voice was louder, more insistent. Sebastian felt drawn to it, and he stumbled forward, his boots thudding loudly upon the solid white floor.

His eyes slowly adjusted to his bright surroundings. It was an infinite ivory corridor, smooth on all sides with no sign of masonry, fixtures, tiling, grout, just perfect smoothness. Light originated from every surface.

Sebastian stepped forward into the hallway. "Who are you? Where are you?"

"Sebastian… come to me…"

Every step Sebastian took, the voice became closer, louder. He must be nearly atop it.

"Come on… you're almost there…"

Sebastian took another stride, and the hallway disappeared; the bright light, the vast white expanse, gone. He was in a completely different place. He rubbed at his eyes, adjusted to the light, and eagerly took in the new scene.

He was outside, in a vast field of knee-high wild grass. It stretched out before him, endless, terminating only at the base of a distant range of majestic, snow-capped grey mountains. He could feel the warmth of the sun, the gentle breeze that ruffled his fur, could hear the faint sound of trickling water from a nearby stream, could even smell the gentle aroma of wild sweetgrass.

He knew this place. He felt safe.

"Are you enjoying the scenery?"

Sebastian turned quickly on his heels towards the sound of the voice, but there was nothing there.

"Are you looking for something?" the voice asked.

Sebastian crouched and took a hesitant step forwards. The ground felt real under his boots, yet there was no sign of the hallway he had come from.

"Where are you?" Sebastian said.

"Here."

The voice came from behind and Sebastian spun around again. There before him lay a simple aerofighter, delta-winged, atop a long strip of tarmac that hadn't been there before. The more Sebastian looked at the aerocraft, the more anomalous it seemed, as if it were a caricature. Or drawn by a child.

Seated at the plane's controls, canopy raised, was a young red fox. The vulpine wore a stereotypical, generic pilot outfit, covered in sewn-on patches, and a full-head helmet with flames painted on it. "You know, I asked you a question," he said.

"Who are you?" Sebastian asked.

The other fox laughed, brushed a length of fur from his eyes, and vaulted out of the canopy. He dropped deftly to the tarmac and removed his helmet, letting his wild russet head fur tumble free. He couldn't have been more than ten. "Well that's a fine hello, isn't it?"

"You look familiar."

"Are you going to answer me or no? Enjoying the scenery, perhaps?"

Sebastian looked around himself. "You won't believe this, but I've been here before."

The other fox smiled. "Do tell."

Sebastian stepped onto the tarmac, gesturing broadly around himself. "Yes! This is Wopat. I haven't been here in so long." He pointed at the mountains. "That's the Craig Range, they stretch from here to—"

"—about a hundred kilometers north of Mursankhovel. Your father used to hunt stag in the snow, he'd take you with him, sometimes let you wander in the wilderness."

"This is my home." Sebastian sighed, and then abruptly snapped his attention back to the other fox. "How did you know that?"

"You've not figured it out? The bright white light, the tunnel, the pleasant memories of your youth, the sense of safety, the companionship of someone familiar who knows your life? Think, Sebastian."

"Sweet Max. I'm dead, aren't I? None of this is real." A sudden wave of nausea overcame Sebastian. He lost his balance and fell to his knees, holding his head with shaking paws.

"Maybe," the other fox said. "Maybe not."

Sebastian clenched his paws on his ears. "No! I can't be dead, you're lying! I'm too young, I'm only twenty-five!"

His companion crossed his arms. "Of all people, you should know there's no such thing as too young to die. Now think harder. When you first arrived here, you felt good, didn't you? Warm and safe. You didn't question what you saw, you just enjoyed it. Now that you're starting to question it…"

Sebastian shook his head slowly, and drew his arms tighter to himself. The sky was clouding over, and a rush of cold air assaulted him. "I don't understand."

The other fox sighed and stared down. "Really, Sebastian, it's not so difficult. You just went through something like this, too."

Sebastian's ears shot up. "We're in my head?"

"More or less."

"Then who are you?"

The other fox struck a triumphant pose, letting the wind tousle his fur. "Don't you recognize me? Stand in awe of the glory."

"You look like me, but younger," Sebastian said.

"Like you!" The other fox scowled, and the scenery darkened around Sebastian. "You still don't get it, do you? I don't just look like you, I am you."

"Me?"

The other fox waved his arms. "Yes, me, you, I'm you! Do you get it yet?"

Sebastian shook his head. "That doesn't make sense."

The other fox's expression suddenly became hostile, his eyes narrowed, teeth bared. "Are you calling me a liar?"

"No! I just don't understand how you can be me. I'm me!"

The other fox sighed and rubbed his head. "Must you be so thick? I'm not literally you, of course, you're right there. I'm more like an avatar of a specific time in your life. I'm what you imagined yourself as when you were a kit. I'm what you wanted to be."

Sebastian frowned. The pieces were starting to fall into place. The caricatured aerofighter, the youthful good looks, the sickening arrogance, the patches: it was what he'd longed for. And that helmet…

As if he read Sebastian's thoughts, the other fox displayed his helmet. He delicately traced a finger along the flames. "Don't you like it? Remind you of anything?"

"Blaze…"

The other fox sneered patronizingly down at him. "That's right, you remember! I'm surprised, what with all the time you spend suppressing it from your memories."

"It's just a silly name I came up with when I was younger!"

"Oh, don't give me that nonsense," the other fox said. "You can't lie to me, you know. I know everything about you, all your hopes and dreams and what you long to be, and now that I'm here, you dare deny me?" The fox sighed and gazed into the distance. "Maybe I'm wasting my time."

Sebastian shook his head and sighed, pushing slowly to his feet. "I didn't mean it like that."

"I know exactly how you meant it. You're just lucky I'm generous enough to continue to grace you with my presence."

Sebastian frowned. "Is there something I can call you?"

The other fox tapped his chin. "Well, you can't very well call me Sebastian, can you? That'd get confusing. Call me… Blaze."

"Must I?"

Blaze shrugged. "Only if you wish to learn a valuable lesson for your life."

Sebastian nodded slowly. "Okay. Then teach me."

Blaze frowned. "I didn't say I was going to teach you, I said you were going to learn. Now then, what do you think of yourself?"

Sebastian looked Blaze over. "I don't understand."

"Don't lie. Do you like how you turned out? You don't want to be me. I make you sick, don't I?"

Sebastian screwed up his muzzle. "For truth? Yes."

Blaze smiled. "And what about me disgusts you so? After all, aren't I perfect?"

"I was never that arrogant!"

"Yet here we are, aren't we? You've always managed to back up your arrogance with raw skills and abilities. You are an excellent pilot, titanist, and top-notch tactician, and yet your troops keep dying. Why do you suppose that is?"

"I don't know," Sebastian said.

Blaze lurched forward and snapped his jaws at Sebastian, sharp enough to make him jump. "Yes you do! You know exactly why it is! The truth has always been in front of you and you keep ignoring it. You can lie to yourself, you can lie to others, but you can't lie to me!"

Sebastian held up his paws defensively and backed away. "I'm not lying!"

"Half-truth! Still a whole lie!" Blaze circled Sebastian, ears folded down, eyes narrowed. "You're careless, arrogant, think you can do anything, anywhere, with anyone! You think you're Max's gift to the galaxy, the second coming and savior of the Volpa genus! That's how you lost your tail!"

Sebastian could only listen helplessly. He wanted to flee, turn and run, but his legs refused to move.

Blaze laughed. "No, you can't get away. You want to run, fly to the forest with your stub-tail between your legs! Curl up into a ball, tuck your head down, and hope everything disappears! You want the mean fox to go away! That's how it is, admit it!"

Sebastian's lips quivered, his ears tucked back. He shook his head slowly.

"You're scared," Blaze said, voice tinged with a growl. "You want to cry, don't you? I can feel it in you. These words I speak are true, and it hurts. Down inside, you feel the pain, the heartache. It wasn't supposed to be like this, was it?"

"No..."

Blaze completed his circuit and stood before Sebastian, arms crossed, looking regally upon him. "The truth is, Sebastian, that you think only of yourself. You're so great and all-powerful, you're really something special. A titanist like you comes along once or twice a century. But you think you can handle it all, so you keep taking on more responsibility, more crewmen, and if things went wrong in your plans, they're expendable, so long as you survive. You're always right, aren't you?"

"I am always right! They just don't understand real strategy!"

Blaze shook his head and sighed. "You know, you can charm them with your charisma, your sprinting looks, sharp tongue and quick wit. You can even prop up your reputation and arrogant claims with your abilities. But you can't fool me!"

Sebastian stammered, paws held up. "Everything I say is true!"

Blaze wagged a finger at him. "You can't go through life blinding everyone to who you really are, Sebastian. Sooner or later, they'll sniff the truth. You'll do something stupid and selfish, try to execute some bold, irresponsible maneuver, and they'll see. You might even come out of it dulcet, but your friends will pay."

"You're wrong!"

Blaze sneered. "No? Should I refresh your memory? How about Arthur Manning? Terrance Burlington? Marlene Johnson?"

"They made mistakes! They should have stuck to my plan!"

"Kirk Williams, Brigotahn Fairchild, Melinda Yale!"

"No."

"Zackary Mellons, Adriana Barstow, Paul Harley, Gary Kesselarri, Tatiana Fortuna!"

"No!"

"Melissa Riverford! Victor Greco! Zef Kelev!"

"Stop it!"

"Adrian Miller!"

Sebastian howled and leapt at Blaze. He snarled ferociously, snapped his teeth onto Blaze's form, but passed unheeded through him. Sebastian collapsed into a heap on the grass and rolled to the tarmac.

Blaze frowned and turned about to stare down at Sebastian's fallen form. "It's actions like that that killed them. You act without thinking. What if you had attacked me and killed me, huh? Did you think about what lessons your impulsiveness may have cost you?"

Sebastian shook, partly in rage, but also in terror. He slowly got to his knees, looking wide-eyed at Blaze. "I..."

"They all died under your command, Sebastian. Your thoughtless actions led them to their deaths. You killed them!"

"They knew the risks when they signed up."

"Did they?" Blaze peered down his muzzle. "They came to you, trusting and high-eared, drawn to your ideals of saving the helpless, bringing freedom to the oppressed of the galaxy. They believed in you and your silly cause, and you used them."

Sebastian slumped onto his legs, his tail low to the ground. "I didn't use them."

"You nearly sacrificed your entire crew to Zef Kelev on a personal vendetta. What if Patricia's aim was a decimeter off?"

"It wasn't."

Blaze growled. "Kelev killed almost a quarter of your crew! You abandoned him on Keller III and created his blood oath, and instead of owning up to your mistakes, you committed a war crime. You bet the remainder of your crew, 308 lives, on your own luck and Patricia's aim."

Sebastian held his head in both hands. "Why are you doing this?"

"Because you need to hear this. You need to face your demons, fight them, or you'll learn nothing and your crew will continue to suffer." Blaze threw up his paws and sighed. "For Max's sake, you're too smart not to think! Did you forget what you said to Greco?"

Sebastian looked up. "What about it?"

"You told him he had potential, that he just needed someone to mentor him. It was a lie."

"I meant that," Sebastian said.

"You said he needed someone like Adrian, but instead you used him. Would Adrian have done that?"

Sebastian clenched his fists. "You leave Adrian out of this."

Blaze smirked. "Or what? You'll run through me again?" He tapped his chin. "You know, if I were you, I'd watch my tongue…"

Sebastian flinched, his ears tucked back. The biting irony was not lost on him. "What should I do? What do you want of me?"

Blaze shrugged. "I can't tell you what's right and what's wrong, Sebastian, only you can do that. It's your job to figure out if you're making the right choices with the power and skills you have, if you're making the lives of people better or worse. You might not come to an answer for triads, months, even years. Look inside yourself, relax, and the solution will come to you."

Sebastian frowned and shook his head slowly. "That's not as specific as I would have hoped."

"The answers in life aren't always obvious. You'd do well to keep an open mind." Blaze pulled his helmet on. "Now, if you'll excuse me, I'm off to save the galaxy."

He stepped around Sebastian, leapt into the cockpit, and pulled the canopy down. Sebastian stared on as the engine throttled to a piercing whine. The aerofighter lurched to a start, sped down the tarmac, and then pulled into the sky, leaving a brilliant blue plasma wake behind.

Sebastian stood, slowly, and watched his counterpart vanish. The air became cold, and a swirling wind cut into him. Almost instantly, clouds engulfed the sky, and he wrapped his arms about himself to stave off the sudden wintry burst. Snow began to fall, slowly at first, then with more fury.

A car squealed to a stop behind him and honked its horn.

"Sebastian! You stapard... get in the car! Now!"

Sebastian's ears wilted. He knew that voice, yet he hoped he was mistaken. He turned slowly to see a large, red sedan, swerving tire tracks behind it in the snow, and a tired, older red vixen behind the wheel.

It was his mother.

"Move your vexing tail, you little cod!" she said. "So help me Max, if you make me get out of this car..."

Sebastian hopped forward through the snow and slid around to the passenger door. He paused at the sight of his reflection in the car's window. He was a youth again, similar to when Alsander forced him through that sour recollection.

He pulled the heavy steel door open and dropped into the passenger seat. His mother didn't wait for him to buckle in before shoving the car into drive, sending snow flying from the rear tires.

"Look at you, you got snow all over my nice seats. You're going to clean that up."

"Yes, mother."

She scowled and pulled back her scarf. "Don't you 'yes mother' me! You were supposed to be in school today, and I find you out here playing in the snow. What have I told you about that?"

Sebastian looked out the window. The mountains he'd seen only a moment ago had disappeared, replaced by an urban landscape, snow-covered, sad little shops and offices. Many were vacant storefronts, several with signs in Volpa indicating their owners had been drafted to the Rimward or Coreward

Fronts. Most would not return. It all felt so empty, few able-bodied men and women remaining. This was his hometown, late in the War.

"You said not to play in the snow."

"You vexing scamp! I told you never to skip school! You know what that makes me look like? You want me to go out there and face all those other mothers? They whisper things. They—"

"Mom! Car!"

His mother slammed hard on the car's brakes, skidded through the snow, and narrowly missed a coupe that turned out in front of them.

She frowned and eased the car back up to speed. "Yeah, I saw it."

Sebastian winced and rubbed where his shoulder-belt had bitten into his arm. He sniffed at the air, and glanced up to his mother. "Have you been drinking?"

"None of your vexing business."

"Mom, you shouldn't drink before driving, psykel can impair your reflexes—"

She slammed the steering wheel with her fist. "Just what I need, a lesson in drinking from my eight year old son! You ungrateful little wretch, don't you ever lecture me!"

Sebastian frowned and looked back out the window. "It's just dangerous, is all."

"What's dangerous is making your mother mad."

Sebastian sighed and gazed outside. An older vulpine soldier in an Alliance duty uniform stood guard on a street corner, flinching under the snowfall. Too old for the front, but young enough to carry a sub-machine gun. A delicatessen stood deserted, a large tan sticker in the window advertising its sale. Its owner wouldn't return.

He tried to remember what day it was, the significance of this place in his past. It could be any one of a number of days. The closer he'd gotten to his draft day and graduation, the more truant he'd become. His mother had started drinking again, so it must be after the Battle of Mera Woods.

He rode in silence, rubbed his paws together for warmth. He'd forgotten how cold their car was in winter. Almost ten minutes passed before his mother spoke.

"You know, that little trollop came by looking for you. What's her name, Elizabeth McMahill?"

Sebastian snapped his head towards her. "She's still alive?"

"Don't talk to your mother that way! Of course she's plenty alive, breathing and everything. She wants you."

"Wants me?" Sebastian asked.

"Yeah," she said, "she's loose, wants some in her, wants to mate you. She's got that look in her eyes, the one I had when I met your father."

Sebastian's ears stood up. Elizabeth was still alive! Maybe he could see her. Maybe somehow he could take her with him.

"You're not going to do it, are you?" she asked.

"Do what?"

His mother rolled her eyes. "Rut her! You know, mate and all that fluffit. You're both too young."

"I'm almost old enough for the military, I should be old enough to choose my own life."

"You're stupid, that's why you skipped school. You're too dumb to start a family, especially at this age. You're what, seven? eight? I don't know, I don't remember."

"You were nine when you mated with dad."

She growled and tightened her paws on the steering wheel. "Yeah, and I got you!"

"Mom?"

"You heard me! Vex you, being born! I was so stupid to fall for your father, but I couldn't resist that uniform, he was so handsome!" She punched the steering wheel again. "Instead of love, I got you, you make me sick! You've been disappointing me since you were born! If it wasn't for you, I'd have gone to art school and been a painter, instead I had to stay home with you! You ruined my life, you're a mistake!"

Sebastian's ears tucked back and he shrunk against the passenger door. The event was starting to come back to him. He wished it hadn't. "I... I didn't mean to..."

"That's your problem, you never mean anything. You disgust me, you're an accident, I wish you'd never been born. You ruined it all!"

Sebastian winced, his muzzle twisted down, eyes wide. "But mom... I still love you..."

"Pish! You only love yourself! I see the way you look at your reflection in the mirror, you never do what I say, you only do what you want! I bought you that vexing hunting rifle for your birthday and all you ever did was complain about how it was too small! It was the best I could get on my salary at the diner!" She stared at him, cold and hard. "We've never been close since you fell out of me."

"Mom! Watch the road! Stop!"

The elder vixen stomped on the brakes, the heavy sedan sliding through a stopped intersection. It swerved haphazardly and skidded to a stop in the middle of the street.

His mother glared at him and growled. "Get out of the car."

"What?"

"You heard me! You think you know better than me, telling me how to drive, how to drink, what I should do with my life!" She reached across him and pushed open the passenger door. "Get out of my vexing car!"

"But... but..."

"You said yourself, you're old enough to choose your own life! Go, go live it!"

Sebastian shook his head slowly, tears welling up in his eyes. He'd tried so hard to forget this day, and here it was, coming back to haunt him. "I don't want to."

"Yeah, and I didn't want you in my life either." His mother turned her eyes away from him, back on the road. "Get out. I never want to see you again. If you come back to the house, I'll have you arrested."

He stared back in shock, lips trembling, teardrops rolling down his muzzle. "P-Please, mom, I love you..."

"Go."

Slowly, Sebastian unbuckled himself from his seat. He stepped uneasily out of the car and into the soft snow. Cars were stopped around them, honking aggressively at the sedan blocking traffic.

Sebastian leaned into the cabin. "Please, mom, reconsid—"

She didn't listen. With a cacophonous squeal of tires on snow, his mother peeled out into the street, and left him behind. She didn't even close the passenger door.

Sebastian wiped a few freezing tears from his face and backed out of the street. He remembered now. He'd never see his mother and father again. Elizabeth's parents let him live with them, provided he mate with their daughter, and he had. Their kindness kept him off the streets until his draft day.

"It's sad, isn't it?"

Sebastian whirled around. There was Blaze, leaning against a concrete wall, snow fluttering through his form.

"You!" Sebastian said. "You're behind this."

Blaze smiled and shrugged. "I didn't do anything. It was all you."

"That's not what I meant! Why did you make me live through that again?"

"As a lesson."

Sebastian growled at Blaze and stalked side to side before him. "What is this, all some game to you? Who are you?"

"I already told you. I'm you."

"This has to be some sort of trick. Have I been captured?"

Blaze shrugged. "By whom?"

"The Dominion?" Sebastian said. "I don't know. This has to be some sort of hallucination. Maybe they've got a clairvoyant who's reading me and trying to get me to reveal military secrets."

Blaze chuckled. "You're quite paranoid, aren't you?"

"Maybe you're Alsander."

Blaze shook his head and huffed. "Even when I try to show you the error of your ways, all you do is wail about how you're the victim. What about the others in your life? What about your mother?"

Sebastian stared at him. "What about her?"

"You miss her."

"Maybe."

"Didn't I say you can't lie to me?"

Sebastian breathed slowly and looked out at the street. Cars crept by, mindful of the snow, the dusting of flakes piling up on the quiet sidewalks. Only a few people walked past Sebastian, yet none noticed him. "So what if I do?" he asked.

"You never visited her."

"You heard her," Sebastian said. "She said she'd have me arrested. What was I supposed to do?"

Blaze stepped into Sebastian's vision. "You don't really believe that."

"Well, she exaggerated sometimes…"

"No," Blaze said. "The reason you never saw her was because you thought she was wrong and you were right."

Sebastian narrowed his eyes on Blaze, his hands tightening. "She was wrong, and hateful! I'm no mistake, she's the one who drank herself into an early grave. She should have quit when I told her."

"You didn't go to her Passage."

"I was busy."

"You intentionally made plans to avoid it!"

"I was on a contract," Sebastian said. "I couldn't have neglected it."

"You were only one system away from Wopat. You could have been on-world in a day, maybe less."

Sebastian frowned. "It was out of our way."

"You didn't even send a message to your family," Blaze said. "You know, Tilly was there."

Sebastian stared at Blaze. "She was still alive?"

"Yes. She died about two years ago, though. You know, she really missed you."

Sebastian sighed. "I missed her too. I think Aunt Tilly spent more time raising me than my own mother."

"Lawrence said you were a coward for not attending."

Sebastian snorted, his wispy breath curling up over his muzzle in the frigid air. "Uncle Lawrence always said that. Everything I did after I left the Alliance made me a coward. I don't know how he ever convinced Tilly to mate him."

"They had twenty-four children."

"Of course they did." Sebastian rolled his shoulders. "He probably called it his patriotic duty, providing more bodies to fight the commies with. Besides, we red foxes are promiscuous."

"You were an only child."

Sebastian turned away from Blaze. "So?"

"So? Do you know how rare that is for a red fox?"

Sebastian pulled his coat tighter; he hadn't noticed he'd been wearing it. He stared at his reflection in a storefront mirror. So young, so frightened. "It's always statistically possible," he said.

Blaze stepped up beside him. "Your father was very distraught that you didn't come to the Passage."

Sebastian growled and stepped away from Blaze, turning down the street. "Why? Wasn't there anyone else at the Passage he could insult and beat? I can't believe he sent me an invitation."

Blaze followed close behind. "You were his legacy. He never said it, but he hoped you'd follow in his footsteps, and become a great military leader like himself."

Sebastian tucked his ears down. "That's ridiculous. He was probably furious that I abandoned the Alliance."

"At first," Blaze said. "But when he saw you succeed, he was thrilled. He bought all the mercenary mags, tracked your career, he even bought some of your stock. He loved to tell his friends about how well you were doing."

Sebastian turned on his heels and growled at Blaze. "Shut up! He hated me! He always yelled at me, he made me stand in the snow when I misperformed!"

Blaze shook his head. "He wanted to instill a sense of discipline, of right and wrong. He wanted you to carry on his heritage."

"The only thing he wanted me to carry was a rifle."

Blaze smiled somberly. "He was crushed that you didn't come to your mother's Passage. He was planning on you being there. He had to make excuses to his friends and family, about how you were running late, probably with mercenary business."

"I don't think so."

"He even redressed your room as it was in your youth."

Sebastian snorted. "You're making that up."

Blaze sighed and looked up to Sebastian. "Do you remember, when you were seven, and you came home with that poster for Tumult?"

"No."

"Yes, you do. Your father took it from you and snarled that rock music would distract you from your studies. He forbade you to listen."

"So?"

Blaze twitched his nose. "He saved that poster. When your mother passed, and he restored your room, he hung it up. He couldn't wait for you to see it. He really cared about you."

Sebastian growled. "No he didn't! He was spiteful!"

Blaze held his head. "Why must you make this so difficult? Why don't you believe me?"

"Because you're lying."

Blaze leaned back on a store wall. "When you failed to show, he took it very hard. He never really recovered. First he sought the bottle, like your mother, but it didn't help. His sorrows were too big to drown. Your actions so saddened him that he hung himself. He even wore his old *Sulla-far Fallara* uniform when he did it."

Sebastian stared hard at Blaze. "Anyone could know that. It was probably in his obituary."

Blaze reached behind his back and produced a single photograph, yellowed with age, and held it out for Sebastian to see. It had curled at the corners, faded with age and wear, its edges rough from frequent usage.

"But this wasn't."

It was a picture of Sebastian as a young kit, smiling, holding a model airplane. His father held him in his lap. It was a gift for Sebastian, on his sixth birthday. His father had built it himself.

Sebastian snarled and tried to swat Blaze's paw away, but his hand passed through it. "Get out of my head! You can't know about that!"

"Vex you, Sebastian!" Blaze said. "I try to enlighten you and all you do is yowl! Your father had that photograph on him every day, from the day you left his life until he died! It was in his breast pocket!"

Sebastian turned from Blaze, waving his paws in the air. "Stop it! Shut up! You didn't know him!"

Blaze reappeared in front of Sebastian. "Listen to me, you bleeding twit! It's your strong-headedness, your inability to compromise or think about your actions, that killed both your parents!"

"I was just a child, vex you!"

"But you grew up, and you still ignored them, pretended they didn't exist! If your father truly hated you, would he have rescued you when you fell into the frozen lake! Did you think about that?"

Sebastian turned away from Blaze and broke into a run. "Muzzle it! I don't want to hear another word!"

Blaze frowned and shook his head. "This isn't working. Maybe something more direct."

The street had frozen over. Sebastian's boots met ice, and he slid and fell to the ground. He didn't get a chance to scream before the headlights were upon him.

***

Sebastian felt like he was falling, but the sensation swiftly gave way to the comforting embrace of solid ground beneath him. He was on his back on the floor of a featureless white room, much like the one he had arrived at when he entered this strange world.

"Get off the floor, Sebastian."

Sebastian scowled and sat upright, but a throbbing pain in his head prevented him from standing. "It feels like I've been hit by a bus."

Blaze smiled and stepped up to him. "Number 743 from the Upper Central route, to be exact, but that's neither here nor there."

Sebastian's ears folded down and he frowned. "Vex it, it's you. What do you want, Blaze?"

"First, I want to know why you're so acid."

"Well, you're somewhat of a yoke, you know?"

Blaze paced around him. "Am I really that strict? Come on, I'm trying to guide you here."

"There's nothing I need to learn."

"Oh, really?" Blaze folded his paws behind his back and leaned over Sebastian. "Didn't your father say there was always room for improvement?"

Sebastian fought back a growl. "You leave him out of this."

Blaze huffed and turned his back, flicking his tail over Sebastian's head. "Oh, pride, the only force more stubborn than inertia!"

"Dorwin Morgette."

"Very good, Sebastian, you remembered."

"Father was quite fond of Chieftain Morgette's speeches."

Blaze nodded. "Yes, he was. He was a fox of principles, convictions, and traditional values. He wanted to uphold the Maxian ways, rather than embrace the inner strife that tears our genus apart. Your father taught you his ways. Your dropship is named after him, isn't it?"

"Yes."

"Morgette once said that a species' culture is only as strong as its military, and a military only as strong as the character of its soldiery," Blaze said.

"I agree."

Blaze turned to face Sebastian. "Morgette freely showed his compassion for his fellow foxes. Your father loved him because he treated strays like you with dignity, just as honorable as the pedigreed. It made him unpopular with the stiffears—"

"Morgette didn't care what they thought!" Sebastian said. "He did what was right and noble, not what the stiffears wanted him to! He wasn't afraid of them!"

Blaze wagged a finger at Sebastian. "Ah, he wasn't afraid, was he? He was never afraid to tell his supporters, or his critics, exactly how he felt. Why, then, are you?"

Sebastian narrowed his eyes. "What do you mean by that?"

"Just what I said. You're afraid to admit your compassion for your troops. You feel for them as if they were your brothers and sisters, and when I ask you of it, you tuck into a ball, raise your hackles, and bark."

"They're my employees."

"Oh no, no you don't," Blaze said. "I told you that you can't lie to me, yet you keep doing it. Who are you trying to impress? I already know everything about you, all your thoughts and feelings, but you're still putting on this feral fox act."

"I don't need to prove anything to you!"

Blaze crossed his arms. "You love your troops like your comrades, and it kills you inside when harm comes to them."

"They're expendable."

"Vex it, Sebastian! They're not expendable! You spent days poring over their dossiers, hand-picking your troops, you can't tell me you did that just to have them die."

Sebastian frowned and shook his head. "They'll die if they must."

Blaze leaned over him. "Oy, you've really gone over the dark-side here, haven't you? Why is 'love' a dirty word?"

Sebastian shied away. "Love is weakness, to show weakness is to invite death."

"That's absurd. You think if you admit you love your personnel, you'll appear weak? To whom?"

"To those who want my destruction."

Blaze rubbed at his muzzle and frowned. "What about Melissa?"

Sebastian rolled his shoulders in a shrug, but remained silent.

"What about Elizabeth?" Blaze asked.

Sebastian growled and jumped to his feet, snapping his teeth at Blaze's intangible form. "Vex it! First I had her, then I had Melissa, and they were taken away from me by events beyond my control!"

"You loved them both."

Sebastian recoiled, frowned, and gritted his teeth. "What is love? I don't believe in love. I never had, I never will."

Blaze sighed softly. "So you'll just pretend they never were real? You can't forget their faces."

"I still see it."

"Your loss still hurts."

"Why shouldn't it?"

"Sebastian, I'm trying to help you, but you don't want to learn. We both know that your life has been tough."

Sebastian scowled and stared at Blaze. "That's putting it mildly."

Blaze frowned and quirked his ears. "Let me analyze you here, huh? Your parents never showed you compassion, so you don't show it for others, you put on this feral act as a defense."

"You sound like Guido."

Blaze smirked impishly and leaned towards Sebastian. "If that's how you want to be. Maybe I can't get through to you, but I know someone who can."

Blaze snapped his fingers, and a doorway opened behind him, a yawning expanse that lead to an abyss beyond. A backlit figure stepped through, a shapely, familiar silhouette of a female red fox. She stepped up to Sebastian, smiled, and looked down upon him.

Sebastian stared up in bewilderment. "Elizabeth?"

"*Fella-Maxfal,*" she said.

Sebastian's ears shot up, and his eyes widened. He reached out a paw towards Elizabeth, and she took it in her own, squeezed it gently. Sebastian whimpered and pulled his hand away.

Elizabeth giggled, soft and warm. "I'm real."

Sebastian held his hand to his chest and nodded. "So I see."

"Did you miss me?"

Sebastian looked into her gaze, his eyes locking to hers. A shiver ran through his body. "More than you can imagine."

Elizabeth smiled gently and nodded. She held out a hand to help Sebastian up to his feet. "*Fassala* is not the same without you," she said.

Sebastian bobbed his head. "We were going to start a family, but then…"

"I know. That's why I'm here."

Sebastian frowned. "I don't understand. You're dead."

"Only physically, Sebastian."

He clutched her black paws in his and squeezed, his fingers entwined with hers. "But you feel so alive…"

She smiled. "To you, I am. My spirit is as alive as ever, though my physical body has seen better days."

"But if you're dead, how are you here?" Sebastian looked to Blaze. "Where is here?"

"We're in the Everlife," Blaze said.

"But you said—!"

"Relax," Blaze said, "you're not dead. She is, but you're not. You're just visiting."

Sebastian whimpered, ears tucked down, and he looked back to Elizabeth. "I don't understand."

"Is it necessary for you to understand, or can you just accept the wonderful gift you've been granted?" she asked.

Sebastian leaned into her, wrapped his arms around her, and hugged her. Her body was warm and solid, and she stroked one hand down Sebastian's back.

"It's been so long," Sebastian said.

"I know," Elizabeth said.

"I'm sorry it had to end."

"Me too."

He looked up to her and sighed. "You're here for a reason, aren't you?"

She gently held him and licked his cheek. "Yes, I am. I've been given a chance to change your mind about your ways."

"My ways?"

"Blaze tried to tell you, but it would mean more coming from me. You still love me, don't you?" she said.

Sebastian nodded timidly. "Yes, I do. I think about you every day."

"When you denied it, a few moments ago, it hurt me. I heard it."

"I never wanted to hurt you. I didn't want to bring you harm," Sebastian said.

She held him tighter and softly nuzzled his face. "Shh, I know. You care about me, don't you?"

"Of course."

"And you care about your unit?"

Sebastian sighed softly. "Yes. They're good soldiers…"

"They're your friends," Elizabeth said. "Don't they deserve to be treated as such?"

Sebastian shook his head. "They don't like me or trust me. It's because I'm a fox."

She tipped his muzzle up to look into her eyes. "Sebastian, they do like you. They're loyal to you for a reason, but they don't trust you now because you've betrayed that loyalty. It's got nothing to do with being a fox."

"It doesn't?"

"No, and when you claim such, it upsets them and their faith in you. They become frightened, confused, rebellious, and distressed. That's how you felt when Adrian died, wasn't it?"

Sebastian winced. "You knew about that?"

She nodded and smiled. "I've seen everything."

Sebastian flinched and glanced down at his shortened tail. "Everything?"

Elizabeth hugged him gently and nodded. "Everything. It was truly noble of you to go through with that. Since I had to leave you, I've been watching you. I miss you too, but you act strange sometimes."

"Strange?"

"You never told Corey about me."

Sebastian frowned. "He didn't need to know."

Elizabeth held him tighter and sighed, her breath washing gently over his face. "Do you remember when Corey gave you the Ankh of Kohoutek? He was sharing his culture and background with you. Even though he'd meant it for Adrian, he still thought enough of you to present it to you instead, and it was a big step for him. Sharing is a way to bridge the gaps between our species, and to help build trust. You didn't, but you could have."

Sebastian looked up. "Who told you all that?"

She smiled. "Max did. He's up here, you know. He's very approachable."

Sebastian's eyes widened. "You've spoken to He Who Watches?"

"All the time. He cares greatly about all of His children, and wants to know how we feel. He has all the time in the galaxy to talk to us. Melissa is up here, too."

Sebastian's nose twitched and his ears stood up. "She is? How is she?"

Elizabeth rubbed his back. "She was scared and confused when she arrived, but she met me, and we talked. I calmed her down. She's very pretty, Sebastian."

"She reminded me of you."

"That's very dulcet, love. She's so kind-hearted. It's a tragedy, what happened."

"May I see her?"

She shook her head. "I'm afraid she's busy right now, but I'll tell her you love her."

Sebastian smiled gently. "Thank you."

Elizabeth gently kissed his cheek. "I'm afraid I have to go now, my time is running out. Please remember, we still love you, and showing affection isn't weakness. Listen to Blaze, he's very smart."

Sebastian shook his head, a tear welling up in his eye. "No, I can't let you go. Please, Beth, don't leave me!"

Elizabeth sighed and gave him a fleeting, tender kiss on his lips. Sebastian struggled to hold to it, but Elizabeth slid away from him, becoming vaporous and distant. "I'm sorry, it's not my choice," she said.

Sebastian cried out as she slipped through his arms, and he stared at her departing form. "Beth!"

"I'll see you again soon, Sebastian. Melissa and I are waiting…"

Sebastian reached out for her, but her body disappeared into the air. He gazed longingly after her, and slowly wiped a tear from his cheek.

"Do you feel any better?" Blaze asked.

"I'm happy she's okay, but the memories still hurt."

"Did you think about what she said?"

Sebastian turned to look at Blaze. He wanted to growl at the other fox, but Sebastian couldn't work up the nerve. Instead, he sighed and nodded. "I never thought of it that way before."

"The words mean more coming from her than me, huh?"

"Well…"

Blaze shrugged. "Don't feel bad. If I were you, I'd rather hear life advice from my beloved mate than from myself."

Sebastian nodded again and looked back at Blaze. Everything felt colder. "I still remember it like it was yesterday. We were newlymates, just after I'd been drafted, and I was out on assignment on Manchester II at our sector's forward firebase, Nomad. Because she was mated to a draftee, she was exempt, but she came too and had to live in the base housing at Point Farway. It was right before the Tariff Conflict, the Dominion was testing our defenses with mercenaries and we were all on high alert..."

Blaze stepped over and gently touched Sebastian's shoulder. "I know. Your aero unit was out on patrol, and a squad of mercenary titans snuck in while you were away and destroyed Point Farway."

Sebastian tensed his fists, ears folding back at the memory. "It didn't make sense, they didn't have to! Point Farway was just a storage depot, we had all our troops up at Firebase Nomad, Farway had no tactical value!"

"I know, Sebastian. You don't need to tell me."

"There was no reason... she should have been out of danger..."

Blaze sighed gently and rubbed Sebastian's arm. "You feel so strongly about this. Why did you never share your feelings?"

"I don't know," Sebastian said. "I guess I was afraid."

"Of?"

Sebastian's shoulders slumped. "Being perceived as weak."

"Are you weak?"

"No, of course not."

Blaze nodded. "You show that with your actions, don't you? What's more important, perceptions or actions?"

"Actions."

"Then use them."

Sebastian forced a smile. "I think I understand now."

Blaze grinned and shook his head. "No, not quite, not yet. We've one more place to stop at."

"Wait," Sebastian cried. "I don't want to!"

Blaze snapped his fingers, and everything went dark, no sight nor sound. Sebastian couldn't move or feel a thing, except the lingering pounding in his head.

A voice called to him from the fog. "Sir? Are you all right?"

Sebastian's eyes snapped open. He sat up swiftly, paws raised, and stared at the speaker.

"Did I startle you, sir?"

Sebastian's chest pounded, his eyes shot open, his ears held back. This couldn't be real. It had to be more of Blaze's tricks.

Slowly, Sebastian reached out and touched the towering young coyote before him. "Zef?"

Zef Kelev canted his head to one side. "Captain? Are you feeling well?"

Sebastian jumped backwards and tripped over a chair. He collapsed into a heap, paws scrabbling for purchase on the cold steel floor.

Zef reached down, grabbed Sebastian's shoulders, and effortlessly hauled him to his feet. "You should be more careful, sir. Is something wrong?"

Sebastian couldn't believe his eyes. He reached out uneasily and pawed across Zef's uniform, to make sure it was real, that it felt as it should. Sebastian traced a finger along the insignia on the breast pocket. He'd recognize the Valentino-Kelev Knights logo anywhere.

"I, um, yeah," Sebastian said. "I'm fine, really. You just startled me."

"I've been here the whole time. Are you sure you're okay? Maybe you've just got some jump sickness."

Zef reached down to feel at Sebastian's throat, and he jerked away from Zef's paw. Zef recoiled, startled.

"Don't... uh, worry," Sebastian said. "I'm perfectly... um, maybe."

"Here, let me help you sit."

Sebastian faltered into the chair he'd tripped over. He began looking the room over; it was spartan, steel, dark and simple. A large briefing table occupied the room's middle.

"I guess it's just a little jump sickness," Sebastian said. "Um, why are we in the briefing room?"

"You brought me here. You wanted to have a final strategy briefing before we got on-world."

Sebastian held his head. They were either in a dropship or some sort of hyperspace transport. He'd been on so many, he couldn't recognize it, but he knew it wasn't the Morgette.

"What world?"

Zef frowned. "Keller III, of course."

No, it couldn't be. He couldn't be here, not again, not after he'd tried so hard to forget what happened here. What sort of fiend would force him to relive this nightmare again?

Sebastian stumbled to his feet. "No, no, we can't, we have to leave, we have to leave now!"

Zef grasped Sebastian by the shoulders and lifted him easily off the deck. "Now I'm worried." Zef dropped Sebastian into a jump seat attached to the bulkhead and strapped him down.

"What are you doing? Let me up!"

Zef sighed and knelt before him. "Please, Captain, relax. You must rest. I'm sorry to strap you in like that."

Sebastian tugged at his restraints. "This isn't what the jumpseats are for! They're for securing oneself during a hyperspace jump, not for restraining people!"

Zef frowned. He reached out and rubbed Sebastian's shoulder. "Try to calm. Are you hungry? Thirsty? Hot? Cold?"

"I'm fine, really, why are you so worried?"

Zef grabbed Sebastian's nose and pressed his thumb to it. "You feel warm. I'm going to get the ship's doctor. If you don't recover soon, we'll have to scrub the mission."

Zef disappeared, leaving Sebastian to his thoughts. He couldn't bear to go through it all again. He had to find some way to get out of this mess. Maybe if he did as Zef said, played sick, they could abort and none of it would have happened.

"Oh no you don't. You're not getting out of this that easy."

Sebastian growled. "Blaze!"

"You seem upset again."

Sebastian turned his head sharply, and flinched in pain. "It's bad enough that you made me talk to my dead mate, but now you're making me relive this."

"She was happy to see you," Blaze said. "Now try and be open-minded."

"Why are you doing this?"

Blaze strolled across the briefing room, grinning impishly as he observed the room's features. He reached up to paw at a light bulb, but his hand went through it. "Think of this as your final exam."

"I listened to Elizabeth!"

Blaze smiled. "But you'll remember better if you apply it to a real situation."

"I don't understand."

"Maybe not, but you will," Blaze said. "Now you're wondering why we're here, aren't you? Don't speak—I can hear your thoughts. It'll be easier for us both if you just sit there and listen, if you're capable of it."

"You're lucky you're incorporeal or I'd—"

Blaze hopped up onto the briefing table. "You're touchy now, aren't you? Let's see here… it's 17 Ophiuchus, 496, you're on board the light transport

CSS Fortitude, a civilian starship designed for carrying dropships, one of which you've been apportioned for this mission." Blaze tapped the table. "As for myself, I'm here because last time I ran you through a test, you didn't do so well. I gave you the chance to apologize to your mother, but instead you fouled it up like the last time, so I brought in some help and thought I'd give you a second chance."

"What's that supposed to mean?"

Blaze slid off the table, strode up to Sebastian, and smiled. "It means, my dear Sebastian, that you're going to get a chance to do it all over again, to put right what once was wrong, and not gunk everything up like an idiot the way you did the first time."

Sebastian shook his head. "How do I do that?"

"That's for you to figure out. If I told you myself, it'd be cheating. Although I would advise you to take this most seriously, because this is your one and only chance to fix this. You mess this up, you won't get another try. I'm giving you a great gift here, and I'd be rather insulted should you decide to waste it."

Sebastian frowned. "Is this real?"

Blaze laughed and gestured across the room. "As real as it ever was, Sebastian. And yes, that means that really is what Zef Kelev was like. He was such a fine officer at one point. How could you betray such a trusting face?"

"I didn't betray him! I had no choice!"

Blaze smirked. "Right. Anyway, there are three ground rules." Blaze counted on his paw. "First, there are no do-overs. Second, you can't scrub the mission by playing sick, this isn't primary school. Ship's doctor Stanislaw Morella will come in here any minute now and blow your fakery wide open, anyway."

Sebastian scowled. "What's the third?"

Blaze smiled pleasantly down to him. "Have you heard of PSCH?"

"No…"

"Psychosomatic cerebral hemorrhage. It's a condition where, during a particularly vivid dream or vision, such a traumatic event occurs that the mind is tricked into believing it real, and suffers a severe stroke."

Sebastian frowned. "You're kidding."

Blaze rolled his eyes. "Would I joke about such a thing? Well, anyway, my point is that if you die in here, you will die in real life. Think about that."

"I don't want to die in my head!" Sebastian said. "Let me go!"

Blaze's eyes darkened and he leaned in over Sebastian's head, looming down on him. "Are you saying you wish to throw away my precious gift?"

Sebastian cowered in his chair. "No! That's not it at all!"

"I assure you that would be a most unpleasant experience," Blaze said. "I like to think of the Dreamworld as my home. You wouldn't think of upsetting me in my home, would you?"

"No."

"Of course you wouldn't! So do as I say, when I say, and I won't get upset. I do bad things when I get upset."

Sebastian's ears tucked down. "Bad things?"

"I've got control of your mind, you know. But let's not think about such unpleasantries. Perform well, learn from your mistakes, absorb your lesson, and you will be rewarded handsomely."

"What's my reward?"

Blaze wagged a finger at Sebastian. "Ah ah ah. You'll have to discover that on your own."

"That's not much help."

"I can't do everything for you, Sebastian, or you'll learn nothing." He pointed at the door. "Now, Zef Kelev and Stanislaw Morella are going to walk through there in about three point six eight seconds. I'll be watching you, so don't do anything stupid."

"What do you mean, stupid?" Sebastian said. "How am I supposed to know what you consider stupid?"

"Who are you talking to?"

Sebastian looked at the door. "What do you mean, who am I talking to? Don't you see him?"

Zef stepped into the room, ushering a Pomeranian with a medical bag forward. "There's no one here except me and Doctor Morella."

Sebastian pointed at Blaze. "He's right there, I'm looking right at him!"

Zef walked up to Sebastian, followed his gaze, and stared through Blaze. "What are you pointing at?" Zef asked.

Blaze smiled and crossed his arms. "They can't see me, you know. Or hear me, or smell me, or feel me. As far as they're concerned, I don't exist."

Sebastian winced and looked quickly back up to Zef. "Nothing, honest! I just thought I heard... and saw something. I'm fine, really!"

Zef nodded hesitantly. "We'll let Doctor Morella judge that."

Blaze chuckled, walked across the room, and stood behind Doctor Morella. "That's a good boy," Blaze said. "I'm sure I don't need to remind you that you're not really suffering from jump sickness, do I?"

Sebastian forced a smile, and deflected the long, narrow instrument in the doctor's hand away from his face. "I'm fine, doctor, really."

Doctor Morella frowned and prodded the device into Sebastian's ear. "You sure? You would not be lying to get to combat, would you?"

Sebastian winced and pulled his head back. "No, I'm perfect, really. The jump was just sharper than usual."

The doctor lifted the device to his face, observed the reading, and slid it back into his bag. He tapped on Sebastian's nose with two fingers, rubbed lightly, and then shrugged. "You're right. You show no jump sickness symptoms. No fever, moisture is fine."

"What do you suggest, doctor?" Zef asked.

"Water, a few minutes rest, and not being so bothersome over petty incidents." Doctor Morella repacked his medical bag. "I've got other duties to be attending to, so you'll excuse me, yes?"

Zef simpered. "Sorry to keep you, doctor."

The Pomeranian scoffed, grabbed his doctor's bag, and departed from the room.

Zef sighed and leaned down over Sebastian, gently undoing his restraints. "What's with you? You've never frazzed out like that over a jump before."

Sebastian stood and winced, a paw shooting to his head to hold his aching skull. "I'm fine, really. Why are you being so helpful?"

Zef ushered Sebastian over to the briefing table. "You're my captain, and my friend. Something is obviously troubling you, what is it?"

"Nothing, really."

"I don't believe you."

Sebastian leaned onto the table and smiled up to Zef. "Have I ever steered you wrong?"

"Hey!" Blaze leaned across the table. "You're doing it again!"

Sebastian stiffened, startled. "Doing what?"

"That whole 'I'm so sweet and innocent' look," Blaze said. "That faux, wholesome charade is what got you into this mess in the first place."

"It's not a charade!"

Zef crouched next to Sebastian and lightly tugged the fox's muzzle to face him. "Sebastian, what's happening?"

Blaze wandered around the far side of the table. "That's an interesting word, isn't it? Faux. It means fake, inauthentic, disingenuous. It's derived from 'fox'. Did you ever think about that?"

Sebastian winced and ignored Blaze. He looked up to Zef and sighed gently. "Nothing, honest. I'm just a little shaken, it's not your fault."

"For a second," Zef said, "it was like you didn't recognize me, like you thought I was someone else. Someone who wanted to hurt you."

Sebastian laughed nervously. "Why would you ever want to hurt me, Zef?"

Zef smiled. "You're the greatest friend I've ever had. You could never do anything to make me want to hurt you."

"There, right there!" Blaze appeared next to Zef. "Did you hear what he just said? Do you see now what you destroyed? That's trust on his face, Sebastian! Trust in you!"

Sebastian frowned. This couldn't be right at all. He'd remembered Zef as brash and proud, yet here he was, caring and altruistic. Maybe it was still some kind of trick, but it was growing harder to ignore. "Thank you," Sebastian said.

Zef stood and gestured towards the briefing table. "Do you think you're well enough to move on to planning? We've got about fourteen hours before the insertion, not including rest."

Sebastian nodded. He flipped the table's reversible surface over to its whiteboard side, pulled out a felt marker from a storage compartment, and began to sketch.

"Remember, Sebastian," Blaze said. "You can't give anything away. You try to warn Zef and I'll pull out of your mind so hard you'll be too damaged to tell what's missing."

Sebastian glanced at Blaze, eyes narrowed. "Yeah. I understand."

Zef looked over the table and smiled. "So what's the plan, sir?"

"The plan is…"

"I've got a positively sporting idea!" Blaze said. "Stick to that stupidly arrogant original plan of yours."

Sebastian drew a large pentagon in the center of the table. He hesitated, reconsidering the line he was about to draw, but finally he followed with a long, thin line to the table's edge.

"We'll come in from the south, drive up to the outer perimeter here." Sebastian drew an X where the line met the pentagon. "Then we'll…"

"Yes?" Zef asked.

A sharp pain shot to Sebastian's head. He reached up and held his skull, gritting his teeth in pain.

"What is it, sir? Is it your headache?" Zef said.

Vague, scattered memories of the ambush rushed forward and engulfed Sebastian's mind. In his head, he could see the laser blasts tearing into his machine, feel the shock of cannon rounds striking his back. The terror of it all, feelings of helplessness, the shock of confusion, the horror of not knowing what to do.

The echoes of Zef screaming as he was killed ran through Sebastian's head.

"You never really did forget, did you?" Blaze said. "I can tell. It really upsets you."

"Captain?" Zef said. "You're hyperventilating."

Sebastian's chest pounded, his fingers locked to the table's edge, and he stared up at Zef. His whole body shook, and sweat matted his fur. "I…"

"Don't tell him, Sebastian, I'm warning you," Blaze said. "You know, people say don't worry, time's a perfect healer. That the nightmares all will come to pass. That doesn't seem to work, does it?"

"I'm just… thinking," Sebastian said. "We could use our laser cannons to cut inside."

"Wouldn't ballistic weapons be more effective against the concrete perimeter wall?" Zef said. "We'd get in faster."

Sebastian gritted his teeth. It hurt to say what he must. "No. If we use our lasers, we'll conserve ammunition. I'm not wasting 200D a round on something that won't shoot back."

"Sounds good to me," Zef said.

"Here, hand me those miniatures."

Zef reached into a cubbyhole and pulled out a pair of model titans, each a decimeter in height. He placed them down onto the map. One was a Comet like Zef's; the other, a Hurricane, like Sebastian's.

"Big brother, little brother," Zef said.

"What?"

Zef smiled and arrayed the two titans together. There was a distinct resemblance between the chassis. Both were squat, torso-forward machines with reverse jointed legs. Each featured dual arm lasers and a center assault cannon, though Sebastian's machine was larger, ten megagrams heavier, and had an ion rifle slung under the nose.

"Big brother, little brother," Zef said. "They're similar, like brothers, one larger, one smaller, yet both great warriors, fighting together. Like us."

Sebastian nodded slowly. He didn't remember Zef being philosophical. "Well, there's a logical reason for that. H.M. Hood designed both, the Comet was specifically designed as a battlefield companion for the Hurricane."

"Wrong."

"Wrong?"

Zef nodded. "They were designed to counter the Lupine Order's order of battle. The Hurricane was conceived as a counter to the lupine Akela titan, as a swift, heavy battle and multi-role titan. The Akela is undoubtedly the more superior machine."

"But the Hurricane contains the best of the Alliance's technology," Sebastian said. "It's the most sophisticated single-seat titan around. The Akela is a two-seater. And the Hurricane's got an assault cannon, where the Akela doesn't."

Zef shrugged. "The Akela is heavier, faster, better armored and shielded, with better radar and a much greater weapons load. It's got two of the largest blaster cannons available for a titan, and it's also got a long particle cannon and missile racks."

"And a machine gun," Blaze added.

Sebastian frowned and glared at Blaze. "And a machine gun."

"It's also rumored to have been first tested in the mid 440's, at least forty years before the Hurricane." Zef held up the Comet miniature in his paw, tilted it between his fingers. "And the Comet, while a formidable machine in the Free States, is designed to counter the Order's Adjudicator in the single-seat, middleweight general purpose and light command functions. Like the Hurricane, it's drastically inferior to the Lupine Order's take on it."

"What's your point, Zef?"

"My point, besides that I'd love to get my paws on an Adjudicator" Zef said, "is that the Hurricane and Comet are just more evidence of the Alliance playing catch-up to the Lupine Order."

Sebastian smirked and snatched the Comet model from Zef's paw. "So we're lucky we're not fighting the Order, huh?"

"We're all lucky we're not fighting the Order."

Sebastian picked up the Hurricane in his other hand and placed both titans near to the pentagon representing the factory. He lined them up shoulder-to-shoulder, and stared at them, silent.

"Zef reminds you of somebody, doesn't he?" Blaze asked. "He looks up to you, he's cheerful, at ease, even playful. He freely questions you, but not to accuse, more to converse."

"Corey," Sebastian whispered.

"They both put their trust and faith in you," Blaze said. "You molded them both to fit a specific role, the one that Adrian filled. In Corey's case, you wanted him to succeed Adrian after he died. In Zef's, you wanted him as a substitute, because Adrian was unavailable, unwilling to set out as a mercenary at the time. You even tried to press Patricia into it, but she doesn't quite fit, does she? She's too rebellious, you snap at her so often."

"I never thought of it before."

"Thought of what?" Zef asked.

Sebastian glanced back to Zef. "Uh, well, I was just thinking, we might be cutting ourselves too close here on this mission, with just you and me."

"But you said so yourself, that doing this mission with as few troops and hardware as possible would work to our best interests. You said it would save us a lot of money in overhead and expenses," Zef said.

"I know, I know." Sebastian waved his paw. "But if we fail, we won't make anything. Isn't it better to be safe than sorry?"

"You've never said anything like that before."

"He's right, you know," Blaze said. "You were always dropping into missions under the minimum recommended weight, sometimes quite far below, in fact. I mean, sure, most contracts give you a bonus for every megagram below the MRW for your squad, but really, do you know how many megagrams you've undercut?"

"No," Sebastian said.

"Nine hundred seventy-four," Blaze said. "Well, that's only up to 496, but you get the idea. That's almost fifty megagrams a mission, you realize that? Zef's Comet weighs fifty-seven and a half."

Zef stepped around the table and stood next to Sebastian. "What are you getting at?"

"Well, we've had some success lately. Maybe we can be a bit less aggressive."

"I suppose," Zef said. "But why bring it up now?"

"Well, I think we should bring another titanist with us."

Blaze laughed and hopped up onto the table, sprawling across it yet not disrupting the items on its surface. "Oh my, aren't we a clever one? I suppose I should have expected nothing less. Here, I'll let Zef tell you you're wrong."

Zef frowned and crossed his arms. "There's nobody else with us. You insisted we only bring us and our machines."

"Did I?"

"Yes, you did. You said it's just a quick hit and run, we'd save if we didn't charter a backup titanist and rig. We're already seventy megagrams undercut, and Wallace is paying us a hefty bonus for that."

"5000D a megagram." Sebastian sighed and leaned onto the table. It was coming back to him now. "Couldn't we just hire someone temporarily?"

Zef shook his head. "A boomer? Now? We're already in system, we'll never find anyone this late, and we'd void our undercut bonus."

"Yeah, you're right. A third of our pay this mission is just undercut."

Zef smiled and playfully shoved Sebastian's shoulder. "But we can do things like that! We're the best! The two of us together are just as good as one, maybe two extra titans, right?"

Sebastian forced a thin smile and pushed back. "We sure are, huh?"

"Is there anything else you want to add to the briefing?" Zef asked.

Sebastian glanced down at the table; Blaze was courteous enough to get out of the way. "No," Sebastian said. "I think that's about it."

"Splendid!" Zef wrapped his arm around Sebastian's shoulders. "Then we've got some spare time. You hungry? I'm hungry." Zef ushered Sebastian towards the briefing room's door. "I hear they've got great venison on board this ship…"

Zef opened the door, and Sebastian stepped through. His feet found no purchase, and he stumbled forward into a bright abyss. He tried to scream, but made no sound; he could feel the ground fast approaching, yet he could do nothing but shield his eyes.

He landed in the cockpit of his Hurricane. The rhythmic shudders running through the seat told him he was in motion, and the scenery outside was clearly not Thanton.

"Nav Baker reached," the computer said.

Sebastian squinted at the landscape. It was broad daylight on a vaguely familiar world. Gentle, rolling hills stretched as far as he could see, broken only by scattered trees and rough patches of dirt. Faint signs of civilization crept up on the horizon.

Before Sebastian realized what he was doing, he had flipped his visor down over his eyes and eased the Hurricane into a right turn. The cross icon indicating his current path settled over the diamond representing Nav Charlie.

"Feels familiar, huh?"

Sebastian jerked up, his concentration broken. "Blaze!"

Blaze was lazily draped across the Hurricane's command console. He smiled pleasantly. "At your service."

"Don't do that!" Sebastian said. "Don't pop up like that."

"Why not? It's fun."

"Why must you taunt me like this?"

Blaze scoffed. "Because I'm you. This is what you would do if you were me."

"I would not!"

"You know, I've told you time and again not to lie to me. I can read every thought you have."

Sebastian glared down at Blaze. "Yeah, well read this."

Blaze gasped and frowned. "What a terrible thing to think! And just because you're too closed-minded to accept what's going on around you…"

"I'm not closed minded, I just don't want to do this again." Sebastian reached down to swap radar modes, but he jerked his paw back. Blaze's legs were in the way. "At least get off my console."

"Why?" Blaze said. "I'm not in your way, I'm intangible. You know where all the controls are, and you never look down in combat, you get all your information from your goggles."

Sebastian scowled and stared at Blaze. "Please?"

"Well, since you ask nicely." Blaze vanished from the console and reappeared, floating, outside the Hurricane's canopy. "How's this?"

"Are you crazy? Get back in here, you'll get hurt."

Blaze laughed. "Oh, you're a funny one! Look, the wind doesn't even move my fur."

"Fine," Sebastian said. "As long as you stay still."

"You didn't say please."

Sebastian sighed. "Fine. Please stay still."

"I don't like your tone."

"Let's just get on with it, okay?" Sebastian said. "Where am I?"

"Didn't you hear the computer? You just reached Nav Baker."

"Can you be more specific? Please?"

Blaze smirked. "Well, since you asked nicely. You're 8.91 meters above ground level, travelling 47.985 kilometers per hour at a bearing of 027.73 degrees. You're 31.14 kilometers outside Nav Charlie, and from there it's 49.03 kilometers to Nav Denver, on the factory wall. Zef Kelev is in his Comet, 8.405 meters away, bearing 146.74 degrees."

"When did you get so technical?"

"I've always been." Blaze glanced to his right, over his shoulder at Zef's Comet. "Look at him, at flank throttle just trying to keep up with you. It's ironic, really. Four years after this date, H.M. Hood introduced the 200-series Comet, with a more powerful engine. If you both had been born five years later, Zef might have been able to escape with you."

"That's not ironic, it's just coincidental." Sebastian shook his head. "Look, just tell me what I have to do so I can get back to my real body without losing my cerebellum or whatever it is you want to take from me."

Blaze sighed and held his head. "I don't really want to hurt you. I want you to take what you've learned about your friends and yourself, and what Elizabeth told you, and apply it to your situation."

"What do you mean?"

"Didn't you see what I just showed you?" Blaze said. "Didn't you see Zef?"

Sebastian chewed on his lip. "What about Zef?"

"I'd rather not have to spell it out for you, Sebastian, but you saw him. He trusted you, implicitly, and he didn't care that you're a fox. Wasn't he nicer to be around, wasn't he a good friend?"

"I can't remember."

"Vex it, Sebastian! You do remember! Zef was your best friend! You saw it in his eyes."

Sebastian gritted his teeth and frowned. He'd seen the way Zef looked at him, the way his eyes shone in his presence. He'd seen the same thing in Corey, the admiration and trust. The last time Sebastian had seen Corey, it had disappeared. Sebastian assumed that this whole exercise was about changing himself for the better. How would he do that?

"Oh, you were so close for a second there," Blaze said.

"I was?"

Blaze sighed. "Sebastian, you've got so much potential, not just for yourself, but for those around you. You've got the intelligence, the skills, the abilities to make life better for millions of people. But you've got to look beyond yourself for once."

Sebastian shook his head and thought. Look beyond himself? Hadn't he already been doing that? Wasn't his choice in mercenary contracts and targets encouraging a brighter world for those around him?

"You almost had it," Blaze said. "It's that qualifier."

Sebastian frowned. "Qualifier?"

Blaze smiled and nodded encouragingly. "Yes, Sebastian. That's it. Every time you think of something, you qualify it against yourself. You think, 'how does this benefit me?' or 'how do I do that'? Even when you think about Melissa and Elizabeth, it's 'how did I fail them'? Everything isn't about you."

That must be it. The other people around him, his friends, family, crew; they were important, too. They weren't just tools to accommodate his needs and desires, things to be used and thrown away. Their lives had value beyond how they could serve him.

"You're getting it now," Blaze said. "Sum it up. Say it out loud, it's got more meaning."

Sebastian looked out the window at Blaze. "It's because I think of myself first that people get hurt. I don't want them to get hurt."

"What about you makes you think of yourself first?"

"I'm arrogant, and reckless, and selfish. That's why my crew keeps dying. I'm a captain of a mercenary unit, I should start acting like it, and take responsibility."

Blaze smiled, broad and encouraging. "The light comes on. You're getting it now. You feel it, don't you?"

The revelation washed through Sebastian, cleansing him, filling him with confidence. He wanted recognition, pride in himself, and he could get it if only he took on the leadership role he'd made for himself.

"Yes, I understand now! I've got a responsibility to help others, and not just search for huge payments," Sebastian said.

Blaze nodded. "That's right. You can be a great mercenary, and earn the honor, the pride, the wealth you seek and desire, without hurting those who love you and care about you."

Sebastian smiled and nodded. "There's only one thing I don't understand. Who are you?"

Blaze just grinned enigmatically. "A smart fox like you can't figure it out? Let's just say that you're one of the very, very few to meet your Founder, and live to talk about."

Sebastian stared at Blaze in shock, eyes wide. Could it be true? "Max? But why?"

"I see in you a great potential, Sebastian Valentino. I want you to reach that potential and, more importantly, I want you to become the fox I tried to be. I, too, was once arrogant, selfish, and disingenuous. Like you, I thought I was using my power to make the world a better place. Instead, I failed my people and set a precedent of greed and dishonor."

Sebastian's ears tucked down against his headset. "But I thought you were perfect."

Blaze shook his head. "Far from it, my dear child. I tried, but failed. Greco was right, you did become the Archetype, the fox I wish I'd never become. I hope you'll transform into who I wanted to be. Do you understand?"

Sebastian nodded and stared at Blaze in awe. "You truly are He Who Watches. But I still have many questions."

Blaze waved a paw. "Sadly, this vision is ending. You know now what you must do. Finish the mission."

"Finish the mission?" Sebastian glanced to his radarscope, then back up to Blaze. "But—"

Blaze was gone.

Now, Sebastian's belief didn't waver for a second. There was no doubt in his mind that he'd talked to He Who Watches, the Founder Himself.

Time skipped forward, and they were upon the factory. Its walls were just as Sebastian had remembered: stoic, reinforced concrete, seven meters tall and a meter thick, topped with barbed wire.

Sebastian keyed his microphone. "Open fire," he said.

Their weapons came to life. The two titans' laser cannons cut into the wall, carving long furrows through a section. Sebastian toppled the weakened portion with a well-placed assault cannon round, and he stepped into the perimeter.

Everything was as he'd remembered: the sunlight, the shadows, the powdered concrete debris flecked on his windscreen. Shivers ran down his spine as the inescapable memory replayed itself.

Just as before, he took precisely twenty-seven steps.

"Titan power-up detected," his computer said.

Sebastian pulled back on his throttle. A trio of red squares appeared on his visor's radar display, all of them to his rear. He glanced over his shoulder, but his titan's structure blocked his view.

"Captain, it's an ambush!"

Sebastian stomped on the steering pedal, and his Hurricane twisted around. There they were, behind embankments near the wall, just as last time.

Zef pulled around Sebastian's far side, arms raised, weapons ready. The Viper charged at them, but the Katyusha kept its distance. There was little room to maneuver in the tight confines.

"Sebastian, if we concentrate our firepower on one target, we can take them!"

Sebastian's eyes shot to the breach in the wall. The Titan III was moving to block their escape; if Sebastian hurried, he could sprint his swifter Hurricane past the massive, sluggish Titan III, and out to freedom.

Zef's Comet pulled back from the Viper. He kept his nose on the enemy titan and fired both his laser cannons into the sixty-nine-and-a-half megagram titan. The Viper's shields shimmered and held, and it brought its dual autocannons to bear.

Time slowed to a crawl. Sebastian's paws tightened on his controls, and his breathing grew ragged. He could see every round the Viper fired, traced their trajectory from the barrel and into the Comet's midsection. Shields did nothing to stop ballistic weapons, and at this range, the Viper couldn't miss.

"I'm taking fire!"

Sweat trickled down Sebastian's forehead, sliding along his visor's viewscreen. Armor tore off the Comet's torso. Zef retaliated with his assault cannon and it hit its mark. The 65mm round buried its way into the Viper's unarmored turntable, exploding up under the armor skirt.

"Captain? Captain!"

Again, Sebastian stared at the hole in the wall. The Titan III wasn't yet into position; there was still enough time to run. His Hurricane had a flank speed over twenty kilometers per hour faster than any of his opponents. Once he was outside the walls and had room to maneuver, he could evade them, disappear into the wilderness before they realized what had happened. He could run away, live to fight another day. It had worked last time.

"Sebastian!" Zef cried. "Attack! Do something!"

Sebastian turned his guns onto the Viper and opened fire. On 17 Ophiuchus, 496, Sebastian's blood spilled upon the vibrant green grass of Keller III.

Honor is a strange thing. One side claims to have it, their enemy denies they lack it, but when they war, there is no evidence of it.

-CenCon Council General Anton Narivo

SCENE FIVE

Sebastian's body heaved. He bolted upright and promptly smashed his forehead into the ceiling of his sleeping alcove.

"Ow! Vex it!"

He let loose a brief salvo of Volpa profanities, collapsed onto his back, and held his head in both paws. It wasn't all that ached. His entire body felt sore from exertion. The mattress, blanket, and pillow were all soaked with sweat.

Sebastian rolled out of bed and fell to the cold steel floor. He unsteadily grasped his command seat and hauled himself up by its shoulders. He was back in his Hurricane. Early morning light crept over the edge of the canyon, casting contrasting shadows outside his cockpit. Clouds teased at the edge of the horizon, tinted red by the rising sun. He was back in the real world.

What of last night? Had it really happened? Had the Founder of the Volpa genus, dead for four and a half centuries, come into his mind and given him a vision to change his ways? Rare, improbable perhaps, but it was not unheard of. Even Luc Vurren, the father of the Lupine Order and the Lupine Way, claimed to have received guidance from the wolf Founder Akela.

It was probably just Sebastian's overactive imagination. Strife was building up in and outside the unit, so it was only natural that he conjure a figure for guidance, someone to reassure him that things would resolve themselves. If Max had really come to him in his sleep, He would have surely left a sign.

Sebastian looked down at his body and screamed.

His uniform was in tatters, slashes crossing his body from his chest down to his legs. Blood welled up from the wounds, staining the white fur of his torso a dark crimson.

Shocked, Sebastian lost his balance and fell. He clutched his chest, pulled on his fur, and found his hands sticky. He lifted a finger to his nose, sniffed at the red fluid coating his black paw pads, and flinched. It was real.

Sebastian stumbled to his cockpit's radio, keyed the transmitter, and called an immediate meeting.

By the time he reached the Freighthog's passenger cabin, the rest of the crew was already gathered, milling about and chattering amongst themselves. Sebastian stepped into the room, and all eyes fell upon him.

"What did you do to yourself?" Udenski said.

"Is this some manner of subterfuge to regain our favor?" Patricia said.

Sebastian sighed and slumped against a wall. "You think I did this to myself?"

"You're desperate, yeah?"

"I'm not that desperate!" Sebastian said. "Now, sit, quiet, listen. Last night I had a… vision, of sorts. Max came to me and told me—"

His crew promptly burst into laughter. "Ah, that's a good one, yeah? I knew you wouldn't give up trying to keep us on," Patricia said.

"Yeah, like the fox Founder has nothing better to do!" Udenski said.

"You don't really expect us to believe that, do you?"

"Now that's just sad."

Sebastian hung his head. Even when he was telling the truth, they didn't listen. Worse still, they mocked his faith. He should have been furious, but by now, he was simply exasperated.

St. Clair stepped up to him, and loomed overhead. Sebastian lifted his head and sighed. "Go on, say it, I don't care," he said. "Nobody should believe me anyway."

"I do."

"What?"

The laughter died down as St. Clair spoke. "I believe you, captain. Such a claim is unlike you, and we wolves take Experiences quite seriously."

"Don't do it, St. Clair, you'll just encourage him," Tracy said.

St. Clair whirled in place and snarled at Tracy. "Interrupt me again and you will be unable to find your head!"

Tracy's ears tucked back submissively, and he held up his paws. St. Clair sighed and turned back to face Sebastian. "As I was saying," she said, "Experiences are important to the lupine psyche. Such messages from our progenitors are sought after, held in close regard. That you were blessed with a visitation from your Founder is not something to be laughed about."

Sebastian looked up at the towering red wolf. "I suppose it's not. I thought it was a dream at first. Then…" He gestured at his wounds.

"It is understandable. You lack training in how to seek or interpret Experiences. Come, sit with me, tell me of it."

Sebastian sat across from St. Clair at the room's table, and relayed the entire story. Now that St. Clair had voiced her support, the rest of the crew listened intently, silently absorbing every word and not daring to question Sebastian.

"It is all quite straightforward," St. Clair said when he'd finished. "Also strange."

Sebastian tweaked his ears. "Howsa?"

"Normally, Experiences are cryptic and vague. The Visited may replay the events of a critical time in their life, with subtle changes, such as having a mysterious stranger intervene to change the outcome. It is up to the Visited to interpret that result."

"But that didn't happen here."

St. Clair frowned. "Your Experience has elements of it, but to have your Founder communicate so blatantly with you, and especially so vividly and lucidly, is quite an event."

"What does it mean?"

"That is fairly perplexing. On one hand, the literal interpretation of your Experience is obvious. You must reconcile your selfish ways, both with yourself as well as your crew."

"And on the other?"

St. Clair shrugged. "The Founder of your species spoke to you, personally, and granted you an audience. That suggests that there is something much more important in the balance than merely personal salvation."

"What are you saying?"

"In all honesty, Captain, I cannot say for sure. Mind you, my expertise is with the lupine and rufine Experiences. I am unfamiliar with what methods may be common to foxes, though I can offer an educated guess."

"Do it."

St. Clair sighed and leaned back in her chair. She massaged her temple with one paw, and stared across her muzzle at Sebastian. "Listen and listen well. There is a distinct, however muted, possibility, that you are a prophet sent to spread the true word of Max, potentially through direct advocacy. Another, greater chance exists that your future actions will determine the ultimate fates of a great number of people."

Sebastian shook his head. "Me? A prophet?"

St. Clair's expression darkened. "There is a third, unpleasant alternative. Max may merely be using you – and, by extension, us – as an instrument to achieve some ulterior motive, rather than out of concern for your well-being."

Sebastian frowned. "I'd hope that's not the case."

"As would I. The thought of being a tool in the paws of the Founders is rather unsettling. We all like to imagine that our Founders wish the best for us, but we must confront the possibility that they have their own plans."

Sebastian nodded and looked down. "What about my death?"

"To be perfectly candid, that troubles me greatly," St. Clair said. "Are you positive that you were killed in your Experience?"

"It's not something I'd overlook."

"My apologies, but one's death within an Experience normally foretells the impending demise of the Visited."

Sebastian pinned his ears against his skull. "I'm going to die?"

"Eventually, yes, as will we all."

"What about my wounds?"

St. Clair shrugged. "The transmission of psychological damage to the corporeal body is beyond my area of expertise. Incidents have been documented, but never conclusively. Assuming you did not inflict such injuries to yourself, I would imagine it as a sign from Max."

"Why?"

"Perhaps He thinks you might forget His message, or dismiss it as a mere dream."

Sebastian examined the frayed, partially melted plasteen ends of his jumpsuit. "It's not something I can ignore. I should probably get into a fresh suit, though. Tracy, fetch me a new uniform, please."

Sebastian rubbed at his head. Everything was happening so fast. Part of him still wanted to believe that last night was a dream, if only to return things to the status quo. Things would be so much simpler. He knew that was impossible, though. He couldn't ignore Max; after all, He would know. He might even know what Sebastian was thinking right now.

"What do we do now, sir?" Patricia said.

Sebastian frowned and stood, slowly, bracing his hands on the table. He pulled his top off, wincing as the fabric chafed over his wounds. "First, fetch a medikit and bandage me up. Please."

Patricia retrieved a nearby kit from a storage compartment. She helped Sebastian up to sit on the table, and then began dabbing at his wounds with antiseptic. She sighed. "Your fur is all matted, you've let it sit too long. It could take an hour or more to wash the blood out."

"Well, try to get it so I can put my uniform back on. We don't have that long."

Patricia swabbed again, and frowned. "This is odd."

Sebastian looked down. "What's that?"

"Well, it's not stopping."

"Howsa?"

Patricia shrugged and started wadding up cotton. "It's really light, but you're still bleeding. It looks like it's not clotting properly. You got any diseases?"

"Not that I know of."

Patricia scowled and pushed a heap of cotton to Sebastian's chest. She grabbed a length of stiff medical tape and started running it around his torso. "I don't know how well this'll hold," she said, "but it should get us off-world. Just don't get into any more fights, yeah?"

"That's not funny."

"It wasn't meant to be."

Sebastian sighed and lifted his arms, flexing his spine as Patricia taped him. "What about the cuts on my legs?"

Patricia tore the roll from the tape and frowned. "Deal with them."

Sebastian stepped down to the floor and experimentally twisted himself. Patricia's treatment drastically cut his mobility, but it would keep the worst of his wounds from exposure. "Thank you, Patricia."

She folded her arms and stared down at him. "So, now what?"

Tracy reappeared and tossed a new uniform top to Sebastian. He put it on. "Now we finish the mission."

Patricia wagged a finger in Sebastian's face. "If you think I'm going to walk into the Sixteenth War Group's teeth—"

Sebastian tugged his uniform into place. "We're finishing the mission, Patricia. That means we're heading to the extraction point at Nav Falcon."

"We're aborting?"

"We're cutting our losses and getting out of here," Sebastian said. "We're not getting paid enough to die on this stinking rock."

Patricia quirked her ears. "For truth?"

Sebastian smiled and patted her arm. "Yes, Patricia. For truth. We're pulling out in thirty minutes."

***

Daylight broke on the Usutka Plain, peeking between mid-morning clouds. Valentino's Star Rangers had packed their equipment in and embarked on their seven hundred kilometer journey to the dust-off zone. There was nothing left for Sebastian Valentino to do but set the autopilot.

The original schedule had called for them to strike the power transformers at Nav Eagle at approximately midnight on the beginning of 2 Leonus. The Canis Dominion doubtless waited for them there, and when they didn't show, they would come looking. By then, the Star Rangers should be two hundred kilometers away.

Sebastian flipped through his radar modes. Aero mode still gave him nothing, but at least he had the ground-targeting band. "My radar's aero mode is still dead. How're you, Patricia?"

"Good enough," she said. "Tracy patched up most of my armor. What about yours?"

Sebastian checked his damage indicator. The blue wireframe was speckled with patches of yellow. "He bandaged up the hole in my nose, but it looks like I've still got some incidental damage elsewhere. Engine looks to be at about 85%. Udenski, how's the radar look?"

"Quiet."

Sebastian sighed and stared out at the landscape. If they'd been headed to Nav Eagle and the city of Walhill, as scheduled, they could have followed the Kinsha River to it. At this elevation, the river cut a chasm through the growing mountains, and the terrain would have helped shield them from aero attacks. Instead, they were forced to abandon its safety in order to cut west across to Nav Falcon. Now they were stuck on flatlands.

Above them rose the Umber Mountains, the sharp grey peaks towering over the plain. Sebastian smiled and looked up to them. "It's pretty out here, with the mountains in front of us," Udenski said.

"It's nice to see them again, it's been a long time," Sebastian said.

"I thought you've been to Thanton recently?" Patricia said.

"The last couple times were on the north hemisphere. I haven't been down here on Lowan for five or six years."

"Happy to see them, yeah?"

Sebastian chuckled. "It means we're getting close to the dust-off zone. You know, they're the tallest mountain range on the planet. Mount Formidable has a vertical prominence of almost five kilometers."

"No wonder the plains are so dry here," Udenski said.

"All this empty space makes me nervous, it's perfect for aerofighters," Patricia said.

"And extraction," Sebastian said. "There's no better place for a dropship to land before the mountains."

"What if we get attacked by aeros?" Patricia asked.

"I doubt it. If I know the Dominion, they'll have all their resources crowded around Walhill."

"And if they don't?" Udenski asked.

"Hopefully we'll be close to the dropship by then," Sebastian said.

"You don't sound too confident," Patricia said.

"I'm not."

Sebastian watched the minutes tick by on his GST clock. Soon, he could assume the Dominion would be hunting for him. Any aerofighters would be coming from Umber City in the south, and they'd probably be searching east of Walhill. The Star Rangers were headed northwest to the dust-off zone; with a little luck, they'd be able to evade any aerofighters long enough to escape.

He waited the time out, watching the progress his squad made on the navigational map.

"It's a little after 0300 now. Prep your shields and weapons, and keep your eyes open for aerofighters," Sebastian said.

"Copy that, sir," Udenski said. "I'll keep you advised."

Minutes faded into hours. The sun peaked overhead and began its descent towards the horizon. The distance to Nav Falcon steadily eroded, with no sign of any enemy activity. The Star Rangers remained the sole occupants of the plateau.

Two meal packs later, Sebastian keyed his microphone. "Udenski, what's going on out there?"

"Absolutely nothing, sir. Completely quiet."

"Too quiet, if you ask me," Patricia said.

"I am in agreement, there is a suspicious lack of activity," St. Clair said.

"Dust-and-runs make me nervous," Patricia said.

"Everything makes you nervous," Udenski said.

"What I mean is, I'd feel better if the dropship were on the ground when we got there, yeah?"

The sun was setting before them, closing in on the mountains. Sebastian tinted his visor to block the glare. "The rendezvous isn't for another two hours. The dropship probably won't be on scope for another ninety minutes."

"I'm picking up an aero contact," Udenski said.

Sebastian sat up in his seat. "Details."

"Well, um, let's see..."

"Udenski?"

"Just a minute, sir. This can't be right."

"Spill it."

"Altitude, 36.5 kilometers, velocity 3300, range 89, coming in hard and hot," Udenski said. "It's the dropship."

Sebastian frowned. "It can't be. It's much too early."

"You can ask it yourself, it'll be overhead in about two minutes."

Sebastian craned his neck upwards to look. Just when Udenski said, he saw it, the glint of sunlight on steel betraying the dropship's presence. It soared overhead at high speed.

"What do you suppose it means?" Patricia asked.

"I don't know," Sebastian said. "An early welcome?"

"I severely doubt that, Captain," St. Clair said. "If our dropship has arrived early, it has no doubt risked identification by Dominion ground radar to do so. There must be an important reason."

"New contact detected," Sebastian's computer said.

"I'm picking them up on my ground-targeting band," Sebastian said. "It looks like they're touching down about seventy kilometers ahead."

"That's short of the extraction point, yeah?" Patricia said.

"By about fifty kilometers. We must be leaving early. Everyone put your shields and weapons on standby, just in case."

"Copy that, sir."

Sebastian targeted the dropship, and watched the wireframe representation in his visor. He cycled through his radio bands, but picked up nothing. The dropship must still be running in silent mode.

"Warning: unidentified titan contact detected," his computer said.

A pair of new targets appeared around the dropship. Sebastian swapped between the two titans; one was a Comet, the other was a model he didn't recognize. A caption beneath its bounding box listed it as UNKN.

"I'm picking up two titan contacts under the dropship, one is a Comet, the other is unknown," Sebastian said.

"What do you mean, unknown? You and your Hurricane know every titan there is, yeah?" Patricia said.

"I thought I did, but I've never seen this one before, and it doesn't register in my databanks."

"I find it most difficult to believe that your Hurricane would fail in this regard," St. Clair said.

"What's it look like?" Patricia asked.

Sebastian watched the wireframe avatar. Both titans were stopped, parked next to the dropship. "It's standard-jointed, torso-up configuration, with some kind of main gun for a right arm."

"It sounds like a Vandal, they're all over the Dominion," Patricia said.

Sebastian tried again. The computer stumbled through a handful of potential model numbers before finally falling back to UNKN. "It's not registering as a Vandal. It's too big, I think."

"If your Hurricane doesn't recognize it, it doesn't exist," Udenski said.

"I'm telling you, it's something that neither I nor my computer have seen before," Sebastian said.

"A better question is whether they're friendly or not," Udenski said.

"I believe that I am more capable of answering that question, Blaze."

Sebastian's blood ran cold. It couldn't be!

"Zef!"

"You did not expect to find me here, did you?"

Sebastian's paws tightened on his throttle and joystick. "I should have known you'd be behind this."

"I must admit a certain amount of flattery that you recognize my handiwork, fox. It is true that I masterminded this scheme, but I confess I had help. The Children of the Dawn, for instance, were eager to supply you with a phony contract in exchange for future work for myself. The Canine People's Army were also quite generous in harassing you the entire way, though I regret they were mostly ineffective. Though I do note you seem to be missing... who is it, Greco?"

"The Whitehats lost six titans, six aerofighters, and thousands of troops," Sebastian said.

"This is true," Zef said. "Of course, none of this would have been possible without the ample tactical advice from my new first officer."

Sebastian scowled and activated his weapons and shields. "What happened to Thompson?"

"I found someone better," Zef said. "Perhaps you know him."

"Greetings, my dear ex-Captain."

Sebastian's breath caught in his chest and a chill ran through his spine. "Corey..."

"Executive officer Corey Delzano, of the Disintegrators, at your service. Did you miss me, Captain?"

Sebastian growled into his microphone. "You traitorous cur!"

"Words, captain," Corey said. "Zef offered me quite a generous employment offer."

"You stapard affakravox! How can you trust him? Don't you know what he's done?"

"I know what he has not done, Sebastian! He has not abandoned his second-in-command to the mercy of the enemy, he has not committed war crimes, he has not used chemical weapons outlawed in every civilized nation, and he certainly did not berate me in front of the crew for my less-than-thorough knowledge of your culture!"

Sebastian hesitated. "You... still remember that?"

"Of course I do," Corey said. "You told me to shut my ugly brown vullisvolk face, called me a stupid dog and a pathetic lappund."

"You've been nursing that hurt all this time?"

"I always thought you were different from the other foxes, Sebastian. I thought you and Adrian were special. But that outburst taught me that you were just like the others."

Sebastian's lips quivered. He felt so violated; how could Corey do this to him? No, Corey wasn't in the wrong. Sebastian had abused him horribly and now he was lashing out. This was all Sebastian's fault.

"You see?" Zef said. "He is a perfect match for me, and smart, too. He has studied your tactics and foretold every move you have made since you landed. Except, of course, your abort. I must say, it fouled our strategy somewhat. I had intended to outright ambush you, but this will do fine."

Sebastian put the throttle forward and pointed his Hurricane in Zef's direction. "I'm happy to upset your plans."

"It is no matter," Zef said. "My new war machine is more than a match for yours at range. I am sure you are curious about it, it must come up on your scanners as unknown."

"I don't give a dusty tail about your new titan," Sebastian said.

"It is the latest from the Canis Dominion's Military Research Lab, the Vandal II. They were gracious enough to sell me one at a steep discount in appreciation for snaring you."

Sebastian slaved his weapons to his left joystick and zoomed his reticle onto Zef's stationary titan. He was still forty kilometers out. "Yeah, they're full of graciousness."

"You do not sound as impressed as I had hoped. Maybe this will change your mind."

Zef's titan lazily turned about, its shoulder cannon pointed towards Sebastian. His targeting computer registered the shot, and Sebastian pulled his titan off-angle. Sebastian assumed the Vandal II came equipped with a large-caliber assault cannon, easy enough to dodge at this range.

Seventeen seconds later, Sebastian was proven wrong. A 30mm solid sphere shot past his left shoulder, leaving a sonic boom in its wake.

"Sweet Max! He must have an EMC on that thing," Sebastian said.

"Indeed I do, Blaze. You will find escape quite impossible. I need not remind you that the Sixteenth War Group is fast approaching in great numbers from your rear," Zef said.

Sebastian checked his radarscope. The vanguard of the Dominion's forces had appeared on the periphery. At least four contacts were closing on him from astern, with many more likely to follow.

Zef laughed. "This time, I have the faster titan, Blaze! There is nowhere to run now, this time you must fight to survive!"

Sebastian switched to short-range radio and pulled his Hurricane to a slow walk. "What do you think, Patricia?"

Over his right shoulder, Patricia kept pace, her Ranger tight in formation. "He makes it sound so noble, yeah? I don't know. There's three of us to his two, but I'm at half my weapons and Udenski's only going to be good if we tear down their shields."

"Zef and Corey are both top-notch titanists," Sebastian said. "I'm not sure if we'll be able to defeat them in our state. We'd have to be very lucky."

"Do you feel lucky?"

Sebastian sighed and watched Zef through his visor. His Vandal II pushed into a run and advanced on him, while Corey's Comet followed suit to his left. Sebastian would be in weapon range in only five minutes.

"I don't."

"Sir?" Patricia asked.

"Look," Sebastian said. "We can assume the dropship is, and always has been, on either Zef's or the Children's payroll. Defeating Zef and Corey would be pointless, the dropship would take off the moment we got close. We'd still be severely wounded and stuck on this plateau, and you can be sure that Dominion aerofighters will be on us in no time. Frankly, I'm surprised they've stayed away so far, though I imagine Zef had some hand in it."

"So what do we do?"

Sebastian forced a smile, his lips quivering. "You've got a bright future ahead of you, Patricia. You'll make a bonny captain."

"What are you talking about?"

Sebastian toggled his shields to full forward, and trained his weapons onto Zef's titan. "Take St. Clair and Tracy and head for the mountains. You're all canines, so you can hide out from Dominion forces until you can rendezvous with opposition forces, they should be able to smuggle you off-world."

"You're joking!" Patricia said.

"Captain, you cannot be serious," St. Clair said.

"Zef isn't going to stop until I'm dead," Sebastian said. "You've all got such potential, and I can't let you suffer any further for my mistakes."

"He'll come after us anyway," Patricia said.

"He doesn't want you, he wants me. If you hurry, you'll stay beyond the radar range of the Dominion titans. You'll have enough time to get to the mountains and away from aero attacks. I'll stay here and distract them all long enough for you to escape."

"No, you can't! That's suicide! We'll stand and fight together one last time!"

Sebastian sighed hard. "Patricia, you know I hate it when you argue with me."

"I know," Patricia said.

"Now do as you're told."

"Sir, please reconsider, we can fight them off, Udenski can drop missiles on them, we can all escape to the mountains…"

"Those are your orders. I expect you to obey."

"You're a braver person than I," Udenski said.

"Captain, I must say it has been an honor and a privilege to serve under your command," St. Clair said.

"She's right, yeah? You were a great friend to me, Captain. I'm sorry about the things I said in anger," Patricia said.

"So am I," Sebastian said. "More than you'll ever know."

"I'll miss you, sir."

A tear ran gently down Sebastian's cheek. "Enough talk, you're wasting time. Go. Good luck."

"Thank you," Patricia said.

"*Yasha-marsa, kehnellya.*"

Sebastian severed the communications link.

He shoved the throttle on his Hurricane hard forward, and the machine heaved into a sprint. He turned north, away from the rest of his squad. Zef and Corey followed pursuit.

By the time they reached his weapons range, Sebastian had pulled them several kilometers from Patricia's group. He kept his throttle up and his back to Zef, forcing him to follow and fire from a distance. Several times, their shots found him. An EMC round tore a large chunk from his back, and a cannon round from Corey hit him in the right arm.

Occasionally, Sebastian twisted around to return fire, but he had no intent of destroying them. He meant only to lure them away. Zef steadily gained on him, and the Sixteenth War Group had entered weapon's range from the east.

He'd been running from both for ten months, one-hundred eighty long days. He was weary and alone, and the hounds were biting at his heels. With his last act, he'd led both sides on an hour-long pursuit to give Patricia time to escape.

Satisfied, he finally turned towards the Dominion's forces. He couldn't give Zef the gratification of killing him.

Sebastian Valentino destroyed four Dominion titans before finally being cut down. His Hurricane gave up, shredded by laser and autocannon fire, and Sebastian narrowly escaped in his ejector seat before his faithful steed succumbed to its damage.

He landed awkwardly on the packed dirt of the Usutka Plain, his leg snapping under the hard landing. Sebastian tumbled onto his back, his tibia jutting out below his knee. It was too painful to move, so he lay on his back and waited, waited for the Dominion titans to encircle him. They arrived before Zef and kept the coyote from his long-desired quarry.

Sebastian stared into the starry night sky; soon, the helicopter would arrive to take him to death row. Maybe it was delirium, maybe traumatic shock, maybe denying Zef his kill with one last act of defiance, but as he lay there, he couldn't help but laugh. He'd charged heedlessly into impossible odds and flaunted his disregard for mortality so many times before. Now, he'd sacrificed himself to save the lives of his comrades.

He still came out alive.

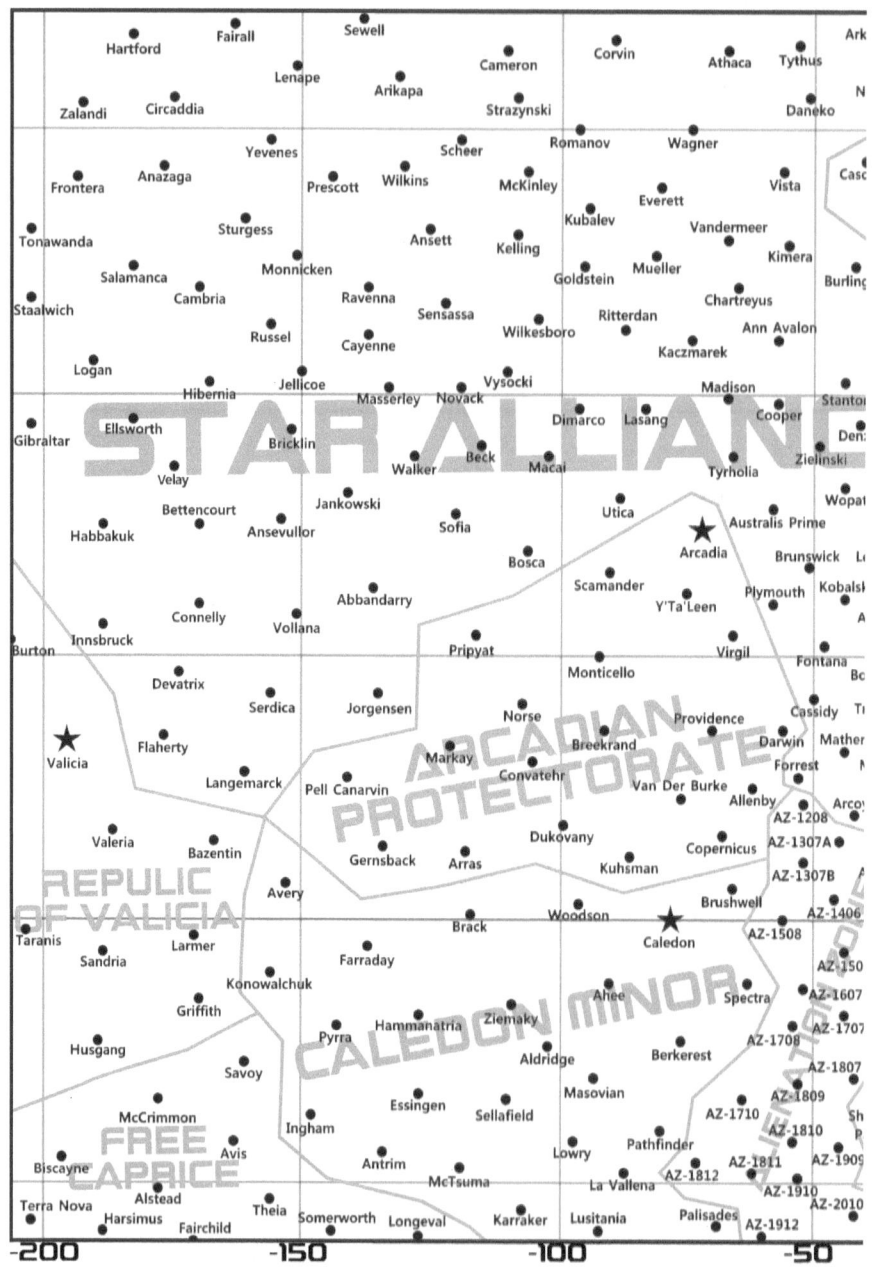

Galactic Map - Theater Le

Property of the Central Concordat (Cencon)

-207, 171 by 126,-60
All units light-years
Borders current as of 505 Post Founding
Contact your local CenCon Administrar Station
for customized projections

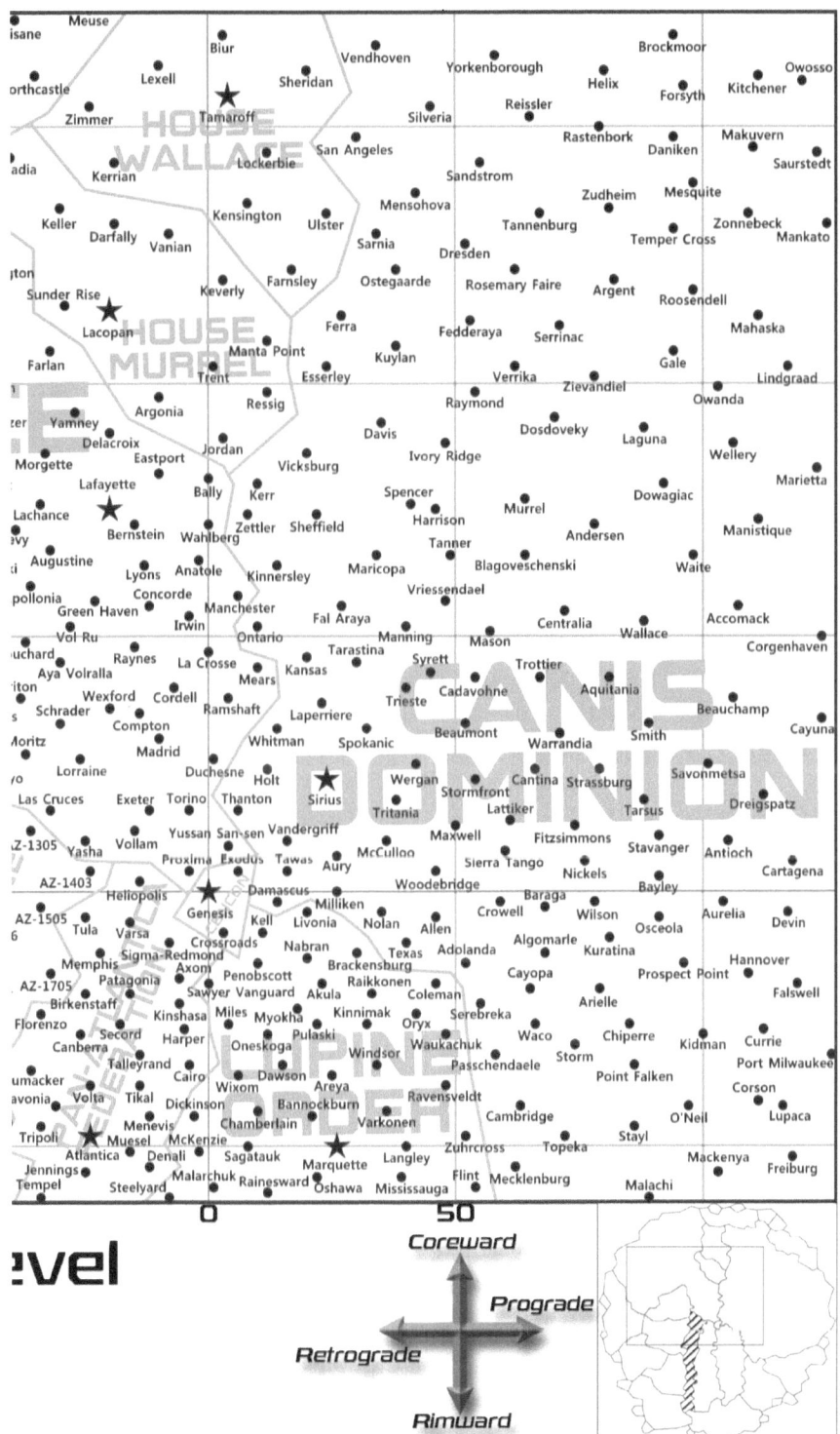

www.ingramcontent.com/pod-product-compliance
Lightning Source LLC
Chambersburg PA
CBHW030403030726
47497CB00002B/456